The shining splendor of o[...] of this book reflects the glittering excellence of the story inside. Look for the Zebra Lovegram whenever you buy a historical romance. It's a trademark that guarantees the very best in quality and reading entertainment.

PASSION'S FIRE

"You're the most stubborn woman I've ever met," said Guy.

Anne's eyes flashed, looking like blue fire. "I didn't ask for your opinion, Mr. Masters. Frankly, I don't give a damn what you think. Now get out."

Anne was pretty, but when she was angry, she was magnificent. Guy stared at Anne in mute fascination. With her full breasts heaving and her eyes spitting sparks, she looked like an avenging goddess.

"Did you hear what I said? I said get out!"

"I'm leaving," said Guy, opening the door. "But just for the record, you won't last a week out here. You'll be begging to go back to Ohio."

"We'll see about that!" she threw back.

Guy turned to go. He'd never met such a high-spirited woman. She wasn't at all what she had appeared to be at first. The engineer in him would have liked to take her apart and find out what made her tick. The man in him simply wanted to find out what it would be like to make love to her . . .

SURRENDER TO THE PASSION

LOVE'S SWEET BOUNTY (3313, $4.50)
by Colleen Faulkner

Jessica Landon swore revenge of the masked bandits who robbed the train and stole all the money she had in the world. She set out after the thieves without consulting the handsome railroad detective, Adam Stern. When he finally caught up with her, she admitted she needed his assistance. She never imagined that she would also begin to need his scorching kisses and tender caresses.

WILD WESTERN BRIDE (3140, $4.50)
by Rosalyn Alsobrook

Anna Thomas loved riding the Orphan Train and finding loving homes for her young charges. But when a judge tried to separate two brothers, the dedicated beauty went beyond the call of duty. She proposed to the handsome, blue-eyed Mark Gates, planning to adopt the boys herself! Of course the marriage would be in name only, but yet as time went on, Anna found herself dreaming of being a loving wife in every sense of the word . . .

QUICKSILVER PASSION (3117, $4.50)
by Georgina Gentry

Beautiful Silver Jones had been called every name in the book, and now that she owned her own tavern in Buckskin Joe, Colorado, the independent didn't care what the townsfolk thought of her. She never let a man touch her and she earned her money fair and square. Then one night handsome Cherokee Evans swaggered up to her bar and destroyed the peace she'd made with herself. For the irresistible miner made her yearn for the melting kisses and satin caresses she had sworn she could live without!

MISSISSIPPI MISTRESS (3118, $4.50)
by Gina Robins

Cori Pierce was outraged at her father's murder and the loss of her inheritance. She swore revenge and vowed to get her independence back, even if it meant singing as an entertainer on a Mississippi steamboat. But she hadn't reckoned on the swarthy giant in tight buckskins who turned out to be her boss. Jacob Wolf was, after all, the giant of the man Cori vowed to destroy. Though she swore not to forget her mission for even a moment, she was powerfully tempted to submit to Jake's fiery caresses and have one night of passion in his irresistible embrace.

Available wherever paperbacks are sold, or order direct from the Publisher. Send cover price plus 50¢ per copy for mailing and handling to Zebra Books, Dept. 3411, 475 Park Avenue South, New York, N.Y. 10016. Residents of New York, New Jersey and Pennsylvania must include sales tax. DO NOT SEND CASH.

ZEBRA BOOKS
KENSINGTON PUBLISHING CORP.

For Evelyn
part sister, part mother,
part friend, part loyal fan.
Thanks for always being there for me.

ZEBRA BOOKS

are published by

Kensington Publishing Corp.
475 Park Avenue South
New York, NY 10016

First printing: June, 1991

Printed in the United States of America

Every morning at seven o'clock
There were twenty Tarriers workin' at the rock
And the boss comes 'long and says, Kape still,
And come down heavy on the cast iron drill,
And drill! and blast! and fire!
Drill, me heroes, drill!

Drill, me Paddies, drill,
Drill all day, no sugar in yer tay
Workin' on the U.P. Rail Road.
And drill! and blast! and fire!
Drill, me heroes, drill!

Traditional Irish railroad workers' song

Chapter One

Anne Phillips gazed out of the train window. The entire landscape was covered with a thick blanket of snow, a world of pristine white stretching from horizon to horizon, not a touch of color to be seen. Even the sky was almost colorless with its low-hanging gray clouds.

Spying the conductor coming down the aisle from the corner of her eye, she turned in her seat and asked, "How much farther to Cheyenne?"

The portly conductor stopped and smiled broadly before answering, "About ten miles."

"Why are we going so slow?" Anne's brother, Jim, sitting across the seat from her, asked the conductor. "Haven't the tracks been cleared of snow?"

"Sure they have," the conductor answered. "The snowplows went out this morning as soon as it stopped snowing, but the rails have ice on them. If we went any faster than this, the brakeman would never be able to stop this train when we reach Cheyenne. We'd just skid clean through the town."

The conductor paused, then asked Jim, "Are you a railroad employee? I kind of figured that, since you're traveling with a railroad pass. Unless you're another one of those reporters?"

"No, I'm not a reporter," Jim answered with a hint of disdain in his voice. "I'm an engineer. I just signed on with the U.P. back in Omaha."

There was no doubt in the conductor's mind that the young man meant an engineer who built railroads, and not an engineer who drove locomotives. Besides being well-dressed and mannerly, the young man's speech was too precise, all marks of a gentleman. The conductor smiled broadly and extended his hand, saying, "Well, welcome to the Union Pacific, young fellow. We're glad to have you. You're working for a top-notch railroad. My name is Amos Johnson. I have the run from Platte City to Cheyenne."

Jim smiled back, took the conductor's hand, and shook it. "I'm Jim Phillips, and this is my sister, Anne."

The conductor's dark, bushy eyebrows rose in surprise. He had assumed the young lady was the man's wife. Remembering his manners, he smiled at Anne and tipped his tall, black hat, with its narrow metal strip across it that read conductor. "Pleased to meet you, miss."

Anne smiled back and nodded her head. Why, she's pretty, the conductor thought, getting his first good look at the young woman's face. Nice even features and a creamy, flawless complexion, and he should have guessed that the two were brother and sister. Both were tall, and they had the same shade of dark blond hair. But it was Anne's eyes that the conductor was the most impressed with. Unlike her brother's, whose were brown, Anne's large, wide-set eyes were hazel, and they seemed to be changing colors right before him, first blue, then green, then gray.

Tearing his gaze away from Anne's fascinating eyes, the conductor sat next to Jim and said, "I sure do admire you engineers, working out there, surveying three hundred miles before the end of the rail, braving the wilderness and the Indians. If if wasn't for you young fellows blazing the trail, we wouldn't be able to build this railroad to the Pacific."

Jim frowned. Gen. Greenville Dodge—the Chief of Engineers, who had hired him in Omaha—hadn't said anything about surveying. It was a dirty, tedious chore that Jim didn't like, crawling through gullies and riverbeds, and climbing over mountains, sometimes in the most adverse weather conditions. He was interested in the actual building of the railroad, not the laying of the route. He liked the excitement on the construction site, and the feeling of power from ordering men around. But Jim wasn't a man to turn down a compliment, even if he hadn't personally earned it. He enjoyed basking in admiration, so much so that he went out of his way to try to impress people. "Thank you."

The conductor gazed off, a look of wonder coming over his chubby face. "It still doesn't seem possible that we're finally building a transcontinental railroad. They've been talking about it for way over a decade now. Imagine, building a railroad that stretches over two thousand miles across the Great Desert and the Rockies."

"Sixteen hundred miles," Jim corrected him in his precise engineer's voice. "And there are still quite a few people who don't think it can be done."

"Oh, we can do it all right," the conductor answered with the utmost confidence, totally undaunted by Jim's correcting him. "If anyone can, the U.P. can. Old Abe knew what he was doing, when he picked us for the job."

"The U.P.'s proposed route was the most logical of the five possible routes," Jim answered. "Any engineer who studied the surveys that Jeff Davis ordered back in the fifties could see that."

"Is that a fact?" the conductor asked, surprised at this bit of information. "I always thought it was because Gen. Dodge knew Lincoln personally. Dodge claims he and Abe met years ago at Council Bluffs, when Abe was still a lawyer and Dodge was surveying a possible transcontinental route. According to Dodge, Abe called him personally to Washington back in '62, just to ask his opinion on where the terminus should be."

"That may be true. Gen. Dodge told me the same story. But I'm sure Lincoln took more than that into consideration when he choose the route. Besides the central route being the most practical from the standpoint of cost, it would obviously serve the whole of the country better than one more northerly or southernly. That was what held up the building of the transcontinental railroad for so long, you know, the different sections of the country arguing over who would get the terminus and whose territory it would pass through. That, and the fact that so many people thought it couldn't be done, that it was just a pipe dream of fools."

"To be honest, I had my doubts there at first, too," the conductor admitted. "Congress passed the Rail Road Act way back in '62. First the U.P. couldn't raise the money to finance it, despite all those land grants and loans from the government. Then, when they did finally start building, things went so slow. Why, by the end of the war we hadn't even lain track out of the city limits of Omaha. It wasn't until Gen. Dodge left the army and took over as Chief of the Engineers that things really started moving.

"Then last winter things came to a complete standstill again. We had a terrible winter, blizzards and all. It was so cold that the Missouri River at Omaha had sixteen inches of ice on it. Of course, in a way, that was good for the railroad. Dodge drove tons of equipment and supplies right over the ice from Council Bluffs and stockpiled it. Saved the railroad a fortune in shipping fees, considering the outrageous prices those steamboat companies charged to ferry stuff across the river. As soon as the spring thaws had passed, we started barreling across the Nebraska plains. Not even those vicious Platte summer storms could stop us. We're moving now, and we aren't going to stop until we reach the Pacific."

"Until we reach the Central Pacific Line," Jim corrected. "Have you forgotten that they're building from the other direction?"

Amos frowned. Why did the young man have to be so persnickety about everything? Besides, U.P. employees liked to think they were doing the entire job. "Well, to the Sierra Nevada then," he conceded. "At the rate we're going, we'll reach those mountains before the C.P. can even finish blasting their way through them. They've been held up in those mountains for years now."

"I don't think it matters where the U.P. and C.P. lines meet," Anne said, joining in the conversation. "What's important is that the first transcontinental railroad is actually being built, and our nation will be united from coast to coast for the first time. I think it's the most exciting, most wonderful thing that has ever happened to this country."

The conductor glanced across at Anne. With her fascinating eyes sparkling with enthusiasm, Anne's entire face was transformed. No longer was she just pretty. She was radiant. "You're dead right, young lady," Amos answered, her excitement firing his own. "Why, if I didn't have so many years into working my way up to this job, I'd quit and hire on as a construction worker, just so I could say I had taken an actual part in building it." He laughed. "In fact, I might still do just that."

Jim wasn't immune to the excitement of his sister and the conductor. He was just as fired-up. If the U.P. and C.P. were successful, it would be the engineering feat of the century, and he hoped to make his reputation as a great railroad engineer through this job. By the time it was over, he would be an important man, a powerful man. The next time he hired on at a railroad, it would be as chief engineer. Why, he knew ten times more than Gen. Dodge did, and he intended to prove it.

For a few moments, the three sat and gazed off into space, each occupied with their own visions of the future. Then, noticing the brakeman signaling him from the back of the car, the conductor jumped to his feet and said, "My goodness! I got so busy talking, I missed seeing the city limits marker."

Anne turned quickly in her seat and looked out the window. The same bleak landscape she had been seeing for days slowly rolled past her. "I don't see any buildings."

"No, miss," the conductor said with a chuckle, "you sure don't. The town is still five miles away. But the citizens of Cheyenne have great hopes for this town, now that the railroad has announced it's planning on building a roundhouse and machine shops here. Why, lots selling for fifty dollars apiece six months ago, are selling for thirty-five hundred now, and the town has a population of ten thousand people. It wouldn't surprise me if Cheyenne turned out to be the capital of a state someday."

As the conductor walked off, being jerked back and forth across the aisle by the rocking movement of the car, Anne stared at his back in disbelief. It seemed impossible that a town that size could mushroom from the flat, desolate prairie in so short a period of time. Yes, she thought, already the face of this country was being changed by the coming of the railroad. It *was* exciting! Certainly the most exciting thing that had ever happened in her dull, dreary life.

Chapter Two

Fifteen minutes later, the train came to a jerking halt. Anne peered out of the window anxiously, hoping to get a glimpse of the town, but all she could see through the steam floating back from the locomotive was the wooden station house. Glancing up, she read the sign that dangled from the station's roof: Cheyenne—Magic City of the Plains. A new tingle of excitement ran through her.

"Hurry, Anne," Jim said impatiently, stepping out into the aisle. "Let's get off this freezing train and into some place warmer. My feet feel like two blocks of ice."

Handing her the wicker basket that had held the lunches they had hurriedly bought at the lunch counters at the stations along the way, Jim picked up the small valise that contained their toilet articles and a change of clothing. Then he rushed her down the aisle, Anne stumbling a bit, her legs stiff from being in the same position for so long. When they reached the door at the front of the car, they had to wait for the passengers before them to alight, an exclusively male gathering except for one other female. Anne stared curiously at her.

The woman's lips and cheeks were heavily rouged, and her dress was much too ostentatious to be of good taste, especially the hat with its elaborate array of ostrich feathers. Had not her appearance given her away, her behavior would have. All during the trip, she had been much too friendly with the male passengers to be respectable. While Anne had lead a rather sheltered life, she wasn't so naive as to not know the woman was one of those "sinful, fallen women" her uncle had often raved about, when he got on one of his hell and damnation tirades. While Jim had been indignant to find such a low creature traveling in the same car with them, Anne had been more curious. She wondered just what the woman did that made her so sinful. She knew it had something to do with men, but her aunt had been very tight-lipped on the subject, other than to say she committed sins of the flesh. Anne had never asked Jim for a further explanation. In some ways, her older brother, although she loved him dearly, could be just as stiff and foreboding as the aunt and uncle who had raised them.

"Make way for the ladies!" the conductor shouted over the raised, excited male voices at the doorway.

The men stepped back, their faces flushed with embarrassment at the conductor's reminder of their lack of manners, and hats flew from heads as if by magic. As the prostitute passed, the men grinned at her. A few even winked. But when Anne passed, they quickly sobered and nodded their heads politely.

Just before they stepped from the car, Anne got a whiff of the woman's perfume. It was so strong that it almost bowled her over. Then, as they stepped into the open between the two cars, a blast of icy wind blew it away, and Anne had to make a quick grab for her tiny hat to keep it from sailing off.

The conductor caught Anne's arm to help her down the steps. "Careful, miss," he cautioned. "There are patches of ice on the platform. Watch your step."

Gingerly, Anne stepped down, still holding her hat in one hand and the wicker basket in the other. Taking a few steps away, so that she wouldn't block the exit, she peered down the platform, seeing the Irish railroad laborers, pouring from the last car and cheering boisterously. A few didn't even bother to wait in line to escape the confines of the car. They threw open the windows and crawled out.

For a few moments, the platform was busy with passengers. Businessmen, merchants, construction workers, disenchanted miners, and a whole barrage of rather shady-looking characters descended upon the station like a swarm of bees, and then dissipated, rushing off in every direction. When the crowd had thinned, the conductor stepped up to Jim and Anne and said, "If you'll give me your baggage claim tokens, I'll have the brakeman fetch your luggage for you."

Jim set down the valise he was carrying, unbuttoned his heavy overcoat, stripped off his heavy gloves, stuffing them into one pocket, and fumbled in his pockets. Then he shook his head in self-disgust and said, "I forgot. I gave you the tokens, Anne."

Anne lowered the wicker basket to the platform. "I forgot, too," she admitted. She reached into the reticule hanging from one arm, pulled out the brass tokens that matched those strapped to their luggage, and handed them to the conductor.

"Well, good luck to you, young fellow," the conductor said to Jim. "Maybe I'll see you around now and then."

"Good luck to you, too," Jim responded. As the trainman hurried off, Jim looked around him, then said in a petulant tone of voice, "I would have thought someone from the railroad would have met us. After all, I'm not a common laborer, like those riffraff Irishmen."

Anne glanced around. The entire length of the platform was deserted, except for the brakeman who was unloading their luggage from the car behind the engine, and the man leaning nonchalantly against the station house a few yards away. Strangely, even in the midst of a crushing crowd and chaotic activity, Anne had been aware of him standing there, with his hands shoved into his heavy sheepskin jacket, his long, booted legs crossed before him, and his hat pulled down over his face. There was something about him that seemed to command attention, as if his presence alone was crowding out everything and everyone. She had never been so acutely conscious of a person.

Then, seeing him push himself away from the side of the building and walk towards them, her breath caught. For such a tall, big man, he had an incredibly graceful walk. As the steady beat of his boots on the wooden planks drew closer and closer, Anne's heart suddenly raced.

The man stepped up to them, seemingly towering over her and Jim, and asked, "Are you James Phillips?"

At the sound of his deep, baritone voice, Anne's stomach fluttered peculiarly. With his height, his jacket straining across his broad shoulders, his hat pulled down low on his forehead—giving the man an almost dangerous appearance—she was acutely aware of his masculinity. His powerful aura of sheer maleness seemed overpowering, and she had never been so aware of her own femininity.

"Yes, I am," Jim answered.

The stranger pulled his hands from his pockets and offered one to Jim. Anne stared at the long, slender hand with the sprinkling of black hairs on the back, thinking that even his hands seemed terribly male. A funny little shiver ran over her.

"I'm Guy Masters, a fellow engineer," the stranger announced.

Jim was disappointed and a little piqued that the superintendent of engineers hadn't met them himself. After all, Jim was an engineer, a person of some importance.

"Sam Reed, our boss, would have met you himself, but he was called out to the end of the rail on sudden business," Guy informed Jim. "He asked me if I would meet you and help you get settled. He'll probably be back by tomorrow morning."

Feeling mollified at knowing the superintendent had planned on meeting him, Jim shook the man's hand and said, "Call me Jim. And this is my sister, Anne."

His sister? Guy thought in surprise. Not his wife? Now, he could see a man bringing his wife along for a brief visit before he went to work. He might not see her again for years. That alone was risky, considering how wild Cheyenne was. But why in the hell would he bring along his sister? Then, belatedly remembering his manners, Guy swept his hat from his head and turned to Anne. "Pleased to meet you."

Anne found herself looking at a ruggedly handsome face with a shock of black, wavy hair hanging over the forehead. She judged the man to be in his late twenties, perhaps four or five years older than Jim. But oddly, the stranger baring his face to her did nothing to relieve her disquietude. He still had a dangerous air about him. Perhaps it was the way he was staring at her. Those coal black eyes seemed to be peering into her soul. She managed a faint nod of recognition.

Guy was doing a little staring of his own. She's not bad-looking, he thought. In fact, she was rather pretty, even if she was taller than most women. And she had the biggest eyes he had ever seen, except he couldn't tell their color in this dim light. Being reminded of the rapidly fading light, Guy abruptly slammed his hat back on his head and picked up the wicker basket at Anne's feet. "I'll carry this for you."

Guy stood and looked over Anne's head, then called to the brakeman pulling a small cart that was loaded down with luggage, "Bring that to the buckboard around back."

The brakeman didn't argue. The man who had called the order had an air of authority about him. As he sharply veered in his course, Guy turned and walked to the side of the station. Anne and Jim hurried to keep up with his long strides.

"I hope Mr. Reed being called out wasn't anything serious," Jim said, wanting to show Guy how concerned he was about railroad business, even though he had just been hired.

"When they have to call in Sam, it's always serious," Guy answered. "But he'll take care of it. He's the best railroad engineer I've ever worked under."

Jim frowned. *He* wanted to be the best engineer on the U.P. payroll, and he didn't like competition, even if it was his superior. "Sam? Is that what the engineers call him?"

Guy didn't miss the disapproval in Jim's voice. Oh God, he thought in disgust, not another one of those stiff, pompous engineers straight out of college and still green behind the ears. "We don't stand on ceremony out here. Everyone calls each other by their first names. On a big construction job like this, it makes for an easier working relationship. Besides, when you live with a man and work with him for months on end, calling him mister seems kind of silly."

Jim bristled, thinking Guy was implying that *he* was silly. Guy was aware of his stiffening. Damn, he's got a chip on his shoulder, too, Guy thought, wishing the superintendent had sent someone else. Acting as hospitality committee wasn't his cup of tea, particularly when the man he had to be polite to was obviously going to be a pain in the ass.

As they rounded the corner of the station, a blast of cold air hit them. Again, Anne's hat went flying, and this time she wasn't quick enough to catch it. But Guy was. He stretched out his long arm and lifted it right out of the air.

Handing it back to her, he said, "Better hang on to it. The wind gets pretty high around here."

Clutching it to her, and aware of Jim holding his hat on his head to keep it from flying off, she asked Guy, "How do you manage to keep yours from blowing away?"

"Pull it so far down on my head that it can't be budged," Guy answered. "Of course, my hat's much bigger than that little dinky thing of yours."

Was he making fun of her hat? Anne wondered, feeling a little irritated. It was one of the few stylish things she had, and her pride and joy. "It's designed to just perch on the top of your head," she answered pertly.

"Well, it doesn't give you much protection from the cold, does it?" Guy responded. "Seems a bonnet that ties under the chin would be more practical. Your ears must be freezing."

He was certainly outspoken, Anne thought, and her ears *were* freezing. But she wasn't going to admit that to the rugged engineer. "Your ears aren't covered either," she pointed out.

"No, but I'm used to this cold."

Was that why he wasn't wearing gloves, Jim wondered, then asked, "Is it always this windy?"

"In these wide open plains, there's nothing to stop it, and during the winter, there's nothing between us and the North Pole. But this is nothing compared to what it is in a blizzard. Then it howls something fierce."

As they rounded another corner to the back of the station, Anne and Jim stopped in their tracks. Before them, stretched out on the prairie in the dim light of dusk, sat Cheyenne. They stared in disbelief, for they had never seen anything like it. There were a score or so of buildings sitting around at random, constructed from rough planking. The rest of the town was made up of log cabins with canvas roofs, dugouts, tin shanties, and tents. Another string of tents stretched out in the distance, following the curve of Crow Creek, the flickering light of campfires barely visible.

Guy turned. He knew by the shocked expressions on Jim's and Anne's faces that this was not what they had expected, but he couldn't resist asking, "What's wrong?"

"We were told that Cheyenne had ten thousand people, that it was a thriving town," Jim answered.

"It does have ten thousand people, at least for the time being. And it is thriving. It has an elected government, a post office, two hotels, three banks, two daily newspapers, a store, a warehouse, and a hundred saloons, gambling joints, and dance halls. Why, it even has its own brass band."

"You aren't serious about the number of gambling halls and saloons?" Jim asked in a shocked voice.

Guy shrugged his broad shoulders. "That's what the count was a few days ago. By now it could be more. They spring up overnight." He turned and gazed out over the town "You're looking at the wildest town west of the Mississippi. Brawling, shooting, killing goes on from nightfall till dawn. Every gambler, confidence man, pickpocket, thief, outlaw, and . . ." Guy hesitated. He had been about to say whore. ". . . lady of the night in the country has come here to prey on the railroad workers. The saloons sell them watered-down whiskey, the gamblers cheat them, the confidence men sell them worthless shares in gold and silver mines, the dance hall girls charge them a dollar for a dance that lasts three minutes, and thieves slip a knife into their backs in darkened alleys or pick their pockets while they're passed out cold someplace. These Hell on Wheels towns attract the scum of the earth, all intent upon relieving the construction workers of their pay by hook or crook."

"Hell on Wheels?" Jim asked. "Why do you call it that?"

"That's a railroad term for these boomtowns that spring up beside construction camps. When we pick up and move farther down the line, they move, too. They strike their tents and break apart their wooden buildings, load them and all of their equipment on wagons, and the next thing you know, they're sitting right on top of us again. They're nothing but transients, trash and outlaws that follow the railroad."

"But can't the railroad do something about it?" Jim asked indignantly. "After all, they're on railroad property."

"Just every other section of land is ours. The rest is government property."

"Then what about the army?" Anne asked. "Can't they expel them?"

"The army is here to protect the construction crews from Indians, not to control that riffraff. However, back in Julesberg, the railroad did finally take things in hand. That town was even worse than this one, so much so that they called it The Most Wicked Town in America. When Gen. Dodge heard a group of railroad directors were coming for an inspection, he ordered Gen. Jack, the chief of construction, to clean up the town. He and about two hundred of his toughest Irish workers went into the town and forcibly expelled the outlaws and trash."

"Then why can't the railroad do that here in Cheyenne?" Jim asked.

"It wasn't exactly legal. You see, when Gen. Dodge asked Gen. Jack how he had accomplished it, the construction chief's only explanation was 'They died with their boots on.' "

"Are you saying they murdered them?" Jim asked in a shocked voice.

"Either that, or they had a shootout. I'll leave you to draw your own conclusions. But the railroad can't continue to police these towns. After Julesberg, more just came to replace them. Besides, we're here to build a railroad, not fight outlaws."

"But what about the law here in Cheyenne?" Anne asked. "You said it had an elected government."

"Yes, a mayor and a few councilmen. They can't hire a sheriff. There's no one stupid enough to take the job. He wouldn't last one night."

While the brakeman was loading the luggage on the back of the wagon, Guy placed the wicker basket he was carrying in it, then the small valise Jim had been carrying. He turned to Anne, still standing on the platform, and, before she could guess his intent, caught her around the waist and swung her up to the buckboard. At her gasp of surprise, Guy explained, "The ground is muddy. You'd sink clear to your ankles in it."

Jim looked down at the brown slush. "You'd think it would be frozen."

"No, it's not cold enough, and here in town, with all this traffic, the snow never sits for long. We get just enough to keep the ground perpetually muddy."

Guy walked around the team of horses and climbed aboard the other side of the wagon, while Jim stepped gingerly through the mud, wrinkling his noise at the squishy sounds he heard, and climbed in the other side. Then, with Anne sitting in the middle, Guy drove the buckboard away.

By the time they reached the town, darkness had fallen, and unlike the little country hamlet Anne had come from—where everyone went to bed shortly after sundown—Cheyenne was teaming with activity. Wagons piled high with lumber and construction materials made their way through the streets, driven by foul-tempered teamsters who cracked their whips above the horses' heads and cursed the unfortunate animals when they got bogged down in the deep mud. A covered wagon passed them going in the opposite direction, its team of oxen doggedly plodding along, followed by several men on horseback and an old, ragged prospector, leading his shaggy mule. From out of a side street, a fancy buggy darted and whizzed by them, slipping and sliding back and forth across the street and slinging mud on pedestrians who were carefully picking their way to the other side, bringing curses and clenched shaking fists from the mud-splattered men.

The boardwalks were crowded with a steady stream of men going in both directions, all intent on getting to their destinations despite the flood of traffic going in the opposite direction. Tough, burly construction workers brushed shoulders with cowhands, mountain men dressed in coonskin caps and buckskins, blue-coated soldiers from the nearby fort, nattily dressed gamblers, and mean-eyed outlaws. Here and there, a farmer in a flimsy, tattered coat or a merchant could be seen. Everyone was in a hurry.

As they drove through Cheyenne, Anne looked about her in fascination. Every other saloon was named Bucket of Blood or Last Chance, the lights from inside spilling out through the windows and swinging doors onto the darkened boardwalk. She craned her neck to see inside the forbidden buildings, but the windows were so grimy that they were just smeared blurs, and all she could see over the swinging doors were the lamps hanging from the ceiling and shrouded in a haze of blue smoke. But the sounds drifted out into the street: men talking loudly and cursing, women laughing shrilly, the muted clink of glasses, shuffling of cards and rattle of casino games. Even in the brisk air, she could smell the stench of cheap liquor, cigar smoke, and unwashed bodies.

They passed a dance hall and the noise was horrendous: yelling, clapping, boots being pounded on the wooden floor, and in the background, Anne could hear the tinny music of a piano in dire need of tuning. The activity was so frenzied inside that the building actually shook.

As one of the dance hall girls stepped outside to the boardwalk, Anne stared at her in amazement. Her face was painted, and her hair, beneath the ostrich feathers she was wearing, was a peculiar shade of bright orange. Her dress was a hideous purple, made of satin and sprinkled lavishly with sequins, the shockingly low bodice and calf-length skirt edged with more feathers. Beneath the girl's dress, Anne could see her black fishnet stockings and purple dancing shoes, with their ankle ribbons tied in a bow. Her garish appearance was enough to make Anne gape, but what really astonished Anne was that the girl was actually fanning herself—despite her bare arms and indecent amount of naked bosom—in the freezing cold.

A little farther down the street, they passed a large tent. A crooked sign over it identified it as yet another saloon. Suddenly, the tent flap flung open, and two men came barreling out, cursing and slinging their fists at one another. A second later, they were in the street fighting, rolling in the mud, and beating on one another. Since the two combatants were blocking their way, Guy was forced to bring the horses to a sharp halt.

As the two muddy men continued to batter one another, Jim asked Guy, "Aren't you going to stop them?"

"Why should I?"

"Those are construction workers. Railroad men."

"They're on their free time. It's their argument, not mine."

Another pair of antagonists exploded from the tent, the two flying through the air and landing in the street with a big *plop* that splattered mud everywhere. From the sounds of the noises from inside—tables being overturned, chairs and glass being broken, loud, angry curses—it appeared the fight was rapidly turning into a wild free-for-all.

Muttering a curse under his breath, Guy backed up the terrified, rearing horses, and guided the unnerved animals carefully around the fracas in the street. As they drove away, Anne glanced over her shoulder and saw men pouring out of every nearby saloon and dance hall to the disturbance, cheering the bloody, muddy contestants on, a few even eagerly joining in, although they had no earthly idea what it was about.

"That was the most disgusting thing I've ever seen," Jim commented, when they turned a corner and left the brawling men behind.

"I told you Cheyenne was a wild town," Guy replied. He shot Anne a meaningful look and added, "Hardly a suitable place to bring a respectable woman."

Jim had been thinking the same thing. He'd had no idea that Cheyenne was such a wild, immoral town. If he had known, he would have never brought Anne with him. But he highly resented Guy pointing out his mistake to him. How dare he criticize me, he thought angrily. It was none of his damn business!

Anne was also feeling a little resentful at Guy's remark. She feared her brother might send her back East, and now that she had gotten a taste of the things going on around a railroad construction camp, she was determined to stay. After her dull life, she found the wild, forbidden things, the noises and all of the activity, terribly stimulating. Why, the air fairly crackled with excitement!

They pulled up in front of a two-storied wooden building. Anne looked up at the sign over it that read Rollins House, and assumed it must be a hotel. After they had alighted—Jim swinging her over the muddy street this time—Guy motioned to a figure huddled in the shadows in front of the building.

Anne gasped as an Indian, wrapped in a heavy buffalo blanket, rose from where he had been crouched in the darkness and hurried forward. Guy pointed to the luggage and then to the hotel. The Indian nodded his head, shrugged off his blanket, and quickly carried the baggage inside. When he returned, leaving a trail of muddy footprints from his soaked moccasins, Guy handed him a coin and pointed to the horses, saying, "Take back to the Great Western."

The Indian picked up his blanket, sloshed through the mud, climbed into the wagon, and drove off. "Is he a *real* Indian?" Anne asked Guy.

"Yes, a Paiute. They hang around town looking for odd jobs. The railroad has even hired a few, but the women make better workers."

"The railroad hires Indian women?" Jim asked in disbelief.

"Yes, as tampers."

"But tamping down the ground around the ties is hard work," Jim objected.

"They're strong. They can do the job just as well as any man. Like I said, they're good workers. The men have a tendency to be a little lazy."

"I thought all of the Indians west of the Mississippi were dangerous," Anne commented, feeling disappointed at the first Indian she had ever seen. "He didn't look at all dangerous."

"Paiutes aren't. They're a Colorado tribe that is rather backward and downtrodden, compared to the fierce plains tribes."

"And Indians actually work for the white man?" Anne asked.

"Yes. The cavalry even hires a few Crows for scouts."

Guy turned and walked to the hotel, holding one of the double doors open as Anne and Jim passed through. The heat of the room surrounded Anne, and she looked around as she relished the welcome warmth. They were standing in a small lobby. In the center sat two leather couches facing one another across the expanse of a small, but expensive carpet. An ashtray on a stand sat beside one couch, a big brass cuspidor beside the second. Other than the black, potbellied stove sitting in the corner, whose coals were glowing red through the grill, there were no other furnishings.

Guy walked to the desk at the back of the room with Jim following. The clerk, a slender, gray-haired man, jumped to his feet. "Ralph," Guy said, "this is Mr. Phillips. I believe Sam Reed made a reservation for him."

"Yes, he did, Mr. Masters. The room is clean and waiting for him."

"Do you have a room for my sister?" Jim asked. "Preferably one next to mine."

The clerk shot Anne a quick glance, then answered, "I have an empty room, but it isn't next to yours. It's down the hall a few doors. Mr. Masters is occupying the room next to yours."

"Then I'll take the one down the hall, and Miss Phillips can have mine," Guy said.

"Yes, sir," the clerk answered, "if that's all right with you." He pushed the registry forward and said to Jim, "If you'll just sign for you and your sister, I'll show you to your room and have my hired hand bring up your luggage in a few minutes."

While Jim was signing the register, the clerk took two keys from the wooden slot on the back wall and placed them on the counter before him. Guy picked them up, saying, "There's no need for you to leave the desk, Ralph. I'll show these folks to their rooms. I have to get my things moved out anyway."

"Well, thank you, Mr. Masters. I'd appreciate that." The clerk rubbed his knee. "My arthritis has been bothering me a bit today, and climbing those stairs is hard on it."

Guy walked up the staircase beside the desk, and Anne and Jim followed. As they passed a wide arch, Anne quickly peeked into the adjoining room and saw it was a dining area. The delicious aroma drifting from it made her mouth water.

When they reached the upper hallway, it was dim, even with the flickering oil lamps that lined its length, and Anne had difficulty reading the numbers on the doors. Guy led them to the front of the building, slipped a key into the lock at the last door, and flung it open. The room was pitch-black.

"Wait here," Guy said. "I'll light the lamp."

Jim was about to say he could do it, but he hadn't the foggiest idea where the lamp was in that inky darkness. Guy walked across the room as straight as an arrow and lit it. As the light flared, Jim commented, "This must be your room, since you knew exactly where the lamp was."

"No, I've been staying next door. I've never seen this room before."

"Then how did you know where the lamp was?"

"I saw it."

"You must have remarkable night vision," Anne remarked.

Sneaking around in the dark to blow up bridges and railroads during the war had perfected it, Guy thought, but made no comment. Instead he shrugged his broad shoulders.

Anne looked around her. The room was unusually spacious. Besides the large mahogany bedstead and bureau, there were two overstuffed chairs with a small table between them sitting off to the side, and on the wall opposite the window, there was a large desk and a straight chair. Maroon velvet drapes, their edges lined with black tassels, graced the windows, and a matching spread lay across the bed. A small, Turkish rug lay on the floor, and there were several lovely hand-painted lamps. Anne had never seen anything quite so luxurious. "I must say I'm surprised at how large and well-furnished this room is," she commented, walking to the window to see the view.

"The Rollins House caters to the elite," Guy explained. "It's much more comfortable than that flea-bitten hotel down the street. If I'm not mistaken, this is the room the railroad bigwigs stay in when they're here on business. The other rooms aren't nearly as large or well furnished."

Jim's chest swelled with self-importance. The superintendent had reserved the best room in the house for him. Then he paled, wondering how much it cost, and if he was expected to pay for it.

Seeing the expression on Jim's face and guessing his thoughts, Guy said, "Don't worry about the bill. I think the railroad is picking up the hotel tab, until you get settled in their facilities."

Despite his relief, Jim's pride refused to let Guy know that his financial position was a little strained. "Well, that's very nice of them, but it isn't necessary. I can afford it."

Guy wondered who Jim thought he was fooling. Hell, engineers didn't make the kind of money to afford rooms like this, particularly not junior engineers. Besides, he didn't miss the sharp, surprised look that Anne had shot her brother at his boast. Seeing her peer out of the window, Guy said, "I wouldn't stand too close to that window if I were you. The Headquarters Saloon, the biggest and roughest in town, is just a short ways down the street, and you never know when there's going to be gunplay. You might get hit by a wild bullet."

While Guy had been talking, he had been unbuttoning his heavy, thigh-length coat. Spying the gun he had strapped around his hip, Jim asked, "Is that why you're wearing a gun? To protect yourself in this town?"

"I wear a gun all the time, both here and on the construction site. We all do."

"But why do you need one on the construction site?" Anne asked, cautiously moving away from the window.

"Indians."

"I thought the Indians had signed a treaty promising to stay a good distance north of the line," Jim said with a deep frown.

"Yes, the Sioux and Cheyenne signed one last September," Guy admitted. "As a matter of fact, the U.P. brought Gen. Sheridan and the peace commissioners right up to the end of the rail line to meet with the chiefs. But that treaty doesn't mean a damn thing to the Indians. Most of the buffalo are south of the line, and the Indians aren't going to let a railroad stand between them and their food supply. Besides, Red Cloud and the other chiefs only agreed to sign, if the army pulled its forts out of the Powder River area and closed the Bozeman Trail that runs through it. That's what they really wanted all along, and they got it. It didn't change their feelings about the railroad one bit. They still hate us for invading their hunting grounds and bringing more white men down on them."

"Then you're still being attacked?" Anne asked.

"Periodically, yes."

"But what about the army?" she asked, "Can't they protect you?"

"They try, but they can't be everywhere at once, and the Indians are crafty. They'll attack one place to draw the cavalry off, while another party attacks us. They have the cavalry chasing around in circles. Besides, we aren't the only people the army is out here to protect. There are still wagon trains going west. They have women and children on them, and naturally, they demand priority."

Guy paused, then said to Jim, "I advise you to buy yourself a six-shooter, like mine. Those single-shot pistols aren't worth a damn in an Indian attack. You don't have to worry about purchasing a rifle though. The railroad supplies every construction crew with Spencers and plenty of ammunition."

"If the railroad provides rifles, why would I need a pistol?"

"Rifles are a pain in the neck to carry around all the time, and if you get busy, you have a tendency to put them down someplace and wander off from them. If you get caught in the open without a gun, you'll wish to hell you had a side arm, and one that fires more than one shot." Guy eyed Jim thoughtfully for a moment, then asked, "You *can* shoot a gun, can't you?"

"Of course, I can shoot a gun!" Jim answered indignantly. "I was in the army."

Guy's dark eyebrows rose in surprise. "Oh? What branch?"

"I served with the United States Military Railroads," Jim answered proudly.

Guy wasn't particularly impressed. True, the service played an important role in transporting troops and munitions across the country during the war, but despite the fact that they carried weapons, they didn't see any fighting, as a general rule. Of course, if Jim had served in construction, at least he'd gotten some experience from the engineering standpoint, which was more than Guy had given him credit for. The North used narrow gauge roads, the South broad, and whole lines had to be torn out and replaced with the correct gauge as the Union Army moved south. Most of the construction had been done by the army engineers, but some had been done by the USMRR.

Guy cocked his head and asked, "Did you work construction?"

Jim wasn't about to admit that he had served only one year, the last of the war, and that the entire time had been spent in a dispatcher's office. For some reason, Guy seemed particularly threatening to Jim. Everyone treated him with respect and jumped when he gave orders. He sensed that Guy was the man he desperately wanted to be, and resented the older engineer for it. "Yes, I did."

Long ago, Guy had learned to watch a man's eyes when he answered a question. He's lying, he thought. But why? Why in the hell was Jim trying to impress him? He was just another engineer, not Jim's superior. Oh, hell! Why was he even wasting his time thinking about it, Guy wondered. Once he turned the young engineer over to Sam tomorrow, he'd probably never ever see Jim again.

Guy turned and said over his shoulder, "Come on. I'll show you the other room."

Jim and Anne followed Guy down the hall to the next door, and waited while he opened it. As he had said, the room wasn't nearly as large or well furnished, as they could plainly see, for Guy had left a lamp burning. There were several maps unrolled on the bed, but no clothing was strewn about. Anne thought Guy was a much neater man than her brother, whose room was always so cluttered and disorganized that she could hardly find her way through to clean it.

Guy walked to one corner of the room, picked up a valise sitting there, and shoved some toilet articles on the bureau into it. Rolling up the maps, he tucked them under his arm and said to Guy, "It's all yours."

"I think I'll let Anne stay in here," Jim responded. "It might be safer, since it doesn't face the street."

Well, he does have some sense, after all, Guy thought, but he wasn't going to make the mistake of agreeing with Jim. It seemed the man took offense at everything he said. "As soon as I dump my things off in the room down the hall, we can go downstairs and get something to eat. By now, the dining room should be open."

Jim turned to Anne. "Are you ready for dinner?"

Since Anne had gotten a whiff of the delicious smells coming from the dining room, she had been ravenous, and the thought of a hot meal after days of nothing but cold lunches teased her appetite even more. "That sounds wonderful to me, but I'd like a moment to freshen up first."

"So would I," Jim agreed.

"Then I'll meet you folks downstairs in about half an hour," Guy responded, then turned and walked from the room. But even after Guy had disappeared down the hallway, his presence seemed to linger. What a strange man, Anne thought. Oh, he was quite attractive with his dark, rugged good looks and his powerful masculinity, but he was so abrupt and businesslike. And so outspoken. Just look at the way he had made that remark about Jim bringing her along, and then giving her brother advice on what kind of a gun to buy, without Jim even asking for his opinion! Apparently he was a man accustomed to giving orders, but he could certainly stand to have a few of his rough edges smoothed over. Why, not once had he apologized for using damn or hell in her presence, and he hadn't even tipped his hat to her when he left. Even the farmers back home had better manners than that.

But, in truth, it wasn't Guy's lack of manners that bothered Anne, or his outspokenness. It was his indifference to her that had disappointed her.

Chapter Three

It was forty-five minutes later, and not half an hour, before Jim and Anne descended the stairs to the dining room. Instead of just washing up and grooming her hair, Anne had decided to change her dress. She wanted to look her prettiest the next time she met the rugged engineer.

When the lobby came into view, Guy was pacing it impatiently. He, too, had changed clothes from the jacket and checked shirt he had been wearing. He was now dressed in a dress shirt, black string tie, and black frock coat, and the dazzling white of his shirt made his deep tan stand out even more. As he spied Anne and Jim, then walked across the lobby towards them, Anne thought he looked even taller than she had remembered him, and the sheepskin coat hadn't padded his shoulders in the least. They were actually that broad. Yes, she thought in silent admiration, he was really a splendidly built man, broad-shouldered and lean-hipped, all hard muscle with not an ounce of fat on him. Then, noticing the thin scar on the left side of his forehead, she stared at it. It did nothing to detract from his looks. If anything, it just enhanced his considerable masculinity, giving him a certain air of mystery.

"I'm sorry we're late," Jim said as soon as Guy stepped up to them, feeling a little irritated at Anne himself for delaying them. He took pride in always being prompt.

"I'm afraid it was my fault, Mr. Masters," Anne said, stepping down from the last step. "My dress was so wrinkled from the long train ride that I decided to change."

Guy had no idea if Anne's dress had been wrinkled or not. With the heavy cloak she had been wearing, all he could have seen was her face. His dark eyes slid over her body. He had assumed, since she was taller than most women, that she would be thin. But such was not the case. All the womanly curves were there. His eyes skimmed over the flare of her hips, the indenture of her small waist, then lingered, ever so briefly, on the thrust of her full breasts. Then glancing up at her face, his gaze settled on her eyes. They're blue, he realized, and not round, like he had thought, but almond-shaped. With their dark brows and thick, long lashes, they were really quite striking.

Anne was aware of Guy's gaze sweeping over her. A warmth suffused her, and it was not one of embarrassment. She had wanted him to admire her. That was why she had worn her prettiest dress, one of the new garments Jim had bought her for this trip. She knew the baby blue wool brought out the blue of her eyes. She hated it when people told her they were gray or green, and she wished her hair were a lighter color and not such a dark shade of blond. Everyone knew men admired dainty, blue-eyed, fair-haired women. But there was nothing she could do about the shade of her hair or her height, and she wouldn't sink to slumping her shoulders to make herself look shorter. No, she just had to make the best of what she had, but she knew she looked attractive. She waited, hoping Guy would compliment her, at least make some mention of her dress.

Anne was doomed for more disappointment. With his usual, abrupt manner, Guy turned to Jim and said, "Fifteen minutes doesn't make that much difference," then whirled around and walked into the dining room.

Anne and Jim had no recourse but to follow. As they stepped into the room, Anne glanced about her. Three men sat at one table in the center of the spacious room, and two at another table in a corner. From their expensive cutaway coats, Anne assumed that they were businessmen of some importance.

"How about that table back in the corner?" Guy asked.

"That's fine with me," Jim answered quickly.

As the three walked across the room, Anne was a little miffed. After all the trouble she had gone to make herself look pretty, she didn't want to be stuck off in some corner. And Guy hadn't even asked her where she wanted to sit. No, he asked Jim instead. Goodness, the man had no manners at all. And a lot of good it had done her to dress up for him. She could have showed up in one of her old rags for all he cared. But the other men in the room did notice. They stared at Anne as she walked across the room, soothing her battered female pride somewhat.

To her surprise, Guy pulled her chair out for her. Then as she sat, he leaned across her shoulder and whispered, "Forgive those men for staring at you so rudely. It's just that respectable women are a rarity in this town."

Anne's female pride took a swift, downward plunge. Here she had been thinking they thought she looked pretty. What a silly little fool she was. It seemed the only men she could attract were the country bumpkins back home.

When Guy leaned over Anne, a sweet scent drifted up to him. He struggled to identify the perfume and then realized—with something of a start—that it was Anne's unique womanly essence. The scent was disturbing, terribly distracting, and for that reason, Guy made a point of sitting across the table from Anne, leaving the chair next to her for Jim.

As soon as they were seated, the three picked up their menus. But Guy couldn't concentrate on his. He found himself peering over it at the top of Anne's head as she read her menu. With the lamp on the wall beside them shining down on it, Anne's honey blond hair seemed to come to life, the light bringing out both the gold and the rich red in the darker strands. He found himself wondering what it would look like in the bright sunlight, if it was so alive in the lamplight, then speculating on how long it might be, for Anne was wearing it enclosed in a hair net at the back of her neck.

"Buffalo steaks?" Jim asked in surprise, drawing Guy's attention away from Anne's hair.

"Yes, they serve buffalo here," Guy informed him, "but I wouldn't recommend it, unless you have a fondness for game. It has a very strong, wild taste."

"What would you recommend?" Anne asked.

Guy frowned. Was it his imagination, or was there a slight edge to her voice? But why in hell would she be irritated at him? "The beefsteak. It's raised on a nearby ranch and is quite tasty."

Jim hadn't noticed the cowhands scattered among the crush of men on the boardwalks earlier. "There are ranches out here in the middle of nowhere?"

"Yes, a few. This is excellent grazing country. I imagine with the railroad coming, giving the ranchers a quick and ready means to the slaughterhouses back East, more ranches will spring up all over this territory."

"But you'd think this country would be too cold for cattle," Jim objected.

"The buffalo have managed to survive out here all these years. The grass is still there, just a foot or two under the snow. All the cattle have to do is dig down for it. Of course, if we have a winter as severe as the one we had last year, it could create a problem. But considering the size of a herd a man could run in this vast, empty country, he could afford to lose a few."

The waiter arrived at the table and poured water into the glasses already sitting there. To Anne's surprise, even he was wearing a string tie and black coat. Plus, when he greeted them, he spoke with a French accent. Yes, she thought, this was a classy place, with its sparkling white table linen and its gleaming china and glittering silverware. She waited while Guy and Jim placed their orders, Guy ordering beefsteak and Jim chicken. Then, to both men's surprise, she ordered buffalo steak.

"Are you sure you really want that?" Jim asked doubtfully.

Anne was still piqued at Guy for not complimenting her. Once more, she had been aware of him putting distance between them when he sat across from her, something she considered just another insult to her feminine charms. She had decided on the buffalo steak to show him just what a low regard she had for his opinions. "Yes, I'm sure. I want something unusual. After all, I can eat beefsteak or chicken any time."

"Well, I suppose it would be a novelty," Jim conceded, "but I hope you won't be disappointed."

"I won't," Anne assured him, shooting Guy an icy look that again puzzled him.

"Would you like a glass of wine with your meal?" the waiter asked the three diners.

"No, thank you," Jim answered stiffly. "I don't drink."

Christ, Guy thought, he was a teetotaler, too? The righteous ass was never going to fit in with the hard-drinking construction crew. He turned to the waiter and said, "I'll have a glass."

"And you, madame?" the waiter asked.

Anne had never been called madame before. It made her feel very cosmopolitan. "Yes, thank you," she answered recklessly.

"Anne!" Jim exclaimed in a shocked voice. "You wouldn't!"

His censure and stern look reminded Anne too much of her hated uncle, and suddenly, a deeply buried rebellious streak came to the surface. "Don't be silly, Jim. Wine isn't hard liquor. Besides, it's good for the digestion."

Anne had read that someplace, and having said it, she felt even more cosmopolitan. If she couldn't impress Guy with her appearance, then maybe she could with her behavior. Yes, she'd play the part of a woman of the world. She sat up straighter in her chair and assumed the most sophisticated expression she could manage.

"If the young lady is going to have a glass, too," Guy said to the waiter, "you might as well bring a bottle."

"Yes, Mr. Masters," the waiter answered, then turned to Anne and asked, "Is there any particular vintage that you prefer, madame?"

Seeing a startled look come over Anne's face, Guy said, "Yes, Rollins House has an impressive selection of wines. You can take your pick. They're listed at the bottom of the menu."

Anne didn't have the slightest notion of what vintage even meant, much less how to chose one. She picked up her menu and looked at the list. Why, she'd never be able to just pick one at random, she thought in dismay. The wines were written in what she assumed was French, and she would make a complete fool out of herself if she tried to stumble over one of those difficult foreign words. She felt trapped. So much for her plan to impress Guy, she thought in utter frustration. Then, as a sudden inspiration came to her, she smiled and said to the waiter, "I'll let Mr. Masters make the selection, since we'll be sharing a bottle."

Guy quickly made a selection, and as the waiter walked off, Anne was feeling very proud of herself for how neatly she had gotten herself out of her predicament. Now Guy would never guess she didn't know a thing about wines.

But Anne's little act hadn't fooled Guy. Even if her brother had not been glaring at her, he would have know that Anne had never drank anything stronger than tea in her entire life. She wasn't the worldly, sophisticated type. Her innocence stood out on her like a red flag. No, like her brother, she had been trying to impress him, but rather than her efforts irritating him, as Jim's had, he found himself admiring her spirit and quick thinking. Strange, he had pegged her for one of those sweet, timid women who were afraid of their own shadow.

Anne was aware of her brother's angry look. She had never defied him before, but when he had censured her in front of Guy and glared at her, something had snapped. She was determined she wouldn't back down. If she did, she would look foolish in front of Guy, and she couldn't bear that on top of his ignoring her. She pretended indifference to her brother's disapproval and glanced up at the wall beside her. "Why, what are those pictures of locomotives doing up there?" she blurted.

"That's a collection that the Rollins House is very proud of," Guy explained, "and since the hotel is frequented by railroad men and their business associates, the pictures generally generate quite a bit of interest."

Looking at a picture that was hanging lower on the wall, Anne said, "But what is that strange-looking machine? Surely, it isn't a locomotive."

The pictures had caught Jim's interest and drawn his attention away from his displeasure with Anne. Before Guy could answer, he said, "Yes, it is. That's a picture of Tom Thumb, the first locomotive built in America."

Anne was grateful for the distraction the pictures had caused. Apparently, her brother had completely forgotten his anger at her, and she decided to make the most of her opportunity to soothe his ruffled feathers. "Really? And you recognized it with just a glance?"

Jim heard the admiration in Anne's voice, and he dearly loved impressing her with how knowledgeable he was. His chest swelled with self-importance as he said, "And that one beside it is a picture of the DeWitt Clinton, the Mohawk and Hudson's first locomotive."

Anne stared in amazement. The locomotive looked more like those she was accustomed to seeing, but the ornate black and yellow cars behind it certainly weren't familiar. "Those cars look like stage coaches."

"Yes," Jim answered with a laugh. "Railroad travel was so new at that time, that no one had any idea how the passenger cars should be designed, so they just copied the stage coaches and put them on iron wheels." Turning her attention to a picture higher up on the wall, he said, "That's the George Washington. It was the first locomotive powerful enough to go to the top of a hill and over it. Before that, the passengers had to get out and push it over the top."

As Jim continued to point out the various great locomotives, Guy paid little attention to him. He, or any other engineer who had specialized in railroad engineering, knew them by sight as well as Jim. Instead, Guy watched Anne's eyes. With them flicking up, then down, then across, they changed colors as the light from the lamp hit them from different angles, first gray, then green, then blue, then gray again. Guy was fascinated, for he had never seen anything that changed colors that way, except a kaleidoscope.

When Jim directed Anne's attention to a picture hanging on the wall behind Guy, and her eye color settled into a shimmering blue, Guy studied her face closer. She wasn't a beauty, he thought, not when you took her features one by one. She didn't have the little turned-up nose that was so much admired, but rather a straight, narrow one. Her chin was a little too square, and her mouth a little too wide. But when you threw all her features together, it was a very attractive face. Then, as Anne raised her head to look at a picture higher up on the wall, Guy noticed the little mole that sat to the side of her mouth. With her lips parted with rapt attention, Guy stared at her soft lips and the tip of her pink tongue. No, her generous mouth was not one made for admiring, he thought, but one made for kissing. Hell, she wasn't beautiful. She was downright seductive with her fascinating, almond-shaped eyes, that damn teasing mole, and that luscious mouth. A sudden heat rose in him.

"That's not a locomotive," Anne said to her brother, her eyes moving higher and giving Guy an excellent view of the creamy skin beneath her chin. There another mole rested, and damn if there wasn't one just below her right ear. Guy's heat rose another notch.

"No, it isn't," Jim agreed. "It's a car. But I can't make out the lettering. Do you know what railroad that car belongs to, Guy?"

Guy started. "What?" he asked in a distracted voice.

"I asked what railroad that car behind you belongs to."

Guy tore his gaze from the intriguing beauty mark on Anne's throat, turned in his chair, and looked up. "That's a Pullman car."

"One of those new sleeping cars Pullman just designed?" Jim asked in amazement, for he had heard of the cars, but never seen so much as a drawing of one.

"Yes, they're really engineering marvels, to say nothing of their beauty."

"You've actually seen one?" Jim asked in surprise.

Guy turned back around in his seat before answering and deliberately directed his gaze at Jim. "Yes, last summer. The vice president of U.P., Thomas Durant, arranged for a large excursion train of congressmen, newspaper reporters, and wealthy men and their families to make the trip out to celebrate our crossing the one-hundredth meridian. They traveled in the new Pullman cars by courtesy of Mr. Pullman. It was some junket. On several occasions, the train stopped and the excursionists poured out on the prairie to dance—

they brought two bands along with them—or picnic, or watch an exhibition of bow and arrow marksmanship and riding skill that a few friendly Pawnees gave them. Durant even arranged for a man-set prairie fire to entertain them, but that was a fool thing to do."

"Why?" Anne asked.

"Because you never know when the wind will change directions on the prairie. If that had happened, they could have been caught in an inferno. Prairie fires are nothing to play around with."

Jim wasn't interested in hearing about the entertainment Durant had arranged, or prairie fires. He wanted to know more about the cars that were the talk of the country. "But you actually saw a Pullman car?"

"A whole string of them," Guy answered. "The last day, Durant took the party on a buffalo hunt, and Sam slipped a few of us engineers on board one of them. I didn't expect to be that impressed, but I was. Pullman's upper berths actually fold up into the ceiling, and they're real beds, not just narrow boards you find in other sleeping cars. I understand he's patented them. The lower berth is spacious enough to sleep two, and both berths are unbelievably comfortable. The car is divided into open compartments, with two seats facing each other. These are converted to beds at night and are lined with curtains to provide the utmost privacy. At both ends of the cars, there are washrooms. Pullman even provides the soap and linens. We were all agog, not only at how neatly everything fit together, but by all the gleaming mahogany, plush red upholstery, and gilded decoration. They're true works of art, as well as engineering. I understand U.P. is planning on using Pullman cars on this railroad when it's finished, and the new dining car he's currently working on. Believe me, it will revolutionize long- distance travel by rail. People will be taking trips to far distances just for the enjoyment of riding in all that luxury."

Jim scowled. "Railroads have never made money on passengers. That's more or less a courtesy to the public. It's the freight that brings in the real money."

"That's true," Guy answered, "but with the Pullmans that

may change. Oh, the railroads will still have their first-, second-, and third-class cars, but the Pullman will bring in a class all its own, a class only the rich can afford. And they'll pay the price, too. Union Pacific is so sure of it that they've already ordered their special china and silverware for the dining cars."

"Does the railroad have many of these excursion trips?" Anne asked, thinking that she would love to travel in all that luxury, and that the trips sounded very exciting.

"Yes, quite a few."

"It sounds like a waste of money to me," Jim remarked disapprovingly, "considering how long it took the U.P. to scrape up the money to build this railroad."

"To the contrary," Guy answered. "It's Durant's way of promoting the railroad, and it works. After that particular excursion went back East, U.P. stock sold like hot cakes."

Jim still had his doubts, but he was curious about something. "Is Thomas Durant really a medical doctor?"

"Yes, a legitimate graduate from one of the best medical schools in the East. But he was always much more interested in railroads than medicine. He was a Rock Island promoter when he got the idea of building a transcontinental railroad and sent Dodge out to survey it. The construction crews laugh at him because he dresses like a dandy and tiptoes daintily through the mud. But I happen to know for a fact that he carries a pearl-handled revolver under his velvet coat and is a dead shot. He's brimming over with energy, a dynamic man who, in truth, is the driving force behind this railroad."

The conversation was interrupted by the arrival of their food. The waiter placed Anne's plate in front of her, then removed the silver dome over it. Anne gasped when she saw the huge steak and baked potato and the heaping pile of green beans.

"Is something wrong with your food, madame?" the waiter asked in a concerned voice.

An embarrassed flush rose on Anne's face. "No, it's just that the servings are so large. I'll never be able to eat all that."

Guy chuckled. "They're used to serving men with big appetites here. You don't have to eat it all."

I should hope not, Anne thought. Why, the portions were so large, they were almost intimidating.

The waiter served Guy and then Jim. When he lifted the dome from Jim's plate, the young engineer frowned down at it, but he had the good sense to hold his tongue until the waiter walked away before he asked Guy, "What's that red gravy doing on my chicken?"

Guy wasn't about to tell Jim that it was a wine sauce, for fear he would insist the waiter take it back and embarrass them all. "It's a special sauce that they serve here. Try it. It's very tasty."

Jim picked up his spoon and tried the sauce. His eyes widened with surprise. "Why, you're right. It's delicious!"

The waiter brought a bottle of wine and two glasses to the table and set them before Anne and Guy. As he poured the wine, Anne glanced quickly over at her brother and was grateful to find he was occupied with his food. She picked up her glass of wine, admiring its deep ruby color before she took a sip. To her surprise, it was warm, and she felt its warmth all the way to her stomach when she swallowed it. She waited a moment, expecting to feel some effect. Then she laughed to herself. Why, it was just like the book had said. Wine wasn't intoxicating. Other than the warmth in her stomach, she felt absolutely nothing. And she hadn't been struck down by God, either, like her uncle had always threatened would happen if she took a drink of spirits.

Anne took another swallow, this one larger, then cut a piece of the buffalo steak, put it in her mouth, and chewed it. The gamy taste was so strong she almost gagged. She made a quick grab for her glass of water to wash it down, but the water did nothing to remove the awful taste from her mouth. She picked up her wine and took a big swallow. Thankfully, it's taste masked that of the strong-flavored meat.

"What are these white things in my green beans?" Jim asked suspiciously.

"Almonds," Guy answered.

"They put nuts in beans?" Jim asked in disbelief.

"Yes, that's they way the French prepare them. The Rollins

House has a French chef they're very proud of. Give them a try."

While Guy was trying to overcome Jim's suspiciousness, Anne took a bite of the vegetable. After the strong buffalo meat, the beans tasted like ambrosia, the flavors of the beans and almonds blending and their contrasting texture complimenting one another. "Try, them, Jim. They're really very good."

"I think I'll just skip them and stick to the chicken and potato," Jim replied a little testily, resenting the cook ruining his vegetable by putting something as inappropriate as nuts in it. "But this sauce on the chicken is really delicious. I wish they had put more on it."

Overhearing him, the waiter returned shortly with a gravy bowl of the sauce and set it at his elbow. "Why, thank you," Jim responded. "That's awfully nice of you."

Jim drowned his chicken in sauce and took a few large bites, while Anne avoided her buffalo and concentrated on her vegetables. Glancing across at her plate, Jim said, "I was afraid you were making a mistake when you ordered the buffalo. You don't like it."

"No, it's not that," Anne quickly denied. "It's quite tasty and surprisingly tender."

"Then why aren't you eating it?" Jim asked between bites of chicken.

"I thought I'd try the vegetables."

"Those vegetables are a waste of time when you've got meat to eat." He ladled several large spoonfuls of sauce on his chicken, adding, "Particularly when the meat is as tasty as this is."

But her meat wasn't tasty, Anne thought. It was awful. She glanced over at Guy and saw the amusement in his eyes. Why, he's laughing at me, she thought. Well, she'd show him. She'd eat the entire steak if it killed her!

She cut another piece of meat, chewed it, then took a swallow of wine. While she continued to eat her steak, washing each bite down with a big swallow of wine, Jim took one of the rolls in front of him and broke it open.

"These are the hardest rolls I've ever seen," he complained.

"They must have been sitting around for a week."
"No, they're French rolls," Guy informed him. "They're supposed to have a thick, hard crust on them."
"Well, Anne could teach that fancy chef a thing or two. She makes the lightest rolls you've ever tasted, and she can turn a pot roast into a feast fit for a king. Of course, she can't make a meat sauce like this, but she can out bake anyone. Her pies and cakes always won the blue ribbon at the county fair back home. No matter how hard those other women tried, they couldn't beat her."
Anne felt like kicking her brother. Here she had been trying to impress Guy on how worldly she was, and Jim was making them sound like country bumpkins. But wasn't that what they were? Country folks? Suddenly Anne felt ashamed of herself. She had never tried to put on airs before, to pretend that she was something she wasn't. She had always prided herself on her honesty. And she had never gone out of her way to attract a man either. But then, she'd never known a man like Guy before. There was something special about him. Compared to him, all the other men she'd ever known looked pale and dull. But that was no reason for her to sacrifice her own self-respect. If he didn't like her the way she was, then that was just too bad.
"You're from farming stock?" Guy asked Jim.
Jim was feeling mellower from the wine, but he hadn't had enough to overcome his deeply ingrained desire to impress others. "No, we're townspeople. Our uncle, who raised us, was a businessman."
"He owned a general store in a small town in a farming community," Anne informed Guy, ignoring the sharp look her brother gave her. "But it was almost as if we were farmers ourselves. The weather and how the crops were doing were the chief topics of conversation."
Guy smiled, a warm open smile that made Anne's stomach flutter. "I'm a farm boy, myself."
Learning that Guy came from such humble beginnings made him seem a little less threatening to Jim. "You don't say? Where were you raised?"
"In Illinois. And you?"

"Ohio."

Jim sopped up his sauce with a piece of roll and popped it into his mouth. As he chewed, he asked, "What made you decide to go into engineering?"

"The Central Illinois put a spur through the valley I lived in when I was a little boy. I spent all of my free time watching them build that road. It fascinated me. Long after the road was finished and the trains were running regularly, I was playing railroad. I had a couple of blocks of wood I'd connected with a string as my train. But I wasn't content to just run it over the ground. I built elaborate roads and tunnels and bridges made from sticks. Even when I got older and gave up my childish games, my romance with the railroad continued. I would lay at night in my bed and hear the engine's lonesome whistle, a sound that seemed to be calling to me, or stand at dusk and look across a snowy field and see the red glow coming from the firebox in the locomotive. Every time a train passed, I'd stare at it, long after the trail of smoke it left had disappeared, wondering what far-off, exciting place it was going, and wishing I was going with it."

Anne was surprised at Guy's revelation. He didn't look or act like any farmer she had ever known. He seemed so much more sophisticated, so much more experienced, so much more exciting. "And so when you grew up, you went to college to study engineering."

Guy swallowed the bite of food he was chewing and took a sip of wine before he answered. "It wasn't quite that simple. My parents didn't have that kind of money. The farm supported us nicely, but there were nine of us kids. I had to work for two years to earn the money. I got a job as a surveyor's helper the first year, then worked on a construction gang laying rails the second, since it paid much better. Then I worked part-time all the way through college." He grinned. "That's how I learned about wines. I cleaned tables at night in a very exclusive restaurant during the school year."

"And in the summers?" Anne asked.

"Back to the construction job."

Anne wondered if that was where he had developed his broad, muscular shoulders, laying those heavy rails. The farmers she had known, as hard as they worked, didn't have his physique.

"Were you in the army?" Jim asked, sopping up his sauce with another roll.

"Yes, I joined the second year of the war. I'd only been out of school two years, so I joined the engineering corps, thinking I could get some experience while I was doing my part for the war effort. But somehow, it didn't turn out like I expected. I landed up in Grant's Army of the Tennessee, leading a squad of raiders."

"Raiders?" Anne asked, having never heard the term. "What did you raid?"

"Our job was to blow up railroads behind enemy lines. Bridges, tunnels, embankments, things like that. It seemed the army had been having a lot of trouble with failures, and in that kind of a situation, you don't have a chance to go back and do the job right the second time, if you failed the first. Once that powder had blown, you had to get the hell out of there, because every Johnny Reb in the area knew you were there and were out to catch you. Some bigwig officer got the bright idea that a railroad engineer could do a better job, because he knew where to place the powder at the structure's weakest point."

No wonder he seemed so exciting, Anne thought. He'd had one of the most dangerous assignments in the war, working far behind enemy lines, dealing with dangerous explosives, then darting back to his own lines with every Johnny Reb on his trail and howling for blood. She imagined there were a few times that he and his men had had to fight their way back. No wonder he looked so comfortable with that gun on his hip.

Jim was thinking the same thing and feeling a little jealous, not that he would have welcomed the opportunity to take such risks. He was terrified of dying or being hurt. But he knew what a high regard the army had for their raiders. They were elite forces, men who did jobs that were beyond the pale of ordinary soldiers, men whose courage, ingenuity and quick-thinking in dangerous situations set them above the others. "Well, you certainly didn't get much experience in railroad construction, did you?" he asked nastily.

Surprisingly, he had, Guy thought. It gave him the opportunity to study many diverse bridge designs, and he got where he could spot a weak point even in total darkness, errors that he'd promised himself he'd never make. But he doubted that Jim would believe him if he told him it had been a learning experience, in both engineering and learning how to lead men, how to command their loyalty and get their best from them. "No, I really didn't get much experience in construction, until the last six months of the war, when I finally got my transfer to the engineering corp."

The three resumed eating. By this time, Anne didn't even notice the terrible taste of the buffalo anymore, but she was so distracted by all Guy had revealed about himself that she continued to automatically wash each bite down with a swallow of wine. Soon, she had downed four glasses to Guy's two.

Aware of Anne's steady drinking and noting the rosy flush on her face, Guy became alarmed. When Jim poured the remainder of the wine sauce over his potato and beans and began to wolf them down, he became even more alarmed. My God, he thought, neither are used to drinking. They're going to get drunk. He considered warning Jim about the contents of the sauce, then decided against it. Undoubtedly, Jim would think he had deliberately misled him and be furious. He held his tongue.

As soon as Jim wiped his mouth with his napkin and tossed it down, Guy asked, "Would you like a cup of coffee with your desert?"

"Dessert? Why, I couldn't eat another bite." Jim turned to Anne. "How about you? Do you want dessert?"

Anne lifted her glass and took another swallow of wine. "No, I'm full, too."

"Then how about just a cup of coffee?" Guy asked hopefully, thinking it might counteract the effects of the wine they had consumed.

"No, it will keep me awake if I drink it at this late hour," Jim answered.

Guy turned to Anne and asked, "And you?"

Anne smiled dreamily over the edge of her glass and said in a silly, singsong voice, "No, thank you."

Guy grimaced, then placed his napkin on the table and signaled to the waiter. When the man arrived at the table, he said, "We've decided against dessert. Just put the tab on the hotel bill." He handed the waiter a gold coin for a tip and started to rise.

"Wait a minute," Anne objected. "I'm not ready to leave yet. I haven't finished my wine."

Guy was tempted to say, You've already had too much, but kept silent, hoping Jim would. However, Jim had been so occupied with his meal that he hadn't noticed how much wine Anne had drunk. He assumed she was just finishing her first glass. Feeling benevolent from the wine he had consumed, he smiled at her fondly and said, "Then hurry, dear. I'm so sleepy I can hardly keep my eyes open."

Anne drained her glass in two large swallows and set it back down on the table. As the men rose, she pushed back her chair and came to her feet before either could make any attempt to play the part of a gentleman. Standing there, swaying slightly, she thought she had never felt so warm and relaxed in her life. Then when she walked across the room, she felt as if she were floating.

Vaguely, as if from a far distance, she wondered why she was feeling so wonderful. Then glancing across at the handsome, rugged engineer walking beside her, she thought she knew. Yes, Guy did have a strange effect on her. Why, she was tingling all over. If only he was as attracted to her as she was to him. The thought was so depressing that Anne almost felt like crying.

Chapter Four

When the three reached the lobby a few moments later, Guy warily eyed Jim and Anne. Both were swaying slightly and had a glassy look in their eyes. "Would you like to take a walk outside?" he suggested. "The brisk air might be . . ." he paused, searching for some word other than sobering, ". . . invigorating."

"Heck, no! It's cold out there!" Jim exclaimed, his speech decidedly thicker. "Besides, I'm beat. All I want to do is go to bed."

Anne didn't feel in the least bit tired. The depression she had felt at Guy not being attracted to her just a moment before had fled as quickly as it had come. Once again, she felt wonderful. Absolutely marvelous! "Oh, let's not go to bed yet," she said in a disappointed voice. A sudden glitter of excitement came to her eyes. "I know! Let's go dancing!"

"Where would we go dancing in this place?" Jim asked, looking about him with bleary eyes.

"There's a dance hall right down the street," Anne answered.

The suggestion didn't sound at all outrageous to Jim, but much too tiring. "Nope. Let's go to bed."

Afraid Anne would push the issue and Jim would relent, Guy quickly said, "Yes, you must be exhausted after your long train trip. And remember, I'm supposed to take you over to the railroad office to meet Sam bright and early tomorrow morning." Half-afraid that Anne would tell her brother to go on to bed and suggest that *he* could take her dancing, Guy turned to her, saying, "I'm sure he'll want to meet you, too."

"Of course, he'll want to meet Anne," Jim agreed. "After all, she's my sister. What time are we supposed to be there?"

God, he's getting more intoxicated by the second, Guy thought, for sister had come out sounding like *shister,* time sounding like thime, and supposed sounding like *shupposed.* "Nine o'clock, but I'll pick you up at eight. That will give us time for breakfast."

"That settles it," Jim said decisively. "We're going to bed."

Taking Anne's arm firmly in his hand, he led her to the stairs, totally oblivious to her glaring at him. Guy followed. When they reached the landing at the top of the stairs, Anne tripped, something that struck her as comical. She started giggling helplessly. Jim seemed to think it was funny, too. He chuckled, until he hiccuped loudly.

" 'Cuse me," he muttered, placing his hand over his mouth. Then they both started laughing again.

"Can you find your way to your rooms?" Guy asked, trying very hard to hide his disgust from the two.

"Of course, I can find my way," Jim answered, starting down the hall in the wrong direction.

Guy caught his arm and turned him around. "It's this way."

"Oops. I guess I got a little turned around. Thanks, old buddy."

Guy's eyebrows rose at the friendly address. Jim was even more intoxicated than he had thought if the testy engineer was being amicable to him.

The three walked down the hall, Anne and Jim none too steady on their feet. When Guy came abreast to his door, he stopped and said, "Good night."

"Good night," Anne answered gaily over her shoulder, while Jim muttered something totally unintelligible.

Guy stood and watched as the two weaved down the hallway, then stopped before Anne's door. Seeing Jim having trouble with the lock, Guy called softly, "What's wrong?"

"The key doesn't fit," Jim called back.

Guy walked to the door and looked over Jim's shoulder. He shook his head in disgust when he saw what the young engineer's problem was. Jim was trying to insert the key into the lock upside down. "Let me give it a try. Some of the locks in this hotel are temperamental."

"I can do it," Jim insisted, jabbing the lock with the key again.

"I'm sure you can," Guy answered diplomatically, "but I had this room last night and figured out the secret. I think I can do it a little faster."

Grumbling under his breath, Jim stepped back and handed the key to Guy. Guy turned his back to Jim (blocking his view), turned the key over, and inserted it in the lock. As he pushed the door open, he was relieved to see Anne had had the foresight to leave the lamp burning. He was anxious to get away from the two. He had better things to do than play nursemaid to a couple of helpless drunks. Turning to Anne, he placed the key in her hand and walked away, calling over his shoulder, "Well, good night again."

" 'Night," the two answered simultaneously; then thinking their saying it at the same time terribly funny, the brother and sister started another bout of senseless giggling.

Filled with disgust, Guy walked back to his door, thinking that there was nothing worse than being cold sober and having to endure the company of two silly drunks, unless it was having to put up with a belligerent one. He supposed he should be glad that the wine had affected Jim as it had, considering the young engineer's normal testiness. At least he was a happy drunk.

When Guy reached his door, he pulled his key from his coat pocket, slipped it into the lock, and turned it. Then he stood, watching Jim staggering down the hall and humming a tune to himself. Might as well wait and see if the ass can get his door open, Guy thought. Seeing the young engineer unlocking his door and stepping inside, Guy breathed a sigh of relief and pushed open his door.

When Anne had found herself standing in the middle of her room after Jim and Guy had left her, she felt terribly disappointed and a little irritated at both men for not agreeing to take her dancing. She didn't feel like going to bed. She wanted to do something gay, something exciting. Listening to the lively music drifting into her room from the dance hall down the street, she began to tap her foot in time to the music, then started dancing a two-step around the room. She didn't need them, she thought. They were no fun at all. She could dance all by herself. She twirled around several times, then bumping into a chair, tripped and fell, thankfully on the bed. Sprawled there, she lay, staring at the ceiling and giggling to herself, not even hearing the burst of gunshots that came from nearby.

Now what had she been doing? Anne wondered groggily when she had recovered. Oh, yes, she was going to go to bed. She stood and slipped off her dress, doing a lot of twisting, turning, and muttering under her breath to find the elusive buttons at the back. Even the tabs on her three petticoats gave her trouble. Finally stripped down to her chemise and drawers, she sat on the bed and attacked her shoes, wondering why her fingers were so numb and tingly.

Finally succeeding in removing the high-topped shoes, dropping them loudly one by one to the floor, she stripped off her chemise and drawers and started walking to her trunk for a gown. Catching a glimpse of herself in the mirror over the bureau, she stopped and stared at what she could see of her naked body, something she would have never dreamed of doing when she was sober. She appraised herself critically, wondering if her waist was really so small she didn't need a corset—as her aunt had always claimed—or if the old skinflint had only said that to save money by denying her one. She placed her hands at her waist and squeezed on both sides, then sucked in her breath as far as she could, thinking to simulate what a corset would do for her. Seeing her full, high breasts jut out even more, she burst out laughing, thinking she looked ridiculous with her bosom popping out like two ripe muskmelons. No, she didn't need a corset. The silly garment would just make her look malformed. It was bad enough that she was too tall. She didn't need to look top-heavy, too.

Anne turned and walked to her trunk, strewing clothing all over the room until she found her nightgown. Slipping the long, flannel white gown over her head and buttoning it, she padded back across the cold floor to the bureau, removing the fishnet at the back of her head as she walked. Standing before the mirror, she picked up her brush and began running it through her waist-length tresses, a nightly ritual she had performed since she was a child, one she suspected had come from her mother, although she couldn't remember her, for Anne's aunt was a stern, forbidding woman who strongly disapproved of any female vanity.

Several times, she knocked herself in the forehead with the brush, something that she again found terribly amusing. Then spying a shaving mug sitting behind the washbasin, she wondered who it belong to. As it suddenly occurred to her that Guy must have missed it when he had gathered his things earlier that day, she set down her brush, picked up the mug, and padded from the room.

Guy had stripped down to his trousers and was lying on the bed reading a construction report when he heard a loud knock on his door. He frowned, wondering who would be calling at this late hour, then rose from the bed. Picking up his gun from the bureau, he walked to the door and stood. In this wild town, he wasn't foolish enough to open the door to just anyone. More than one man had been jumped on and knocked senseless by a robber before he even knew what hit him. "Who's there?" he called cautiously.

"It's me. Anne."

Guy couldn't believe his ears. What in the hell did she want, and didn't she have better sense than to be wandering about the hallway at night? Rollins House might be the best hotel in Cheyenne, but that didn't mean it was a safe place. As a matter of fact, thieves were prone to lurk about in its darkened hallways at night, knowing the men who frequented the hotel would be good pickings.

Guy threw back the door. Anne stared at his impressive chest with its mat of dark hair that tapered to a fine line at the waistband of his pants. She had seen Jim without his shirt many times, but her brother's chest certainly didn't look as manly. Nor did Jim have such muscular arms. A peculiar warm curl formed in the pit of her stomach. Then spying the gun Guy held in his hand, she giggled and asked, "Are you going to shoot me?"

Guy had been stunned when he opened the door and saw Anne standing there in her nightgown. Recovering from the shock, he stepped forward, glanced up and down the hall, and, catching her wrist, jerked her into the room. As he pushed the door shut behind her, he asked, "What in the hell are you doing running around the hallway in your nightgown?"

The reminder of how inappropriately she was dressed had absolutely no effect on Anne. All her foggy brain could concentrate on was what she had come for. She smiled broadly and held up Guy's shaving mug. "You forgot this in my room. I brought it to you."

As she handed it to him, Guy said, "Thank you, but that wasn't necessary."

"But, of course, it was. You couldn't shave in the morning without it." Anne leaned forward and peered at his jaw. "And you're going to need a shave by morning. I can already see a faint beard."

Guy seriously doubted that she could see anything, as tipsy as she was, but when Anne leaned forward, he had caught a whiff of her scent, a scent that did strange things to him. Suddenly very aware of her femininity and the total inappropriateness of her being in his room, Guy only wanted to get rid of her. He stepped back and said stiffly, "Thank you."

"You're welcome."

When Anne continued to stand there with a dreamy smile on her face, Guy said, "I think you'd better go back to your room now."

"But it's boring in my room. There's nothing to do there," Anne objected with a little pout.

Guy was acutely aware of her full lower lip sticking out. He felt the sudden urge to take her in his arms and nibble that tempting flesh. Fighting down the urge, he said, "You could go to bed."

"That's not exciting, and I'm not in the least bit sleepy."

Guy knew Anne had no idea what she was doing, but she looked so damned desirable with her long hair hanging around her shoulders and her eyes half-closed with languor, making them look even more seductive. And he was acutely aware that she must be naked beneath her gown. His heat rose, and he felt a tightening in his loins.

"Anne, it's late, and you have no business being in my room, particularly dressed like that."

Anne glanced down at herself. "What's wrong with the way I'm dressed?"

"You're in your nightgown!" Guy answered in exasperation.

"But I'm covered. Besides, my brother sees me in my nightgown all of the time."

"I'm not your brother," Guy answered tersely, "and I'm not a saint," he added ominously. He tossed his gun on the bed and reached around her, opening the door. "It's dangerous for you to be here. Now, go back to your room."

Guy's reference to his not being a saint and the danger she was in went right over Anne's head. She had no idea of what he was implying. All she felt was a keen disappointment. She had hoped . . . Anne wrinkled her brow, trying to remember what she had hoped. Then as it came to her, she smiled and said, "I won't leave until you kiss me good night."

Despite Anne's silly smile, there was a determined set to her chin, and Guy knew he wouldn't get rid of her until he did what she requested. Muttering an oath, he bent forward and quickly pecked her on the forehead.

"That's not the kind of kiss I meant," Anne complained with another little pout. "I meant a *real* kiss."

To Guy's horror, she stepped boldly forward and slipped her arms around his neck. He sucked in his breath sharply at the feel of her soft breasts pressing against his chest, seemingly making a mockery of the material of Anne's gown between them. Feeling his manhood begin to harden and rise, Guy thought, Christ! Doesn't she know what she's doing to me?

He reached up to pull her arms away, but Anne had a death grip around his neck. She pressed even closer, their bodies touching from chest to thigh, stood on her tiptoes, and lifted her mouth in a silent invitation.

A cold sweat broke out on Guy's forehead. Feeling his passion rise at an alarmingly rapid speed, he tried desperately to pry her arms loose, saying harshly, "Anne, stop it! You don't know what you're doing!"

"Don't you like me?" Anne asked with another little pout.

At that moment Guy liked her too damn much for her own good. He groaned and answered, "Yes, but you're playing with—" Guy stopped in mid-sentence when Anne's eyes, which had been closed in anticipation of his kiss, suddenly flew open. Alarmed at her fixed stare, he asked, "What's wrong?"

"The room," Anne answered in a dazed voice. "It's spinning all around."

Anne's arms went limp and slipped from Guy's neck. As her knees buckled, he caught her and swept her up in his arms. Seeing her head loll back over his arm, Guy muttered, "Christ! She's passed out cold!"

Shaking his head in disgust, Guy walked to the door and peered both ways down the darkened hallway. Seeing no one, he walked down the hallway, saying a silent prayer that no one would come out of their room or up the stairs and catch him carrying Anne down the hall in her nightgown and him partially nude, particularly not Jim. He shuddered to think what that ass might do if he caught him in this embarrassing, if not compromising position.

Guy breathed a sigh of relief when he saw Anne had left her door open. She was a dead weight in his arms, and it would have been difficult to get the door open without dropping her. Stepping inside, he kicked the door with the heel of his foot, walked across the room, and set Anne down on the side of the bed, holding her firmly around the shoulders with one arm, while he stripped the bed linens back with his other hand.

Having succeeding in getting Anne in a prone position on the bed, Guy stood and gazed down at her. Despite the fact that she was unconscious, Guy still thought her desirable and tempting as hell. With her long hair spread out around her like a shimmering reddish gold cape, her dark thick eyelashes laying like fans across her flushed cheeks, and her luscious mouth parted, she looked very pretty and very inviting. The soft material of her gown molded her full breasts, leaving nothing to Guy's imagination. He could even see the outline of her rosy nipples, and the steady rise and fall of the mounds seemed to be daring him to reach out and touch them. Feeling his heat rise again, Guy quickly jerked up the covers and firmly tucked them around Anne's shoulders. The movement roused Anne slightly. She moaned and rolled to her side.

The new position gave Guy an excellent view of the mole on her creamy neck just below her ear. He couldn't resist the temptation. He bent his head and kissed the spot, then breathed deeply of her sweet essence, a scent that left his senses reeling.

Suddenly, Guy realized what he was doing. Stealing kisses from a stuporous woman. Christ! How low could he sink? Filled with self-disgust and cursing Anne for being so damn desirable under his breath, he walked quickly from the room, closing the door firmly behind him.

Chapter Five

When Anne woke up the next morning, she felt absolutely wretched. Her head was pounding, the weak winter light coming in through the window hurt her eyes, and every time she moved, she felt nauseous. Even more distressing, she couldn't remember how she had gotten into bed. The last thing she recalled, she had been brushing her hair.

There was no doubt in Anne's mind as to what had caused her malady. She had drank too much wine and was paying the price for her indulgence. My God, she had actually gotten tipsy! No, she admitted, remembering how silly she had acted, she had been *soused.* She wondered what Guy must have thought of her, and was mortified. Why, he was probably totally disgusted with her. The realization that she had made a complete fool out of herself in front of the rugged, exciting engineer made her very depressed.

After lying in the bed a good half-hour brooding over her embarrassing downfall, Anne finally managed to force herself to get up and dress. She'd die before she'd let Guy know she was suffering from a hangover. That would only be more humiliating. Looking at the clothing she had strewn all over the room, she shook her head in disgust, then quickly regretted the movement of her head as another wave of nausea came over her.

She was sitting on the bed and wondering if there was some graceful way she could beg off from going to meet Jim's boss, when a knock sounded at the door. She winced, for the noise seemed inordinately loud, then rose and slowly walked to the door, careful to make no sudden movements for fear it would upset her stomach even more. When she opened the door, she saw her brother standing there and rubbing his head. "What's wrong?" she asked.

"I don't know," Jim answered with a deep scowl on his face. "I woke up with the most god-awful headache this morning. My head has never pounded like this before. You didn't by any chance bring one of Aunt Mae's headache powders with you, did you?"

"No, I never have a headache," Anne answered, thinking, *except for this morning.* Having no more idea than Jim as to what ailed him, she said, "I hope you're not coming down with something."

"So do I, what with starting a new job and all. That's certainly no way to impress a new boss."

Suddenly becoming aware that Guy wasn't with Jim, Anne asked, "Where's Guy?"

"I wasn't finished dressing when he came by. He said he'd meet us in the dining room."

Anne was relieved at the reprieve. It gave her a few more minutes to prepare herself for their meeting.

When Anne and Jim walked into the dining room a few minutes later, Anne had second thoughts. The smells of the food made her feel even more nauseated. She wondered if she shouldn't beg off after all, even if it would make Guy suspect she was suffering from a hangover. That wouldn't be nearly as humiliating as if she got sick in front of him. But Anne found it was too late to turn back. Her brother took her arm in a firm grasp and hurried her across the room to the table where Guy was sitting.

As Guy rose from the table, Anne felt a twinge of resentment. How dare he stand there looking so healthy and robust, when she was feeling so wretched. He'd drank just as much wine as her, or at least she thought he had. She forced herself to look him in the eye, but to her surprise, she saw none of the disgust she had expected. If anything, he looked a little uncomfortable.

"Good morning," Guy said to Anne.

"Good morning," she answered, managing a smile.

She doesn't remember coming to my room, Guy thought with relief. He didn't notice my disgusting condition last night, Anne thought with equal relief.

Jim pulled her chair out, and Anne sat. Then the two men seated themselves and ordered hardy breakfasts. When Anne only ordered tea and toast, Jim asked, "What's wrong? You usually eat a much bigger breakfast than that."

Anne wasn't about to admit how badly she felt. Apparently her brother hadn't noticed her condition last night either, and she wasn't going to take any chances of arousing his suspicions. "I'm just not hungry after that big dinner we ate last night."

"Well, you know what Aunt Mae always said. That breakfast was the most important meal of the day. Are you sure you won't reconsider?"

His mentioning of their overbearing aunt and her annoying sayings didn't help Anne's disposition any. "No, I'm quite sure," she answered a little testily.

While Jim had no earthly idea why Anne was acting so irritable, Guy did. He had noticed how wan she looked when she walked into the room, and suspected she was feeling under the weather from the wine she had consumed. He found himself feeling sorry for her and deliberately drew Jim's attention away from her by initiating a conversation concerning engineering with him.

As the two men talked while they ate their breakfasts, Anne was relieved that they were totally ignoring her with their technical conversation. It was all she could do to concentrate on forcing the dry toast and tea down, but she had to admit that it did seem to settle her stomach a little, enough so that she ordered a second cup of tea. By the time they stepped outside into the cold air, she was feeling a little more human.

When they were settled into the buckboard and driving through town, Jim asked Guy, "How come you live at the hotel and aren't staying in the accommodations the railroad provides?" He assumed that the older engineer must be well-off despite his humble beginnings, if he could afford such luxurious quarters.

"I don't usually stay at the hotel, but I just got back from a year in the field surveying, and I'm giving myself a little treat."

"You were a whole year in the field?" Jim asked in a shocked voice.

"Yes."

Jim scowled deeply. "I wasn't told anything about being expected to do surveys. I should think U.P. would consider it a waste of talent and money to expect their engineers to do something an ordinary surveyor could do."

"Surveying is an important part of railroad engineering. We're not just doing ordinary land surveys, you know, plotting out lots and tracts of land. We're laying out the route for a railroad, where the highest rise can't be more than five feet every hundred and the steepest grade on every curve has to be less than ten degrees. And we have to be sure our cuts will yield enough material for our fills. That demands an advanced technology that the ordinary surveyor doesn't have the training for."

"Yes, but I didn't hire on with the U.P. to do surveying. I want to do construction."

"We all do. We're all much more interested in the actual building than the planning, but without that planning, the whole project could be a failure. Besides, if you're worrying about having to do surveying, I think you can forget it. That part of the job is almost done. The surveying party I left up in the Rockies ought to be able to finish it up this spring."

"Is that where you just got back from, the Rockies?" Anne asked Guy.

"Yes, a few days ago."

"But it must have been terribly cold up in those mountains," she commented. "You'd think it would be too cold to work outside."

"It was a little chilly," Guy admitted, "but the eastern side of the Rockies doesn't get the snowfall that the western side does. It's the Central Pacific up in the Sierras that's really got it rough. Last winter, they had forty feet of snow dumped on them. It was so deep that they had to tunnel their way from their living quarters to the tunnel they were blasting. Those Chinese laborers didn't see the light of day for the entire winter."

"The Central Pacific is using Chinese laborers?" Jim asked in surprise.

"Yes."

"But why?"

"Because they're incredibly hard workers, and they don't give the railroad the labor problems that the Irish workers did. They wouldn't dream of striking, and they never miss work because of drunkenness. The strongest thing they ever drink is tea. And the Chinese will do dangerous things that you could never get a white man to do."

"Like what?" Anne asked.

"The Sierra Nevada aren't like ordinary mountains. They don't rise gradually. They go straight up in the air, and they're made of solid granite. The only way the Central Pacific could cut their way around those mountainsides was to hand chisel a ledge into them. They accomplished that by lowering the Chinese in little wicker baskets over the sides of the mountains, where they whittled away until they could get a hole big enough to place a charge of black powder. The white laborers were too terrified of the heights, to say nothing of the blasting. More than one time, those Chinese weren't pulled up fast enough after a charge had been set, and they were blown to pieces. Also there were many times that the ropes on those baskets broke, and the Chinese were plunged to their deaths. No one else but them would do it."

"Do they lay rails, too?" Jim asked.

"Yes."

"But they're such little men," Jim objected. "You wouldn't think they'd be strong enough."

"It's true that they're little. Not many weigh much more than a hundred pounds, but they're strong. The Irish construction workers laughed at the first gang of Chinese that arrived on the construction site. Like you, they thought they were too small to be good workers. But the Chinese put the Irishmen to shame. When Charlie Crocker, the C.P.'s chief of construction, saw what they could do, he made arrangements for five thousand to be shipped over from China. Now the C.P. uses Celestials almost exclusively."

"But still, it doesn't seem right, using Chinese to build a

railroad here in America," Jim remarked, his voice tinged with scorn.

Guy refrained from commenting, knowing Jim's opinion was based more on blind prejudice than anything else. Harvey Strobridge, Crocker's chief, shared the same low regard for the Asians, and drove them like slaves. The Chinese were terrified of him. But Crocker knew their value and appreciated them. For that reason, they were known as Crocker's Pets.

By this time, the trio had left Cheyenne behind and were driving into a busy railroad yard. Wagons piled high with construction materials were everywhere, and Guy had to weave their way around them and through crowds of construction workers dressed in leather jackets and high boots, with picks and shovels slung over their shoulders. Locomotives sat about on the various tracks, their smokestacks sending up puffs of grayish white smoke. One blew its whistle, making Anne jump at the sudden, unexpected sound, then chugged away from the coal bin where it had been loading up.

Staring at several construction workers walking in front of them, Jim suddenly spied something that he hadn't noticed before. "Why, that man is wearing a pair of Confederate trousers. What's that Johnny Reb doing here?"

"The war is over, particularly out here," Guy answered in a hard voice. "The U.P. hires both Yankee and Confederate veterans, and they're damn glad to have them, since they know how to handle weapons and most are good shots. As far as the railroad is concerned, knowing how to defend yourself against an Indian attack is a lot more important than which side of the war you fought on. We're here to build a railroad. Nothing else. Any man who doesn't remember that doesn't belong here."

Jim held his tongue, but Guy's answer angered him. Who did Guy think he was, lecturing to him like that? Guy might be able to forget the war so quickly, but Jim couldn't. As far as he was concerned, those Rebels were still his enemy.

When Guy pulled the wagon up to one of the many cars sitting on the tracks and reined in, Anne was surprised. She had expected the railroad's offices to be housed in a building.

As they climbed from the wagon, Anne was acutely aware of the construction workers and teamsters, sitting on the wagons eyeing her curiously. Having no idea how unusual it was for a lady to be seen visiting the yard, she thought their stares terribly rude. Then, when she reached the stairs of the car Guy led them to, she found, to her dismay, that there was no step stool. She was still pondering over the dilemma of how to reach the bottom step of the stairs and yet maintain her modesty, when Guy picked her up by the waist and lifted her to the stairs.

Anne sucked in her breath sharply. As he stepped up beside her, Guy said, "Sorry. I guess I should have warned you."

It wasn't that Guy's picking her up had surprised her. Anne had caught her breath because his hands had seemed to burn her right through her layers of clothing. And he was standing much too close, so close that she could feel his heat and smell his scent, a mixture of tobacco smoke, shaving soap, leather, and a faint, utterly masculine scent that made her senses reel. She was vastly relieved when he stepped away and opened the door at the back of the car.

As they walked into the car, Anne quickly glanced about her, seeing it was furnished with two battered desks, a few overstuffed chairs, and a large table. Several maps hung on the walls, obscuring a few of the windows, and there was a big potbellied stove at the back of the car. Other than that, the car was empty.

"I guess Sam must have been called away for a minute," Guy commented. "Make yourselves comfortable."

Anne sat down in one of the overstuffed chairs, while Jim walked to one of the maps and peered at it. "Is this the route the U.P. will be taking?" he asked.

"Yes," Guy answered, sitting in another overstuffed chair and crossing his long legs in front of him, "all but the last fifty or so miles, which haven't been surveyed yet."

"When will we reach the Rockies?"

"Actually we've already laid tracks through a spur of them, the Black Hills, just east of Cheyenne. We had a devil of a time finding a pass through those hills, even with the Mormons helping us."

"I didn't realize there were any Mormons in this territory," Jim remarked. "I thought they were all in Utah."

"No, there are a few scattered around in the Nebraska Territory, particularly the part between here and Utah. But as I said, not even they knew a pass through the Black Hills. It was Gen. Dodge who found it, while he was still in the army. He'd been sent out here to clear the area of Indians, or rather, since he had an interest in the U.P., had *arranged* to be stationed in the Black Hills, and while being chased by a bunch of Sioux, his scout, Jim Bridger, took him back to the fort by way of a circumspect route, around crags and boulders, skirting Crow Creek here and Lodge Pole Creek there. According to the story, Bridger complained that they damn near got caught and scalped, because Dodge was so busy taking notes on the scenery, but by the time they had gotten back to the fort, Dodge knew he had found the pass. If he hadn't, we might still be sitting back at Platte City and completely stymied."

"Why did Dodge leave the army, anyway?" Jim asked.

"For two reasons. When the government made that last peace treaty with the Indians, he was thoroughly disgusted. He's a die-hard Indian hater, and if he had his way about it, the army would wipe out every Indian in this country. Second, the chief engineer of U.P. at that time, Peter Dey, quit, and the railroad offered Dodge ten thousand dollars a year to take the job."

Jim was impressed at the princely sum the railroad had offered Dodge, and was even more determined to prove himself chief material on this job. "Why did he quit? I understand he's one of the top railroad engineers in this country."

"He is, but he couldn't stand anymore of Col. Seymore's interference. Seymore is Dr. Durant's assistant and doesn't know a damn thing about building railroads. None of the engineering staff have much use for him, nor do the construction workers. He rides a horse they call Knock 'em Stiff, and carries an open umbrella to keep off the sun when he's making inspection trips. Besides looking ridiculous, he asks a million stupid questions. But he doesn't interfere as much, now that Dodge in is command. Dodge outranked him in the army and doesn't put up with any of his foolishness."

The door opened and two men walked in. Guy rose to his feet and introduced Jim and Anne to Samuel Reed, Superintendent of the the Engineers, and John Caseman, Chief of Construction. After the amenities had been finished, Anne stared at Caseman. Reed was an ordinary-looking, middle-aged man, but Gen. Jack, as Casemen had quickly said to call him, was like no other man Anne had ever seen. He was a short man, five-feet-four inches, and almost as broad as he was tall, with a thick, bushy black beard. He was dressed in a fur cap, leather coat, and high surveyor's boots, and his belt was bristling with revolvers, to say nothing of the long, black whip he carried. To Anne, he looked more like a wild cossack than a construction chief.

"Well, Jim, I'm pleased to have you," Reed said politely. "I assume you're ready to go to work."

"I certainly am, sir."

"That's not necessary," Reed answered with a friendly smile. "Just call me Sam, like the rest of my staff does. Any particular phase of railroad engineering that you're interested in? I try to keep my engineer's preferences in mind, but let me warn you, I'll have to use you where I feel you're the most needed."

"I prefer building bridges, sir."

Sam frowned at Jim's persistence in calling him sir, then said, "I don't know if there is an opening there or not, particularly since Leonard Eicholtz, my head bridge engineer, requested that I bring Guy back from the surveying team he was working with. You see, Leonard was so impressed with the bridge Guy designed over the Loop River that he insisted I call him back, now that we'll be running into more streams and rivers, and building more bridges and trestles. Guy's bridge took a tremendous battering in the spring floods last year, but miraculously held. Leonard insists Guy's rather radical design was the reason for it."

Jim highly resented Reed praising Guy and the admiration he saw in the chief engineer's eyes. "Still, sir, I'd like to work on bridges," Jim said stiffly. "I have some rather revolutionary ideas myself."

"Do you now?" Reed asked with interest. "Well, we certainly can use men with innovative ideas out here. We're coming up against some engineering obstacles we've never encountered before, what with the steep mountainous ravines and all. Not even the Alleghenies presented us with so many challenges. I'll talk to Leonard and tell him to give you a try."

"Thank you, sir. When will I begin work?"

"We should be pulling out the day after tomorrow."

"So soon, sir?" Jim asked in surprise.

"Yes, with the chinook wind blowing now, things should be warming up quite rapidly."

Jim had no idea what a chinook wind was, but he wasn't going to show his ignorance by asking. Anne, however, had no qualms, and did ask.

"It's a warm wind that comes over the Rockies in this part of the country," Reed explained. "It was named after an Indian tribe in Oregon. Once those winds start blowing, like it did today, spring is just around the corner. Even Gen. Jack will be moving his rolling factory town in two days."

"I beg your pardon," Jim said in confusion. "Rolling factory town?"

"You haven't seen my rolling town yet?" Gen. Jack asked in a booming voice. "Well, come on, folks. I've got something to show you."

Gen. Jack led Anne and Jim from the car, with Sam and Guy bringing up the rear. They walked across several railroad tracks, and then Gen. Jack turned and pointed to the long line of cars they had just left. "That's it," he said proudly, "my rolling town. The two flatcars in front hold all our tools and my blacksmith shop. Those four three-decker boxcars behind them are where the construction workers sleep. They hold four hundred men. The car behind it is the dining car," he said, pointing to an unusually long boxcar. Motioning to a string of smaller cars, he said, "Next is the cookhouse, behind that the bakery, then the butcher shop, the storeroom and general store, a bar for the construction workers, my office, and last, the engineers' office we just came from. Everything's on wheels. Except for striking a few tents, we can move the entire construction camp out in a moment's notice."

Jim and Anne were amazed. It *was* a town on wheels. The only thing it lacked was a barber shop, a post office, and a church.

Jim was relieved to hear that they would be pulling out soon. He didn't like the idea of Anne being in Cheyenne for any longer than absolutely necessary. But there was something he couldn't figure out. "You said that all you had to do was strike a few tents. What about the families' quarters? Don't you have to dismantle them?"

"What family quarters?" Sam asked.

"Why, the houses the railroad workers' families live in."

"We don't provide any quarters for our workers' families," Sam informed him. "If they come out here, they only come for a short visit. Then they stay at a hotel in the nearest town."

"Are you saying you don't have any families living near the construction site?" Anne asked, looking obviously distressed.

"No, we don't," Sam answered.

Anne shot her brother a sharp look. "I'm sorry, Anne," Jim said. "I didn't realize the railroad didn't provide quarters for families. I'm afraid you'll have to go back to Ohio."

A stunned expression came over Sam's, Gen. Jack's and Guy's faces. All had assumed that Anne had just come for a brief visit before her brother went to work. Not one of them could believe that the young engineer had actually brought his sister along to live with him in a construction camp.

But as stunned as the three men were, Anne was even more so. She couldn't go back to that dull, dreary little country town, where the most exciting thing that ever happened was the county fair. The place had been nothing but a prison. But even more important, she couldn't go back to living with her hateful aunt and uncle. She had felt like she was on the brink of insanity when her brother had rescued her and told her she could live with him from now on. No, she couldn't go back to that. She *wouldn't* go back! "No, Jim, I won't go back."

"Didn't you hear what Mr. Reed said? There's no place for you to stay out here."

"I'll stay in Cheyenne."

"No, you won't," Jim said in an adamant voice. "I

won't have you living in that wicked, dangerous town. It's no place for a respectable woman."

Anne looked around desperately. Then, spying a large woman standing in the doorway of the dining car, she asked, "Who is that woman?"

"Why that's Big Bertha," Gen. Jack answered, "my head cook."

"You hire women cooks?" Anne asked in surprise.

"I sure do. Of course, most of my cooks are men, but women are a lot more reliable. They don't drink, except for a little nip now and then, and they don't take off every time they hear about a new gold or silver strike someplace."

An excited glitter came to Anne's eyes. "Can you use another cook, Gen. Jack?"

Gen. Jack cocked his head and asked, "Are you talking about yourself, young lady?"

"I certainly am."

Jim gasped, then said in a shocked voice', "Anne! You can't be serious!"

"Of course, I'm serious!" Anne retorted. "If I hire on with the railroad, too, I can go with you."

"Not exactly, miss," Sam said, breaking into the conversation, "If Jim is working on a bridge crew, he'll be twenty or thirty miles in front of the end of the line. You'll hardly ever see him."

"But I will see him occasionally," Anne countered.

"I won't allow it, Anne," Jim said in a firm voice. "I won't have you working around all these rough men without me here to protect you. It's too dangerous."

"Now just a minute, young fellow," Gen. Jack said in a stern voice. "Let me get something clear here. I don't allow any of my men pestering my women workers, They mind their manners around them, or they answer to me. And you can take my word for it. There isn't a man within fifty miles of my construction camp that will tangle with me."

Jim didn't doubt the tough construction chief's word for one minute. He was a terrifying-looking character, with his wild beard and his arsenal of guns. "But you have no decent living quarters for women."

"I can pitch a tent right outside my office for her. That's where the Indian women I hire live, in their own tepees. Or she could bunk in with Big Bertha in the cookhouse. But I don't think she'd want to do that, not the way Big Bertha snores."

"You can't be seriously considering hiring her?" Jim asked in horror.

"Well, that just depends upon how good a cook she is." The construction chief turned to Anne and asked, "Are you a good cook? You know the men won't tolerate one that isn't. They'll flat run them right out of camp."

"I'm a good cook, Gen. Jack," Anne answered. "I promise you won't be disappointed in me."

The construction chief smiled broadly behind his black, bushy beard. "Then you're hired, young lady. You can report to work the day after tomorrow. But you'd better get here early. We'll be pulling out at noon."

Anne beamed at his answer, while Sam, Guy, and Jim looked on in utter disbelief. Finally, Jim recovered and stepped forward, saying to Gen. Jack, "Now, just a minute. I think I have something to say about this. I absolutely forbid my sister to hire on with the railroad." Seeing Anne opening her mouth to object, Jim cut across her words, saying in a stern voice, "No! I don't want to hear another word about it! It's settled. You're going back to Ohio."

Anne was furious at her brother. Here she had just gotten out from under two domineering people, and now he was trying to tell her what to do. She glared at him with impotent fury. Jim glared back.

Gen. Jack glanced from brother to sister. Obviously, the little lady wasn't going to take her brother's dictate sitting down, and he had a feeling Anne had a determined streak a mile wide in her. "I tell you what. You two talk it over privately." He turned to Anne and said, "If you want the job, it's yours. You know where my office is."

Jim was livid at Gen. Jack. How dare the construction chief tell Anne he'd hire her over his objections. He had no right to interfere in family business. He took Anne's arm in his hand and said, "She won't be taking the job, Gen. Jack—and that's final!"

Jim turned and firmly led Anne away to the buckboard. Gen. Jack grinned. He had a feeling he was going to see Anne again—real soon. He turned and walked back to the line of railroad cars, calling out to several construction workers who were passing the time of day discussing the big fight in Cheyenne the night before, "Get to work, you damn Tarriers! The railroad isn't paying you Paddies to stand around and loaf!"

As the big Irishmen scurried off, Guy said to his boss, "I can't believe Jack would actually hire her."

"You know Jack," Sam answered. "He'll hire anyone. Disgruntled farmers, disappointed miners, gamblers down on their luck, Indians. He's desperate for workers, especially good cooks."

"But Anne's not like those other women. They're tough old cougars, as tough and rough as the construction workers. She's led a sheltered life. She's never been exposed to such crude, ill-mannered men. Why, their vile language alone would shock her."

"I know. I can't say I approve myself. But I don't think the men would harm her, even if General Jack wouldn't be putting her under his protection. You know yourself that they have a strange chivalry out here, a deep respect for women, all women. I've never seen it anyplace but here in the West. Why, they won't even lay a hand on a prostitute who robs them."

"But still, a construction camp is no place for a respectable woman," Guy persisted.

"Well, I don't think we're really going to have to worry about it. You heard what Jim said, that he absolutely forbade it. He'll handle it."

Guy gazed off at the brother and sister in the distance. Anne's back was rigid with fury, and he hadn't missed seeing the determined set of her chin when Jim led her away. Guy strongly suspected Jim was going to have a hell of a fight on his hands, and actually felt sorry for the younger engineer.

Chapter Six

The ride back to the hotel was an uncomfortable one for Guy. Anne and Jim both sat rigidly on the buckboard, staring straight ahead, neither uttering a word. Guy could feel the anger that was seething in both of them, and felt like he was sitting on top of a keg of black powder, about to explode at any minute.

It did explode, and Guy wasn't out of hearing distance when it did. No sooner had the door to Anne's room closed behind them, than Guy heard Anne shriek out at her brother, "How dare you! How dare you forbid me to hire on with the railroad. How dare you forbid me to do anything! I just got rid of two domineering people in my life, and now you're trying to tell me what I can or can't do. I won't tolerate it. I won't!"

"Sssh! Lower your voice."

"No! I won't lower my voice. I'm not going to do any damn thing you tell me to do. I'm tired of people ordering me around."

"Anne!" Jim said in a shocked voice. "Watch your language. Do you know what you just said?"

She had said damn, and it had felt good to say it. As angry as she was, no other word was strong enough to express her feelings. "You're damn right I know what I said, and I'll say it any time I damn well feel like it!"

Jim stared at his sister in stunned silence for a moment, then asked, "What in the world has gotten into you? I've never seen you like this. So angry, so . . . so unreasonable!"

"Unreasonable? Is it unreasonable for me to want to make my own decisions for a change, to run my own life? I'm sick and tired of being told by everyone what to do. First Uncle Ben and Aunt Mae telling me what to do, what to think, what to say, even what to wear. And now you're trying to boss me around. Dammit, I'm not a child! I'm a grown woman."

"I can understand your feelings about Uncle Ben and Aunt Mae. They're both incredibly domineering people. But there's a big difference in them and me. I'm your brother. I love you. I'm genuinely concerned about your welfare."

"Then how can you ask me to go back to that, to living with them? You know how they are. So bossy, so narrow-minded, so penny-pinching. My God, they treated us like we were slaves, instead of relatives! We ran around in rags, working ourselves to death, and they begrudged us every morsel of food we put into our mouths, and we both know our father left money for our support. Why, if Uncle Ben could have figured out a way to cheat you out of your inheritance to go to college, he would have taken that, too. But *you* got to get away from them! I didn't! It wasn't until you brought me along on this job that I finally got away and saw there was another world out here, a world I never dreamed existed. I can't go back, Jim. I can't!"

"I don't want you to have to go back," Jim said in all sincerity, "but you can't stay out here either. Working for the railroad is no place for a respectable woman."

"Why not? You work for them. You're respectable."

"For Christ's sake, Anne," Jim said in exasperation. "I'm a man. That's different."

"Why is it different? Do you think women don't have any sense of adventure? Do you think only men should lead exciting lives? No, Jim. There are important things going on out here. Exciting things! And I want to be a part of it, too. I won't go back to that dull, dreary town living with those mean, hateful people. I'm going to take the job Gen. Jack offered me."

"You'll do no such thing!" Jim bellowed. "I won't allow it!"

"And just how are you going to stop me?" Anne asked, her anger once more on the rise. "I'm a grown woman. I'm twenty-two years old. You can't stop me. No one can!"

"You'd defy me?" Jim asked in utter disbelief. "You'd deliberately do something you know I disapprove of?"

"Yes, I would, Jim. But not because I want to spite you or hurt you. It's something I'm doing for myself. I want to be in complete control of my life."

"But I'm your brother! I'm responsible for you."

"No, Jim, I'm responsible for myself. That's what I'm trying to tell you. I'm a grown woman. I want to live my own life as I see fit."

"But you'll be making a big mistake!"

"If it's a mistake, then I can only blame myself for it. But I'm going to take that job."

Suddenly, Jim realized that the Anne he was talking to was a total stranger to him. He'd never dreamed that his sister had such a strong will, that once she had set her mind to something, she could be so determined. Utterly exasperated, he threw up his arms and yelled, "All right then! Be stubborn about it! Take the damn job! But don't say I didn't warn you!"

Jim stormed from the room, slamming the door shut behind him.

Down the hall, in his room, Guy heard Jim's angry footsteps outside his door and then going down the steps. He had also overheard the entire conversation, for the rooms had thin walls, and Jim's and Anne's voices had been raised. He was just as exasperated with Anne as Jim was. Crazy fool, he thought. She doesn't have the slightest idea of what she's getting into.

He wondered if he should try to reason with her, since her brother had gotten absolutely nowhere. If Anne was his sister, he'd make her leave, even if he had to hogtie her to a seat on a train going back East, and order the conductor not to untie her until they had reached Omaha. But Anne wasn't his sister. She wasn't his responsibility. It really wasn't any of his business.

But the longer Guy thought about it, the more convinced he became that he should give it a try. Maybe Anne would be more receptive to reason from someone who wouldn't get so emotionally involved. Unlike Jim, he would remain calm and cool, presenting the reasons for her not to accept the job in a logical manner. Right now, the prospect of working for the railroad looked exciting to her, but when he presented the hard, cold facts, surely she'd relent. She hadn't struck him as being stupid.

Guy rose from where he was lying on the bed, walked to the door and down the hall to Anne's room. Hearing the knock on her door and thinking it was her brother, Anne frowned. Had Jim come back to resume the argument, or to apologize for getting so angry at her? She hoped it was the latter. They had never had a disagreement before, and it upset her knowing that he was displeased with her. But she wouldn't back down, she promised herself. No matter what.

She opened the door and saw Guy standing there. "May I talk to you privately for a minute?" he asked.

Stunned by his request, Anne stepped back.

As Guy shut the door behind him, he said, "I don't mean to pry into your business, but I couldn't help overhearing you and Jim. I can understand why you want to take the job with the railroad. What's happening out here *is* exciting. But I don't think you have any idea of just how much work the job involves."

Anne highly resented Guy's interference. "You're right, Mr. Masters, it isn't any of your business," she said in an frosty voice. "And for you information, I'm not afraid of a little work."

Jesus, Guy thought, she could freeze hell over with that icy look. "Please, call me Guy. After all, we're friends. For that reason, I feel I should warn you about what you'd be getting yourself into. I'm not talking about a little work, Anne. I'm talking about hard labor. You'll be expected to lift heavy sacks, to work long hours over a hot stove, to—"

"I worked from dawn to dusk in my uncle's store, and I lifted more than one feed sack," Anne interjected. "I'm stronger than I look."

Guy frowned. Things weren't going the way he had expected. "All right, so you're stronger than you look," he conceded, seriously doubting her claim, "but have you ever lived in a tent? I have. Believe me, they can get damn hot in the summer and terribly cold in the winter. And there's a lot of dust around a construction camp. Besides choking you and making your eyes water, it sits an inch thick on everything. Water is scarce. There's not enough for bathing. The only full bath you'll get is when we hit a creek or a river. That's the only time you'll be able to wash your clothes, too. You're not used to such harsh living conditions, Anne. Why, I bet you've never slept on a hard cot in your life."

Anne doubted if anything could be harder than the narrow little bed her aunt and uncle had provided for her. And she'd be more than willing to put up with a few inconveniences to get away from them. Besides, Guy trying to talk her out of it was only making her more determined to take the job. "Thank you for warning me, but I still intend to take the job."

Guy felt his frustration rise. Why in hell wasn't she listening to him? He had presented all the facts to her, and she had shrugged them aside as if they were nothing. "It's too dangerous! There are Indian attacks, buffalo stampedes, prairie fires, outbreaks of cholera."

"I can take care of myself."

Her overly confident answer infuriated Guy. Hell, she was a woman, as vulnerable as they came. "Sure you can," he said sarcastically. "The first night in Cheyenne you got drunk. Is that how you take care of yourself?"

He had noticed, Anne thought in mortification, but she was determined she wouldn't admit it. "I did no such thing!" she denied hotly.

"Like hell you didn't! I bet you don't even remember coming to my room."

Anne's eyes widened in surprise. "I thought not," Guy commented. "Yes, you came to my room later that night, dressed in just your nightgown, and you wouldn't leave until I had kissed you."

Anne was horrified. She wouldn't do that, not even drunk. "You're making that up!"

"No, Anne, I'm not making it up. Then you passed out, and I had to carry you back to your room."

That's why she couldn't remember going to bed, Anne thought, feeling sick with humiliation.

"So you see, you aren't capable of taking care of yourself. If I hadn't been a gentleman, I shudder to think of what could have happened to you. It's too dangerous out here for you. Go back to Ohio."

Guy's last words seemed too much like a command to Anne. Her anger rose like a monumental wave. "Who in the devil do you think you are, ordering me around? If I won't let my brother boss me, I'm certainly not going to let you tell me what to do."

"Haven't you heard a damn thing I've said? It's too dangerous for a woman like you out here. You could get hurt. Everyone isn't a gentleman. Something could happen, something you couldn't defend yourself against."

"Like what?" Anne threw out recklessly.

"Like this," Guy answered, stepping forward and sweeping her into his arms.

He kissed her hard and savagely, wanting to frighten her, wanting to prove how helpless she was against a man's strength. Anne struggled, and Guy tightened his arms, molding her soft curves to his long body. But taking her into his arms had been Guy's undoing. Subconsciously, he didn't want to hurt her; he didn't want to scare her. Ever since the night before, when he had held her in his arms, he wanted to make love to her.

Insidiously, without Guy even realizing he was doing it, his kiss softened, his lips coaxing and wooing. The change from fierce demand to gentle seduction bewildered Anne. When his tongue glazed her bottom lip, then her teeth, she melted into him, opening her mouth instinctively. As his tongue darted into her mouth, plundering her sweetness, Anne became wildly excited. She had never been kissed so masterfully, so skillfully, so totally. She stood on tiptoes in a silent, but eloquent plea for more.

Guy was intoxicated by the sweet taste of Anne's mouth, her drugging womanly scent, her incredible softness pressed against him. He slipped his hand between them and cupped her breast, then slid his thumb over the crest. Feeling the nipple spring to life and hearing Anne moan, Guy's passion rose, hot and urgent. He ground his hips into hers. It wasn't until he felt his manhood harden and press almost painfully against his tight pants that Guy finally came to his senses. My God, what in the hell was he doing? If he didn't stop now, he wouldn't be able to!

He jerked his mouth away and stepped back. Her senses still reeling, Anne swayed. Holding her with one hand, but still carefully keeping his distance, Guy said in a roughened voice, "That's what could happen, Anne. That and a hell of a lot more. And there wouldn't be a damn thing you could do to stop it."

His words were like a dash of ice water on Anne's heated senses. Why, he had only kissed her to teach her a lesson. How dare he! How dare he arouse her passion like that, then toss her aside. "No! You just caught me by surprise."

"And what's to keep another man from catching you by surprise, Anne? Women are scarce in these parts, and the men working on those construction crews are hungry for women. I stopped at a kiss. They wouldn't."

"You heard what Gen. Jack said, that he didn't allow the men to pester any of his women workers."

"The other women cooks aren't as young and pretty as you are. They aren't as much of a temptation. What are you going to do if Gen. Jack isn't around to protect you? He can't be nearby all the time. He has a job to do. What will you do then? A man whose dead set on having you can overpower you. You simply aren't strong enough to fight him off."

"Then I'll get a gun and wear it all the time, like those women I saw out in the street."

The women Anne had seen were prostitutes. They all wore a derringer strapped to their waist, guns they were dead shots with. It wasn't their virtue they were protecting, but their purses, and they weren't protecting them from the railroad workers, but rather the other scum of the earth. Guy laughed harshly. "What good would that do you? You don't even know how to shoot one."

"Then I'll learn!" Anne retorted.

Christ! Guy thought. No matter what argument he had, she had some smart comeback for it. She was the most exasperating woman he'd ever met. He didn't blame Jim for getting angry with her. "You're the most stubborn woman I've ever had the misfortune to encounter."

Anne's eyes flashed, looking like blue fire. "I didn't ask for your opinion of me, Mr. Masters. Frankly, I don't give a damn what you think. And what I do is none of your business. Now get out!"

Anne was pretty, but when she was angry, she was magnificent. She seemed to grow taller right before Guy's eyes, and with her full breasts heaving and her eyes spitting sparks, she looked like an avenging goddess. He stared at her in mute fascination.

"Damn you! Did you hear what I said? I said get out!"

Almost too late, Guy saw the washbasin that Anne picked up and threw at him. He barely had time to duck before the missile flew over his head and hit the door behind him.

Seeing Anne pick up the water pitcher, he put up his hand and said, "Whoa, there! I'm leaving."

Guy opened the door and turned. "But just for the record, you won't last a week. You'll be begging to go back to Ohio."

His words were like a gauntlet thrown down at Anne's feet. She was even more determined to prove him wrong. "We'll see about that!" she threw back. "Now get out!"

Seeing her raise the water pitcher, Guy quickly stepped into the hall and pulled the door shut. Hearing the pitcher hit the wooden panel with a loud crash, he muttered, "Christ! What a hellcat!"

Guy turned and walked down the hall. Well, he'd tried to reason with her, he consoled himself. If anything happened to her, it was her own damn fault. He sure as hell wasn't going to worry about her. He had a lot better things to worry about than some hardheaded, crazy female.

But secretly, so secretly that he would have never admitted it to himself, Guy was glad Anne wasn't going back to Ohio. He'd never met such such a high-spirited woman, or one that seemed as complex as Anne. She wasn't at all what she had appeared to be at first. The engineer in him would like to take her apart and find out what made her tick. The man in him simply wanted to find out what it would be like to make love to her.

Chapter Seven

Two days later, early in the morning, Jim and Anne climbed into the buckboard that he had arranged for to transport them to the railroad yards, while the driver of the rented wagon loaded their luggage into the back. As they drove off, Anne glanced over at her brother and knew he was still dead-set against her taking the job with the railroad. Jim was sitting stiffly on the seat and staring straight ahead; he had hardly spoken a civil word to her all morning. Considering how angry he was at her, she supposed she should be glad that he had even agreed to take her with him, and not force her into having to hire her own transportation to her new job.

Anne was torn between two emotions; excitement at starting her new job, and regret that Jim wasn't in accord with her. There had never been a rift between them, but then, she had never gone against his wishes before. This was the first time she had ever shown any independence, but it was a heady feeling, one she was determined she wouldn't relinquish. Not only that, but she could even earn her own money. From now on, she would be in complete control of her life, and her brother would have to learn to live with that fact. After all, she didn't try to tell *him* what to do. Surely she deserved the same consideration. And deep down, Anne knew he loved her. He'd relent in time.

Putting aside her regret that she and Jim weren't in accord, Anne turned her attention to her surroundings. The town itself was quiet. The only people Anne saw were a merchant, sweeping the boardwalk before his store, and a sleepy bartender, yawning as he stood between the swinging doors, before he turned and made a beeline for his bed. But when they reached the railroad yard, the place was in a frenzy of preparations for departure, for although construction had continued during the long, cold winter, it was beginning in earnest now that spring was right around the corner.

A line of covered wagons were drawn up before a large warehouse, where they were being hurriedly loaded with food supplies, blankets, tents, guns, and ammunition for the grading and bridge parties that worked far ahead of the end of the line. Several flatcars sat on a track beside another warehouse and were being loaded with iron rails, wooden ties, and barrels of spikes and bolts. All around them, tents were being stuck, the sounds of the hammers rang out over the hiss of steam coming from the locomotives that sat on several tracks and the rumble of wagons filled with graders and bridge roustabouts, who were already pulling out. Everybody on foot was hustling about, and the air crackled with excitement.

"Where do you want me to drop you off?" the driver asked Jim.

"At the engineers' office," Jim replied, remembering that Gen. Jack had said his office was next door.

The driver drove the wagon up beside the car and stopped, then jumped down and started piling Anne's and Jim's luggage on the ground. Anne and Jim climbed down, and while Jim was paying the driver, she looked around her, wondering if she should report to Gen. Jack's office or wait for him here.

Her dilemma was solved when she saw the burly construction chief hurrying across the yard towards her, sending construction workers scurrying out of his way. And no wonder, Anne thought. With his size and all that black hair on his face, he looked rather like a locomotive barreling down the rails. And to think that this huge, fierce-looking man was going to be her boss. A little tingle of fear ran over her.

"Well, hello there, young lady," the construction chief thundered, as he came to a stop in front of her. "Did you decide to take the job?"

His booming welcome left Anne's ears ringing. She smiled bravely and answered, "Yes, I did, Gen. Jack. I'm ready to go to work."

"Well, I'm mighty glad to hear that. As soon as you say good-bye to your brother, I'll take you to the cookhouse and introduce you to Big Bertha. She'll take charge of you. You just give me a call when you're ready."

As the construction chief rushed off, Anne turned to her brother and said, "Well, I guess this is good-bye for a while."

At Anne's words the cold, forbidding expression on Jim's face was replaced with a deeply concerned one. "Oh, Jim, don't worry about me. I'm going to be fine. It's not like you're leaving me all alone. You heard what Gen. Jack said. I'll be under another, older woman's care. And please don't let this come between us. You're all I have in this world."

"I know," Jim admitted with a hangdog expression on his face, "and you're all I have, too. But I sure wish you wouldn't do this, Anne."

"Let's not get into that again. It will only spoil our parting."

Jim reached into his coat pocket and pulled out a handful of bills. He handed them to Anne, saying, "If you change your mind, this should get you back to Ohio."

Seeing Anne about to object, he said quickly, "No, don't argue. Please take it. It would relieve my mind, knowing that you weren't stranded out here until I got back."

Anne decided it would be better to keep her mouth shut and take the money. She accepted it, stepped up to her brother, and kissed his cheek. "Thank you."

"You will be careful?" Jim asked.

"Yes, and you be careful, too."

Jim looked about him, then seeing Sam motioning to him from where he was standing by a wagon loaded with men in the distance, he said, "Well, it appears we're ready to pull out. I'd better go."

He turned and quickly kissed Anne on the cheek, then picked up his two valises and rushed off, calling over his shoulder, "I'll see you in a few weeks."

Anne watched her brother thread his way through the crowd. When he reached the wagon, a man standing on it bent down and offered him his hand. She knew only one man with shoulders that broad. Guy. It dawned on her that the only two people she knew out here were leaving her behind with total strangers, and she felt a twinge of fear. Sudden doubts assailed her. Then, when Guy rose, and their eyes met over the distance between them, Anne remembered his last words to her. No, she thought, firming her resolve, she wouldn't go running like a scared rabbit. And she wouldn't fail. She'd show that bastard a thing or two.

"Anne?"

Anne almost jumped out of her skin at the loud sound of her name. She turned and saw Gen. Jack standing there.

"Are you ready to go meet Big Bertha now?"

"I'm ready," Anne answered, her heart still pounding from the fright he had given her.

As Anne started to bend to pick up her two cardboard suitcases, Gen. Jack made a quick grab for them. Then he turned and walked down the line of cars, with Anne hurrying to keep up with him. Goodness, she thought, with such short legs, you wouldn't think he could move so fast.

When they reached the cookhouse, Gen. Jack stood politely to the side of the wooden stairs, so that Anne could go up them first. Well, despite all his gruffness and his terrifying appearance, he's a gentleman, Anne thought. She climbed the stairs and stepped into the cookhouse. Then she came face to face with a woman who could only be Big Bertha.

When Anne had seen the woman across the railroad yard two days before, she had known she was large, but she had never dreamed she was this big. The head cook towered over her by a good foot, and her shoulders were as wide as a man's. As Anne's eyes quickly skimmed over Bertha's body, she realized that the rest of her fit her impressive frame. She wasn't fat. She was just big all over. Why, she was a giant!

"Big Bertha, this is Anne Phillips, the young lady I was telling you about," Gen. Jack said.

"Well, howdy, honey. I'm pleased to meet you."

Big Bertha took Anne's hand in her big calloused one and shook it roughly. It was all Anne could do to keep from wincing, for she felt like the woman was going to jerk her arm out of its socket. She forced herself to smile and looked up, then found herself gazing into a rather homely face covered with freckles and creased with a smile a mile wide. It was the smile that made Anne feel more comfortable. "I'm pleased to meet you, too."

"Well, I'll leave you two to get acquainted," Gen. Jack said, setting Anne's luggage down. As his boots pounded down the stairs, he called over his shoulder, "You better make sure you've got everything secured tightly, Big Bertha. We'll pulling out in fifteen minutes."

"Don't you be telling me my job, you big, ornery cuss. You mind your business, and I'll mind mine."

Anne gasped at the cook's audacity to talk so disrespectfully to the construction chief, but not just because he was the boss. Why, she didn't think *anyone* would have the nerve to call him an ornery cuss to his face, as terrifying as he was, not even a giantess. But apparently Gen. Jack thought Bertha's saucy retort amusing. He chuckled as he lumbered off.

Anne turned and saw Bertha's brown eyes twinkling with sheer deviltry. "I just love trying to rile him," the huge cook explained to Anne, pushing a wisp of fiery red hair from her forehead.

"I should think that would be a little dangerous," Anne commented.

"If one of his men said that to him, he'd knock 'em to kingdom come, but he don't mind it from me. He knows I'm a big tease. Of course, I don't allow no fooling around from the men cooks under me. I gotta keep a firm hand on them, or they'd be taking advantage of my good-naturedness and loaf on the job. They don't like a woman bossing them around, you know, so I have to act real tough."

Anne didn't think Bertha had to act tough. She strongly suspected that the big woman *was* tough.

Big Bertha eyed her up and down where her cloak was open, then asked, "Did you bring any other clothes with you? That suit is mighty pretty, but it ain't very practical for a cook."

"Oh, I have plenty of suitable clothes in my luggage," Anne answered. "Old housedresses."

"Now, that sounds more like it. It don't matter if you get them all dirty. Of course, it don't hurt to wear an apron, like I am," she motioned to the full-length apron she was wearing over her faded calico dress. "You bring any of those along with you?"

"Yes, I did. You see, I planned on keeping house for my brother, who just hired on as an engineer with the railroad."

"Then you didn't just come out here to get a job?"

"No." Anne explained how Jim had been under the misconception that the railroad provided living quarters for families, and how she had happened to learn about the job, ending with, "So I accepted Gen. Jack's offer."

"How did you brother feel about that?" Big Bertha asked.

"He wasn't pleased with me," Anne admitted. "In fact, he was furious. He wanted me to go back to Ohio."

Big Bertha wasn't surprised. Anne didn't look like the kind of woman who applied for a cooking job with the railroad. She looked too fragile, too ladylike. But Big Bertha wasn't going to hold that against her. She was a firm believer in giving a person an opportunity to prove themself. She wouldn't be in her position if Gen. Jack hadn't given *her* a chance. She owed Anne the same opportunity to prove her mettle. Besides, she'd stood up to her brother, hadn't she? And Big Bertha knew only too well how domineering they could be. She'd had four of them to contend with, the ornery brutes.

"Yeah, that sounds like a man," Big Bertha answered. "They think they know everything. Even my husband was that way. Sometimes I felt like slugging him."

"You're married?" Anne asked in surprise.

"I was, but I ain't now. He got killed in the war, the big dumb Irishman. But he sure was a hunk of a man. I fell in love with him the first time I saw him laying rails. God, he was a good-looking bastard."

"Then you were working for the railroad at the time?"

"Nope. The railroad was putting a spur through my hometown in Tennessee, and he was working on the construction gang. My ma didn't want me to have anything to do with him, him being one of those foreigners, and a Papist to boot, but I went after him like a thirsty horse does a trough of water after a long day's work. I snagged him, too. That's how I got the railroad in my blood, from following him from railroad town to railroad town After the war, when I heard the U.P. was hiring women cooks, I picked up stakes and came out here. Ain't regretted it either. That's one thing I'll say for the railroad. They pay good."

"Just how much does the job pay?"

"You mean you didn't ask?" Big Bertha asked in disbelief.

"No. I guess that sounds pretty foolish," Anne admitted, "but I was so excited about getting the job, that it never even occurred to me to ask."

"Well, naturally they pay me more than they will you, since I'm head cook, but you'll be making the same money a construction worker does. Thirty-five dollars a month."

Anne was stunned. It sounded like a fortune to her. "Why, that's wonderful!"

"It ain't bad, honey, but believe me, you'll work just as hard as a construction worker does for it. The railroad pays good, but they expect their money's worth in exchange." Big Bertha paused, then said, "Now, you'd better step back into my bedroom and change your clothes, before the train starts moving. The springs on this damn car ain't so good, and it bounces around something awful."

"Maybe I should wait until we get where we're going?"

"Nope. When we pull up to where we're heading, we're gonna have to get busy getting supper ready. Those Tarriers out there will only put up with missing one meal a day, and then only on moving day."

"Where did you say I should change?"

Big Bertha stepped aside and pointed to an area in one corner of the car that was enclosed with two blankets hung from the ceiling of the car. "Back there."

Anne only glanced at the area. Then her attention was caught by the first sight she'd had of the rest of the cookhouse. Lining the entire length of the back side of the car were stoves, and Anne had never seen such massive stoves in her life. With twelve burners apiece and huge ovens on each side of the firebox, they made the one she had cooked on at home look like something that belonged in a doll house. On the opposite side of the car were large, floor length cabinets, where Anne assumed they must keep their pots and pans and cooking utensils, and in one corner, next to Big Bertha's "bedroom," a built-in pantry. In the middle of the car was a long bare table. Then Anne realized they were alone. "Where are the other cooks?"

"Up on top of the car," Big Bertha answered in disgust. "They're just like little boys. They get a big kick of riding up there in the open. Even Henry does."

"Who is Henry?"

"He's one of my bakers, my only one at the present time. You've never seen such a sour man. Doesn't talk, just grunts. And he's always frowning. But he makes good bread."

"Do you have any other women cooks?"

"There's one or two off with the grading parties, but I'm the only one here in Gen. Jack's rolling factory. Nope, all I've got is those ornery men. Be kinda nice to have a woman around for a change."

Anne bent to pick up her luggage. Big Bertha grabbed one suitcase, saying, "I'll carry this one for you."

When they reached the big woman's sleeping quarters, Big Bertha pushed back one of the blankets for Anne to enter. Anne looked about her, seeing a single bed, a small chest of drawers, and a trunk which she assumed contained the rest of Bertha's clothing that wasn't hanging on wooden pegs on the wall. There was hardly room enough for her to set her suitcase down.

Seeing the expression on her face, Big Bertha said, "I know it ain't much. Gen. Jack offered to put me up in a tent, but I like being here in the cookhouse, where I can keep my eye on things. Besides, I'm one of those people who can't sleep unless I've got good solid walls around me."

"Where do the other cooks sleep?"

"They bunk in the sleeping cars with the construction workers, except they don't really have beds. They sleep in hammocks."

"Where did you get your furniture? Did you bring it with you?"

"Nope. The railroad provided it. You see, they keep furniture around for when the company bigwigs make an inspection trip out past the end of the rail. Store it in one of their warehouses until the occasion arises, and then ship it by rail out to the end of the line, then by wagon to the construction site, and put it in a tent. Some of it is right fancy, too. I could have had a much bigger bed, except there wasn't hardly enough room in here for this one."

And there certainly wouldn't be room enough for another bed, Anne thought. It seemed she really didn't have any choice about where she would sleep.

Big Bertha placed the suitcase she was carrying on her bed and said, "I'll leave you to change your clothes. Better hurry, though. They way I figure it, you've got about five minutes before the train pulls out."

Anne quickly changed into a calico dress that was even more faded than Big Bertha's, donned one of her aprons, and tossed a shawl over her shoulders. She had just strapped her suitcase closed when she heard the sound of a whistle. Then, with a sudden jerk that almost threw her off her feet, the train pulled out.

She pushed the blankets aside and saw Big Bertha sitting before the open boxcar door. Seeing her, the big cook said, "Come on over here and sit down beside me. We can watch the scenery pass by, providing you don't mind a little cool wind."

Anne carefully walked across the swaying car and remarked, "I'm surprised it's so warm in here."

"We've banked the fires in all the stoves. That way we don't have to start out from scratch when we get where we're going. Of course, we have to chain the doors to the fire-boxes closed, or we'd have sparks flying everywhere."

Anne sat down beside Big Bertha. "How far is it to where we're going?"

"To the end of the line? Oh, about sixty miles or so. Gen. Jack generally moves us about every fifty, but Cheyenne was our winter camp, so we stayed here a little longer."

For a few moments, the two women watched the scenery passing by, then as the train picked up speed, the car began to shake back and forth violently, sending the kerosene lamps hanging from the ceiling swaying. Seeing the horrified expression on Anne's face, Big Bertha laughed. Over the noises of the clattering rails, the pots and pans banging in the cabinets, and the rattling of the chains holding the fireboxes and the ovens closed, the head cook said, "Now you know why I sit on the floor. It's impossible to stand. The railroad must have picked the most dilapidated freight car they could find for this cookhouse."

"Then why don't you ride in the bakery car?"

"Hell, it ain't any better. None of 'em are."

"I'm surprised the stoves aren't moving."

"They would be if they weren't bolted down. So would that table. That's why we have to put everything up when we move. If we didn't, things would be flying everywhere. Why, on one trip, my bed walked clean to the other end of the car."

Aware of a terrible noise coming from outside the car, Anne asked, "What's that awful banging?"

"The wooden steps. They hang them on hooks outside the car when we're moving."

Anne looked out the doorway. The scenery was whizzing past them. "I've never traveled this fast before."

"Nope, I don't reckon you have. When Gen. Jack moves us, he don't believe in wasting time. Of course, he burns up a hell of a lot of coal, making that locomotive push so fast."

"Push? Are your saying the locomotive is pushing us, not pulling?"

"That's right, honey. Didn't you know they could do that?"

"No, I didn't," Anne admitted. "But why isn't it pulling?"

"This way it can push us right up to the end of the side track where we'll be parked, and still be free to back up. Hell, we might be sitting in that same spot for weeks. Can't tie a locomotive up doing nothing for that long. They're expensive pieces of equipment."

Unbelievably, the train picked up even more speed, and Anne and Big Bertha had to hang on to the door to keep from being thrown out or flung across the car. Anne was bouncing so hard her teeth were rattling, and the wind was flapping her clothing wildly around her. It was a little frightening, but terribly exciting. Now she thought she knew why the men were riding on top of the car. They were probably having to hang on to the catwalk for dear life ,and getting a dangerous but thrilling ride.

When the train reduced its speed, Anne asked in disappointment, "Why are we slowing down?"

"We've probably reached the foothills of the Laramie Mountains. You can't go that fast around curves, particularly when the engine is pushing those top-heavy, three-decker cars ahead of us. They're liable to tumble over. If you think this car rocks, you oughta ride in one of them. Swings those Tarriers in their hammocks all over the place, and bangs them up something awful. But they love it, just like they love a good fight." Big Bertha shook her head. "Sometimes I think those Paddies don't have good sense."

"I've heard the Irish called Paddies before, but I've never heard them called Tarriers. Why does everyone call them that?"

"That's what they call themselves. What they're really saying is *ter*riers, but with their thick brogue it sounds like *tar*riers."

"But why would they call themselves terriers?"

"Have you ever seen a terrier digging for a bone? He throws dirt everywhere, and he can dig faster than any animal on earth. That's what those trackmen say they're doing, digging their way across the country. They've even got a song about Tarriers, that they sing while they're working."

For a few moments, the women watched the scenery passing by. Here, in the gently rolling hills, the snow had piled up much thicker, and an occasional fir tree could be seen, its snow-laden branches drooping under the heavy weight. At one place, the tracks curved around a hill, and the embankment was so close that Anne could have reached out and picked up a handful of snow. Seeing a spot where the snow looked like a giant honeycomb, she asked, "What made those strange tunnels in the snow over there? Some burrowing animal?"

"Nope, the chinook wind does that. Cuts holes right through the snow. Peculiar-looking, ain't it? I never saw anything like that back in Tennessee. And we didn't have any of those back home either," Big Bertha said, pointing to several lavender and purple patches in the snow farther up on the embankment, "at least not that I ever saw."

"Why, they look like flowers," Anne said in astonishment.

"They are. They're the first flowers to come up in the spring out here. They're called pasqueflowers. Wish you could see one up close. They're real delicate-looking. I think it's amazing that they can bloom in the snow."

Anne had never seen such flowers before and was amazed. Suddenly, it occurred to her that she would be seeing a lot of things out here that she had never seen before, had never dreamed existed, and not just wild railroad towns. Why, it was a wilderness that up until recently few whites had seen, and they had been almost exclusively male: miners, mountain men, a few ranchers, soldiers stationed at the outlying forts. Other than the women who passed through on wagon trains or the few hardy Mormons who made their homes here, it was an isolated country that still existed in its wild, natural state, untouched and untamed by civilization, one that few females had been privileged to see. And she was one of the first. Why just viewing all the new things this country had to offer was as exciting as the building of the railroad, an added boon to her exciting adventure that she had not yet considered.

Big Bertha broke into her thoughts. "I think we ought to talk a little business. I need to have an idea of just how much cooking you're used to doing."

"Well, I cooked all the meals at home and did all the baking." I also did all the house cleaning, washing and ironing, and worked as a clerk in my uncle's store, Anne thought bitterly.

"Baking, huh? What'd you bake?"

"Everything. Bread, dinner rolls, sweet rolls, pies, cakes, cookies."

"Are you pretty good at pies?"

"Yes, if I do say so myself."

"Well, I sure am glad to hear you say that, honey. I lost my pie man a week ago. He just took off for the gold fields. Here one day and gone the next. Henry has been baking the pies, but he's lousy at them. His crusts are as hard as a rock, and the Tarries have been raising hell about it. They don't mind

Gen. Jack running them like an army, but they're dead-set they ain't gonna be fed like one. Good grub is what keeps a lot of them here, and that's what our job is, keeping their bellies full and the food tasty. So if you ain't got any objections, you can bake all the pies."

"Is that all you want me to do, just bake pies?"

"Yep, that will keep you busy. We go through two hundred a day."

"Two hundred?" Anne gasped in disbelief. "Pies?"

"Yep, we're feeding four hundred hungry men."

"But that's a half a pie apiece!"

"Sure is. We cut them in sixths, and they eat a slice at breakfast, one at dinner, and one at supper. And you'd better believe if any man doesn't get his pie allotment for the day, he raises hell about it."

"And they actually eat pie for breakfast?"

"They eat the same meal three times a day. Meat, potatoes, vegetables, canned fruit, bread, and pie."

"They eat all of that for breakfast?" Anne asked in disbelief.

"Yep, and come roaring back for more at noon and sundown."

Anne was still thinking about the two hundred pies and felt overwhelmed. Why, she'd never baked more than three at a time, and that lasted the family a whole week. "Why don't you bake cakes? They go farther."

"Most men prefer pies to cakes. Besides, cakes need eggs, and where are we gonna get them out here?"

"You could bring them in by rail."

"We tried that. They were all broken, every last one of them. I never saw such a god-awful mess in my life."

"They could pack them more carefully," Anne pointed out.

"Hell, they ain't gonna go to all that trouble. Nope, the only time we have cake is fruitcake at Christmas, and only because they don't need eggs."

Anne felt defeated before she had even begun. "I don't know if I can manage two hundred pies a day. Why, I wouldn't even begin to know how to measure out the ingredients."

"Just take your pie crust recipe and multiply it times ten.

That's about all the dough you're going to be able to handle at one time. I'll give you a hand the first day or so, until you get the hang of it. And I'm sure gonna have to help you today, since you'll be getting a late start."

"But I shouldn't have to bake two hundred pies today," Anne objected.

"Sure you do. We bake them a day in advance. That's so Henry can have the ovens at night to bake his bread. He gets his dough mixed and kneaded in the morning, then lets it rise all day, and starts throwing it into the oven in the evening when the pies are done. He's got six hundred loaves of bread to make, you know."

"Why, that's a loaf and a half per man!"

"Yep. Those Tarriers have big appetites. They're doing hard labor, you know. They have to keep up their strength."

Big Bertha glanced out of the car, seeing a wooden water tower pass by. Then noticing that the train's speed had slowed considerably and that they were rolling down a side track, she said, "Brace yourself, honey. We're at the end of the line, and when these cars hit that barrier at the end of this side track, we're going to be in for a good jolt."

Anne had already had a good jolt. She'd have to bake two hundred pies a day? My God!

Chapter Eight

No sooner had the train come to a neck-snapping stop than Big Bertha jumped to her feet, leaned out of the wide door, and yelled to the men on top of the car, "All right, you lazy bums! Get the hell down here! We've got work to do!"

She turned to Anne, who was struggling to her feet, and said, "I'll be with you in a minute, honey. I've got to get things going in here. And you better step back from the door."

As Big Bertha rushed off, Anne wondered at her last words. Then she jumped back in fright as a man's booted feet came flying through the air. He landed on the floor with a loud thump, followed by two more men as they swung down from the top of the car. As the three men came to their feet, they stared at Anne as if they didn't believe their eyes.

"Stop gaping, you dumb apes," Big Bertha said from where she was unlocking the doors on the ovens and fireboxes. "You've seen a woman before. This is Anne Phillips, our new cook. And you'd better mind your manners around her, too, or I'll knock your heads together. Anne, this is Pete, Carl, and Johnny. Don't ask me their last names. They never told me, and I couldn't care less. Pete and Carl are the cooks here in the cookhouse, and Johnny's our potato peeler."

"How do you do," Anne said politely, thinking that Pete and Carl did look something like apes with their huge shoulders and arms and the bushy beards on their faces. Johnny, however, was clean-shaven, and just as thin and wiry as the other two were massive. And there was something about the blank look in his eyes that disturbed her.

As the three men continued to stare at her, Big Bertha,

said, "You heard what I said. Stop gaping and get busy. We've got a meal to get on the table. Unless you want to be tarred and feathered by those trackmen out there, when they find their supper ain't ready."

Apparently the two big men took Big Bertha's threat seriously. They scurried off, Pete jumping to the roadbed and placing the wooden steps back in place before the door, and Carl scooping up a big bucket of coal from the bin at one side of the car and feeding it into the fireboxes in the stoves. When Johnny continued to stare at Anne, Big Bertha gave him a little shove, saying in a gentler voice, "Go on now, Johnny. Get your work done."

As he ambled off, Big Bertha stepped up to the door of the car, stuck her head out, and yelled, "Hey, you water boys! Get me some barrels of water in here. And get a move on! We ain't got all day."

Johnny carried two huge, battered pots from the cabinet to one end of the car, dumped them on the floor, then disappeared through a door there that Anne hadn't noticed before. A few moments later, he came back carrying a sack of potatoes over his shoulder, that was almost as big as he was. He threw it down on the floor, pulled a knife from a scabbard at his waist, sliced the burlap open, turned one of the pots over for a stool, and sat down. Anne watched in amazement as he peeled a potato. She had never seen anyone peel anything that fast. Potato peelings flew through the air, and what seemed like a second later, the bare potato hit the bottom of the pot beside him. A second later, another potato went flying into the pot, and then another, and another.

Big Bertha stepped up to Anne. "Come on, honey. I'll take you to the bakery now. Can't do nothing else in here until those blasted butchers deliver our meat."

As they walked through the door at the end of the car, Anne said, "I've never seen anyone peel potatoes as fast as Johnny can."

"Well, he oughta be fast. That's all he does all day."

"Just peel potatoes?"

"Yep. We've gotta have plenty of potatoes. Those Tarriers dearly love their potatoes."

"But you'd think he'd get terribly bored, sitting there and peeling potatoes all day."

"An ordinary man would, but Johnny ain't quite right in the head. You see, he got hit by a bullet there during the war. He ain't dangerous or anything, but it left him a little dim-witted. He can't handle anything but a simple job, one where he just does the same thing over and over. He showed up at the railroad back in Omaha asking for a job, but Gen. Jack was afraid to put him out on the construction site, for fear he'd get hurt. You have to be able to move pretty quick out there to get out of the way, with all the wagons and horses and locomotives going up and down. So he put him in here peeling potatoes."

"That's a shame," Anne said with compassion. "Why, before the war, Johnny was probably perfectly normal."

"Yep. The war left a lot of crippled men looking for work. That's one reason I admire Gen. Jack so much. If he can possibly find a job for them, he does. Why, he even has a one-armed blacksmith working for him. Can you imagine that?"

And to think she'd thought Gen. Jack looked so terrifying, Anne thought. Why, he had a heart as big as his body.

The two had been standing on a small wooden platform between the cars. Bertha pushed the door of the bakery open and walked in. "Well, here's where you'll be working."

Anne looked about her. The car looked much like the cookhouse with its cabinets, pantry, coal bin, and long table in the middle, except the stoves' ovens were much larger and half of one side of the car contained floor-length metal racks.

Bertha walked to a cabinet and unlocked it. Swinging the door open, she said, "Here's where we keep the pots and pans and mixing bowls. And you'll find the spoons, rolling pins, measuring cups, and anything else you might need for mixing in that drawer there."

Anne stared at the stacks and stacks of pie and bread pans, then looked at the huge tin mixing bowls and pots. Again, she felt overwhelmed.

Bertha unlocked the pantry and opened the door. "And here's where you'll find everything else you need, and when you run out, just send Henry to the storehouse for it."

Anne didn't think that would sit too well with her fellow baker. She should pull her own weight. "Oh, I'm sure I can carry it."

Then she stepped around the door and looked into the pantry, seeing the huge, hundred-pound sacks of flour and sugar and tins of lard that came up to her hip. She gasped.

"Yeah, I figured you didn't know what you were saying," Bertha remarked. "I ain't never seen such big sacks and tins either, until I came to work for the railroad. Like I said, send Henry after them."

"What are in those other sacks?" Anne asked.

"Dried fruits, since that's the only kind of pie we can make without eggs. You'll find apples, peaches, pears, apricots, raisins, and prunes." Big Bertha pointed to a shelf, saying, "You'll find all your spices up there."

Anne looked at the tins of spices. Even they were oversized. "What about the butter? Where do you keep it?"

"I'm afraid you ain't gonna be able to dab any butter on your fruit. It has to be kept cool, and we don't have any coolers here."

"Then how do you keep your meat?"

"All the pork we get has been cured. So has the corned beef. The rest is delivered to us fresh daily from the ranchers or the professional hunters that supply us with game."

"You mean buffalo?" Anne asked, wrinkling her nose in remembrance at how awful it tasted.

"Yeah, and deer and antelope and bear. We even get turkeys every now and then, but I pretty much put a stop to that. The hunters deliver the meat already dressed, but we have to pluck those damn birds. The last time we had to dress a hundred turkeys, I told them not to bring them anymore, except at Thanksgiving and Christmas. That was just too much work on top of our cooking, and we had turkey feathers everywhere. It took us a week before we got the last of them swept out of the cookhouse."

A tall, thin man with a gaunt-looking face walked into the bakery. "This is Henry," Big Bertha informed Anne. "Henry, this is our new cook, Anne Phillips. She's going to take over baking the pies."

If Henry was relieved to be rid of the awesome chore, he showed no sign of it. There was absolutely no change in the sour expression on his face. He grunted, turned, and whipped an apron from a peg on the wall, tying it around his waist.

As he reached into the cabinet and pulled out a huge mixing bowl, Big Bertha whispered to Anne, "Don't pay no attention to him. That's just his way."

Anne didn't feel particularly insulted. Big Bertha had already warned her. "I guess I'd better get started on my pies, too. What kind should I make? Apple, peach, or apricot?"

"Hell, make some of everything you've got. That way, everyone can have his favorite. But go easy on the prune pies, honey. Too many of them give the men the runs."

An embarrassed flush rose on Anne's face, but Big Bertha didn't notice. She was looking over Anne's shoulder at the open side door. "Well, it's about time you got here with those water barrels."

Anne turned and saw a boy about nine years old, carrying a heavy water barrel up the stairs to the car. She held her breath for fear he'd fall or drop it, but apparently he was much stronger than he looked. He sat it down with a big thump inside the door, then disappeared in a flash.

"Why, he's just a boy," Anne said. "What's he doing here?"

"Working for the railroad."

"They hire children?" Anne asked in a disapproving voice.

Big Bertha cocked her head. "Where are you from?"

"A little town in Ohio."

"You ever been to a big city?"

"Just Omaha."

"Well, let me tell you something. They hire kids a lot younger than that in the factories back East, and they work them a lot harder than the railroad does its water boys, and pay them a hell of a lot less. Besides, we feed them, and they're out in the fresh air and sunshine."

"But how did they get out here? There are no towns around."

"A few came along with their pas. But most are runaways, who came out here to work on the railroad."

"Well, if they're runaways they should be sent back home. Why, their parents are probably worried sick about them."

"Not these boys. Gen. Jack told me all about them. Most are city urchins, whose parents didn't give a damn about them. They'd been fending for themselves for years, raiding garbage cans for food and rags to clothe themselves, and sleeping in the streets. And they've got a brighter future ahead of them out here than those kids they left behind. When they grow up, they can work on the construction gangs. They've got a job waiting for them."

Anne was horrified. She had never known about such things. Yes, she thought, she *had* lead a sheltered life, and she felt ashamed of herself. Why, compared to those poor children, she had lived a life of luxury.

"Well, we'd better get the fires going, so we can get your fruits stewing," Big Bertha said, walking to one of the stoves and unlocking the chain that had held the firebox closed. "I tell you what. I'll take care of that end of it, while you get your pastry started."

Anne's first day on the job was an experience she would remember the rest of her life. In the first place, she had never worked with so much pasty dough at one time. Cutting five cups of lard into fifteen cups of flour, until the mixture was the size of small peas, was laborious enough, but stirring the mixture after the water had been added was almost more than Anne could manage. Then the pasty had to be rolled out. By the time Anne and Big Bertha had made fifty pies and had them in the ovens baking, Anne's arms and shoulders were aching; by the time they had completed a hundred, Anne's back was aching, too, and she was drenched with sweat from the heat in the car and covered with flour; by the time they had finished a hundred and fifty, Anne's feet were killing her and her arms were numb, and by the time they had finished the last pie, Anne was beyond any feeling at all.

"That's it for today, honey," she heard Big Bertha saying, as if the voice was coming from far away. "And I'm proud of you. Just look at all those pretty pies you put out."

Anne looked at the racks where all but the last of the pies were cooling. The thought that she would have to repeat the awesome chore the next day brought tears to her eyes. "Oh, Bertha," she wailed, "I can't do it! I'll never be able to make two hundred pies all by myself."

"Sure you will, honey, when you get used to it. And you won't have to rush so much from now on. You'll have all day, so you can take you a little break now and then. Now, what do you say to us stepping in the cookhouse and having a bite to eat?"

"I'm too tired to eat."

"Yeah, you do look pretty beat. You go on to bed then, and I'll clean up in here. Things will look a lot better in the morning, when you've had a good night's sleep."

"What about the pies still in the oven?"

"I'll take them out. You go on to bed. Gen. Jack set you up a tent right outside his office. You can't miss it. It's the only one sitting that close in. He said to tell you he was sorry all he could provide tonight was a cot, a few blankets, and a wash cabinet. But he promised he'd have some decent furniture shipped up by tomorrow." Big Bertha paused, then asked, "You ain't gonna get scared out there, all by yourself, are you?"

Anne had never been alone in a house at night, much less in a tent in the open. Ordinarily she might have been a little apprehensive, but at this point, she was too tired to even care. "No."

She turned and took a few steps towards the cookhouse. "Where are you going?" Big Bertha asked.

"To pick up my suitcases."

"You don't have to worry about them. Gen. Jack carried them down there when he dropped by to tell me he had your tent all set up."

Anne didn't remember seeing the construction chief, and as huge as he was, he would be hard to miss. "When was that?"

"About two hours ago. I guess you were so busy you didn't even see him."

Or too exhausted, Anne thought. She turned and walked to the door. Big Bertha whipped Anne's shawl from a peg on the wall where she had hung it much earlier and handed it to her. "Better put this on. It's a little nippy out there."

Anne took the shawl, but she didn't wrap it around her. She simply didn't have the energy. As she walked wearily down the steps, she thought the cold air a blessed relief after the stifling heat of the car, and wondered how she would endure it in the summer.

At the bottom of the stairs, she paused. She hadn't realized that it was dark, and wondered just how late it was. There wasn't a soul about. She peered down the line of cars sitting on the track and saw the vague outline of a tent, then turned and trudged toward it.

"Here, honey," Big Bertha said, coming down the steps and handing her a kerosene lamp. "You'd better take this with you. You might trip on something in the dark."

Anne took the lamp, and as she walked away, Big Bertha said, " 'Night, honey."

"Good night," Anne muttered.

Despite the circle of light the lamp threw out around her, Anne stumbled several times, both from sheer exhaustion and the slippery loose gravel along the roadbed. When she reached the tent, she pushed back the flap and stepped in, then stumbled again, this time almost falling to her knees. She looked down to see what had tripped her, and saw that the tent had a raised planked floor.

She lifted the lamp and looked about her new quarters. She judged the tent to be about fourteen feet square, and it looked very empty. A cot with a pillow and blankets on it sat to one side of the tent, and a wash cabinet and barrel of water on the opposite side. Other than that it was bare, except for her suitcases, a chamber pot, and a kerosene lamp hanging on a pole in the center of the tent, that helped support the canvas ceiling. She peered closer at the pole, seeing a tin of matches was nailed on it. Well, thank God for that, she thought. She certainly didn't carry matches around with her. But she wished they had provided her with a stove. Despite how good the cold air had felt when she left the overheated bakery, it was now freezing.

Anne walked to the cot and sat the lamp down beside it, then stripped off her dress and tossed it aside. Sitting on the cot, she removed her shoes and stockings, but she couldn't summon the energy to strip off the rest of her clothes, wash off, and don her gown. She was simply too exhausted. She extinguished the lamp and, still wearing her petticoats, collapsed on the cot and pulled the covers over her. She was dead to the world the minute her head hit the pillow.

Anne was rudely awakened by the sounds of a bell ringing loudly and men's shouts. She bolted to a sitting position, her heart racing as she looked wildly around her. It took a moment for her to orientate herself, for it was still dark. Why, we must be being attacked by Indians! she thought.

She threw back the covers and ran from the tent. Standing in front of it, she looked about her. Lights spilled out from the doors of the line of boxcars and the windows of the bunk cars, and she could see the sleepy construction workers stumbling out of the boxcars in the distance. Several men were kicking and shaking men sleeping under the cars and yelling, "Get up!" And all the while, the bell was ringing urgently. She looked about wildly, wondering which direction the attack was coming from, for she could see no savages riding down on them.

"What are you doing standing out in here in the cold?" a voice behind her boomed out.

Anne jumped a foot in fright and then whirled around. Seeing Gen. Jack standing there, she felt weak with relief. "Oh, thank God, you're here. I've never been in an Indian attack before. What should I do? Where should I go?"

"Indian attack?" Then realizing why she thought they were under attack, Gen. Jack laughed and said, "No, young lady. We aren't being attacked. The bell is ringing to wake the men for work."

Anne felt foolish at first, then thought in self-defense, but what had she been expected to think in the middle of the night? "I didn't know you worked at night."

"We don't. It's morning, or almost. It's five-thirty, time for the men to get up, if they're going to eat breakfast and start laying rail by seven."

"It takes them an hour and a half to eat?" Anne asked in astonishment.

"It does when they have to eat in three shifts. The dining car only holds a hundred and fifty men." Gen. Jack looked her up and down and said, "You'd better step inside and get some more clothes on, young lady. You're going to catch your death standing out here dressed like that in this cold air."

Anne glanced down at herself and was horrified when she realized she was only wearing her underclothes. She darted back into her tent, again stumbling on the raised floor. She limped to her cot and sat on it, rubbing the bruised spot on the top of her foot. Then realizing how cold it was and that she was shivering, she pulled her blankets up over her shoulders. She couldn't believe it was almost morning. It seemed like she had just gone to bed. She wondered if she was expected to start work this early, too. Probably. But she was still so tired, and her shoulders still ached. She considered laying back down and sleeping just a little longer. She'd gladly give up her breakfast for just a few more winks. But she knew if she did, she would sleep much longer than that. She'd hate to be late her second day on the job. Groaning in resignation, she rose and fumbled in the dark for the lamp.

Chapter Nine

Thirty minutes later, Anne walked into the cookhouse, carrying the lamp Big Bertha had loaned her the night before. The place was a beehive of activity. One tall, skinny cook was ladling out steaming potatoes and vegetables into tin bowls as large as washbasins, while another short, fat one was slicing meat from a monstrous roast and piling it on platters. Several adolescents, hardly more than boys, were carrying the huge bowls and platters out of the door at the end of the car that faced the dining car. Other than Big Bertha, who was slicing loaves of bread in half and piling them on another platter, Anne had never seen any of the car's occupants.

Spying her, Big Bertha stopped with her knife in midair and said, "Well, morning, honey. What are you doing here?"

"I thought I'd bring back the lamp before I went to work.;"

Big Bertha placed the knife on the table, shoved the platter of bread stacked a foot high across to an adolescent reaching for it, and said to Anne, "How come you're going to work so early? As exhausted as you were last night, I'd have thought you would have slept later than this."

"I heard the bell. I thought I was supposed to go to work."

"Yeah, that bell would wake the dead," Big Bertha answered with a chuckle, "but you don't have to get started this early. Dawn is soon enough for you." Seeing Anne casting curious glances at the others, Big Bertha said, "These are my night cooks, Slim and Sam. They fix breakfast, and then hang around to help get dinner going before they go to bed. Those boys are my dishwashers and general handymen here in the cookhouse."

Big Bertha looked around, then said, "Well, I reckon that's it for the first go-around. Go ahead and ring the bell, Sam."

The short, fat cook waddled to the door, leaned out, and rang the big bell that was bolted to the side of the boxcar. The call to breakfast was hardly necessary. The track layers were already standing ten deep before the dining car, huddling against the cold air with their hands shoved in the pockets of their leather coats.

"Come on in the dining car with me," Big Bertha said to Anne. "This is something you won't believe unless you see it for yourself."

Anne followed Big Bertha from the cookhouse. When they stepped on the small wooden platform between the two cars, Anne asked, "Why is the door to the dining room off to the side?" she asked.

"You'll see," Big Bertha answered, opening the door for Anne.

Anne stepped inside the dining car. Beneath the dim light cast by the lamps hanging from the ceiling, a long table stretched the entire length of the eighty-foot car, both ends butting up against the ends of the car. Anne looked at the wooden bench that ran beside the table at the back of the car and asked, "How do they get back there to sit? They can't walk around the ends."

"They go over the table. Step on the bench, then in the middle of the table, and right over."

Seeing the expression on Anne's face, Bertha laughed, saying, "Yeah, I couldn't believe it either. Have you ever heard of anything so dumb? But that's the only way they can get to the other side."

"But why didn't they leave the ends open when they built the table, so the men could go around?"

"This way they can sit four more men at the table. Now you know why that door is off to the side the way it is, and that was only because I threw a fit. When I took this job, they didn't have a door going to the cookhouse. We had to bring everything around from the outside, no matter what the weather. I told Gen. Jack he had to put me some doors between these cars, or I was gonna flat quit."

Anne looked at the table that was laden down with huge metal bowls of vegetables, gallon tins of canned fruit, pies, heaping platters of bread and meat, then asked, "What in the world is in those wooden buckets?"

"Coffee. It's faster for them to just dip their cups in buckets, than for us to pour it from a pot."

Anne glanced down at the table beside her, then took a second, closer look. The tin plate was nailed to the table. Seeing her look of disbelief, Big Bertha said, "It's easier washing them that way, and we don't have to reset the table. The dishwashers just swap them out with a dish mop."

Anne was horrified. While it might be quicker, it didn't sound very sanitary.

Big Bertha turned to the two lads waiting beside the closed door at the side of the boxcar and said, "Okay, boys, roll it back."

The big door creaked as it was rolled aside. A second later, a human tide of construction workers came pouring through the doors. It was the closest thing Anne had ever seen to a stampede. They came rushing in, shoving the men before them, and without ceremony, stepped on the bench, then the table, and over, surprisingly without one bowl being overturned or one platter disturbed. As soon as they were seated, it was every man for himself as they speared meat, potatoes, and canned fruit, grabbed the thick hunks of bread, dipped their cups into the buckets of steaming coffee. Long arms reached out over other outstretched arms reaching in the opposite direction to grab pitchers of syrup, which they liberally poured over their bread. When their plates were heaping, they gobbled the food down, so intent on their eating that not a word was muttered and not a glance was given to the two women standing at the end of the car. Then, having eaten their fill, they grabbed a piece of pie in their hand and, if they happened to be sitting at the back of the car, supported themselves on the shoulder of the man seated next to them, stood on the bench, and stepped across the table, the two men on the opposite side leaning over to make room for them to pass, while still shoveling food into their mouths.

Big Bertha opened the door, and the two women stepped back out on the platform. "Now, you've seen what a hundred and fifty rough trackmen look like when they're eating," the big woman commented. "Polite bunch, ain't they? And I swear those Tarriers' stomachs are bottomless pits."

"Are they really all Irishmen?"

"There're a few Germans and Slavs among them, but I'd say a good eighty to ninety percent are Paddies, and at least half of them are newly arrived in this country. The railroad is about the only place they can find work, other than the army. There's a lot of prejudice against them in this country, because they're Papists and foreigners. The railroad don't care what religion a man is, or if he speaks English or not, as long as he's got a strong back."

After a breakfast of meat and bread—Anne just couldn't face up to vegetables and pie that early in the morning—she and Big Bertha walked into the bakery. Looking around her, Anne asked, "Where is Henry?"

"Sleeping. He didn't get the last of his bread outta the oven until two this morning. He'll come in about mid-morning and get the bread started for tomorrow. Do you think you can get things going in here by yourself, while I finish up seeing to breakfast in the cookhouse?"

Started, but not finished, Anne thought, dreading the chore. "Yes, I think I can."

By the time Henry entered the car later that morning, Anne already had a forth of her pies baked and was covered with a fine coating of flour, her apron splattered with fruit fillings. She greeted her taciturn fellow baker, but Henry's only response was a sour grunt. Soon he was up to his elbows in bread dough at the other end of the long table. As he viciously punched the huge ball of dough, then flopped it over on the table with a big slap and punched it some more, Anne wondered if he was simply kneading dough or pretending that it was his worst enemy. If he was that rough with pie dough, it was no wonder his pastry was so tough.

It was almost sundown by the time Anne finished her chore,

and she was almost as exhausted as she had been the day before. She stepped down from the car, relishing the feel and the smell of the cool, fresh air after the stifling heat and the heavy, sweet odors of the bakery, thinking that she couldn't stand the thought of looking at another pie, much less eating one. However, she wasn't so weary that she didn't take note of her surroundings, for this was the first time she had seen the camp in the daylight.

Gen. Jack's factory of cars sat on a side track about a hundred yards from the main track. Between it and the main track, and on the opposite side of the new rails, there were tents and wooden toolsheds scattered about at random, and here and there were water barrels and piles of wooden ties. On the main track were several flatcars loaded down with iron rails, and in the distance, towards the east, she could see a locomotive sitting beside a large water tower.

She turned her attention to the opposite direction, where the new track was being lain. To her disappointment, the construction was finished for the day, and all she could see was a crowd of trackmen standing beside the dining car, a few smoking while they waited their turns to eat, but the majority champing at the bit to get into the car, a few even yelling to the men inside to hurry, or making threats that if they didn't leave enough for them, they'd break their heads open. Their boots covered with mud and their clothing splattered with it, they looked a sight, just as Anne knew she must look a sight with all the flour and sticky fruit juices on her.

She turned and walked down the roadbed to her tent, gazing off in the distance as she did so. The camp lay in a small valley surrounded by rolling, sparsely timbered hills. To Anne's surprise, she saw that most of the snow had melted, leaving patches of white against the brown. For the first time she realized that the breeze did feel much warmer than it had the day before, and hoped that it would stay so once the sun went down. It had been miserable bathing and dressing in the cold tent that morning.

As she neared her tent, Anne noticed the three tepees that sat about fifty yards to the side of hers. She stared at them curiously, thinking they were much smaller than she had always envisioned a tepee to be, and wondering if the symbols painted on the buffalo hides had any special meaning. Then she laughed, thinking that she would have never dreamed that someday her nearest neighbors would be Indians and a huge man who looked like a wild cossack.

Anne pushed back the flap on her tent and stepped inside. Then she looked about in surprise. A big double bed sat to one side, and a small bureau, chifforobe, and wash cabinet sat to the opposite side. There was also a small potbellied stove at the back of the tent, with a coal can sitting beside it. Thinking she must have entered someone else's tent by mistake, she was about to back out, when she spied her luggage in one corner and her hairbrush sitting on the wash cabinct.

"Well, how do you like your new quarters?" a deep voice boomed out behind her. "Looks a little better than it did yesterday, don't it?"

Anne jumped a foot in fright, then wished Gen. Jack would stop slipping up behind her and scaring the daylights out of her like that. She turned and smiled at the huge man, saying, "It's very nice. In fact, I can't believe it."

"Sorry I couldn't get it up here yesterday, but I wasn't sure you were going to take the job until you showed up. I told them back in Cheyenne before we pulled out to send everything they would if a railroad director was visiting. You'll find bed linens, blankets, and towels in that box over there. If I'm not mistaken, there might even be some soap in there, too."

"But won't you be needing all this if a director *does* come for a visit?"

"Aw, hell, we've got a warehouse loaded with furniture in Cheyenne, and even more back in Omaha. They won't miss this. Besides, a cook is more important to getting this railroad built than one of those idiots. All they're good for is nosing around and asking stupid questions. Why, I bet they couldn't find their way out of a sack if their lives depended on it."

Anne was a little shocked at how disrespectfully the construction chief talked about the directors, and the chief knew it by the expression on her face. "I don't work for this railroad on a full-time basis like Gen. Dodge, and I don't own any interest in it like he does, even though he has all the shares in his wife's name. I'm a private contractor, so I don't to have to bow to them. If they mess with me too much, I'm just liable to up and quit on them, and they know they can't build this railroad without me. They might know how to bring in the money, but I'm the man who knows how to get the work done. Not just anyone can handle those rough, tough construction men out there."

Anne didn't doubt his word for one minute, but she was curious about something. "If Gen. Dodge owns shares in this railroad, why did he put them in his wife's name?"

"Well, just between you and me, I suspect there's some skullduggery going on at the top, some skimming of government and stockholders' money that's going into the bigwigs' pockets and not to the railroad. I think Dodge is playing it safe. If the railroad makes it big, he'll bring in a heap of money from his stock, but if there's ever an investigation as to where he got the money to buy that much stock, he can claim he didn't have anything to do with it, since the stock was in his wife's name." Gen. Jack frowned, making his bushy, black eyebrows meet over the bridge of his big nose. "I'm just a simple man. I'm not smart enough to figure out just how they do it, but I know things aren't on the up and up there. For one thing, a lot of that money is being used to bribe congressmen to increase the land grants and speed up the loans. For another, Dr. Durant is funneling a lot of that money to himself and buying stock like mad, even though it's supposedly restricted to two hundred shares per man. But I will have to say one thing for Dodge. He's not as greedy as the rest of them. He has to fight a constant battle against the directors. He wants to build the shortest, cheapest route possible, but they want to make the line longer to qualify for increased government loans and more land. Hell, they weren't content to just own every other section ten miles to each side of the track, they wanted twenty. And they got it, too."

Anne was shocked. She had no idea so much corruption was going on. "Why, that's terrible!" she said in outrage. "The building of this railroad should be for the good of this country, not for a few ruthless, grasping men to become rich and powerful."

"That's the way it is, all over the country," Gen. Jack answered with an unconcerned shrug of his massive shoulders.

"All of the big businesses are doing it. It's just part of this industrial boom that started after the war. And this railroad *will* be for the good of the country. It's going to open up the West to everyone. The common man may not get as wealthy, but he'll benefit, too. Why, just look at this country around us. I haven't ever seen such good farming land."

Anne had to agree, but she still hated to see a noble cause tainted by men's greediness. Unlike the general population who admired men who amassed fabulous wealth and turned a blind eye to their corrupt and shoddy methods, Anne couldn't. She had high principles and expected the same of others.

"Well, I'd better be going," Gen. Jack said. "I imagine my dinner is waiting for me in my car."

"Then you don't eat with the other men?" Anne asked in surprise.

A look of horror came over the construction chief's face, before he boomed out, "Hell, no! Why a man could be stomped to death or squashed just trying to get into the dining car, to say nothing of having his arm bit reaching for something, or his hand stepped on by some big Tarrier coming over the table. Why, that place is downright dangerous."

As Gen. Jack stepped from the tent Anne had to laugh. As huge as he was, she seriously doubted that he could be squashed or trampled underfoot in a crowd of burly men, nor would anyone dare bite his arm or step on his hand.

She walked to her bed and sat down on it. Never had she felt such a soft mattress, not even back at the Rollins House in Cheyenne. Gazing about the tent, she decided it was an improvement all around to her bare little bedroom back home. Why, it was quite cozy. And it was all hers.

It was a heady thought, having her own quarters where she would have complete privacy, away from her overbearing uncle and equally bossy, snoopy aunt. Why, she could fix it up just as she pleased. Yes, working for the railroad wasn't at all bad, she thought. They gave her room and board and a handsome salary. Then she remembered how she had to earn that keep and money and was filled with despair. She'd never be able to do it, she thought, not without Big Bertha's help. She was going to fail.

Then she remembered Guy's prediction. No, I won't fail, she vowed fiercely. I won't!

Wearily, she rose from the bed to build a fire.

The next afternoon, Gen. Jack paid them a visit in the bakery. This time Anne didn't miss him. She couldn't. He exploded into the car and roared out at Big Bertha, "Which one of your cooks is responsible for that riot in the dining car this morning?"

"Well, I reckon it was Anne here," Big Bertha answered calmly, "since she's baking the pies now."

Anne hadn't been aware of any riot. From her tent, she hadn't heard the men beating on their tin plates with their forks and yelling. Terrified she had down something wrong, she swallowed a lump in her throat and asked, "Was something wrong with the pies?"

"Wrong?" the construction chief yelled out, making Anne wince at the loud noise and her knees shake even harder. "Why, hell no! The men are raving about your pies and demanding more."

"That's right, honey," Big Bertha said. "They were beating on their plates and yelling for more pie at the top of their lungs. I never heard such a racket in my life. I was mighty pleased with you, and you should be proud of yourself. Why, if you wanted to, you'd have a job with the railroad for life, the way you make pies."

Anne was glad the men liked her pies, but terrified that Big Bertha might have bowed to their demands. "What did . . . did you say?"

"Why, I told them to hush up, that no matter how much racket they made, they weren't gonna get more pie. Then I told them to get the hell out of the dining car, that they were holding up the other men."

Anne went weak with relief, until she heard Gen. Jack ask, "Are you sure you won't reconsider that, Big Bertha? I like to keep the men happy, and you know yourself that this outfit runs on their stomachs."

"Hell no, I ain't gonna reconsider! I ain't gonna work my

cooks to death just because they're pigs. Three slices of pie a day is enough for anyone!"

When Gen. Jack started guffawing, Big Bertha realized he had been baiting her. He enjoyed trying to rile her, just as much as she enjoyed riling him. She grinned, then said, "Now, get out of here, you big bully, before I take that whip of yours to you. You may not have work to do, but we do."

After the construction chief had left, Anne asked, "Does he use that big whip on his men?"

"Nope. I think he just wears it for show. He doesn't run his men by terrorizing them, like the construction chief for the C.P. does. He knows how to handle men. He's tough but fair, and he'll get right in there and work beside them. He don't ask them to do anything he wouldn't do himself. That kind of a boss demands respect and loyalty. Those Tarriers would do anything for Gen. Jack."

Anne thought Big Bertha the same kind of boss. She didn't just sit back and give orders. She dug in and helped, not just Anne, but all of the cooks. Yes, it did make a difference. If her aunt had treated her as kindly and fairly as the head cook did, Anne wouldn't have resented her nearly as much.

Over the next week, Anne's job got easier and easier, as her muscles adjusted to the hard labor and she discovered little short cuts. She had the awesome chore down to a fine art, not wasting a moment or a movement. She worked like a well-oiled machine, her arms flying as she rolled out the dough, filled it with fruit, then rolled out the top crusts. After a while, she didn't even have to check the ovens to see if they were done. It became second nature. Other than stopping to stretch her back, the only time she took a break was for lunch, which she ate with Big Bertha. Since she started well before dawn, because she could never go back to sleep after being rudely awakened by the loud bell, by the end of the week, she had her chores done several hours before sunset. That gave her some time to herself.

Anne would have liked to have seen the construction gangs at work, to view the actual building of the railroad, but by that time, the rails had already been lain a good ten miles away. The closest she ever came to seeing anything that even remotely dealt with the building of the railroad, was the construction gangs coming back to the camp on the flatcars at sunset, or the locomotives pushing cars loaded down with rails and ties through the camp. So she passed her free time washing out her clothes and cleaning her quarters and laying in her bed and thinking.

Invariably her thoughts turned to Guy. She tried to keep her mind off of the tall, rugged engineer, to concentrate on her brother instead, but it simply didn't work. She remembered everything Guy had said, every movement he had made, every nuance about him. But what haunted her most was the memory of his kissing her. She couldn't believe she had let him kiss her so intimately, and had let him do something as indecent as touch her breasts, but she had never known anything as thrilling.

Anne hated herself for daydreaming about the darkly handsome engineer. She hated herself even more because she couldn't feel angry at him for taking such liberties with her. All she could feel was regret that he hadn't kissed her out of genuine feeling, but a desire to frighten her. He was undoubtedly the most exciting man she had ever met. Overbearing, yes—he had no right to try and stick his nose into her business—but terribly exciting.

Chapter Ten

After ten days in their new camp, Big Bertha was standing in the bakery and talking to Anne, when she glanced out of the door and said in disgust, "Well, I wondered how long it would be before they showed up."

Anne turned from the oven where she was taking out pies and asked, "Who?"

"That riffraff that follows us from camp to camp," the big woman answered, now standing at the boxcar door. "They're pitching their tents and putting up their buildings across the main tracks. I wonder what name they'll tag onto this Hell on Wheels town? And they brought their damn yapping dogs with them, too. You'd think those mutts would be used to the locomotives by now, but they always raise a ruckus every time one passes through. I guess that's the last peace and quiet we'll see for awhile."

Big Bertha turned from the door and said, "You'd better give that town a wide berth, honey. Stay on this side of the main tracks. I don't trust any of those shady characters as far as I can throw them. Now, if any of them tried any funny business with me, I'd flat lay them out, but you're not as big and strong as I am. They ain't gentlemen like our men are."

Anne couldn't believe her ears. Then she laughed. "You're calling those construction workers *gentlemen?*"

"Oh, I know they ain't got no table manners, and they're rough-talking and hard-drinking cusses, but when it comes to women, they're downright gentlemanly. They show respect for us. That trash out there don't." Big Bertha paused, then asked, "Ain't any of the Tarriers been pestering you, have they?"

"No, I'll have to admit they've been very polite to me. They tip their hat and stand to the side when I pass. Of course, they still stare at me."

Big Bertha laughed. "Well, you can't expect them not to look! They're men, and naturally, they're gonna look, particularly at a young, pretty little thing like you."

Anne had never considered herself little, but she supposed compared to Big Bertha, she was. She looked at the head cook thoughtfully, wondering how old she was. Anne would guess in her early thirties, certainly not too old for her to be attracted to a man. "Do any of them ever stare at you? I mean, like they might be interested?" Anne added quickly, thinking they all must have stared at Big Bertha's size when they first saw her.

A flush rose on Big Bertha's face, making her freckles stand out even more. "Well, believe it or not, a few of them *have* tried to cozy up to me. I guess they must be pretty desperate for a woman. I ain't a young girl anymore, and I've put on some weight these past few years."

Anne didn't think a man showing interest in Big Bertha would have to be desperate. Quite a few of the trackmen were giants themselves, and Big Bertha's good nature and kind heart more than made up for her homely face. And when she smiled with that big mouth of hers, she brightened everyone's day. Anne was becoming quite fond of her, and thought she would make a man a fine wife. "Are you interested in any of them?"

"Nope. After my husband, they all seem kinda pale. I guess I'm just what they call a one-man woman." Big Bertha paused for a moment and gazed out into space, then said sadly, "I sure wish that dumb Mick hadn't gotten himself killed."

Anne was filled with compassion. It must be terrible to love someone so much and then lose them, she thought.

Big Bertha wasn't one to wallow in self-pity. She laughed and said, "But that's all past history. How about you, honey? Did you leave a beau back East?"

Anne had been courted by several men, but like Big Bertha, none of them interested her. Her full energies had been spent in trying to avoid them, not attract them. There was only one man who had caught her attention, and he wasn't interested in her. "No, I guess I'm like you. I'm a one-man woman, except he . . ." her voice trailed off.

"Except he what?" Big Bertha prodded.

Anne didn't want to tell Big Bertha about Guy. She was afraid the big-hearted woman would feel sorry for her, and she had too much pride for that. She shrugged and said, "Except he hasn't shown up yet."

"Well, you just keep waiting and watching. He will. And when he does, don't you let nothing stop you from nabbing him. That's what I did with my husband. I had to be a little brazen, but when you want something that bad, you have to go after it with all you've got. That's one time it don't pay to be meek." Big Bertha laughed. "Poor bastard. He didn't have a chance."

Anne didn't think those tactics would work with Guy. He was most definitely a man with a mind of his own. Besides, she wasn't the kind to run after a man.

Big Bertha glanced out of the door once more, then said, "And remember what I said. Stay away from that town."

Anne remembered what she had told Guy in Cheyenne. "I was thinking that I might get a sidearm and wear it."

"What for?"

"To protect myself from those men you're talking about."

"Hell, they won't come over here. Why, if they set one foot across that main track, Gen. Jack would blow them to bits, because he'd know they'd be up to no good. A few of them tried that back at North Platte, snuck across the tracks to steal some equipment. There wasn't enough left of them to bury by the time he got through with them." Big Bertha cocked her head and gazed at Anne thoughtfully before saying, "But that might not be a bad idea. You don't need no side arm, but you oughta keep a rifle in that tent of yours, in case of an Indian attack. That's why we have those over there by the door. You'd be in a hell of a fix, if you got caught out there without a gun."

"Then you fight off Indians, too?" Anne asked in surprise.

"Sure do. Everyone does, even the boys. Do you know how to shoot a gun?"

"No, but I thought maybe my brother could teach me when he came for a visit."

"I don't think you oughta wait until then to learn. I'll teach you."

"But when?"

"How about tomorrow afternoon, since it's Saturday? Now that that riffraff has arrived, you won't have to bake so heavily for Sunday. Most of the men sleep right through breakfast and dinner, after their night on the town. You oughta be finished by noon, if you only have to bake half the pies you usually do."

"Are you saying that I'll have Saturday afternoons off from now on?" Anne asked in an excited voice.

"As long as that trash across the tracks is around. Besides, you oughta have at least a half a day off, if those trackmen get all day Sunday. Sure burns me up. They get a whole day off, and us cooks have to keep going. Why, we work as hard as they do. Of course, I try to arrange for the men under me getting a Sunday off, too, every now and then. They like to unwind, too."

As Big Bertha walked from the bakery, Anne wondered what to do with her new free time. The town was off limits for her, and her laundry and housecleaning wasn't all that much. She'd use the time to sew some new work dresses, except that she couldn't get any yard goods out here. She had already visited the general store and discovered that. They catered to a strictly male clientele. All they sold was men's clothing, cards, checkers, tobacco, and a few handguns. There wasn't a newspaper or a dime novel to be found; even the passenger trains had boys carrying a basket of books around for the passengers to occupy their time with. Curious to know why there were no reading materials, Anne had asked and been informed there was no demand for it. Except for a very rare man, the construction workers were illiterate.

Well, it seemed she would have even more time to daydream about Guy, Anne thought morosely. No, she wouldn't let herself do that, she vowed. That was futile and silly. She'd spend her new free time learning how to shoot a gun, then practice until she was a dead shot. That would be better than laying around, mooning over some man, particularly one who couldn't care less about her. It was demeaning to spend so much time thinking about him. So what if he was the most manly creature she had ever met? So what if he was the most exciting? So what if just thinking about him sent tingles up her spine? He was just a man, and out here, they were a dime a dozen.

That afternoon, when Anne walked to her tent, she was distracted. But for once, she wasn't thinking about Guy. An idea had occurred to her on how to occupy her free time, and she was anxious to put it to work. She had decided that she would keep a journal detailing all of her experiences since she had come West, and all the exciting things she had seen and had yet to see. Someday her children or grandchildren might enjoy reading about her adventure, and she had a lot of writing to do to catch up.

For that reason, Anne didn't hear the wagon, until it was almost on top of her. Catching a glimpse of the horses from the corner of her eye, she jumped aside, her heart racing in fright, then yelled at the driver angrily, "Watch out where you're going, you damn fool! You almost ran me down!"

The driver, who had been looking over his shoulder and frowning at the new town across the tracks, reined in hard and turned his head. Anne's breath caught. It was Guy.

She stared at him, thinking he was ever more handsome than she remembered. His skin was tanned even deeper, and his black, wavy hair shone beneath the bright spring sunlight. And that strange male magnetism hadn't been a figment of her imagination. Even from where she stood, she could feel his strong sexuality, a raw, utterly masculine appeal that seemed to be crying out to a deep, primitive part of her.

Guy was the first to recover from his surprise. "I'm sorry. I'm afraid I wasn't paying attention to where I was driving. Hello, Anne."

The sound of his deep, rich voice washed over her, and Anne felt a tingle run over her. As he stepped down from the buckboard beside her, she smelled his scent, and her senses swam. His effect on her irritated her to no end. Damn him! she thought. She had promised herself that she wouldn't give him the time of day, and here he had reduced her to a quivering mass in just seconds. Why, her silly legs were even trembling. She stepped back and jutted her chin out defiantly. "I'm still here."

Guy didn't want to get into a spat with Anne. He had volunteered to come to the camp in the hopes that she might still be here, and that he'd be able to see her. "Yes, I can see that. I guess it's a good thing I didn't make any bets on it. I would have lost. I'm afraid I underestimated you. How's the new job?"

Guy admitting that he had been mistaken about her mollified Anne. "Well, I'll admit it was a little tough at first," she acknowledged, then quickly added, "but I'm adjusting to it. What are you doing here?"

"They sent us a few barrels of the wrong size nails. I came to exchange them."

It never occurred to Anne that it might be a little odd to send a valuable engineer for something that any bridge monkey could have picked up. "How is Jim doing on his new job?"

Guy wondered if he should tell Anne the truth, that the other engineers disliked her brother as much as he did, and that they all tried their damndest to avoid him. It was Jim's know-it-all attitude and the chip on his shoulder, but Guy didn't want Anne worrying over her brother. "He's doing fine. I would have offered to bring you a letter from him, but he was away from camp when I left."

"Would I be imposing to ask you to take one back to him?"

Guy wished he hadn't mentioned a letter. He'd rather that Jim not know that he'd come to the main construction camp. Undoubtedly, Jim would want to know why *he* hadn't been asked to make the trip, and Guy knew, that even if Jim had volunteered, the boss wouldn't have allowed it, for fear he would get lost. Jim had absolutely no woodsman's knowledge, and his sense of direction was lousy. He had wandered off from the construction site one day and gotten lost. Guy was the one who had finally found him, and he knew Jim would never forgive him for that. Knowing that Anne was waiting for an answer, he replied, "No, I don't mind."

"Thank you, I'll hurry."

As Anne turned to rush off, Guy caught her arm and turned her. "I'm not in that big of a hurry. I can't get back to our camp by nightfall anyway. Just as long as I make it by dawn." He paused for a moment, then asked, "Well, Anne, is building this railroad as exciting as you thought it would be?"

Anne frowned, then admitted, "Well, I haven't actually seen any building."

"Why not?"

"The first few days on my job, I didn't get through in the bakery until dark. By the time I picked up speed and finished earlier, they were laying track miles away. I guess I'll just have to wait until we move to the end of the line again to see it."

"But that might be weeks away. You don't want to wait that long, do you?"

"I don't really see where I have any choice."

"I could drive you to the end of the line. There's still several hours of daylight left. It shouldn't take us over an hour to get there."

"But by the time you did that and brought me back, it would be dark."

"So I'll drive back to my camp in the dark. I would have had to make a part of the trip that way anyhow."

Why was he being so persistent? Guy wondered. Seeing Anne was one thing. Putting himself in a position where he would be alone with her was quite another, and there was a long, lonely stretch between here and the end of the line. He hadn't been able to forget her, particularly what she had felt like in his arms, what it had been like to kiss her. The memory of it had haunted him, especially at night, so much so that he went to sleep with his loins aching. In view of that, he'd be a fool to drive her to the end of the line. Hell, he'd be playing with fire. She wasn't some whore, to be taken for a quick tumble and then forgotten. She was a respectable woman, and he sure as hell wasn't contemplating courtship. But despite his doubts, Guy wanted to spend some time with her. He wanted more than just a quick hello and good-bye. When he saw her hesitating, he said, "Come on, Anne. This is something you don't want to miss. It's exciting."

Anne had been hesitant because she didn't know if it would be appropriate to drive off into the countryside with Guy. A woman who did that with a man she wasn't engaged to back home would have her reputation ruined. Just what might happen, other than kisses and his touching her breasts again, Anne wasn't quite sure. That provoking man and woman mystery again. But this wasn't home. The rules no longer applied. She had thrown them out the window when she had taken the job, and that's why she had come out here, to see new and exciting things. "All right," she agreed with a radiant smile. "I'll go."

"Good," Guy said, taking her arm to help her into the buckboard.

Suddenly realizing that she looked a sight, Anne asked, "Can you give me a few minutes to freshen up?"

"Sure. While you're doing that, I'll drive over to the storehouse and exchange these nails."

"I'll hurry," Anne promised and rushed off to her tent.

Anne quickly stripped off her soiled dress, brushed the flour out of her hair, and washed up. She had just finished dressing and was slipping the hair net back over her long hair, when she heard the crunch of wagon wheels outside her tent and knew it had to be Guy. Snatching up her shawl, she walked to the tent opening and tossed back the flap, feeling a little taken aback to find Guy standing there.

But instead of looking at her, Guy was gazing over her shoulder at the inside of her tent. Seeing the surprised expression on his face, she said, "It's not bad, is it? I have all the comforts of home here."

"You certainly do. This place is a castle compared to our quarters."

Anne was acutely aware of Guy's eyes on the double bed and wondered if he envied her, but somehow, she sensed his intent interest in it had nothing to do with that. His staring at it made her feel peculiar, all fluttery inside. He jerked his eyes away, took her arm in his hand, and hurried her to the buckboard, saying rather roughly, "We'd better get going." Anne was bewildered by his sudden abruptness.

As soon as they were settled on the wagon seat, Guy picked up the reins and snapped them. The horses trotted off at a brisk speed. Soon they had left the construction camp behind and were following the shiny, new rails through the valley, then around curves and turns when they reached the hills. Anne looked around her. From the camp, the hills had looked brown, but up close, she could see the new tender shoots of grass that were lifting their heads to the warm spring sun. In another week or two the entire area would be covered with grass. She imagined it would be very pretty, if there were only more trees. Those that were standing were mostly short, scrubby-looking things.

"Is there some reason why there aren't more trees out here, and they don't grow very tall?" she asked Guy.

Guy glanced at the hills around him. "I'm afraid that's man's doing, not nature's. When we surveyed this area, it was heavily wooded, but we've just about stripped it for our ties and trestles. Until we reached these hills, every piece of wood had to be shipped in, and that was costing the railroad a small fortune. What's left are the rejects, trees that were too short or twisted to get a decent piece of wood from. However, when we reach the Laramie Mountains, a little farther west, you'll see more timber, particularly higher up where it wasn't so easy to get to."

"It seems a shame to strip the land to build a railroad," Anne commented, thinking the countryside must have been beautiful in its natural state.

"I'm afraid that's the price we have to pay for progress. The shortage of wood in this area has been our main problem, that and getting materials to build the roadbeds. The gravel had to be shipped in from back East, too, first by rail to the end of the line, then by wagon up to where we're grading. It won't be until we reach the Rockies and start blasting our way through them, that we'll be able to provide our own ballast, as we call it."

Anne still thought it was a shame to strip the land. Surely they could have left a few more trees. "I shouldn't think just any old tree would do."

"If we had a choice, we'd be more particular. We'd much prefer hardwoods, cedar or oak, but there wasn't much of that out here. We had to settle for a lot of cottonwood, which is a soft, pulpy wood. At first, it wasn't working out at all. It rotted too fast. Then we discovered that we could preserve it by soaking it in a solution of zinc chloride, a process we call burnettizing. Since then, we've been using the cottonwood ties in a ratio of four junkwood to one good."

Anne frowned. She'd never stopped to consider what problems the railroad was encountering with just construction materials. Why, everything had to be transported for hundreds of miles, right down to the last nail and bolt. She supposed she really couldn't blame them for using what they had at hand, whether it be timber or the remnants of a mountain. And it was more than just an exciting project. From the construction and engineering standpoint, it was an awesome one. No wonder there were so many people who believed it couldn't be done.

"How far is it to the end of the rails?" she asked.

"About ten miles from the main camp. If we were building on the wide open prairie, we'd be much farther by now, but all these curves through these hills have slowed us down. Each rail has to be pounded by hand into the correct shape, you know."

Anne hadn't known. Again, it was something she had never thought of. "Why don't you just blast your way through the hills?"

"Believe it or not, blasting takes more time. It's easier to go around if you can."

Anne noticed the creek that seemed to be paying peek a boo with them, running next to the tracks for a short distance, then wandering off for a mile or so, then beside the tracks again. It didn't look like much of a waterway. "Is this the creek you're building your bridge over?"

"No. The railroad doesn't cross it anywhere. We're building over a dry ravine. Actually, building a trestle over a ravine can be trickier than one over a river or stream. There's no well-defined waterbed. You have to try to predict how much water will come down that ravine during a heavy rain or spring thaws, and how much of a battering the trestle will have to withstand. If you've never seen a flash flood in hill country, you can't imagine it. The water doesn't just rise, like it does in a river. It comes down those ravines in a tremendous wall of water, with such force that it sweeps everything out of its way."

As they rounded another hill and came into a flat, level area, Anne spied the construction sight. The place was in a frenzy of activity. Anne thought the workers looked like ants swarming over an anthill beneath the cloud of dust that hung over the area. As they drove closer, wagons rumbled up and down the roadbed, and foremen on horses darted here and there, shouting orders to the men. Water boys scurried to the thirsty Tarriers calling to them, sloshing water from their buckets at they ran and nimbly dodging the wagons and men on horseback.

They passed a locomotive, sending puffs of white smoke into the air like an Indian's smoke signals, and Anne thought the engineer leaning with one arm on the windowsill of his wooden cab was the only one who wasn't working at a frenzied pace. If anything, he seemed bored to tears. But such was not the case with his black-faced fireman, who was standing behind him and madly shoveling coal into the furnace. Then, as a mangy dog standing in the doorway of the cab let out a sharp bark, Anne jumped in fright, for she hadn't even noticed the animal.

Guy chuckled. "I guess he thinks we're getting a little too close to his territory. All of those train mascots are that way, terribly protective, and every train crew has one. It seems to be some kind of unwritten railroad rule."

Guy veered the wagon from the main stream of traffic and off to the side of the construction site a fair distance. Reining in, he said, "I think this is a good spot to see everything, and it looks like we arrived at an opportune moment. The locomotive is about to push up another car of rails and materials. Each of those large flatcars carries enough to lay two miles of track."

Anne watched as the locomotive pushed the big flatcar of rails forward; it came to a stop behind a small boarding car. As the stakes on each side of the large car were pulled out, the rails rolled off onto the ground, sounding like a bombardment as iron hit iron and making her cars ring. The noise was still echoing through the hills as the trackmen hurried to the pile and loaded sixteen rails, together with a keg of bolts, spikes, and a bundle of fishplates (used to hold the abutting ends of the rails together) on the small boarding car. The rail crew jumped on and the car was pulled to the end of the rail by a team of fast horses. Before the car had come to a full stop, two husky men leaped from it on each side, seized the forward end of the five-hundred-pound rail with their tongs, and trotted forward, the metal scraping against metal until the rail cleared the car, where two more men caught those ends with their tongs.

"Ready! Down!" the foreman yelled over the noises.

The two parallel rails were dropped on the ties with a loud *clang.* No sooner had they hit them than the track straightener, with his notched wooden gauge, set the rails precisely at four-feet-eight-and-half inches, and the boarding car was rolled forward for another pair of rails to be laid. Behind the boarding car, a man dropped spikes into their holes, and a spiker gave the long iron pins three hard blows with his maul, while the tampers beat the ground around the ties, and the bolters secured the fishplates where the two rails met.

Anne was amazed at the trackmen's speed and precision. They performed like a well-trained drill team, every man doing his job without a moment's hesitation or a glance at his co-worker, not a motion wasted, unless it was to wipe the sweat from his eyes. Over and over, the procedure was repeated, a sweaty, dusty, backbreaking, muscle-straining job, until the boarding car was empty of its rails. Then the car was tipped on its side to the ground, and another car with rails came thundering down to the end of the line, while the empty car was pulled to the rear by another team of galloping horses to be reloaded, leaving in its wake yet another trail of choking dust.

The trackmen were a colorful group with their checked and plaid shirts and their bright neck scarfs. Both the blue of the Union army and the butternut brown of the Confederate were seen in their pants, along with gray and black twill of those men who had not fought in the recent war. But it was their hats that were most amazing. Every kind imaginable was present: leather caps, ragged forage caps, battered slouch hats, shiny black derbies, cowboy hats, the tall gray and blue hats that the ex-officers wore, even an occasional white Panama hat, and a broad-brimmed sombrero. It seemed the workers were exhibiting their rugged individualism in their dress, for no two were dressed alike, except for their dusty, high black boots.

Anne turned her attention westward, where the golden sun was dipping below the hills and turning the sky a rosy color. There, about a quarter of a mile ahead of the trackmen, a crew of laborers were taking ties from a wagon and placing them on the graded roadbed. As soon as they hit the ground, "pioneers" butted the ties to a rope line measured from the track center spikes (set by the surveyors months before) and shoveled gravel beneath the ends to act as a cushioning. Beyond them, the roadbed stretched into the distance, its iron surveyors' spikes glittering like gold as they reflected the light of the setting sun.

As Anne took it all in, her eyes darting here, then there, Guy watched her fascinating, kaleidoscope eyes. Then his gaze drifted upward to her hair, and his breath caught. In the oblique light of the setting sun, it was all fire and gold. He remembered how soft it had felt, tumbled down her back the night he had held her in his arms, and had the sudden urge to caress it. Without even realizing what he was doing, he reached up and touched a stray lock hanging over her forehead.

Anne started at his touch and turned her head to look him in the eye. "I was afraid you might not be able to see with your hair falling over your eyes like that," Guy said quickly, jerking his hand away.

Anne pushed the lock back and said, "I'm glad I came. It's amazing how fast they work. And they never stop. Why, they must have laid a quarter-mile of rails just since we've been sitting here!"

Guy smiled at her exaggeration. "Not quite. That would be a hundred rails, and I'd guess they've laid about forty. But each rail does put us twenty-eight feet closer to the Pacific."

At the reminder of where they were heading, a thrill of excitement ran through Anne. Yes, she thought, and she was actually seeing it happen! She was really a part of this great feat, even if she wasn't out there laying rails. Her job was just as important as theirs, for without food those men couldn't do what they were doing. She was glad she had insisted upon staying, and vowed she'd see it through to the end. No matter what happened, she wouldn't be cheated of her claim to building this great railroad. They'd do it, despite what the skeptics said. They'd show the nation and the entire world what stern stuff they were made of. They wouldn't let the Indians or the wilderness or anything defeat them.

She jumped when the locomotive shrilly blew its whistle. The noises on the construction site seemed to be suspended in air, before silence reined for a split second. In that brief time span, there was no clattering of rails being dropped, no ringing of spikes being driven, no scrapping of shovels, no pounding of earth, or thudding of horses' hooves. Then a resounding cheer came from the workers, the deafening noise bouncing off the surrounding hills and reverberating through the small valley before the trackmen took off at a dead run for the empty flatcars, each man carrying his shovel or maul or tongs with him.

As the men clamored on the flatcars, shoving and pushing, Guy said, "Well, that's it for today. I guess we'd better be getting back to camp ourselves."

Anne glanced about her and saw the long shadows being cast by the hills, as the sun sank below the horizon. Disappointment filled her. She would have liked to watch the work a little longer. But even more disappointing was the fact that her time with Guy was coming to an end. He would take her back to the camp, and there was no telling how long it might be before she'd see him again. Or maybe she'd never see him again. They had met by accident, and he would have no reason to seek her out. With this gloomy thought in mind, she responded, "Yes, I suppose so."

Chapter Eleven

As Anne and Guy rode from the construction site, the workers were still climbing on the flatcars, many cursing each other as they struggled for a place to sit on the crowded car. A few scuffles occurred, and more than one man found himself rudely pushed off. In that case, his only recourse was to dash for another car and join the men shoving and pushing to board it. Several men leading several sweaty horses passed their wagon, the animals needing no urging, for they knew their supper awaited them back at camp also. Then, as Anne and Guy were leaving the little valley, the train passed them by, the trackmen seated on the flatcars yelling and whistling at them, while the engineer tooted his whistle, and the train dog barked ferociously at them.

While Anne didn't understand much of the crude remarks the rough men were yelling, she was embarrassed. She understood just enough to know that the trackmen apparently thought she and Guy were much more than friends. Did they think they were courting, since they were out here alone? *If only we were,* Anne thought morosely, her misery surrounding her like a heavy shroud.

Guy was embarrassed, too, on Anne's behalf, and angered, for much of what the men were yelling was unfit for a decent woman's ears. If he could have gotten his hands on them, he would have gladly slammed his fist into a few ugly faces. They had no right to assume she was anything less than a respectable woman. Yet, he knew, that's what all the construction workers thought to some degree. They judged Anne by the other women cooks, women they assumed were just as immoral as the prostitutes that flocked to the Hell on Wheels towns, just because they were out here in the wilderness, and because they were as rough-talking and crude. As far as Guy knew, it was a false assumption. None of the women who worked for the railroad were sporting women, not the cooks or the few female telegraph operators. If they were, they wouldn't be slaving away at their jobs, since prostitution was much more lucrative. Of course, none of them were particularly attractive either, but if a man was horny enough, that didn't matter. If they bedded any of the male workers, they were discreet about it, and in truth, there was little—if any—foundation for the men's low opinion of them. Like the nurses who had served in the war, they were condemned simply because of their presence in what the men considered an all-male venture. The only difference was out here the women were generally treated with respect, if you could call a man's behavior respectful when he tipped his hat and entertained evil thoughts at the same time. No, the workers wouldn't harm Anne or attack her, not physically. But that didn't stop them from thinking, and knowing what they were thinking infuriated Guy.

As the train faded from view, a silence fell over the two—Anne brooding over Guy's lack on interest in her, and Guy seething with anger. The only sounds were those of the wagon wheels squeaking and the hooves of the horses on the packed ground. Then darkness fell.

Alone in the darkness, Guy's acute awareness of Anne sitting beside him overrode his anger. Her sweet scent drifted across to him, and every time the wagon hit a hole and their thighs and shoulders brushed against one another, he was conscious of the brief, titillating touch. Damn, he wanted to kiss her so bad he could taste it, and the thoughts going through his head were far from pure. Hell, he was no better than those crude trackmen. Maybe worse. He knew Anne was a decent woman, but that didn't stop his passion from rising. What was there about her that brought out the animal in him?

Damn her! Why hadn't she gone back East, where she belonged? She had no business staying out here and tempting him. It had been close to a year since he'd had a woman, for he wouldn't sink to going to a prostitute out here. The fear of disease was one thing that kept him away, his innate good taste the other. The sporting women out here were of a much lower class than those back East, and he found their loud laughter and coarse language repulsive. Besides, he was a man who had always prided himself in keeping his passion in check, and yet every time he got anywhere near Anne, he had to fight himself. He'd known this was a mistake, even before he saw that double bed in her tent and those thoughts of making love to her on it had started flitting through his head. He should have found some excuse to get out of it then.

While Guy battled himself, sitting stiffly on the wagon seat and staring straight ahead, Anne wondered at his silence. Was he regretting the time he had lost by bringing her out to see the construction going on? By now, he could have been halfway back to his camp. When he urged the horses to a faster speed, Anne thought he was anxious to be rid of her and sank into an even deeper gloom. By the time they arrived at the camp, she was so dejected, she was on the verge of tears.

Guy was anxious to be rid of Anne, but not for the reasons she thought. He was rapidly losing his battle against himself. He pulled up in front of her tent, jerked the horses to a halt, and jumped from the wagon. As he helped her down, he steeled himself to the feel of her soft hand in his.

Anne turned in front of her tent and said, "Thank you for taking me."

"You're welcome," Guy said curtly, wishing to hell she'd go inside. Her scent was driving him crazy.

He can't wait to get rid of me, Anne thought, and felt tears stinging at the back of her eyes. Terrified that he might see them, she turned and pushed back the tent flap, saying over her shoulder as she stepped inside, "Good-bye."

Guy frowned. The word had such a final tone to it. Suddenly, he didn't want to leave her. Without even stopping to consider what he was doing, he said, "I'll light the lamp for you."

Guy stepped past Anne, walked to the lamp, and lit it. He turned and saw her standing just inside the tent, the light from the lamp bringing out the reddish highlights of her hair, and her hazel eyes shimmering from her unshed tears. He stared at her for a moment, thinking she looking very beautiful, then, noticing that she was holding her shawl tightly around her, said, "I'll light a fire for you."

As Guy turned, Anne stepped forward and caught his arm, saying, "That's not necessary. I won't need it, since I'll be going straight to bed."

Guy glanced at the bed and found himself plagued with the same thoughts he'd had that afternoon. Anne's hand on his arm seemed to burn right through the material of his shirt. His mouth turned dry. He turned to leave and found Anne blocking his path. With something akin to a groan, he abandoned his struggle and swept her into his arms, kissing her hungrily and molding their bodies together tightly.

Anne never knew what hit her. No sooner had she recovered from her surprise, than she was falling under the heady magic of Guy's passionate kiss. The tent spun dizzily around her as his tongue ravaged the sweetness of her mouth, an incredible excitement filling her. Dropping her shawl on the floor, she curled her arms around his broad shoulders. She wasn't even aware of him slowly backing her towards the bed. All she could think of was his fiery kiss and his hard male body pressed against her.

When they reached the bed, Anne tumbled backward on it. Guy followed her without even breaking the torrid kiss and lay halfway over her. Vaguely, Anne was aware of their intimate position, of her breasts flattened against his muscular chest, of his thigh between hers. From a small corner of her mind, she thought to protest, but the feel of Guy caressing her breasts robbed her of the thought. Tingles ran over her, and the thought flitted away.

Guy kissed her cheeks, her temples, her eyelids, her forehead, then dropped his head to nibble on the enticing mole beneath her ear. God, he thought, she tasted so sweet, and her skin was so soft and silky. He wanted to explore every inch of her body. Remembering the mole beneath her chin, he slid his mouth across her throat and supped on it, his hand working on the buttons on her bodice.

Anne's senses were spinning. Not until she heard Guy mutter thickly, "God, your breasts are beautiful," did she regain some semblance of reason. She looked down and saw her breasts were bared, then watched with mortification as Guy flicked his thumb across one rosy nipple and it rose eagerly to his touch. Alarmed at how far and how fast things had progressed, she opened her mouth, but no sound left her lips. Rather she sucked in her breath sharply as Guy bent his head and his tongue lashed out over the turgid nipple like a wet whip, feeling a bolt of fire rush to her loins. As Guy bent his head and took the throbbing peak into his mouth, she was awash with sudden new sensations, each tug of his lips intensifying the burning feeling in her loins. She caught the back of his head and arched her back, glorying in the feelings he was bringing her. Then as his hand massaged the other breast and his slender fingers rolled that nipple, Anne felt she couldn't bear the burning throbbing between her legs anymore. Instinctively, she arched her hips, seeking some way to ease the almost painful aching.

She felt it then, pressing against her hip, long and hard and seemingly scorching her. The blatant proof of his arousal was an unknown to her, for the time he had kissed her before, she had been too enthralled with the kiss itself to notice. Whatever it was, it seemed enormous and very threatening. A tingle of fear ran through her, and she cried out.

Guy heard Anne's soft cry. He, too, was very aware of his hard, throbbing flesh pressing against her soft hip, a part of him that he ached to bury inside her warm depths. With his senses dulled by his passion, he ignored her cry and continued his feasting at her breasts, but he did have enough presence of mind to shift his weight.

With that strange, frightening part of him no longer pressing against her, Anne once more fell under the spell of Guy's attack on her senses. His hands seemed to be everywhere, caressing her arms, her hips, her thighs, and leaving a burning sensation everywhere he touched. The feel of his lips and tongue at her breasts were an exquisite torture that left her weak, with hot waves running up and down her. It was wonderful, and she was trembling all over. A low roaring filled her ears. She wished he would never stop.

But Guy did stop. While Anne's soft, fearful cry didn't bring him fully to his senses, the loud call of a trackman passing by the tent did.

"Hey, Sean, wait fer me!" the man called to one of his drinking buddies, heading for the Hell of Wheels town across the tracks. "What's your damn hurry, man? So what if you have to be waitin' in line fer a poke? We've got all night!"

The loud words were like a dash of ice water on Guy's heated senses. Suddenly he realized what he was doing, and who he was doing it to. This was Anne, and not some whore he paid to "poke," as a few of the trackmen called it, having picked the crude term up from some of the cowhands. He jerked back from her and hastily covered her breasts with the bodice of her dress, then flew to his feet beside the bed.

Anne looked up at him with passion-glazed eyes, then sat up and looked about herself in bewilderment, as if she was wondering how she had gotten on the bed. Fearing that when she recovered her senses she would be angry with him, and knowing he deserved it, Guy muttered, "I'm sorry. Forgive me for getting so . . . so carried away."

Guy turned and rushed from the tent without another word. Long after he had driven away, Anne stared at the tent flap. As reason returned, she felt acutely embarrassed at the liberties she had allowed him to take. Why, she'd never dream of letting another man do those things. In fact, she had never even dreamed men did those things. But she was too honest to deny that she had enjoyed it. She had wanted Guy to kiss her, desperately, and all those other things he had done to her had been marvelous. Then, as she realized he had kissed her because he wanted to, and not to try and frighten her, a thrill ran through her.

Anne didn't sleep much that night. She was too thrilled at knowing that Guy was attracted to her, and she was filled with a consuming curiosity to know what would have happened if he hadn't stopped! She sensed that the sensations he had aroused in her were just the tip of the iceberg. Damn Aunt May! Why did the old biddy have to be so secretive about it?

* * *

The next afternoon, Big Bertha took Anne behind Gen. Jack's rolling factory to teach her how to shoot a rifle. Tossing a large empty fruit tin a distance away, Big Bertha handed Anne the gun and said, "See if you can hit that can."

"Is the gun already loaded?" Anne asked nervously.

"Yep, and that ain't no musket that has to be loaded through the muzzle and only fires one shot. That's a Spencer carbine, a seven-shot, tube-fed, breech-loader that has a lever action."

"What does all that mean?" Anne asked in confusion.

"It means you load it from the butt, by slipping a tube of seven cartridges into it, and you have to pump the lever to load the bullet into the barrel. If you don't do that, you can stand there and squeeze the trigger until doomsday, and nothing will happen. Now then, push that lever forward and back."

Anne did as Big Bertha directed her, and found that it took quite a bit of strength to do so.

"Now aim it and pull the trigger."

Anne knew enough about guns to know that she had to get the target between the sights on the end of the barrel. She lifted the gun, centered the tin can between the sights, and pulled the trigger. The tremendous explosion left her ears ringing, and recoil sent her staggering backward.

As Anne rubbed her aching shoulder, Big Bertha said, "Yeah, that's the trouble with those rifles. They got a kick like a mule, but you'll get used to it."

"Did I hit the target?" Anne asked, peering through the cloud of smoke.

"Nope. Didn't come anywhere close."

"But I had it between my sights," Anne objected.

"You *thought* you had it between your sights. It takes a heap of practicing. Now pump that lever and try again."

By the time Anne had emptied the gun, she still hadn't hit her target, and she was disgusted with the whole thing. Besides the shots leaving her ears ringing, and the gun's painful kick, the irritating gun smoke was making her eyes water. "Well, I guess that's it for today," she commented, feeling somewhat relieved.

"Why do you say that?"

"The gun is empty."

"So we'll just reload it," Big Bertha said, slipping a tube of cartridges from the canvas bag she had slung around her neck.

Showing Anne how to reload the gun, she handed it back to her and said, "Now, try again, but this time put the can a little lower in your sights."

Anne shot again, and again. Both bullets missed their mark, much to her disgust. Then, hearing someone laughing, she turned and saw two of the cooks, several of the dishwashers, and one of the butchers, standing on one of the cars and watching them.

"What's so damn funny?" Big Bertha shouted.

"Women can't shoot worth a damn," the big, burly butcher shouted back. "You oughta stick to your brooms. At least you can knock the Injuns over their heads with them."

His answer brought another loud laugh from the others.

"So you think a woman can't shoot, do you?" Big Bertha asked angrily. "Well, we'll see how funny you think this is!" She grabbed the gun from Anne and aimed it at the spectators. Anne was amazed at how fast she pumped the gun and fired. The bullets tore into the wood at the butcher's feet, sending splinters flying and making the man jump about wildly to keep from being hit. Within seconds, the others had leaped from the top of the car.

"You damn-fool woman!" the butcher yelled angrily at Big Bertha. "Be careful with that thing. You might have hit me!"

"If I'd meant to hit you, I would have! Now, you get the hell out of here, before I load this gun back up and do some serious shooting!"

Seeing Big Bertha slipping another tube of cartridges from the bag, the butcher beat a hasty retreat. Big Bertha laughed and said, "Well, I guess we showed them."

"You showed them," Anne corrected. "I'll never be able to shoot that well."

"Sure you will, honey. All it takes is practice."

"But isn't it a waste of ammunition for me to just practice? The railroad may not appreciate that."

"Aw, hell, the railroad has tons of ammunition. And if it means you killing just one of those lousy redskins, it will be worth it. Now, give it another try."

Anne shot ten rounds of ammunition, and finally managed to hit her target twice, sending the tin can skittering across the ground. Her success pleased her no end. Then she missed the next five shots. Feeling frustrated, she turned to Big Bertha and asked, "What am I doing wrong?"

"You're probably just tired. After shooting for a while, your arms get to shaking. I reckon that's enough for today."

Anne thought it was enough, too. Her shoulder was aching something awful, and she had a pounding headache. She handed the gun back to Big Bertha.

"Be careful," Big Bertha cautioned. "You almost touched the barrel, and after all that shooting, it's as hot as an iron."

Anne wiped the sweat from her brow and said, "I thought it was the sun that was so hot."

"Well, that, too, I reckon." She glanced up at the sun sinking below the horizon and said, "Jesus, I hate to see summer come, if it's this hot in the spring."

As they walked back to the camp, Anne asked, "How many Indian attacks have you seen?"

"Two or three. Then once, we had the Injuns come for a friendly visit, or so they claimed. I think they were just nosing around to see how many guns and ammunition we had."

"Where did that happen?"

"Near Grand Island. Chief Spotted Tail and a bunch of his Sioux came for a visit. Gen. Jack showed them around. He made a point of showing them all the stacks of ammunition in the cars. Then the Injuns showed us their skill with bows and arrows. I'm telling you, those damn redskins could put an arrow through the hole in a shovel handle from sixty feet away. Every blasted one of them was a dead shot. I guess they were trying to impress us with their firepower, too. Gen. Jack invited them into the chow car and fed them. If you think those Tarriers have got big appetites, you ain't seen nothing. I thought they were gonna eat the table, and when syrup was passed around, they drank it right out of the pitcher. Damndest thing I ever saw in my life. Then Gen. Jack invited Spotted Tail into the locomotive for a ride, and his braves all lined up to race the engine. At first, it looked like they were beating the engine, and they gave a big whoop. Then the locomotive pulled ahead of them and left them behind. I think they left feeling kinda discouraged, but you'd think by then they'd know they couldn't pit their horses against the Iron Horse. Months before that, they'd strung a rope across the rails, held by sixteen chiefs. The engine raced right by, taking the rope and a few of the chiefs with it."

"You make them sound foolish."

"It ain't that they're stupid. They just don't understand any kind of machinery. They can't figure out where it gets its power."

Anne laughed. "I guess I can't fault them. My brother tried to explain how a locomotive worked to me. He might as well have been talking Greek. Something about the steam pushing pistons that turned the wheels. It still didn't make sense to me. I guess I don't have a mechanical mind."

"Most women don't, and neither do those Injuns. But that don't mean those red devils ain't cunning and dangerous."

As they walked around the end of cars sitting on the track, Big Bertha spied a group of trackmen walking towards the town across the tracks. "Well, there they go, all gussied up for their night on the town, with their black silk neck scarfs and their hair slicked down. Hell, that bunch didn't even bother to eat first." Big Bertha gazed thoughtfully at the men for a moment, then shook her head. "I never could understand men. Why they think getting drunk, gambling, and whoring was so much fun. If that rotgut whiskey don't make them so sick they puke their insides up, it makes them mean, and they get into a fight. They come back looking like they've been run over by a locomotive. And they're damn fools to gamble with those card sharks. What money those slick gamblers don't take from them, the whores do. It's bad enough they come back flat broke, but they're downright stupid to risk having their thing rot off from some disease they caught from one of them women."

"What thing?"

Big Bertha shot Anne a sharp glance, then said, "You know—that thing between their legs."

Anne knew males and females were built differently. When they were small children, she had seen her brother naked. But what she had felt pressing against her hip the night before didn't seem to bear any resemblance to what she had seen. Why, it was huge and as hard as a rock. "How do they catch a disease?"

"Why, honey, those whores all carry diseases. When you're doing it with every Tom, Dick, and Harry that comes along, that's the price you pay."

"Do what?"

Big Bertha stared at Anne in disbelief, then asked, "Don't you know what happens between men and women?"

"No, I don't. The aunt that raised me would never tell me anything."

"Well, what about your girlfriends? Didn't they know? Hadn't they heard things?"

"I didn't have any close girlfriends. They were so busy on their farms, and I was so busy in my uncle's store, that we rarely saw one another."

"Well, what about animals? Ain't you ever seen them mating?"

"No. There was just our store, a blacksmith shop, and a church in our village. The blacksmith hated dogs and cats. He chased them away. He said they spooked the horses he was trying to shoe."

"Christ, honey! I didn't know you was so damn innocent. Why, you might as well have been living in a cave. I'd tell you, but I don't think I'm the one to do it. I'm so plainspoken."

"Oh, Bertha, I'm tired of being put off. I want to know what all of the big mystery is about. If you don't tell me, who will?"

"Why don't you ask your brother?"

"Jim? Why, he's as bad as my aunt, or worse. She was just tight-lipped, but any time I even vaguely approached the subject with Jim, he looked so embarrassed it made me uncomfortable."

"Yeah, I reckon it ought to come from another woman. And if someone don't tell you, you're gonna be mighty shocked on your wedding night. Why, if you don't know what's coming, it might even scare the daylights out of you." Big Bertha glanced about her, then said, "But this ain't the place to do it. Let's step inside your tent, where it's more private."

The two women walked to Anne's tent and stepped inside. Anne lit the lamp, since the light was so dim, and the two sat on her bed. Then Big Bertha bluntly explained the sex act. Anne *was* shocked. She had never dreamed that men and women did that!

Seeing the expression on her face, Big Bertha said in a flustered voice, "Oh, hell, I knew I shouldn't have told you. I'm too unladylike. I don't know to be delicate about it. Now you've got the idea it's dirty, and it ain't that way at all. Why, it's the most natural thing in the world. That's the trouble. Most women think it's dirty, something they should be ashamed of doing. They don't know how to relax and enjoy it. They got the idea in their heads that only the man is supposed to like it, and that there's something wrong with a woman who does."

Anne remembered Guy's erection pressing against her. She couldn't imagine him putting that inside her. "Doesn't it hurt?"

"The first time I was a little sore," Big Bertha admitted. "Everything had to stretch. But after that, it was a plumb good feeling. But I reckon that depends upon how good a lover the man is. I've heard some women say their husbands didn't even give them time to get het-up, that they were in and out as quick as a rabbit. Sounds to me like those men was nothing but a bunch of selfish brutes, just interested in themselves. It takes a woman longer to get in the mood. They ain't as naturally passionate as men are. They like a little kissing and cuddling along with it. And they ain't like men. They gotta have some feelings for the man. That's why I never could understand those whores. How they could do it with just anyone and everyone. Why, it's plumb unnatural for a woman. But then, they ain't doing it for the fun of it, they're doing it for the money."

"Are you saying that a man's passion can be aroused without him really caring for you?" Anne asked.

"Sure can. That's why you gotta watch yourself around them. Hell, they get all het-up, and there ain't no stopping them. Why, they can overpower you and force themselves on you. Of course, passion goes along with love, too. That's what it's really all about, a man and woman loving each other, or at least, it should be."

"But how do you know the difference? How do you know if a

man cares for you, or he just . . ." Anne's voice trailed off.

"Just wants to satisfy his lust?" Big Bertha asked, finishing the question Anne couldn't find the words for. "Well, I reckon that's a problem. A lot of women can't tell the difference. I reckon a lot of men can't either. They marry a woman thinking they love her, when actually they're just lusting after her. Men are strange creatures. They seem to be more driven by their passion than their hearts."

Seeing the perplexed expression on Anne's face, Big Bertha said, "Well, I reckon I didn't answer your question, did I? You still don't know how you're gonna know the difference, do you? I'd say it depends upon how the man treats you otherwise. How considerate he is with you."

Long after Big Bertha had left, Anne pondered over what she had learned. Now she knew what the big mystery was about, but she was even more confused. Just because Guy had kissed her, just because he had become aroused, didn't necessarily mean he cared for her. He might have been just acting like a man, being driven by his passion. She remembered how anxious he had appeared to be rid of her. That wasn't very considerate. And he had kissed her so suddenly, he had just pounced on her!

Anne's spirits sunk to a new low, before anger came to her defense. How dare he! How dare he treat her like that, when he had no feelings for her! He had just taken advantage of her stupidity. If she ever saw that bastard again, she'd scratch his black eyes right out of his head!

Chapter Twelve

A week later, Anne found her brother waiting for her outside the bakery, when she had finished for the day. A feeling of joy rose in her, for she desperately needed someone she knew genuinely cared for her. Believing Guy couldn't give a fig about her, had been a hard blow to her self-esteem.

After she had hugged Jim tightly and kissed him on the cheek, the two retired to her tent. Then seated side by side on the bed, Anne asked, "Well, how is your new job going?"

An angry look came over Jim's face. He slammed to his feet. "Terrible! And it's all *his* fault!"

"Whose fault?"

"Guy! He thinks he's so damn smart. That he knows everything. What's more, he's got the chief engineer completely fooled. Any suggestion I make, the chief ignores, and I've made some good ones. But any crazy idea Guy comes up with, he goes along with. Do you know what that idiot proposed? That we widen that ravine we were bridging! Have you ever heard of anything so crazy? Guy had some stupid theory about the runoff flowing slower if it were wider. It was nothing but a waste of the railroad's money. By the time we finished blasting, we had an expanse that was twice the size of what we'd started with. And as if that weren't bad enough, then he proposed some radical bridge design. Why, it was so radical it was absolutely absurd! It didn't follow any of the principles of trestle building. I couldn't believe the chief accepted his proposal and not mine. Why, it wouldn't surprise me if that bridge collapsed the first time a train went over it. And do you know what Guy said when he overheard me telling the others what I thought of it? He took me aside and advised me to keep my opinions to myself, until I learned a little more about building bridges in this country. Then he had the audacity to say that my criticism about how things were being done was only making me look foolish."

Considering Anne's own hard feelings toward Guy, it didn't take much to fire her anger. She came to her brother's defense like a lioness to her cub's. "Why, that's awful! You're an engineer, too, and entitled to your opinions. And you're just as smart as he is, or smarter. Who does he think he is, anyway? God? That he can do any damn thing he wants, or say anything he wants? He's not your boss! Honestly, he's the rudest man I've ever met. I thought that from the very first. Why, he's nothing but a . . ." Anne searched her mind for an apt description of Guy, her anger at him for taking advantage of her naivete taking precedence over all, ". . . a sneaky opportunist."

"That's exactly what he is!" Jim agreed readily, so angry his face was mottled with red. "He's trying his damndest to get ahead of the rest of us, and he has absolutely no scruples at all. There's nothing he wouldn't sink to in order to make himself look good—even lying. I know he's been talking to the others behind my back, trying to turn them against me. That's the only explanation for them avoiding me the way they do. My expressing my opinions isn't making me look foolish! He is! Why, there's no telling what kind of lies he's been telling them. And I know why he's doing it. He knows I'm smarter than he is, that I'm the far better engineer. I'm a threat to him. He's been trying his damndest to get me fired, just like he did Bill."

"Who's Bill?" Anne asked.

"He's a bridge monkey I've become friends with. He hates Guy, too, and he sees right through him, just like I do. Guy almost got him fired. He accused Bill of not putting enough nails in a section of the trestle that he was working on. He said Bill was lazy and doing sloppy work. Bill said it was a lie, that Guy had it in for him. For two cents, I'd quit this job and go back East, before that bastard ruins my professional reputation."

Alarm quickly replaced Anne's anger. If Jim quit and went

back East, he'd expect her to do the same, and Anne didn't want to do that. Her job gave her a sense of worth that she had never had, and she enjoyed her independence. For the first time in her life, she had money to spend, not that there was much to spend it on in the construction camp, but someday, there would be a time and a place. Besides, she had promised herself that she would stick it out no matter what, that she would prove her mettle and place her claim to the part she had played in the building of this great railroad. And it was dull back East. Why, there was nothing exciting going on back there. She'd die of boredom. "You wouldn't really do that, would you?" she asked fearfully. "Let Guy chase you off? Why, this is the biggest opportunity you've ever had. You said so yourself. You should stand up and fight!"

"Yes, it is the biggest opportunity I've ever had, and it infuriates me that he's ruining it for me, and all just because he's jealous. But you're right. I shouldn't let him chase me off. That's what Bill says, too. That I should beat the tar out of him!"

Anne hadn't meant physical fighting. She was even more alarmed, for she knew her brother would be no match in a fistfight with Guy. The rugged engineer had worked on a construction gang, and was as hard-muscled as any of the trackmen. And undoubtedly, he knew all of their fighting tricks, while Jim knew nothing of the art of self-defense. Jim could be badly hurt. However, Anne knew better than to point this out to her brother. Instead, she said, "I don't think that's the solution. You wouldn't want to let him reduce you to brawling, would you? Make you look common and crude? That's beneath you. No, sooner or later, he's bound to make a serious mistake, and they'll see him for what he is, nothing but an arrogant show-off. I'd just bide my time and let him hang himself."

In essence Jim was a coward, but between his twisted thinking and his new friend's encouraging his anger, he was on the verge of doing something rash. He had never been so frustrated or disappointed in his entire life. Nothing was working out as he had anticipated, and he was too blind to his own inadequacies to admit that it was his fault. Instead, he blamed it all on Guy, the man who seemed to be getting all the attention and glory. He stewed silently for a moment, then said, "I'll stick it out for a little longer. But if things don't change soon, I'm quitting and going back East. At least, they know how to appreciate a good engineer back there."

Hoping to take his mind off his agitation, Anne told him about her job. Jim didn't act the least happy about her doing well, nor was he impressed that she managed to bake two hundred pies a day. His refusal to acknowledge what an awesome chore she was performing irritated Anne. Why was it that men always thought they were the only ones who worked hard? she wondered. Why, she labored just as hard as any trackman on her job, and certainly harder than any of the engineers, who mostly supervised. And why did men always think their job was more important? She had seen that irksome male attitude back home in the farmers. The men worked from sunup to sundown, but the women's work was never done; yet, when the farm was a success, it was the man who was given credit for it. Even the male cooks, who she would expect to know better, were under the mistaken impression that they worked harder and that their jobs were more important than hers. Men were such arrogant creatures!

Seeing that Jim wasn't in the least bit interested in her job, Anne turned the conversation to the subject of her lodgings, thinking that her brother would at least be glad to see that she had a fairly decent place to live in. Such was not the case. He seemed to resent her having better quarters than he, and launched into a sour recitation of how crude and crowded the living accommodations for the engineers were. By the time Jim left, saying he and his new friend were going on an overnight hunting trip, Anne was glad to see him go. His visit had done nothing to encourage her or raise her spirits. If anything, she felt more downcast after he had left, and she was worried sick that he might quit and go back East. It seemed that he was disgusted with everything about the job, and angrily she blamed Guy for it. If the rugged engineer weren't treating Jim so badly, maybe her brother would have been able to overlook the discomforts of the job. Yes, she decided, if he weren't for Guy undermining Jim, her brother would be much more contented. Damn Guy! Now she had a double reason to hate him.

* * *

The next week was unusually warm for spring, and the bakery was like one big oven. By the end of the day, Anne was soaking wet with perspiration, and the flour that covered her was caked to her skin and clothing. One day, when she had just finished putting the last of the pies on the rack to cool and was preparing to leave, Big Bertha wandered in, took one look at her, and said, "Jesus! You look like something the cats dragged in and decided they didn't want."

"I know," Anne replied wearily, pushing a wet strand of hair from her forehead. "This heat is killing me."

"Well, you'd better get used to it, honey. It's gonna get a hell of a lot hotter this summer."

It was a thought that Anne could hardly bear. She sat on a stool by the door, hoping to catch a breath of cool air, and said, "I'd give anything for a real bath right now. Not a sponge bath, but an honest-to-God bath. How much longer until we reach a river?"

"From what I've seen so far, there ain't many rivers out here. About the most you'll see is a creek."

Anne remembered the creek she had seen when Guy had driven her to the end of the line. "There isn't any way we could borrow a wagon and drive over to that nearby creek is there?" she asked hopefully.

"I don't think that would be too good an idea, honey. Some of the men do it every once in a while, but there might be Injuns lurking about, and two women alone would be easy pickings for them. We'd better wait until we camp beside a creek."

"But that might be weeks!"

"Yep, it might, but I think I got a solution."

"What?"

"Come on back to the store room and I'll show you."

Big Bertha took Anne back to the crowded car that served as a storeroom. There, among sacks of coffee, flour, and dried beans, and crates of tinned fruit, she pulled a short barrel forward and said, "You could use this empty vinegar barrel for a bathtub. I thought about using it for myself, but I was too big to fit in it. Seemed a shame to throw such a nice sturdy barrel away, so I hung on to it. It will be a tight squeeze, but I think you can make it. You're a long-limbed gal, but you ain't near as broad as I am."

The prospect of a real bath sent a thrill through Anne. Then she remembered something. "I don't know if I should. I already feel guilty about the water I use to wash my clothes in."

"Hell, you shouldn't feel guilty about that. It ain't like you're one of those Tarries out there. Wouldn't do them no good to wear fresh clothing every couple of days, like we do. They're just gonna turn right around and get dirty again. But we cooks have gotta keep reasonably clean. Of course, those men working under me may change their clothes more often, but they sure ain't bathing regular. Have you ever got a whiff of them? Why, it's enough to bowl you over! But then, men ain't as particular about cleanliness as women are."

Anne didn't mention it, but she changed her clothing every other day, and she always wore a fresh apron. "But still, it would take a lot of water to fill that barrel."

"You wouldn't have to fill it plumb full. Just to your waist. Hell, by the time you got in it, that would only be a foot of water. Then, when you got through, you could wash your clothes in it. That way, you wouldn't be wasting it. Besides, water can't be all that scarce. If it were, the railroad would fix that big leak in the water tank. That's where I've been going when I can't stand myself no more. Sneak over to the water tank at night and stand below that leak. Of course, it ain't as relaxing as sitting in a tub."

Anne was a little shocked to learn Big Bertha stripped naked and bathed right there in the camp, but then she supposed the big woman was relatively safe from prying eyes. In the middle of night, no one was about, the men so exhausted from their hard work that they were dead to the world. On some nights, when the wind was in the right direction, she could even hear their loud snores from her tent, and wondered how they could sleep with all that racket around them. But bathing in the open in the middle of the camp was something that Anne could never do. Why, she'd be terrified someone would catch her. But Big Bertha was her boss, and if she said it was all right to use the extra water, she'd be a fool to turn the barrel down. She grinned and said, "You talked me into it."

Big Bertha grinned back. "Good. Ain't no reason for us to go around smelling to high heaven, just because these men do. I swear most of them are like little boys, whose mas have to take a stick to them to make them take a bath. Sometimes I think all that business about water being scarce is just an excuse. Males are sorta like cats. They seem to purely hate water."

Guy was the one who had told her water was scarce. Was he using it as an excuse not to bathe? Anne wondered. Then she remembered that he always looked neat when she saw him, and the smell coming from him had been far from disagreeable. No, he was as inclined as she was to personal cleanliness. The remembrance of Guy's disturbing scent made Anne's stomach flutter, a reaction that irritated her to no end. Damn him! Why couldn't she forget him?

"Come on, honey," Big Bertha said, tearing Anne from her thoughts. "I'll help you carry this barrel over to your tent."

The next Saturday, Anne decided to forgo her target practice in favor of a long, leisurely soak in her new "bathtub." After she had washed her hair and bathed, she looked down at the water, thinking that she should wash her clothes while it was still relatively warm, but she wasn't in the mood. She decided to put it off until Monday, when she took her next full bath. After her hair was dry, she dressed and walked from the tent for a stroll before going to the cookhouse for supper.

As soon as she stepped from the tent, she saw several men climbing down from a wagon parked beside one of the boxcars a short distance away. Dressed in white shirts and string ties, she knew they weren't trackmen. Her breath caught when the driver rose from his seat and she realized that it was Guy. Then, remembering the way he had treated both her and Jim, her anger rose.

When Guy had agreed to come to "town" with a few of his fellow engineers for some unwinding, he had promised himself he wouldn't seek Anne out. Their last meeting had almost ended in disaster, and he had vowed he would keep his distance. Since he couldn't seem to control his passion when he was around her, he would stay away from her. The solution to his problem seemed simple enough, but as soon as they drove into the busy camp, he found his eyes straying toward her tent. For that reason, he spied her as soon as she stepped from it. A spontaneous smile crossed his lips, a smile that quickly turned to a frown when he noted the murderous look that came over her face when she saw him.

She's as mad as a wet hen for the way he'd behaved, Guy thought. But dammit, it wasn't all his fault. A respectable women had no business looking so damn seductive. She should look sweet and docile, but with Anne's hazel eyes flashing, and her body held rigid, she looked more like a spitting wildcat, and Guy found he longed to tame that wildcat. The realization that Anne's anger only served to excite him filled Guy with self-disgust. He should turn his back on her and walk away. After all, he'd apologized, and he'd be damned if he'd repeat it. He wasn't a man to grovel to anyone.

He climbed down from the wagon, fully intending to ignore Anne and catch up with the other engineers, who were already walking toward the town. But when one of his friends looked over his shoulder and asked, "Aren't you coming?" Guy found himself saying, "I'll join you in town. I have some business to attend to here in camp first."

Hating himself and having no idea what he was going to say, Guy walked up to Anne. He felt like a damn fool when he stopped in front of her, smiled, and said, "Hello, Anne."

The green sparks in her eyes turned to blue, then green again. "How dare you talk to me!"

"I've already apologized for what happened the other night, Anne," Guy replied stiffly, feeling his own anger rising.

"And that's supposed to make it all right?" Anne threw back hotly. "You think all you have to do is apologize?"

"Dammit, Anne, I'm a normal healthy male. I'm not made of stone, and you're a very desirable woman. Besides, if I remember correctly, you weren't objecting. You did nothing to try and stop me. It was as much your fault as mine that things got out of hand."

Was it partly her fault? Anne wondered. Should she have tried to stop him? Deep down, Anne knew she had let her passion get the better of her, but that had only happened because she thought he cared for her. But she could never admit that to Guy. He would think her a silly little girl, and that would be even more humiliating. But she found that she couldn't let go of her anger. She brushed his objection aside and asked, "And what about the way you've been treating Jim? I suppose that's not your fault either?"

Guy frowned. "What are you talking about?"

"Oh, don't act so innocent!" Anne snapped in disgust. "Do you think he doesn't know what you're doing? That everyone but you is stupid? He knows you're talking about him behind his back, turning the others against him, trying to get him fired. Of all the low, despicable things to do. You can't compete with him in the open, so you resort to sneaking and lying."

Guy was willing to take the blame for his part in what had happened between him and Anne, but he wasn't going to be blamed for something he hadn't done. "When did he tell you that?"

"When he visited me, two weeks ago."

"It's a lie, Anne. I've never done any of those things to him."

"I didn't expect you to admit it," Anne answered contemptously.

Guy's anger rose. "Are you calling me a liar?"

"Yes, I am!"

Guy's anger turned to fury. That damn Jim and his crazy twisted thinking. And now he's got Anne thinking crazy. He glanced around him and saw several men staring at them curiously. He took Anne's arm in his hand and said, "Come on."

As Guy firmly lead her towards the wagon, Anne jerked her arm and asked, "What do you think you're doing? Let go of me!"

"No, Anne. We're going someplace where we can talk this over."

"I'm not going anyplace with you!"

"The hell you aren't! We're going to hash this out, and we're going to do it in private."

Anne looked around her, seeing the men gaping at them. They *were* making a spectacle of themselves, she realized, arguing in public, but she had no intention of going anywhere with

Guy. She jerked on her arm again, but Guy's hold on it was like iron. She dug in her heels and said coldly, "That's not necessary. I have nothing further to say to you."

Guy turned to her. "Well, I have plenty to say to you. You either come willingly, or I'll force you."

"You wouldn't dare!"

"Wouldn't I?"

The words were said softly, but there was steel beneath them. Anne looked up at Guy. Towering over her with his black eyes glittering with anger, he looked very determined and very dangerous. She considered screaming for help, then thought better of it. She knew Guy would tolerate no interference. There was no telling what he might do if one of the trackmen made the mistake of trying to come to her aid. He looked furious enough to kill.

"All right, I'll go with you," she agreed reluctantly, then—trying to salvage some of her pride—added, "But it won't change anything. You might be able to fool the others with your lies, but you can't fool me!"

Guy fought down a new wave of anger. God, she was the stubbornest woman he'd ever met. She was determined she wasn't going to listen to him, just like she had been determined she wouldn't listen to reason when he had tried to talk her into going back East. But he was equally determined.

Guy helped Anne into the buckboard, then climbed in on the other side. As he drove off, she sat stiffly on the seat, staring straight ahead. Guy guided the horses around the end of the string of boxcars and across the flat area behind Gen. Jack's rolling factory toward the hills.

For a while, Anne was so furious that she didn't even notice how far they had traveled. Guy was nothing but a big bully. Then, becoming aware, she glanced back over shoulder and saw that the line of boxcars was far away. "This is far enough. No one can hear us here."

Guy ignored her and kept driving.

"Did you hear what I said?"

"I heard."

"Then stop!" Anne demanded.

Guy was just as just as strong-willed and as stubborn as

Anne. "Not until I deem it's the right place."

By this time, Guy was driving the wagon up into the hills. "If you don't stop, I'll jump out!"

"I wouldn't advise that. You might break a leg."

Anne glanced to the side of the wagon. The hill they were climbing was steep, and she could see sharp rocks poking up here and there through the tall grass. Once more, Guy was driving at a good clip. She might injure herself if she jumped out. Finally realizing that she was at his mercy, she fumed silently as the wagon bounced up one hill, then down, then up another.

Guy brought the wagon to a stop at the top of the hill, climbed down, and walked around it. When he offered Anne a hand to help her down, she brushed it aside angrily and alighted by herself, then walked away from him, deliberately putting her back to him. "Say what you have to say and get it over with."

Guy looked at Anne's rigid back where she had come to a stop beneath the shade of a small tree. God, she was exasperating, he thought. He walked up to her and asked, "Why are you being so damn stubborn about this?"

Anne whirled around to face him. "I'm *not* being stubborn!"

"Yes, you are. All I'm asking is a chance to defend myself against Jim's accusations."

"Then defend yourself and get it over with!"

"All right, I will!"

Anne glared at Guy, and he glared back. Hazel and black eyes meet in a furious clash of wills. Neither wavered. Throwing up his hands in disgust, Guy said, "Oh, forget it! You're determined you're not going to listen to anything I say. You've tried and convicted me, and that's that! I'd just be wasting my breath. Besides, I don't know why I even give a damn what you think." Guy paused, then added, "But I do."

His admission that he cared what she thought of him disarmed Anne of a good deal of her anger. She wondered why. She knew he wasn't a man who went out of his way to please others, and he had gone to a lot of trouble to plead his case. Seeing the puzzled expression on her face and sensing that she might be more receptive to him, Guy decided to give it another try. "Anne, I haven't done anything to Jim. I'm not lying to others about him or talking behind his back. Where did he ever get that idea?"

"Because the other engineers avoid him."

"They avoid him for the same reason I do, Anne, and not because of anything I've said to them. As a matter of fact, I've tried to gloss over the way he behaves to the others."

Anne scowled. "Are you saying they don't like him?"

"Anne, I'm going to be perfectly honest with you, even at the risk of making you angry again. No, the other engineers don't like Jim, and the construction workers feel even more strongly about him. It's his superior attitude that irks them. You don't come on a new job and start criticizing everything and everyone. No matter how smart and able you may be, they're going to resent you walking in and trying to run the show, particularly if you're just a junior engineer. That in itself is bad enough, but it seems no matter what anyone says, Jim wants to argue about it," then he gets angry if he doesn't win the argument. Jim even argued with the chief of engineers when he turned down his proposed bridge design, and that simply isn't done. The chief is the boss because he's more experienced than any of us. How the bridges are built is his decision, and his alone. He might ask for suggestions from the rest of us, but that doesn't mean he has to accept any of them. Jim was furious with him, and with me, just because the chief happened to pick mine. I guess that's why he singled me out, why he blames everything on me. But I'm not talking behind his back and trying to turn anyone against him. Jim is doing that to himself. And I'm certainly not trying to get him fired. I can't imagine where he got that idea."

"His friend, Bill, told him that. Jim said you tried to get him fired, that you had it out for him."

A surprised expression came over Guy's face. "Are you talking about Bill Turner, a bridge monkey?"

"I don't know what his last name is, but yes, he is a bridge monkey."

"And you say Jim and he are friends?"

"Yes, that's what Jim said."

"Well, I guess that explains some of the crazy ideas Jim's gotten into his head about me, if Bill has been feeding him tales. Bill hates me, and I did try my damndest to get him fired. I caught Bill doing sloppy work on the trestle we were building. He was only putting two nails in beams that should have ten or twelve. I warned him about it and made him correct his mistake. Then, a week later, another bridge monkey fell, when one of the beams collapsed, and broke his leg. When I investigated the accident, I found Bill had been doing the same thing again. It infuriated me. Not only was he endangering his fellow construction workers, but the entire project. I went to the chief about it, but Bill swore up and down that he hadn't done it. It was his word against mine. Rather than fire him, the chief took him off the job and put him to work removing some of the rubble we had blasted. Since then, Bill's been bitterly complaining to everyone about it, and naturally, he's been swearing he was innocent. But the rest of the men ignore him. They know he's lazy, and they know he's trying to get back at me."

What Guy had told Anne put everything in an entirely different light. She strongly suspected that Bill had befriended Jim only to use him as a means of getting revenge on Guy, that the bridge monkey was deliberately fueling Jim's resentment towards Guy because of his own hatred. Why, Bill had even encouraged Jim to fight Guy, something that could have led to Jim being injured, if not fired. But then, if Jim was arguing with his boss, he might be fired anyway. Alarmed, she asked, "Is Jim in danger of losing his job? You said he argued with his boss."

"No, I don't think so, Leonard is an amazingly tolerant man. He believes in giving every man a fair chance. He just credited Jim's arguing with him to disappointment and immaturity. But I don't think Bill is a good influence on Jim. He's just using him, you know."

"I know. The next time I see Jim, I'm going to warn him about it.

"If you do, don't mention me. As suspicious as Jim has become, he'll think I put you up to it."

Anne frowned. Jim did seem overly suspicious. She would have thought that he could see though Bill's ploy, if everyone else made light of the irate bridge monkey's claim to innocence.

Now that she thought about it, Jim's picking Bill for a friend seemed peculiar. Her brother had always looked down on the construction workers, thinking them crude and much beneath him, and he really had nothing in common with them. "I wish Jim got along with the other engineers better," she said, voicing her thoughts.

"So do I, but it's hard to be friendly to a man who seems bent on impressing you, then resents everything you say if you don't happen to agree with him. Friendship is a give-and-take situation."

Anne's frown deepened. She knew her brother had always been that way to some degree. He wanted so badly for people to admire him, and Anne had played his game. She was the only one in the family who had fed his ego. Not once had her aunt or uncle praised him. Like her, nothing he did pleased them. But it hadn't seemed to bother her as much as it had Jim. He had been hell-bent to become a successful engineer, if for no other reason than to prove them wrong.

Now it seemed he was trying to prove his worth to the whole world, and going about it in the wrong way. Instead of impressing people, he was turning them against him. Why, he didn't have a real friend in the world, except for her, and she had to admit that she probably wouldn't like him either, if she didn't love him. Love had a way of making you overlook faults. She wondered if he would have turned out differently if their parents had lived and raised them. Surely if there had been more love, more praise in their childhood, Jim wouldn't have been so driven to prove himself. Maybe that was even what was driving her, why she was so determined to see this job through to the end. Like him, she needed to feel important, except that she wasn't demanding admiration and respect. She knew it was something that had to be earned.

Now that Guy had vindicated himself in Anne's eyes, he realized he *had* been a little overbearing in forcing her to come out here with him, but the thought of her thinking badly of him was something he couldn't accept. He wondered at it. He was a man who let his deeds speak for themselves. He rarely made explanations, particularly not on a personal level. If people couldn't accept him the way he was, he didn't worry about it.

Then why was he bending over backwards to try to get Anne's approval? It was a disturbing thought, one that probed too deeply into emotions he had yet to recognize, much less accept. He shook it aside and said, "I'm sorry I rushed you off that way. I never ever considered if you were on your way to work or not. I hope I didn't get you in trouble."

"Oh, I'm through with my work for today. I have every Saturday afternoon off, since most of the construction workers don't bother to eat on Sundays. They're too busy sleeping off Saturday night."

"But what about Saturday night supper? Don't you have to help with that?"

"I don't cook meals. I work in the bakery. On Saturdays I only have to bake a hundred pies for the next day."

"A hundred pies?" Guy asked in a shocked voice. "That's impossible! No one can bake a hundred pies a day."

Anne laughed, feeling pleased that Guy recognized what an awesome chore it was. "I didn't think so either at first, but I found out differently. Actually, except for Saturdays, my daily quota is twice that many."

Guy was astonished. His mother did a considerable amount of baking on the farm, for their family was large and everyone had a hardy appetite because of their hard labor, but what Anne was telling him she baked on a daily basis seemed phenomenal. "There's no one to help you?" he asked, still finding it hard to believe.

"Big Bertha helped me the first few days. She's my boss."

"Yes, I know who Big Bertha is, but you'd think it would be too much for just one person."

"It's mostly a matter of organization," Anne said modestly.

And a hell of a lot of hard work, Guy thought. He'd known Anne would have to work hard. Everyone on the railroad did. But he had never dreamed that she'd have to work *that* hard. Apparently, she wasn't as delicate as she appeared. And she did look delicate, with her fine bone structure and creamy skin, he thought, his eyes sweeping admiringly over her.

Anne was aware of Guy's look. Knowing that he was admiring her strength as much as her appearance, gave her a warm glow of price. She knew he wasn't appraising her just as a woman, any woman, but was seeing her for herself. It was a heady feeling.

She basked in his admiration for a moment, then glanced around him and looked back toward the camp. To her surprise, she couldn't see it, for the hill they had traversed hid it from her view. She turned and gazed out over the landscape. As usual, the rolling hills had a haze over them, and they were covered with a lush green grass that was sprinkled with splashes of colorful wildflowers, blue here, pink there, yellow elsewhere. The flowers came as a surprise to Anne. She hadn't realized they were blooming. And above it all, the cloudless sky was a searing blue. "It's beautiful here," she remarked.

Guy's eyes swept over the landscape. "Yes, this is a pretty place. Seeing as it is now, I guess you can't blame the Indians for not wanting to give it up. My blanket is in the back of the wagon. We were planning on sleeping in the open tonight. I could spread it on the ground for us to sit on. That is, if, you'd care to stay awhile and admire the view," he added quickly.

Guy held his breath for fear she would insist upon going back to the camp. When he had brought her out here, his only thought had been to clear himself of Jim's accusations, but now that she was in a more amiable mood, he didn't want to take her back. Not yet. He wanted to enjoy her company just a while longer.

Anne didn't want to go back to the noisy, dusty camp. It was so beautiful, so peaceful here. It occurred to her that Guy might try to kiss her again, might even do some of those other things to her, but the thought didn't disturb her. Knowing that he admired her as a person as well as a woman seemed to put a different light on everything. Besides, she wasn't as naive as she was before. If things got out of hand, she'd quickly stop him.

Having no idea that she might be playing with fire, she said, "I don't see why we can't stay for a little while and watch the sunset. They're so beautiful in this part of the country."

As Guy walked to the wagon for his blanket, he felt ridiculously happy. The feeling irritated him. If he didn't watch out, he was going to end up smitten with Anne, and that would never do. He wanted no emotional entanglements with any woman.

Anne didn't notice the frown on Guy's face when he walked back with the blanket and spread it on the ground under the tree. She was too busy admiring the view. Still occupied with that, she sat down, pulled her legs up, and wrapped her arms around them, gazing out at the spectacular sunset. For a while, Guy stood, pretending interest in the scenery while he tried to decide whether to risk sitting down on the blanket beside her. In view of his usual reaction to her nearness, that might be a bad mistake. Dammit, why did she have to be so desirable?

"Aren't you going to sit down?" Anne asked.

For the life of him, Guy couldn't think of a likely excuse to stand, and he certainly wasn't going to admit that he was afraid to sit beside her. Hell, a man who couldn't control his passion was no man at all. He sank down on the blanket, carefully putting a foot or two of distance between them, leaned against the small tree trunk, and crossed his long legs before him. The minute he'd settled down, he knew it had been a mistake. Anne's sweet scent drifted across to him, and he was acutely conscious of her breasts, pushed up against her bodice where her legs were pressing against them. Remembering only too well how soft they had felt and how sweet they had tasted, he jerked his eyes away and found himself gazing at a tendril of hair that had come loose from her hair net. The breeze was ruffling it, making it brush lightly across the enticing beauty mark below her ear, and Guy found himself watching it with envy. Feeling his heat rise, he again tore his eyes away and stared straight ahead, cursing himself under his breath.

"Look at that bird up there," Anne commented.

Guy glanced up at the bird soaring high in the brilliant blue sky. In the oblique light of the setting sun, its wings were rose-colored. "It's an eagle."

"It's beautiful, the way they glide across the sky."

Guy glanced across at her. Her hair had seemed to pick up the fire of the sunset, and with her head thrown back to watch the eagle, he got an excellent view of the beauty mark that seemed to be begging to be kissed. He couldn't resist the temptation. He bent forward and kissed it softly.

A thrill ran through Anne. She held her breath, desperately wishing he would kiss her mouth. When he made no further movement, she lowered her head and looked him in the eye, acutely conscious of their lips being just inches apart and him staring at her intently. What's he waiting for? she thought wildly, then parted her lips in silent invitation.

Guy gave up the struggle he had been fighting with himself. One arm slipped around Anne's shoulders as his lips brushed back and forth across hers. The feel of her lips trembling beneath his, excited him even more. He lowered her to the blanket, his mouth softly playing at hers, his hands running over her breasts, her hips, her thighs.

When Guy nibbled at the corners of her mouth and his tongue flicked out with sensual promise, Anne went weak with longing. Her legs slid limply to the ground, and she turned her head to meet Guy's mouth, wanting him to kiss her, really kiss her. But he continued to tease and torment her, running his tongue slowly over her lips, her teeth, then nibbling on her full bottom lip. Feeling unbearably frustrated, Anne slipped her arms around his broad shoulders and tried to capture his lips with hers, but Guy slipped away from her, kissing her cheeks, her brow, the tip of her nose.

She didn't even realize he had unbuttoned her bodice and pushed aside her flimsy chemise, until he blazed a trail of kisses down her throat, across her shoulders, then over the soft mounds that were rising and falling in quick, ragged breaths. By the time she did realize, it was too late to object. His soft kisses and licks as he slowly circled one mound were making her ache for the feel of his mouth on her nipple, as much as her lips had ached before. Would he never reach his objective? She couldn't stand anymore of this delicious torment. Did he mean to drive her crazy? Then when he did finally take the throbbing nipple into his mouth, she sighed in esctasy, loving the glorious feelings his lips and tongue were invoking, awash in a shimmering, tingling warmth that ebbed and flowed.

Anne was drifting on a warm hazy cloud, when Guy undressed her, stopping to kiss and caress each inch of skin he exposed. When he sat back on his heels and his hot eyes devoured her nakedness, Anne couldn't rouse herself from her passion-drugged state to feel embarrassment, even though she knew he could see everything in the dim twilight. She knew he thought she was beautiful, and that in itself was heady stuff. When he stripped off his shirt and bared his broad, muscular chest, she stared at it hungrily, then followed the fine line of dark hair that tapered to his waist and disappeared beneath his belt. She saw it then, the huge buldge that was straining at the material of his pants. Instead of the sight frightening her, it excited her unbearably, sending her heart racing and her pulses pounding. She lifted her arms to him in a silent but eloquent appeal. Then when he took her back in his arms and the dark hairs on his chest brushed against her aching nipples, she gasped, feeling as if a bolt of lightning had raced to her loins, leaving her aching and burning there.

Guy's breath had caught, too, as he felt the sensuous caress. One hand cupped the back of her head as he kissed her deeply, thoroughly, passionately, his tongue making hot forays in and out of her mouth, Anne felt that searing, demanding kiss clear to her toes. The soles of her feet burned, and her blood turned to liquid fire. Her lungs felt seared, and the marrow in her bones seemed to melt.

She whimpered when Guy broke the torrid kiss to rain kisses over her face and shoulders. Guy stroked her thighs, marveling at the incredible softness of her skin, his hand slowly inching upward. When Anne felt his fingers brush the curls between her legs, then touch her there, she stiffened in shock at his boldness. "No!" she gasped.

But Guy gave her no time to further object to his touching her so intimately. His fingers were already sliding through the wetness there and gently separating the soft lips to stroke the tiny bud that was the most sensitive spot on her body. "My God!" Anne whispered, her eyes flying wide in wonder as a whole new barrage of sensations attacked her senses. It seemed that every nerve ending in her body had suddenly shifted to the area between her legs. She was on fire. Her muscles tensed in anticipation. And then the sweet ripples began, growing to powerful undulations, as shock wave after shock wave coursed through her.

When it was over, she felt as limp as a dishrag. She wasn't even aware of Guy slipping off his pants. It wasn't until he took her back into his powerful arms and she felt his erection pressing against her, that any semblance of reason returned. She should stop him now, before it was too late, a little nagging voice told her from the corner of her mind. But the feel of that hard, hot man-flesh was exciting her unbearably, bringing an answering throb to the core of her womanhood, an ache that she knew only Guy could ease. When he started nibbling on her earlobe while his hands caressed her breasts, fresh tingles of intense pleasure rushed over her. Then, when he raised his head and she saw the desire blazing in his dark eyes, she knew she couldn't stop him. She couldn't because she didn't want to. She wanted him as badly as he wanted her.

Guy had no intention of stopping. Never had a woman fired his blood the way Anne had. He was intoxicated by her scent, the feel of her silky skin, her incredible softness. He had to have her. He had to sink himself into that warm, wet velvet his fingers had just explored and find relief. He'd explode if he didn't. His entire body was quivering with need.

When he felt Anne press herself against him, caressing his long, rigid length, he sucked in his breath sharply. He needed no further encouragement. He rose over her, slipped his hands beneath her soft buttocks, and positioned himself between her legs. He entered her slowly, cautiously. When he felt the thin membrane, he hesitated for a just a second before he plunged in.

Anne had been prepared for pain of some kind. But still the sharp, jabbing pain caught her by surprise. She cried out softly and tears came to her eyes.

Guy had never made love to a virgin before. In the past, he had limited his sexual encounters to experienced women, either women who were free with their favors, or those who openly sold them. He wasn't prepared for how tight Anne was, or for the gut-wrenching feeling her cry brought him. "I'm sorry," he muttered. "I didn't mean to hurt you, but it couldn't be helped."

Anne hardly noticed his apology. Once the brief stab of pain had passed, all she could feel was a dull ache, before she became acutely aware of his hot length filling her. It seemed impossible that he was actually inside her, that her body had stretched to accommodate him. Why, he felt immense! Then when he lay inside her, kissing and caressing her, she wondered if it were over and felt a keen disappointment. Surely that wasn't all there was to it.

Guy had deliberately waited for Anne to become accustomed to him and relax before he continued. When he made his first movement, Anne knew it wasn't over. Her breath caught at the exquisite sensation of pleasure that jolted her. Instinctively she moved with him, would have quickened the pace, if Guy hadn't held her back as even more wonderous and exciting sensations filled her. More shock waves traveled up her spine with each deep, masterful stroke. The earth seemed to turn on its axis, spinning crazily, as she was thrown upward into a swirling vortex, a terrible, urgent pressure building inside her. She strained against Guy, seeking something that she knew nothing of, every muscle in her body taut with expectation, her heart racing, feeling as if she were being consumed with fire. Suddenly Guy stiffened, his groan of esctasy filling her ears, then collapsed over her.

Anne knew it was over. She had felt him emptying himself into her, a hot scalding feeling deep inside her. As Guy lay with his head buried in the crook of her neck, the strange tension drained from her. It had been thrilling, exciting, wonderous, but she still felt a twinge of disappointment that she couldn't explain.

Guy kissed her ear, then raised his head and looked down at her, a puzzled expression on his face. He had never had such a white hot release, such a soul-shattering experience as he had with Anne. Why, of all women, had she brought him such ecstasy? She had been a virgin, untutored in the art of making love. Yet not even the most skilled ladies of the night, women who knew every sensuous, erotic trick of the trade, had brought him such intense pleasure. Deep down, Guy knew the answer. With Anne it had been more than just a physical joining. There had been feelings involved that he had never felt for a woman before. But Guy wasn't willing to probe too deeply. The most he would admit was that he cared for Anne. Becoming aware of her silence, he wondered if she was regretting it and blaming him. Damn, he should have known better than to get himself involved with a respectable woman. Now the recriminations and demands would come.

"Are you having regrets?"

Guy's question tore Anne from her musing. She briefly wondered at his hard tone of voice, then considered his question. She supposed she should regret it. She had wanted him to kiss her, then foolishly had let her passion get the better of her. But strangely, she couldn't seem to summon up any regret or guilt for what she had done. It had seemed so natural, so right. Nor could she summon up any anger at Guy. She was as responsible for what had happened as he.

She stroked his muscular shoulders, slick with perspiration. "No, I guess we both let things get out of hand."

Guy should have felt relieved that Anne was letting him off the hook by accepting part of the blame for what had happened, but he didn't like Anne calling what they had just shared something that had simply got out of hand. It hadn't been passion for passion's sake, not on his part *or* hers. He knew a woman like Anne would never allow a man to make love to her unless she had some feelings for him. He wanted her to know that he hadn't been simply using her. "I didn't mean for this to happen, Anne. I didn't plan it. But I don't regret it either. It was . . . it was special."

Did that mean he cared for her? Anne wondered, a thrill running through her. But she refused to let herself get too excited, for fear she would be reading more into his words than he meant. "It was special for me, too."

Her answer brought a smile to Guy's lips. Of course, it was special to her. It was her first and only time. Damn, he wished he hadn't hurt her and that it had been better for her. He knew she hadn't reached fulfillment.

He glanced over his shoulder and saw that the sun had set and darkness was falling. "We'd better get back to camp. There might be wild animals out here."

Anne was disappointed, but she knew what he said was true. The surrounding hills were filled with wild animals who roamed at night. More than once, she had heard wolves howling, and one trackman had been attacked by a bear in the dark and severely mauled.

When Guy rose from her and stood, Anne was grateful for

the concealing darkness. Now that her senses weren't dulled by passion, their nakedness embarrassed her, and even though she didn't think Guy could see anything, she dressed quickly.

As they rode back to the camp, Anne felt uncomfortable and awkward. Guy was silent, and she couldn't think of anything to say. If only she knew how he really felt about her.

Guy was pondering over where to go from here. He knew he wanted to see Anne again, but feared if he did, he would only be getting himself further involved. He had his plans for the future laid out, and they didn't include a woman in any shape, form, or fashion. In view of that, the best thing to do would be to put an end to it right now.

A sliver of moon had risen by the time they drove into the camp and came to a stop before Anne's tent. She waited while Guy climbed down and walked around the wagon to help her alight, her nerves jumping. When he held up his hand to her, she felt a fresh wave of desire run through her. God, she was a shameless creature, but she didn't want him to leave.

Guy had felt a electrical jolt run up his arm when their hands touched. Christ, now I can't even touch her without getting aroused, he thought in alarm. No, this was the time and the place to end it. He stepped back from Anne and said stiffly, "Good night, Anne."

Tears stung at the back of Anne's eyes. How could he share something with her that he'd admitted was special, and then just walk away? Wasn't he even going to kiss her good bye? She forced the words through a lump in her throat. "Good night."

Guy knew his abrupt behavior had bewildered and hurt Anne. He felt like a first-class heel, and did a complete turn around. He took her in his arms and kissed her. It was a sweet kiss, meant to comfort, not arouse, and Anne clung to him.

When he lifted his head, he heard himself saying, "I don't know how long it will be before I get the chance to see you again. We've finished the bridge we've been working on, and will be moving on to build a bridge over the Laramie River. As soon as Gen. Jack moves his factory up and closes the gap, I'll try to get back."

As Guy turned and walked away, Anne wasn't disappointed knowing it would be awhile before she saw him again. What mattered was that he was promising to come back. He did care. He had to!

Guy waved as he drove away, and Anne waved back. Then when he disappeared into the darkness, she hugged herself tightly to keep from bursting from happiness.

Chapter Thirteen

The next day, Big Bertha wandered into the bakery. For a while the two women talked about the usual things that occupied their conversations, the big woman filling the pie pans with warm filling, while Anne continued to roll out pie crust. Then abruptly Big Bertha asked, "Who's that fellow I saw you driving away with yesterday?"

Anne was so stunned by the unexpected question that she almost dropped her rolling pin. She'd never stopped to consider that Big Bertha might have seen her leaving the camp with Guy. Did the head cook suspect what had happened? An embarrassed flush rose on Anne's face. Then she realized that Big Bertha had no reason to suspect anything had happened. Just because she went for a ride with a man didn't mean anything. And there had certainly been no outward change in her to give her away. Inward, yes, for there was still the soreness between her legs that was testimony to that, but not outward.

"His name is Guy Masters." Anne answered. "He's an engineer, like my brother. He met us at the train when he arrived at Cheyenne, and helped us get settled. You might say he's a family friend, of sorts."

Big Bertha strongly suspected that Guy was more than a friend. She had noticed the change in Anne and figured it had something to do with the handsome engineer. A visit from a family friend didn't make a girl's eyes sparkle. Why, Anne had been positively glowing when she had walked into the bakery that morning. "I figured he was an engineer, when I saw him riding up with the others. Engineers are the only ones who wear white shirts and string ties when they go out for a night on the town. That's because they're gentlemen, I reckon." Big Bertha paused for a moment, then said, "I've seen that handsome cuss before, back in Cheyenne. A woman couldn't help but notice him, even in a crowd. He's the kinda man that sends tingles up her spine just looking at him."

Seeing Anne's startled expression, Big Bertha laughed and said, "I don't know why that should surprise you. Hellfire, he's as handsome as sin and just oozes masculinity. A woman would have to be blind not to know he's all man and then some. And she'd have to be dead and buried not to react."

Anne couldn't deny Guy's considerable masculine appeal. She had noticed him immediately on the railroad platform. But she refrained from making any comment, for fear that Big Bertha might guess she hadn't been perfectly honest with her when she had claimed Guy was only a friend.

"I sorta figured he might be courting you," Big Bertha commented when Anne remained silent.

Was he? Anne wondered. He had promised to come back to visit her, and wasn't that what men did then they courted a woman? And she knew he cared for her. A thrill ran through her. But she was too cautious to admit her hopes to Big Bertha. It would be humiliating if it turned out that Guy was only being friendly. "No, it's nothing like that. He just offered to take me for a drive through the country to relieve my boredom."

Big Bertha felt a twinge of disappointment. She sensed Anne's strong attraction to the handsome engineer, even though she claimed he was only a friend. What a shame, she thought. What in the hell was wrong with the cuss? Was he blind? Why, Anne was a beautiful girl, and a hard worker. And there wasn't a selfish bone in her body. She'd make some lucky man a fine wife.

Two weeks later, Gen. Jack moved his rolling factory to the end of the line. As they chugged away, Big Bertha looked at the town across the tracks and said, "Well, I reckon that's the last of Rock Springs. Like most of the Hell on Wheels towns, it'll dwindle down to nothing but a water tank, a dilapidated station house, and a heap of tin cans."

The ride through the Laramie foothills was a pleasant one, despite the the terrible rocking of the boxcar they were riding in. Then as the train came around a curve, Big Bertha's face paled and she said, "Oh, Jesus, here comes a bridge! Hang on for dear life, honey."

The train whizzed over the bridge. Anne made the mistake of looking down at the deep ravine. The ground seemed a hundred miles away. For a moment, she was seized with pure terror. And then an excitement filled her. With their speed, the wind rushing past her, and nothing below her, she felt like she was flying. It was wonderful, and she felt a keen disappointment when the ground appeared beside her again.

Big Bertha opened her eyes, breathed a sigh of relief, and said, "Well, that one wasn't so bad. Most of the bridges shake something awful, and I'm always terrified they're gonna collapse right under us. You reckon that was the bridge your brother worked on?"

"I suppose so."

"Well, you'll have to give him my compliments, honey. That was the smoothest ride I've ever had on this railroad, bridge or no bridge."

Anne knew that it was Guy, and not Jim, who deserved the credit. He had designed the bridge, and then seen to it that it was constructed safely. And thank God for that. If the beams couldn't support the weight of one man because of that incompetent bridge monkey, they certainly couldn't support the tremendous weight of a train. Guy was right. Bill should have been fired on the spot.

Anne wondered if Bill was still using Jim to get revenge on Guy. She had seen nothing of her brother and was anxious to warn him about the man. The fact that Jim seemed to have forgotten her hurt Anne. After all, he was her only living relative, for she refused to count their aunt and uncle as relatives, because of the hateful way they had treated them. He could have at least come for a visit before he moved on to another bridge site. Guy had come. Why, if it hadn't been for him, she wouldn't even have known they were moving, and by now, she would have been worried sick about Jim. But then, she should be seeing him soon. And Guy, too. Gen. Jack had said they were moving right up to the Laramie River.

The thought of seeing Guy again sent tingles running over Anne, and brought a warm curl to her stomach. Then a horrible thought occurred to her. What if Guy and Jim came to visit her at the same time? That would never do, not the way Jim felt about Guy. Visions of Jim attacking Guy plagued her mind. She was so distracted that she didn't even notice the Laramie Mountains with their thick pine forests.

It turned out that all of Anne's worrying was for nothing. The bridge across the Laramie River was almost completed, and she learned that the engineers had moved on to another bridge site on the Medicine Bow River, further west. She was both relieved and disappointed.

The construction camp settled down beside the river. Within a week, the riffraff had settled down beside them, and a new Hell on Wheels town had mushroomed, this one named Laramie City. It turned out to be one of the roughest of the railroad boomtowns, totally dominated by the man who owned the largest saloon and had made himself mayor and justice of the peace. Ace Moyer—along with his brother who he appointed sheriff—ran the town, robbing people in fake trials or just simply murdering them and burying their bones under his saloon. Far into the night, Anne could hear noises coming from the rowdy town: the faint sounds of tinny piano music, boisterous laughter, yells, shouts, screams . . . gunshots. The latter always disturbed her deeply, for she feared some poor Tarrier had met his death. There wasn't a Monday that went by where one or more of the railroad men simply didn't return. She could hardly wait for Gen. Jack to make his next move, and she could get away from the wild, lawless town.

It came sooner than Anne had expected. This time the end of the line was situated in a broad valley beside the Medicine Bow River, and Anne learned that the engineers had once more moved on, this time to the Platte River, thirty miles away. Anne was disappointed. It seemed she was never going to catch up with Guy and her brother. And neither had come to visit her, but it was Guy's absence that disturbed her the deepest. Had the rugged engineer lost interest in her?

Two days after they had moved to the new location, Big Bertha stood at the bakery door, gazed out over the construction camp, and said to Anne, "You know, I think this is the prettiest spot we've ever settled on, with all that lush grass out there and the view of the Medicine Bow Mountains in the distance. Have you ever noticed the way the wind waves that grass? That's what the ocean must look like."

"Yes, it's very pretty," Anne agreed in a distracted voice.

Big Bertha frowned. She had hoped she could cheer Anne up. The girl had seemed so depressed the last few days, and Big Bertha thought she knew what ailed her. She was pining for that man. Bertha's big heart went out to her.

The next day, Big Bertha, accompanied by Gen. Jack, stepped into the bakery. Anne knew immediately by the expressions on their faces that something was drastically wrong. Big Bertha looked like she was going to burst into tears, and Gen. Jack was strangely subdued. Anne held her breath, sensing they were bringing bad news.

Big Bertha glanced expectantly at Gen. Jack. The giant shuffled his huge feet, looking extremely uncomfortable. Big Bertha took a deep breath and said, "Well, it looks like I'm gonna have to be the one to tell you, since Gen. Jack ain't got the guts." She stepped up to Anne and took her flour-covered hands in her big ones. "Your brother is dead, honey," she said gently.

Anne had known bad news was coming, but nevertheless, she was shocked. *"Dead?"*

"Yeah, honey. There was an blasting accident up on the Platte. He and another man got killed outright. A rider just arrived with the news. His boss knew he had a sister working for Gen. Jack. He thought you'd want to know right away."

Anne couldn't believe it. It seemed impossible that Jim was dead. For a long moment her mind struggled to accept the terrible reality. But it had come so suddenly, so unexpectedly, that Anne was in a daze. Maybe it was a mistake, she thought, clinging to a last thin thread of hope. Maybe it wasn't Jim. "Will . . . will they be sending the body back?"

Big Bertha grimaced at her question, and Gen. Jack shuffled his huge feet again and stared at the floor. "They can't, honey,"

Big Bertha answered gently. "There ain't enough left of him to bury. You see, he was the one doing the blasting."

Anne had assumed that Jim had been killed by flying rocks or buried under rubble. "But Jim doesn't know anything about blasting," she objected. A sudden anger filled her. "Why was he doing it? They should have sent someone else."

General Jack heard the anger in her voice and quickly came to the railroad's defense. "Jim wasn't authorized to do it. Leonard Eicholtz doesn't allow any of his engineers to mess with the stuff, except Guy Masters, and that's only because he had so much experience with it in the war. Blasting powder is dangerous stuff. You can't set a long fuse on it. You have to know what you're doing, and you have to be able to run like hell once that fuse is set. There's been many a man—even experienced ones—who didn't run fast enough. No one seems to know why, but your brother took it upon himself." Gen. Jack paused, then said, "I sure am sorry to hear about it."

Anne knew that was the closest the huge, gruff man could come to expressing his condolences. But the words sounded so empty. Being sorry couldn't bring Jim back. But then nothing anyone said could do that, and Gen. Jack did look miserable. "Thank you," Anne muttered.

"Do you want me to wire the news to your folks?" he asked.

Anne didn't feel particularly obligated to tell her aunt and uncle. She knew they wouldn't mourn Jim. No, she was the only one who would. But she supposed she owed them that much. "Yes, if you don't mind. But it's not my parents. We were raised by an aunt and uncle."

Gen. Jack pulled a rumpled piece of paper and a stub of a pencil from his shirt pocket, and said, "If you'll just give the names and town, I'll see that a wire gets off right away."

After Gen. Jack left, Anne walked to a stool and sat, staring out into space. She wished she could cry, but the tears wouldn't come. The pain was all balled up inside her, and there was an icy feeling in her chest. "I still can't believe it," she said half to herself. "He was too young to die."

"I know how you feel, honey," Big Bertha said softly, laying her huge hand on Anne's shoulder. "That's how I felt when I heard the news about my husband. I just couldn't believe it either. I kept hoping they'd made a mistake. I think it's easier to accept if you can actually see the body, but they buried him off in one of those military cemeteries." But at least he got a burial, Big Bertha thought grimly. That's more than Anne's brother got. Jesus, of all the ways to go, being blown to bits. A shudder ran through her.

When Anne was silent for a long time, Big Bertha asked, "What are you gonna do now, honey? Go back East?"

Jim's death hadn't changed the way she felt about her aunt and uncle. It hadn't changed anything. "No, I still want to work for the railroad. I promised myself I'd be there when this railroad was completed for . . . personal reasons."

"I'm glad to hear that. I sure would miss you, if you went back. Now, why don't we go on over to your tent, so you can rest up."

"But what about the rest of the pies?"

"I'll take care of them. You ain't gonna be able to keep your mind on your work. You need time to recover from your shock."

As Anne and Big Bertha stepped to the ground beside the bakery, something caught Big Bertha's attention from the corner of her eye. She turned and saw a rider tearing past the trackmen who were laying rails further down the line, jumping his horse over any wagons or obstacles that were in his path, and veering his mount to keep from running several men down. "Hellfire, I don't know who that cuss is, but he can sure ride. Only people I ever saw that could keep their seat racing that way was Injuns."

Maybe he is an Indian, Anne thought, catching a glimpse of the man's black hair.

The man brought his mount to stop beside the dining car, his mount rearing and pawing the air at the sudden stop. Even before the horse's front hoofs had hit the ground, the man had jumped from the saddle. As the cloud of dust that surrounded the man and animal cleared, Anne recognized Guy.

Guy looked around him, then spying Anne standing with Big Bertha beside the bakery, he started walking rapidly towards her. His chest was still heaving from his wild ride, when he came to a stop before her and said, "I was out of camp when it happened. I came as soon as I could." He looked her deeply in the eyes and said, "Christ, Anne, I'm so damn sorry it happened."

As he opened his arms to her, Anne walked into them, knowing that was where she belonged. Then the tears came as if a dam had burst, torrents of them; her entire body shook with soul-wrenching sobs. Guy held her, gently stroking the back of her head with one hand, while desperately wishing he could take the pain away.

Tears ran down Big Bertha's cheeks. Over the past days, she had cursed Guy for not coming to visit Anne and for hurting her, but his opportune appearance earned him complete forgiveness. He had come when Anne needed him the most, riding into the camp as if all the bats in hell were after him to get to her. Why, it was like a damn fairy tale, she thought, with something akin to awe. He was like a knight in shining armor, coming to the aid of his ladylove.

Seeing some of the construction workers staring at them curiously, Big Bertha dried her tears with her apron and stepped up to the two. "Take her on over to her tent," she said to Guy. "It's more private there."

The big woman walked away, knowing Anne was with the one person who could comfort her the best.

It took a while for Guy to maneuver Anne into her tent. At first, she refused to budge, clinging to him as if her life depended on him. When he did get her to move, she walked beside him with her face buried in his shirt, sobbing as if her heart would break. Several times she stumbled, and would have fallen if Guy had not been supporting her with his arm around her shoulders. Finally Guy picked her up and carried her into the tent.

When he sat her on the bed, Anne wouldn't relinquish her hold around his neck. He sat beside her and pulled her onto his lap, rocking her and crooning soothingly while she cried.

Anne cried until there were no more tears left. Then she just sat with her head resting on Guy's broad shoulder, feeling weak and drained. When she did become aware of her surroundings, the first thing she noticed was that Guy's shirt was sopping wet from her tears. "I'm sorry I got your shirt wet."

"It doesn't matter."

"You've got flour all over you from me."

"That doesn't matter either." Guy kissed the top of her head, then asked, "Are you feeling better?"

"Yes, a little. I had to get it out, but it wouldn't come."

Guy wished he was feeling better. Maybe getting his feelings in the open would relieve him, too. "Oh, God, Anne, I feel so bad about it, so damn guilty."

Anne looked up at him with surprise. "But why should you feel guilty?"

"The only reason I can figure Jim did it, was because he was trying to compete with me, because I was blasting."

"Then his feelings about you hadn't changed?"

"No, if anything, they just got worse. He seemed to be obsessed with me. Anything I did, he had to do, and he had to do it better, or so he seemed to think. That wasn't the first time he had done something risky. Because I went up on the trestles without the benefit of a rope around my waist, like the other engineers, he had to try it. But I'm as used to climbing around on those trestles as the bridge monkeys. I did it during the war. For me, it wasn't that risky, just like blasting isn't."

"Do you think Bill was putting him up to it?"

"It's possible. They were as thick as thieves."

An angry expression came over Anne's face. "If I could get my hands on that man, I'd kill him!"

"He's already paid for his treachery, Anne. He was with Jim when it happened. I don't know what in the hell they thought they were doing. We weren't even blasting in that area that day."

Anne thought over what Guy had told her, then said, "There's no reason for you to feel guilty, Guy. It didn't happen because of anything you did to Jim. He did it to himself. He seemed to be driven by an almost fiendish desire to be admired, to be a success. It was his jealousy of you that killed him. It was like a devil riding his back."

Guy was aware that Jim's competitive spirit had reached an abnormal plane. Jim had seemed more interested in trying to prove he was better than Guy than doing anything productive, and Guy suspected that Jim had talents that he had never shown. It seemed a terrible waste that all of his energies had gotten misdirected. But even though Guy knew Jim had picked him as his nemesis—through no fault of Guy's—he had still felt guilty about the young engineer's death. Anne's words eased him of that awful burden. He was glad he had brought it out in the open, instead of keeping inside.

For a long moment the two sat in silence. Then Anne heard a rumbling sound coming from outside the tent. It didn't sound like the bombardment noise that the rails made when they were being dumped from a flatcar to the ground. "Is that thunder?" she asked in surprise, for rain seemed to be a rarity in this part of the country.

"There wasn't a cloud in sight when I rode up."

Guy gently lifted her from his lap and walked to the tent opening. Pushing the flap aside, he stepped outside and looked up at the sky. The sun blazed down on him. He looked across the tracks where a few camp followers were already erecting a saloon. There didn't seem to be anything coming over the horizon behind them. The rumbling was a continuous roll now, and several other people in the camp were looking up at the sky.

"It seems to be coming from the other direction," Anne commented, stepping from the tent.

Guy saw several of the trackmen yelling and pointing in that direction, but his view was blocked by Gen. Jack's boxcar office. He turned and walked to the end of the car, then seeing the thick cloud of dust in the distance, he knew what was making the noise. "That's buffalo stampeding!"

"Buffalo?" Anne asked in disbelief. "I don't see any."

"You can't see them yet, but they're there all right, and judging from the size of that cloud, there's thousands of them. And this camp is right in their path," he added in an ominous tone of voice.

"But won't they go around us when they see all the cars sitting on the tracks?"

"Buffalo are so damn nearsighted, they're practically blind, and once they get to running, nothing on this earth can stop them. A herd of stampeding buffalo can bowl over everything in their path—cars, towns, even locomotives."

By this time, Guy could see a faint dark line below the cloud of dust that was moving toward them at a frightening rate of speed. He wasn't the only one who had figured out what was happening. Every bell in the camp was sounding the alarm, the frantic clanging joined by the sound of locomotive that sat further down the line blowing its whistle shrilly. "Damn, I wish the rails were laid across that bridge," Guy said over the deafening noises. "At least we could try to get these cars across the river."

Before Anne could make any comment, he took her arm, turned, and rapidly walked past Gen. Jack's office, saying, "Get across the bridge to the other side of the river. With those steep banks on both sides, it should be safe there."

"What about you? What are you going to do?"

"What every other man in this camp is going to do. Try to head them off."

"But you said they bowled over everything. You could be killed!" Anne said, her voice shrill with fear.

"We've got to at least try to save the railroad's equipment. These cars alone cost thousands of dollars apiece." He pushed her towards the river. "Now, go on. Run for the other side."

Anne was terrified that Guy would be killed. If anything happened to him, she didn't want to live. She never stopped to wonder why his death would be so much more unbearable than her brother's. "I'll stay and help, too."

"No, it's too dangerous for you here."

When Anne refused to budge, Guy said, "Dammit, Anne, this is no time for you to get stubborn on me. Do what I told you! And you *stay* on the other side of side of the river! Do you hear me? If I see you step one foot back over on this side before this is over, so help me God, I'll throttle you."

Anne's anger came to the rise. How dare he threaten her and accuse her of being stubborn! "You can't order me around!"

Guy was so exasperated he felt like screaming. He quickly gave in to the impulse. "The hell I can't!"

As Anne glared at him defiantly, Big Bertha ran up to them. Seeing her, Guy pushed Anne towards her and said, "Get her out of here!"

As Guy ran off, Big Bertha pulled on Anne's arm, saying urgently, "Come on, honey. We can't do nothing here. We'll only be in the way."

Anne's anger at Guy fled as quickly as it came. She watched as he raced away, her eyes filled with fear for him. "But he might get killed!"

"He can take care of himself better than most. Now, come on," Big Bertha said with firm determination, once again pulling on her arm. "We've got our own job to do. Gen. Jack said for us to round up the water boys and get them across the bridge."

Chapter Fourteen

Anne and Bertha raced towards the river, fighting their way through the steady stream of construction workers, going in the opposite direction trying to head off the stampeding herd of buffalo. As they ran, they gathered the water boys from the crowd of men and relayed Gen. Jack's orders. Most of the boys were ashen-faced with fright and obviously relieved when Big Bertha told them they were to run for safety with them, but a few balked at her words, and the big woman had to threaten to box their ears if they didn't obey her. In all but one case, just the sight of the huge woman towering over them and looking very stern was enough to make the boys quickly change their minds. The boy who wasn't impressed with her threat—a big, strapping twelve-year-old who was determined to stay and help the men—rapidly found out that Big Bertha was a woman of her word. When he stubbornly refused to obey the second time, the head cook hauled off and slugged him, a powerful, deadly earnest blow that sent him flying to the ground. When he recovered from his shock, he jumped up and followed, apparently having decided that prudence was the better part of valor.

The group tore off for the bridge, following the roadbed of the newly laid rails, passing wagons racing in the opposite direction, the horses wall-eyed with fright at all the excitement. The locomotive that had been sitting at the end of the line raced past them, the engineer still blowing his whistle shrilly, while the fireman frantically shoveled coal into the firebox. Anne didn't glance back to see if the buffalo were still coming. She didn't have to look to know that they were closer. The thundering noise of thousands of hoofs hitting the ground pulsated in the air. The prairie shook.

When they reached the area where the pioneers had been working, they jumped over the scattered ties and the picks and shovels that the men had tossed aside, then came to a halt when they reached the bridge. It was shaking from the tremendous beating the ground was taking.

"Jesus," Big Bertha said, her face draining of all color and making her freckles stand out even more than usual, "look at that damn thing. It looks like it's gonna break apart at any minute."

The timbers did seem to be creaking ominously to Anne. She looked down at the river. It seemed a long drop. A tingle of fear ran through her. She turned and actually saw the herd of buffalo for the first time. Even though they were still far away, it was a terrifying sight. The herd seemed to stretch from horizon to horizon; a solid wall of tremendous animal energy racing down on them that quickly made her decide to take her chances on the bridge. Given her choice, she would rather fall to her death than be crushed beneath those pounding hoofs.

She turned and said, "Hurry! Let's get across before the bridge shakes even worse."

Big Bertha was terrified of heights even under normal conditions. That's why she closed her eyes every time they rode over a bridge. "Wait a minute, honey. Maybe we can just wait here and see if the men can't turn the herd."

Anne glanced at the frightened boys around her. The lads' lives were in their hands, an awesome responsibility that Anne took very seriously. "No, we can't wait. If they don't manage to turn the herd, it might be too late for us to cross. Come on."

Anne stepped out on the bridge and took a few steps. Realizing that no one was with her, she turned and said to the group, "Dammit, don't just stand there! Do you want to die?"

"We might fall off the bridge and get killed," one terrified boy answered.

"You won't fall. The ties on this bridge are almost five feet wide. Stay in the middle, crawl if you want to, but dammit, move!"

When there was no response, Anne reached out, caught the

wrist of the closest lad, and jerked him forward. She turned and walked away, calling over her shoulder, "Watch us. If we can do it, you can do it!"

Anne walked slowly across the shaking bridge, pulling the terrified boy behind her. Everything seemed to be trembling: her, the boy, the bridge, the ground, even the shimmering water far below her. Maintaining her balance on the wooden ties with nothing to hold on to was difficult, for the preservative that the ties had been soaked in left an oily film that was slippery, but she was determined to cross. Hearing the boy sobbing behind her, she said over her shoulder, "Stop that! Just pretend you're a tightrope walker in a circus. Don't think of anything but putting one foot in front of the other. You can do it."

A few steps later, Anne sensed the boy had gathered his courage. She glanced over her shoulder and saw he was still pale, but had stopped crying. She gave him a wide, reassuring grin and said, "Let's show those fraidy cats back there a thing or two. Remember, we're tightrope walkers."

Anne dropped the boy's wrist and spread out her arms the way she had seen a tightrope walker perform. Better-balanced, she was able to walk much faster on the shaking bridge. She heard the boy behind her laugh nervously and say, "This is fun, lady. A little scary, but fun."

"Yes, it is," Anne agreed, for it was frightening but exciting. "And just look at how brave we are."

The boy's chest swelled with pride. No one had ever called him brave before. He called back to the others anxiously watching, "I ain't afraid! You fellas ain't nothing but a bunch of yellow bellies."

It was a challenge that the other boys couldn't resist, for the boy on the bridge was the youngest and smallest. Determined not to be outdone, the lad Big Bertha had cuffed, stepped forward, calling back, "Watch out who you're calling yellow belly, you little fart!"

As the big boy walked out on the bridge, the others followed. Big Bertha brought up the rear, even though she was still terrified. The narrow bridge seemed a mile long, and the walk across it an eternity. When the big woman stepped off at the other side, she was as white as a sheet and shaking almost as badly as the bridge. She ignored the boys around her, who were jumping up and down and cheering at their feat, and said to Anne, "I'm plumb ashamed of myself. Thank God you took charge. Gen. Jack would skin me alive if he knew how I balked back there."

Anne didn't even hear Big Bertha's words. Her full attention was on the prairie as she craned her neck to see what was going on across the river. Now that she had the boys safely across, her fear for Guy had once more taken precedence over everything.

Seeing her worried expression, Big Bertha looked back, then said, "We can't see much from here. Let's go over to that cliff that juts out over the river there."

The two women ran to the cliff, followed by a few of the boys. The others scampered into nearby trees to get a better view.

When they reached the cliff, Anne could see where the construction workers had rushed out onto the prairie behind Gen. Jack's rolling factory. Standing in the tall grass that came to their thighs, many were discharging their guns into the air, while others were beating on metal objects to try and frighten the herd away with the noise. It seemed a wasted effort to Anne. She seriously doubted that the buffalo could hear the noises for the thundering of their own hoofs, and all the men seemed to be accomplishing was making more of a din. No, if anyone was going to turn the herd, it was the men who had raced their mounts and wagons out to meet it.

"Where's the locomotive going?" a boy standing next to them asked.

Anne glanced off into the distance and saw the big locomotive racing away, leaving a thick cloud of black smoke in its wake.

"I reckon it's trying to outrace that herd," Big Bertha answered. "That engine is the most expensive piece of equipment we've got. If we can't save nothing else, we gotta save that." Then her eyes widened, as she watched the fireman crawling from the cab, and inching his way along the narrow running board that ran along the boiler.

Anne saw him, too, and was terrified for him. If he should fall at that speed, he would be killed for sure.

"What in the world is he doing out there?"

"He's filling the cylinder caps on the boiler with hot tallow, so the wheels will turn faster," Big Bertha answered.

The two women and the boys watched fearfully while the fireman filled the cylinders with his tallow can. Suddenly the wheels spun so rapidly that they shot sparks from the rails, and the engine sped off like a streak of lightning.

Anne held her breath until she saw the fireman scamper back into the cab. She let out a deep sigh of relief, and turned her attention from the rapidly disappearing locomotive back to the scene on the prairie. The men who had rushed out to meet the herd were firing their guns at the buffalo, some from horseback and others from the wagon they were riding on, and although many of the huge beasts at the head of the herd were falling, it made no difference to those behind them. Blindly they ran on, trampling the fallen animals beneath their sharp hoofs, headed straight for the camp like an arrow.

"They ain't gonna be able to turn that herd," Big Bertha observed grimly. "Hellfire, there must be at least five thousand buffalo in it."

Anne would have judged the herd even larger, for as far as she could see there were buffalo, and the huge shaggy beasts were running so close they looked like a solid mass. Anne would have never thought that such a big, top-heavy animal could run so fast, but the herd was sweeping down on them like a huge, tawny, never-ending wave. She could see now why Guy had said they bowled over everything in their path. Nothing on earth could stop them. Why, there must be thousands and thousands of tons of wild, terrified beasts coming down on the men out there. "Why don't they turn and run?" she asked in stark fear.

"They are!" Big Bertha cried out.

There was a mass exodus on the prairie as the men gave up their efforts to turn the herd. The construction workers on foot turned and ran for the river, pushing and shoving those in front on them in their haste, and more than one man was knocked to the ground. The men who had ridden out also turned and raced back, the wagons bumping wildly and almost throwing the men from the back, as the drivers whipped their horses to an even greater speed. Several of the mounted men overtook the men on foot running beside the tracks, their horses' hoofs spraying loose gravel from the roadbed in the runners' faces and bringing loud curses from the injured parties. Not that anyone heard the curses. Between the thundering of the herd and the drumming of the men's boots and horse's hoofs, the noise was horrendous, and the ground shook even harder.

It was then that Anne noticed that not all of the men had deserted the cause and fled. Four mounted men remained on the prairie, still firing their Spencers at the oncoming buffalo. Sitting on their horses slightly to the left side of the herd, close to the river, they seemed to be concentrating their fire to that side of stampeding animals. Anne knew that one of the men was Gen. Jack, for no one else was that huge. Two of the men were blonds, their hair shining like beacons in the bright sunlight. The fourth was dark-haired, and Anne knew with a sinking certainty that it was Guy.

As the men fired their rifles, the sharp cracks rang out over the continuous roll of the pounding hoofs; twenty, forty, then sixty buffalo fell. Anne had never seen such deadly expertise. Obviously each man was a sharpshooter and utterly fearless. They pumped the levers of their Spencers with lightning speed, slammed a new cartridge into the butt, then fired another round, as efficient and methodical as if they were machines and not men, giving the impression that they were totally impervious to the terrible danger they were in. But while they appeared cool, calm, and utterly fearless of the wave of buffalo coming down on them closer and closer, their mounts weren't unafraid. Terrified by the sight of what was rushing down on them, the horses tried to rear and turn, and the men were forced to fire from their whirling mounts as they tried to control them with only their knees. One of the fair-haired men was unseated by his horse. His mount turned and sped away through the tall grass for safety, before the man even hit the ground. Jumping to his feet, the man looked wildly about him. Then, realizing he had no means to make a mad, last-minute dash for safety, he turned and ran for the river, too.

That left three men on the prairie to face the herd. The buffalo fell by the scores. No longer could Anne hear the distinct crack of their shots. They came so fast now that they seemed to blend into one. A solid line of dead or wounded thrashing animals lay to one side of the onrushing herd, but still they came.

In the meanwhile, the men on foot ran for their lives. Those who first arrived at the river tore across the narrow bridge, at times a man bowling over another and sending the unfortunate slower runner falling to the river below and splashing in the water. When a larger group of panicky men arrived, a scuffle occurred at the end of the bridge. Fists flew to settle who would be first to cross. Soon a fight involving at least a dozen hot-tempered Irishmen was blocking the bridge. Those behind them simply swarmed down the steep river bank, dived in the water, and swam across.

Anne's full attention was on Guy. Why didn't he turn his horse and make a dash for safety? In a minute it would be too late to escape, for the herd was almost on top of the three men. Oh, damn him! Why did he have be so hardheaded? To hell with the railroad's equipment! *Run!* she screamed silently, her heart racing in fear.

Down on the prairie, Guy had no intention of turning and running. But it wasn't the railroad's equipment he was trying to save, not at that point. It was the men on foot fleeing for their lives. He knew that unless the herd was turned, many of those men would be trampled to death. In part, his staying behind to protect their escape came as second nature to him. Many times during the war he had acted as rear guard for his fleeing squad. Without even fully realizing that he was cutting off his own avenue of escape, Guy swung down from his wildly whirling horse, faced the herd, and grimly kept firing, pulling one tube of cartridges after another from the bag he had slung around his neck.

The buffalo were so close now that he could see the whites of their eyes and feel the scorching heat that their running was generating. The noise was deafening, so loud it made his ears hurt. The ground shook so hard that he had to grip his rifle tightly to keep from dropping it; it was a struggle to maintain his balance. He could smell the animals' fear and the stench of their sweaty fur. He kept firing, aiming for the center of their massive shaggy heads, squinting to see through the gun smoke that settled in a heavy cloud around him.

Then, in a rush of hot air that almost knocked him over, they swept past him, and he momentarily marveled that he hadn't been mowed down. One beast, a rare, pure black "silk robe" ran by him, so close that he thought he could have reached out and touched it. He pivoted, firing at the head of the herd, until he was engulfed in a thick cloud of choking dust that made it impossible to see.

To Guy, it seemed an eternity for the herd to pass. Sweat drenched him. The dust was so thick he couldn't breath. His ears were ringing, and his head was pounding. If he could have figured out which direction was away from the herd, he would have staggered away, but, between his watering eyes and the swirling dust, he couldn't see a damn thing. He stood, coughing so hard his sides ached. His lungs felt seared, and his brains as if they were being shook from his skull.

From where she was standing on the cliff over the river, Anne saw the first of the herd sweep past Guy and the other two men. As a thick cloud of dust fell over the prairie and obscured her view, she had no way of knowing if they were still alive or not. But she—like everyone else breathlessly watching from that side of the river—knew that the three brave men had somehow managed to make the herd veer. It was just enough to turn the stampeding buffalo so that they missed Gen. Jack's rolling factory. But they didn't miss the flatcar loaded down with rails further down the side track. The raging animals slammed into it with a horrendous crash, sending the iron rails flying through the air like toothpicks, then hit the main track, sending ties and more rails flying into the air. Scores of beasts fell to the ground, either injured by the flying rails and ties, or stumbling on them. In turn their bodies were trampled beneath the onrushing herd, which smashed into the water tower and obliterated the saloon that the riffraff had been erecting just a short time earlier. After that Anne could see nothing else because of the thick cloud of dust. And then the entire valley was thrown into a strange reddish semidarkness as the dust blotted out the light of the sun.

It took a moment for the laggards who were still running for the safety of the river to realize that the herd was passing them by and that the camp had been saved. They came to a halt, looked about them in disbelief, then cheered. A resounding answering cheer came from the crowd standing on the river bank. Then, as the dust began to settle and the sound of the thundering herd faded into the distance, the men hurried back to the camp.

Anne and Big Bertha still stood on the cliff over the river, the big woman's mouth gaping in disbelief. Finally, she said, "Hellfire, I could have sworn they wouldn't be able to turn that herd. I thought Gen. Jack and those two other fellows were goners for sure. I wonder who they were?"

"One was Guy," Anne answered, her eyes still glued fearfully to the spot where she had last seen him. "And they might be dead for all we know."

Big Bertha glanced over at Anne. The girl looked like she was going to burst into tears at any moment. Bertha peered down at the cloud of dust that still hung heavily over the trail where the buffalo had run. At first she could see no sign of movement or life. Then she distinguished the vague outline of three forms, one of the shadowy figures moving toward another. "They ain't dead, honey! I can see them plain as day. Well, almost," Big Bertha added. Then a big grin split her freckled face and she said, "Hell, I should of known it would take more than a herd of buffalo to kill Gen. Jack. Why, it's a wonder they didn't turn tail and run in the opposite direction when they saw that big brute with his ugly face."

An immense wave of relief ran over Anne, leaving her feeling weak and her legs trembling. Then she laughed and said, "You should be ashamed, talking about Gen. Jack that way. Why, he's a hero!"

"Oh, God," Big Bertha groaned, "don't you ever tell him that. If you do, I'll have a hell of time shaving him back down to size." The big woman turned and said over her shoulder, "Come on, honey. I just remembered I left the pies in the oven. If we don't hurry and they burn, we'll have a riot on our hands tomorrow."

When Guy first saw a shadowy figure lumbering heavily toward him through the thick dust, he thought it was a buffalo who had gotten separated from the herd, since the figure was so large. Then he recognized Gen. Jack.

The big man slapped Guy on his back so hard that it almost knocked him off his feet. Then, realizing that the giant was saying something to him, Guy knocked his ear with the heel of one hand to try to clear his hearing and said, "I can't hear you. My ears are still ringing."

"What?" Gen. Jack yelled, the question sounding to Guy as if it came from a great distance.

"My ears," Guy yelled back. "They're still ringing."

"Yeah, so are mine. I said I didn't know you were in camp, until I saw you out here. What are you doing here?"

All of a sudden, Guy's ears stopped ringing. He winced at Gen. Jack's shouting and answered, "I came to give my condolences to Anne."

The giant scowled and said, "Yeah, that was a terrible shame, wasn't it? And quite a shock." His expression brightened. "But I'm damn glad you showed up when you did. Thanks for helping us out."

A slender, fair-haired man walked up to them through the thick dust. Guy recognized him as the other man who had stayed to turn the herd till the bitter end. "Guy, this is Tom Miller, one of my foremen. He served under me during the war and was one of my best officers. Don't guess I have to tell you why. You saw for yourself. Tom, this is Guy Masters, one of our best engineers."

As the two men shook hands, Gen. Jack turned, peered off in the distance, and said, "Wish you two had time to get better acquainted, but I'm afraid we've got work to do. Let's go see what a mess those buffalo left."

The stampeding herd had left a swatch a half-mile wide where not a blade of grass remained standing. Scattered all over were pieces of ties, battered rails, and dead buffalo that were trampled almost beyond recognition. Looking at gory mess that had once been a buffalo, Gen. Jack said to his foreman, "Better get the men busy dragging off all these carcasses, before they get to stinking to high heaven."

As the foreman rushed off, Gen. Jack looked at where the

main track had stood, and shook his head in disgust. "Hell, we're going to have to rebuild that whole section before we can go on with what we were doing. Those goddamned buffalo! They're just about the stupidest creatures God ever made, and the spookiest. I wonder what in hell touched them off?"

Guy glanced back in the direction the buffalo had come from, and saw a thick cloud of black smoke in the distance, through the reddish dust that was still floating in the air. "There's your answer," he said in an ominous voice.

Gen. Jack turned. His eyes widened. "A prairie fire? But what in the hell started *that?* It couldn't have been lightning. There isn't a cloud in sight." Then as a sudden dawning came, a furious expression came over the giant's face. "Those god-damned Indians!"

Gen. Jack ran off, bellowing, "Sound the alarm! Prairie fire! Get everything that will hold water! Come on, you stupid Tarriers, move your asses!"

Guy stood and looked at the dark cloud of smoke in the distance for a moment. It seemed that they had survived one disaster, only to be threatened by yet another. Damn, it was going to be a long day.

He turned and rushed off after the construction chief.

Chapter Fifteen

Anne and Big Bertha had just finished taking the last of the pies from the oven, when they heard the camp bells ringing wildly once again. They exchanged startled glances, then Big Bertha asked, "Now, what do you suppose all that racket is about?"

She walked to the wide door on the boxcar and called to a foreman she saw rushing by, "Hey, you! What in hell is going on?"

The man whirled around and answered, "There's a prairie fire coming down on us. That must be what stampeded those buffalo." He paused, then asked, "Have you got any pots and pans or barrels in there that you can spare? If so, toss them down to me. Gen. Jack said to fill up everything we could find with water."

Anne and Big Bertha collected every pot, pan, barrel, and empty tin they could find and tossed them out to the waiting man, who loaded them on the back of a wagon. As the wagon drove rapidly away for the river, Anne asked, "What will we do now? Go back to the other side of the river?"

"No, honey, not this time. We can help here."

"How?"

"First of all, we're gonna help the men wet down these cars, then set up a table with coffee and food on it out back. There ain't gonna be no time for a sit-down dinner today. The men will just have to grab a quick bite, when they can find a minute or two."

The two women hurried out of the bakery and around Gen.

Jack's office car. As soon as Anne saw the dark rolling smoke in the distance, she asked, "Why are we wetting down the cars now? The fire is nowhere near us yet."

"A prairie fire can be miles away and still blow cinders on us. For some reason or another, they always whip up a big wind."

Anne and Big Bertha helped the men splash water on the sides of the cars, while others passed buckets up to several men on the roofs. One wagon after another came racing up from the river, with every kind of imaginable container in the world on it. In their haste no one was particularly careful where he aimed his water. If someone happened to be in the way, he simply got drenched, instead of the cars. Soon the ground all around them was a quagmire.

Gen. Jack stopped Big Bertha just as she was about to toss a big pot of water on the dining car, and asked, "What do you do with all those big gunny sacks the potatoes and things like that come in?"

"We throw them away in the trash heap. Why?"

"We haven't got near enough blankets. Take a few men with you, and see what you can dig out from the trash for me."

Anne went along with Big Bertha and the half-dozen burly Tarriers she enlisted to help her. The trash pile was a good distance from the main track, and contained not only tin cans, discarded broken barrels and boxes, rags, yellowed newspapers, and gunny sacks, but garbage from the kitchen and wastes from the butcher shop. It was covered with swarming flies and reeked to high heaven. It was all Anne could do to force herself to pull the sacks from the stinking pile. Then, seeing something darting out from the bottom of it, she jumped back and shrieked in fright.

"It's just a little field mouse, honey," Big Bertha said, having been much more frightened by Anne's shrill cry than the furry animal.

Aware of the Irishmen around her grinning with amusement, Anne countered, "Well, it looked more like a rat to me. I've never seen mice that big."

"Well, most mice don't eat as well as that one has. Guess he is a little bigger than most, but they won't hurt you."

"Well, what do they need these sacks for, anyway?" Anne

asked testily, irritated at having the daylights scared out of her and the Tarriers laughing at her.

"You can't fight a prairie fire by *pouring* water on it. The only way it can put out that way would be with a hard rain. It's gotta be beaten out, with wet blankets and sacks."

Big Bertha turned back to the trash pile and the chore at hand. Anne wanted desperately to walk away, but felt to do so would be cowardly. It would only be adding fuel to something the Tarriers seemed to think so terribly funny—the big, grinning apes! She gritted her teeth and gingerly reached down for the corner of another gunny sack, then gave it a mighty yank that disrupted the entire pile. Scores of mice ran out. Anne bit back another scream and stood frozen as they scurried past her. One ran up the leg of an Irishman, whose pants had come out of his boot on one leg. The man went wild, jumping up and down, shaking his leg, cursing, then beating on his leg, and all the while the other Irishmen laughed hilariously. The mouse finally fell out and ran away, but Anne took satisfaction in seeing the Tarrier's face pale with fright.

When all of the sacks were removed from the pile and loaded on a wagon, Anne was relieved. She could hardly wait to get away from the stinking pile and its repulsive inhabitants.

By the time Anne and Big Bertha got back to the factory, the other cooks had set a table with coffee and food on it, in the mud behind the dining car. Construction workers crowded around it, grabbing a hunk of meat, or a slice of pie, or half a loaf of bread, gobbling it down as they ran off and splattering mud everywhere. Anne could see that the fire had gotten much closer. Flames shot up into the sky; heat waves radiated from it, and the smell of smoke was strong in the air.

She turned her attention to the men out on the prairie fighting the fire. Most had stripped off their shirts, and their sweaty skin glistened in the sunlight as they beat at the flames with their dampened blankets and sacks. A few were using their shovels to beat out the flaming grass, and wagons sped back and forth from the river, bringing more barrels of water to the scene.

Half an hour later, the fire had gotten still closer, despite the men's valiant efforts to stop it. A pall of thick, choking smoke lay over everything. A weary worker would rush up to the table, grab a quick bite to eat or down a few cups of water—his skin blackened with smoke and his clothing drenched with sweat—then hurry back to the grim task at hand. Anne and Big Bertha set up an emergency medical center, where they smeared lard onto the burns of those men whose hands and forearms had been blistered. The wind generated by the fire whipped their skirts around their legs.

By the time another half-hour passed, it was beginning to look hopeless. The fire raged less than two hundred feet from the boxcars, and had already jumped the tracks that lay on the other side of the barren area that the buffalo had left. Angry orange flames leaped fifty feet into the sky; the air was scorching; the irritating smoke so thick their eyes watered and every breath was a struggle. Red hot cinders flew all around them, making a sizzling noise when they hit the wet boxcars, and causing multiple tiny burns on their exposed skin. Their clothing looked moth-eaten from the burn holes in it. The wind was almost gale force, kicking up dust and whipping their clothing.

"I reckon we'd better go on over to the other side of the river," Big Bertha said grimly to Anne. "It don't look like they're gonna be able to stop it."

Anne looked about her. The men were still working at a frenzied pace, those farther away frantically beating at the fire, and those who were again wetting down the boxcars. A sudden fierce determination filled her. She'd be damned if she'd give up the fight before they did.

"No," she said in a firm voice, "I'm not leaving yet."

"But there ain't nothing we can do here," Big Bertha objected.

"The devil there isn't! We can fight the fire as well as the men can."

"Fight the fire?" Big Bertha asked in disbelief. "No, honey, that's too dangerous for women."

"Not for me, it isn't."

Anne ran out on the prairie where the men were fighting the fire. Big Bertha gaped at her back, then ran after her. When Anne reached one of the wagons where the steaming blankets and gunny sacks were being rewet in the barrels of water, she grabbed a sopping gunny sack and ran towards the flames.

A hand reached out and caught her arm, whirling her around. Guy stood before her, his face, bare chest, and arms black with smoke, and the ends of his hair singed. "What in the hell are you doing here?" he thundered. "I thought I told you to go to the other side of the river."

Anne was vastly relieved to see Guy. She'd had no idea where he was, or if he might have been injured by the fire. "I did go, but I came back after the buffalo had passed."

And all this time he had been thinking she was safe on the other side of the river, Guy thought. "Then get back over there. Now!"

"No, I'm going to fight the fire, too."

"Dammit, will you do what I told you? Now, get to the other side of the river, where it's safe. I've got enough to do without worrying about you."

He pushed her in the direction of the river, turned, and rushed back to the line of fire fighters, his newly saturated blanket dripping water. Anne glared at his back. Who did he think he was, ordering her around?

She turned and walked off in the opposite direction. Guy glanced over her shoulder as he ran and thought she was obeying him, since she was walking in the direction of the river. But Anne had no intention of doing that. She was going to the the other end of the line.

She picked a spot between two big Irishmen, who gave her startled looks when she stepped between them. Anne glared at them defiantly, clearly telling them she would tolerate no interference from either of them. Then she began to beat at the flames licking at her feet.

Anne quickly found out that it was an exhausting chore, beating and beating and beating. It seemed for every flame she extinguished, two more jumped from the ground in its place. The heat was unbearable, drenching her with sweat within seconds, and plastering her hair to her head. Her face and hands felt like they were scalded, and the hot air burned her lungs. But she held her ground, refusing to give an inch. And then, no longer was she content to just keep the fire at bay. It seemed to have a will and life of its own, a raging, roaring monster that was determined to destroy her. Then it became an enemy. A very personal enemy. And Anne was filled with determination to beat it back, to kill it. She beat at it wild vengeance, cursing it beneath her breath, an almost fanatical gleam in her eyes.

The two Irishmen beside her felt that they couldn't give ground to the fire if Anne didn't, despite their utter exhaustion. It was beneath their male dignity to be outdone by a woman. Instead of gradually stepping back from the fire—as they had done all afternoon—they began to beat at it just as fiercely as Anne was, smothering it little by little, moving forward inch by inch. Seeing them make headway against the fire, the men next to them increased their efforts, and so on down the line.

They advanced a foot, a yard, two yards. After four yards, the flames began to die down, the ravenous fire no longer having anything to feed on. What meager flames remained could be stamped out with their feet. They stood in the smoldering embers and drifting smoke and looked about in disbelief. Then a deafening cheer went up, and one of the Irishmen next to Anne caught her by the waist and swung her around.

Setting her down, he grinned from ear to ear and said, "By the saints, we did it! Ah, lass, ye were magnificent!"

"Aye, that she was," the other Tarrier agreed. "I was about to give up me fight, 'til she came along. Ah, lass, 'tis a mean swing ye have there. I'd hate to be yer husband, an' have ye mad at me and a-swingin' yer broom. 'Tis a bloody pulp, I'd be."

Anne was so tired she could hardly stand, but she had to laugh. She turned and saw Big Bertha rushing toward her, her face and hands as black with soot as the others. Then the big woman pulled Anne into her arms and gave her a bear hug that threatened to crack her ribs.

Stepping back from her, Big Bertha said, "I lost you in the crowd, honey. Was worried sick about you. But I didn't have time to come looking for you. I was too busy fighting that damn fire. I'm glad to see you're all right. Of course, you look like hell, with all that soot on you."

"You don't look so great yourself," Anne replied. "I may be covered with soot, but at least I don't look like I've been rolling in the dirt."

"That's cause you ain't, and I have been." Big Bertha pointed to her skirt. A good quarter of it was missing, the edges burned to a crisp, and her petticoat was scorched. "I got too close to the flames, and my skirt caught on fire," she explained. "I was trying to beat them out with my gunny sack, when the fellow next to me threw me on the ground and started rolling me in the dirt. I reckon he saved my life, but he didn't have to be so rough about it. He threw me down so hard, he damn-near broke my neck, and now I got a crick it in," the big woman finished, rubbing her neck with one hand. She paused, then added, "Funny thing about that. He was a short, skinny little fellow. I'd never have thought he could be that strong. I ain't exactly a lightweight, you know."

"A short, skinny Irishman?" Anne asked in disbelief.

"He ain't a Tarrier. He ain't a German or a Swede either. He's homegrown."

"How do you know that?"

"Because I could understand him. He don't have a lick of an accent."

Big Bertha looked about her and saw the men wearily trudging back to camp. "I'd better get back to the cookhouse and get their supper going. After they've rested up a bit, they're gonna be as hungry as bears."

Anne thought they were always as hungry as bears, but undoubtedly they had worked up an appetite. "I'll come help, as soon as I've washed up a bit and changed my clothes."

"Don't bother, honey. Hell, those men have been eating and breathing soot all afternoon. A little more in their food won't hurt them."

The following activity in the cookhouse was almost as frenzied as that on the prairie had been earlier, as the cooks hurried to prepare an evening meal. Since everyone had been occupied with fighting the fire, they were running hours behind, time that had to be made up, for each and every one knew that once the Tarriers decided it was time to eat, no force on earth could reason with them. To attempt to do so would be risking one's life. Gen. Jack's declaring that drinks were on the house in the company bar, as a reward for the men's hard work, bought them some time. As they worked, they could hear the racket coming from the bar several boxcars down, boisterous laughter and cheers that made the male cooks grumble under their breaths because they were missing out on the celebrating. Big Bertha finally had to promise them a bottle apiece, if they'd shut up their complaining and move faster. But the construction crew's preoccupation with their celebrating didn't last near long enough. Apparently the liquor only whetted their appetites. Too soon, they were banging on the door on the dining car and demanding entrance, forcing the cooks to serve the meat half-raw. Not that the ravenous Tarriers noticed. They wolfed it down and yelled for more.

"I reckon you can go on now, honey," Big Bertha said to Anne, seeing how exhausted she looked. Poor thing, she thought. First hearing that awful news about her brother, and then everything else piled on top of it. "It's been a hard day for you."

Anne was exhausted, both emotionally and physically, but she didn't want to desert the others. "I can stay and help awhile longer."

"No, you go on. We've got things under control here now, as good as we're gonna. As soon as those apes in the dining car are through, we're going to bed ourselves. The night crew can clean up this mess. They got a little sleep this morning."

Anne was really too tired to argue. She nodded her head and walked towards the bakery.

"Where are you going?" Big Bertha asked.

"To get a lantern from the dining car. It's dark out there."

Big Bertha had lost all track of time. She glanced out and saw that the fire on the other side of the swatch laid bare by the herd was still burning in the distance, sending flames leaping into the air and turning the dark sky a rosy color. "I wonder how far that damn thing will burn?" she asked, half to herself. "What a waste of good grass. You'd think those Injuns would have better sense than to do something like that. What are those buffalo they're so damned fond of gonna eat?"

At that point, Anne could have cared less about the buffalo. She stepped into the dining car, found the lantern in the darkness, and lit it. But before she could pick it up from the table, she heard someone coming up the stairs. She turned and saw

Guy standing in the doorway, looking absolutely furious.

Guy *was* furious. After the fire had been put out, he had spent a frantic several hours searching for Anne. He'd looked on the other side of the river, in her tent, in the bakery, and through the entire camp, his fear for her so strong he could taste it. Then, in the crush of men standing outside of the bar, he had heard two Irishmen telling the story of how one of the women cooks had bravely fought off the fire between them. As the men had praised her strength, courage, and determination, Guy had thought they were talking about Big Bertha, for they'd made the woman sound bigger than life. But the minute he saw the light in the bakery and stepped into it, he knew it had been Anne. She was as black with soot as he was. And immense wave of relief had rushed over him, to be quickly replaced with anger.

"You didn't obey me, did you?" he asked, his black eyes boring a hole into her.

Anne stuck out her chin defiantly. "No, I didn't. I was needed here."

Guy glanced down at Anne's hands and saw several blisters on them. A mental picture of her fighting the fire flashed through his brain, and his fear for her rose like a monumental wave and merged with his anger. "Dammit, you could have been killed!" he roared. "What in the hell do you know about fighting fires?"

"I know as much about it as anyone else. I did my part."

"It was unnecessary. It was foolish to risk your life that way."

Anne highly resented Guy's saying her part was unnecessary. Why, the men next to her had praised her for her efforts. How dare he belittle what she had done, when he hadn't even been there to see for himself! And everyone had risked their lives, not just her. "Everyone put their lives in jeopardy. Including you!"

Guy wasn't concerned about himself, or anyone else. At that moment his only concern was for Anne, a woman who brought out powerful protective urges in him. "That's different. We're men. It's our job to do dangerous things. A woman doesn't belong here, certainly not a woman like you."

"A woman like me?" Anne threw back angrily. "What does

that mean? Are you saying I'm weak? Well, I'm not! I'm just as strong as Big Bertha."

Deep down, Guy knew Anne wasn't weak. She had shown a strength and determination that he hadn't credited her with, but she looked so damned feminine, so vulnerable—something that Big Bertha didn't—that his protective urges completely overrode his reason. "No, you aren't. Big Bertha is a tough, hardy woman. She's used to roughing it. You aren't. You weren't raised that way."

"I don't see how I was raised has anything to do with it!"

"Well, it does. It has everything to do with it. It's too dangerous for you out here. When are you going back East?"

His abrupt question took Anne aback. "What do you mean, when am I going back East?"

"Jim is dead. There's no reason for you to stay out here."

His reminder of her brother's death brought a wave of sadness to Anne. Had it just been that morning that he had been killed? It seemed eons ago.

"Did you hear what I said? There's no reason for you to stay out here."

Guy's persistence tore Anne from her brooding. "Being close to Jim wasn't the only reason I hired on with the railroad. I have reasons of my own."

"Yes, I know. You think it's exciting. But it's too damned dangerous! I should think you would realize that after today. Christ, you could have been killed twice!"

"I'm not going back East," Anne answered stubbornly.

"The hell you aren't! You're going, if I have to put you on the train myself."

It was the third time that day that Guy had tried to boss her around, and Anne was sick and tired of his domineering attitude. "Just who in the hell do you think you are, bossing me around? What I do or don't do is none of your damn business."

"It is my business."

"And why do you think that?" Anne demanded.

"Dammit, Anne, you must know I care for you. That night, up in the hills, should have proven that."

If he cared, really cared, he wouldn't be sending her away, Anne thought. Why, if she left, she'd probably never see him again. But then that probably wouldn't bother him. Caring wasn't an admission to loving someone. No, it was a far cry from it. You cared about friends, about family, even pets, but that wasn't the relationship she wanted with Guy. She wanted much more. A deep hurt filled her, and she wanted to wound Guy in return. "And so you think our sharing an hour of passion gives you the right to tell me what to do? That you own me now? Well, it doesn't! What I do is none of your damn business. I'm running my own life now. Not you, or anyone else is going to boss me around. Not now. Not ever!"

An hour of passion? Guy thought in shock. Was that all it had meant to her? And here he had been playing it up for something much more, actually mooning over her like some asinine adolescent. Why, she had made a total fool out of him!

Guy's body went rigid with cold fury. His black eyes glittered, as he said in an icy voice that was much more biting for its lack of heat. "Well, that's fine with me. You've relieved me of all responsibility, and now I can stop worrying about you. You're on your own, Anne. You can get yourself killed, for all I care."

Guy whirled and bounded down the stairs. A moment later, Anne heard his horse tearing from the camp. So, she thought, it was just as she had suspected. He didn't care, not deeply. And apparently, he had felt his making love to her had made her his responsibility in some way, nothing but an unwanted burden. Yes, it had just been passion on his part, and he'd felt guilty, just like he had felt guilty about Jim. Even his coming to console her had been false. He'd only come to ease his conscious, just as he had used her body to ease his passion.

Anne felt terribly betrayed. Tears streamed down her face, leaving white lines where they washed away the black soot. Angrily, she swiped at them She didn't need him in her life, she thought. She didn't need anyone. And she hoped to God she never laid eyes on the big brute again!

Chapter Sixteen

The next morning the sun came up and cast its bright light over the prairie, the better part of which was blackened or beaten bare. Only a thin strip of grass by the river remained of what had once been a virtual sea of grass. Smoke still drifted in the air. By the afternoon, a wind had come up and added gritty ashes and particles of dirt, blotting out the sunlight and leaving a thin coating of dust and ashes on everything and everyone. The vast grassland had been turned into a dust bowl.

Anxious to get out of the choking dust and the gloomy atmosphere, Gen. Jack was determined to repair the destroyed track as quickly as possible. That meant the construction crews had to climb on wagons and be driven eastward to the end of the line—wherever that happened to be—for they had no materials to build with. They pulled out that afternoon, leaving the cooks and a score of men to guard the camp from a possible Indian attack.

The construction gangs were gone for days on end, and Anne thought she would go out of her mind for something to do. It gave her too much time to brood over Jim's death and what she felt was Guy's painful betrayal. She turned her energy to her journal, viciously striking out every mention of Guy, then rewriting it so that it was an impersonal chronicle of what she had seen and heard since she had come west.

Within a week, the construction crew had replaced the destroyed track and returned to camp, many still marveling that the fire had not only left the ties charred embers, but had actually melted the iron rails in some places. Behind them came a locomotive, pulling flatcars loaded down with shiny new rails. But Gen. Jack gave the men no respite. He pushed them hard to lay the rails westward, and as soon as the bridge had been crossed and several miles of new track lain, he moved his factory. Everyone agreed that the new camp was a blessed relief from the dust they had been eating, breathing, sleeping, and working in. To be able to breath fresh air and see the sun seemed a small miracle.

They crossed the flat Great Divide Basin in the heat of the summer. The sun beat down on them unmercifully, the terrible heat draining their strength as much as their hard labor. Everyone – including the cooks who suffered just as much in their hot boxcars, was ordered to take salt pills. Those men who foolishly refused to follow Gen. Jack's stern order, soon found out the folly of their stubbornness. They fell like flies from heat exhaustion.

Anne threw herself into her work. When she was finished with her pies every day, she insisted upon helping in the cookhouse with the evening meal. However, it wasn't her dedication to her job that drove her. She wanted to be exhausted at night, so that she would fall asleep as soon as her head hit the pillow. That way she wouldn't be plagued with memories of Guy, and most particularly not tormented by the memory of his making love to her. Damn him! He had awakened her passion and left her with physical yearnings for which there was no relief. She'd never forgive him for that, or for toying with her affections.

One hot day in August, Big Bertha was standing in the doorway of the cookhouse and fanning herself with her apron, when Gen. Jack rode up and reined in. "What are you looking so sour about?" Big Bertha asked the giant testily, for the heat did nothing to sooth her disposition. Nor did it improve any of the construction workers. Tempers flared in the blazing heat, and not a day passed when there wasn't at least one fistfight among the men.

"By damn, don't tell me you're in fighting mood, too," the giant threw back. "And don't rile me! Not today. I've got a problem I need to talk over with you."

"Well, I'd ask you to come in out of the heat, except it's a hell of lot hotter in this damn car than it is out there. Jesus, you'd think they could have put some windows in this car. There ain't a breath of air in here."

"Are you just going to complain, or are you going to listen? I said I had a problem."

"Well, spit it out then! I ain't got all day."

Gen. Jack glared at Big Bertha, a look that would have sent one of his biggest and bravest workers scurrying away in fear, but had absolutely no effect on the woman. Her utter lack of fear of him usually delighted the construction chief, but today, he was feeling a little testy himself. "You've got a sassy mouth on you, Big Bertha."

"That ain't news. I've always had a sassy mouth. Now what is it you wanted to talk over with me?"

Gen. Jack whipped off his hat and wiped the sweat from his forehead with his forearm. "Have you got any cool water in there?"

"Is that what you wanted to ask me?"

"Hell, no! But my mouth is so dry I can't hardly talk."

"Is that a fact? Well, you sure could have fooled me."

Seeing a look of exasperation come over the giant's face at her sarcasm, Big Bertha said, "Aw, come on in, you big ape. I'll fetch you a drink. But it ain't gonna be cool."

By the time Gen. Jack had dismounted and walked up the steps, shaking the car with his heavy tread, Big Bertha had a cup of water waiting for him. He quickly downed it, then dunked the tin cup into a bucket of water sitting on the table and drank that. Wiping his mouth with his sleeve, he said, "I just got word from one of the bridge camps up in the foothills of the Wasatch Mountains that their cook upped and quit on them. They want me to send them another cook. Can you spare one?"

"The foothills of the Wasatch Mountains?" Big Bertha asked in surprise. "Ain't that a part of the Rockies? I didn't know we had any bridge camps that far west."

"Well, we do. They're working even farther west than the graders, building a bridge over a creek."

"Ah, so there is another stream in this dad-blasted country? I was beginning to think we'd never see another one. Ain't seen so much as a gully since we left the North Platte. That's the damndest river I've ever seen. Seems we've crossed it two or three times."

"Goddammit, will you stop yapping about rivers! I asked you a question. Can you spare one of your cooks?"

"Why take one of my cooks? Why don't you wire back to Omaha and have your brother send you one?"

"Hell, Dan don't hire cooks. He's my supply chief. Besides, even if he did, it would be weeks before he could get one out here, and that bridge those men are working on is one of the most important ones down the line. It crosses Black Creek, and it's a real bastard of a job. That's why they're working so far ahead of the graders. It's gonna take months to complete. And we've got to keep those men happy, or they'll be quitting, too."

When Gen. Jack said the bridge was a real bastard of a job, Big Bertha immediately thought of Guy. She knew he had a rapidly rising reputation as an outstanding bridge engineer, and wondered if he could be working on that bridge. "Who's the construction chief on that bridge?"

"What the hell difference does that make?" Gen. Jack roared out.

"Because I ain't sending any of my cooks to the ends of the earth unless they're gonna be treated right!" Big Bertha yelled back.

"Well, you can stop worrying about that. Guy Masters is the construction chief on that bridge, and he's about the fairest man I've ever met. He's like me. He don't ask his men to do nothing he wouldn't do himself."

"I didn't know Guy was a construction chief," Big Bertha said in surprise.

"He is now. Sam thinks so much of him, he put that bridge entirely in Guy's hands, since he designed it."

Big Bertha's eyes lit up. With Guy in charge, it was even better than she had hoped for. That meant he wouldn't be transferred, and Gen. Jack had said the bridge would take months to build. She had overheard Anne's and Guy's argument the night of the fire, and thought it was a shame. She had been wise enough to recognize Guy's anger as fear for Anne, but couldn't for the life of her understand why Anne had gotten so angry. He'd told her he cared for her, and coming from a cautious man like Guy, that had spoken volumes. She'd considered bringing it up with Anne, then discarded the idea. The girl had a stubborn streak in her a mile wide. Just look at the way she had rushed out on that shaky bridge and then off to fight the fire. No wonder Guy was worried about her, if she was that reckless. Then, too, Guy could be pretty stubborn himself. It seemed to her that the whole spat had been because they were both too strong-willed, and neither was going to give an inch. But she knew Anne hadn't been happy since that night. That was why she drove herself so hard. Now, if the two could get together again, maybe they could work out their differences, particularly if they were thrown together for months. After all, deep down, they both really cared. Hell, the two young fools were probably in love, and didn't have enough sense to know it. Not only were they as stubborn as mules, but they were just about as dumb, too.

"Okay," Big Bertha said, "I'll help you out and send one of my cooks. I'll send Anne."

"Anne?" Gen. Jack asked in shocked voice. "But why her? Why don't you send one of the others?"

"Because she's my best all-around cook, and you said you want to keep those men happy."

"I want to keep the men happy here, too. If she leaves, who's going bake the pies?"

"Henry."

"Henry! For God's sake, do you want the men in this camp to mutiny?"

"Oh, his baking ain't that bad. Besides, I'll help him."

Gen. Jack hesitated, wondering if he should risk it. Sending a young woman that far up the line didn't set particularly easy with him. As isolated as that bridge camp was, it was terribly vulnerable to Indian attacks.

"You gotta make up your mind who's more important, that bridge crew or this bunch of rowdy apes," Big Bertha said, not wanting to give him too much time to consider.

If that bridge didn't get finished on time, the entire project would be set back for weeks, Gen. Jack thought. Besides, if there was any man who could protect Anne, it was Guy, what with all his war experience. That was another reason Sam had assigned him the job. The superintendent knew Guy could fight off any Indian attacks. Not only did the young engineer know how to handle men, but he didn't know the meaning of fear. He'd seen him that day the buffalo had stampeded, facing up to them on foot, no less! Christ, even *he* wouldn't have been that bold.

Aware that Big Bertha was waiting for an answer, Gen. Jack said, "All right, send Anne. I'll find a man to drive her up there."

"What about her tent? You gonna let her take that? There ain't no living quarters for women up there."

"Yes, she can take that and her furniture, too. I'll tell the man to strike the tent and load everything on the wagon, as soon as she has her things packed. On second thought, they might as well leave in the morning. Can't get much traveling in this late in the day. But it sure would be a lot easier, if you'd send one of the men cooks."

"I told you, she's my best cook. Unless you want me to send Henry."

"Can he cook meals any better than he can pies?"

"Nope, but he's hell with bread. Reckon they could live on that?"

"Goddammit, you know better than to ask a stupid question like that! Send Anne."

As Gen. Jack stomped down the stairs of the bakery, Big Bertha grinned from ear to ear. Now, if she could get Anne to consent to go.

Anne was putting the last of her pies for that day in the oven, when Big Bertha walked into the bakery and said, "Well, ain't you the lucky one."

Anne gave Big Bertha a puzzled look, then asked, "What are you talking about?"

"Gen. Jack needs a cook to replace one that quit at one of the bridge camps up in the foothills of the Wasatch Mountains, and he picked you. Sure should be a lot cooler up in those hills than it is here. I envy you."

Bridge camps? Anne thought. Why, Guy might be there.

"Then why don't you go?"

"Oh, hell, honey, you know I can't go. I'm the head cook here."

"Then send one of the other cooks."

"Nope, I'm afraid that's impossible. General Jack said he wanted my best all-around cook, and that's you. Of course, if you want to argue with him, you can, but I wouldn't advise it. He *is* the boss, you know," Big Bertha added ominously.

"Are you saying he might fire me if I refused?"

"Well, he don't like having his orders questioned. The last man that did that was sent packing. Of course, if you've got real good reasons, like you're afraid to go that far off into the wilderness or something, maybe he'd reconsider."

The only thing Anne feared was running into Guy, and she could hardly tell Gen. Jack *that.* The giant might ask questions, and what had happened between her and Guy was much too personal to discuss with anyone. Besides, Guy might not even be in that camp. Engineers didn't just build bridges. They helped supervise everything, to see that the railroad was being built according to their specifications. He might be in a grading camp, or off blasting a tunnel. Either way, it wasn't worth risking her job over. "All right," she conceded, "I'll go."

"I'm glad to hear you say that, honey. I'm going to miss you something awful, but I really think it's for your own good."

"In what way?"

Big Bertha realized she had almost given herself away, and if Anne ever realized she was deliberately sending her to Guy, she'd be furious with her. "Why, it should be a much easier job than baking all these damn pies. You'll only have to cook for that bridge crew. Of course, you'll be your own boss, and it will be a lot more responsibility. You'll have to plan all your meals and do your own ordering and keep records of what you're spending. But who knows? With the experience you get there, you might be a head cook someday, like me."

Anne was growing bored with her job, and she *did* have to look to her own future. She certainly didn't want to bake pies for the rest of her life. And she didn't want to settle for being a head cook either. They still had bosses over them, and she wanted to be totally independent. With the money she had saved and would continue to earn on this job, maybe she could buy her own restaurant somewhere. Providing . . . "Are you absolutely sure the money the railroad is paying us is legal tender?"

"Jesus, honey, you've asked that question every single payday. I told you, the government allows the railroad to print its own money, and it's good anywhere. Why, it's probably more solid than those greenbacks the government prints. Ain't nobody got more debts than the government. And that's another advantage of this job. You'll probably get a raise. The railroad values its cooks way out in the boondocks more than it does those here, except for me, that is."

Yes, Anne thought, taking the new job would certainly be to her advantage. Not only would she be earning better pay, but she would be getting experience that would be invaluable in the future. "I think you're right, Big Bertha. This new job is an opportunity I can't afford to turn down."

Chapter Seventeen

Anne left the camp just as the sun was rising the next morning. Her tent, furniture, and personal possessions were piled in the back of the wagon she was riding on, in the company of a grisly old man who looked more like a fierce mountain man than a driver, with his arsenal of weapons and wild, bushy beard. They followed the newly laid rails across the prairie, passed tbe trackmen busy at their work and already sweating up a storm in the heat, then drove by the men laying ties. From then on, they followed the roadbed, which stretched into the distance as far as the eye could see.

Anne quickly found out that her driver and guard was almost as taciturn as Henry. Apparently, he took his job of protecting her very seriously, for he was constantly scanning the horizon for Indians. She wished he wasn't quite so conscientious and a little more talkative. The scenery was monotonous, just miles and miles of grass, dotted with patches of red Polly Mallow, vivid reddish orange Butterfly Weed, and huge sunflowers, and an occasional butte in the distance that shimmered as it reflected the heat of the sun. She was bored to tears, and almost wished a band of Indians would attack them, just to liven things up a bit.

They camped that night on the prairie and slept beneath the stars. Before the sun even came up the next morning, they were on their way again, being guided only by the light of a quarter moon. A few hours later, Anne spied something she hadn't seen since she had left the North Platte. Trees! As they drove into the cool shade of the rustling cottonwoods, Anne saw the camp before her and assumed this must be their destination. But to her dismay, the driver drove right through the camp, then took a bumpy, winding road that led down to a wide waterway.

As they waited for a ferry to cross the water and carry them across, Anne looked at the trestle being built in the distance, and wondered if the driver knew what he was doing. This was obviously a bridge camp. "What's the name of this stream?" she asked suspiciously.

"Ain't a stream. It's the Green River."

"Then how much farther is it to Black's Creek?"

" 'Bout twenty miles."

"Then we should be reaching it by nightfall?" Anne asked, feeling vastly relieved.

"Nope. That's where the railroad first crosses the creek. Gonna cross it four times. That's jest 'bout the windingest creek in this here territory. It's the last crossing we're headin' fer. Won't get there 'til tomorrow afternoon."

My God, Anne thought, she *was* going far out into the wilderness. But then, she had managed to get more information out of the closemouthed driver in one minute than she had in two days. She supposed she should be grateful for that.

They slept beneath the stars again that night, and when the driver woke her up before sunrise, it was all Anne could do to rise from her blanket. Every muscle in her body ached, from bouncing over the prairie in the daytime and sleeping on the hard ground at night. Then, when the sun came up and revealed the landscape around them, she looked about in amazement. No longer was the ground as flat as a pancake. There were rolling hills all around her. And wonder of all wonders, the hills were heavily wooded. At least she had a change of scenery to occupy her time.

The roadbed meandered through the hills like a lazy stream, climbing higher and higher. In the distance, Anne got a glimpse of the Rockies, towering mountains that looked blue from where she sat. Later that morning, they passed a grading camp, and Anne avidly took in all of the activity going on, for this was the first time she had seen that part of the railroad construction. A steady stream of wagons lumbered into the camp and dropped their heavy loads of rock into a crushing machine; this reduced them to gravel and spit out the rubble at the opposite end into huge piles. From these piles, the workers loaded their wheelbarrows, then sped to the surveyor's spikes, and dumped them at the feet of the men there, who spread the gravel and built the roadbed higher and higher. All the while, Anne could hear the explosions of the blasting going on the hills around them.

They left the grading camp behind them, now following just the surveyor's spikes that wound through the hills. About an hour later, they came upon a group of workers trudging beside a wagon loaded down with barrels. Anne knew that they must be a blasting crew on their way to a new site, for their clothes were covered with soot and dirt. As they marched along carrying their picks and heavy iron drills, they sang. Anne listened closely as they drove by, for almost without exception the Irishmen had beautiful singing voices. She recognized the tune they were singing, she had never heard these verses, originated with the building of the transcontinental railroad:

> Every mornin' at seven o'clock
> There were twenty Tarriers workin' at the rock
> And the boss comes 'long and says, "Kape still,
> And come down heavy on the cast iron drill,
> And drill! and blast! and fire!
> It's drill, ye Tarriers, drill.
>
> Drill, me Paddies, drill,
> Drill all day, no sugar in yer tay
> Workin' on the U.P. Rail Road.
> And drill! and blast! and fire!
> Drill, me heroes, drill!

As the sound of the voices trailed off, Anne smiled. She hoped she could remember the verses and add them to those she already had in her journal.

About an hour later, the surveyor's spikes came to a sudden

stop at the foot of a large steep hill, that looked like it was made of solid rock. "What happened to the spikes?" she asked the driver in alarm.

"We'll pick 'em up on the other side of this hill. They're plannin' on blastin' a tunnel through here."

As the driver drove the wagon up the steep, rocky incline, Anne looked down and thought wildly, *This is no hill. It's a mountain!* The drop to the bottom seemed miles away. She clung to the seat of the bouncing wagon for dear life. Their descent was even more terrifying, for the grade was so steep that the horses and wagon slid down it. Anne feared the wagon would overrun the poor animals, despite the fact that the driver had the brake on. Twice, the wheels smashed into big rocks that threatened to overturn them. She was pale with fright when they reached the bottom, and trembling like a leaf in a windstorm.

Shortly thereafter the ground leveled out a little, and they came to a creek. Anne knew it had to be Black's Creek. They'd already crossed it twice. Looking about her, she asked, "Where's the ferry?"

"Don't need no ferry. The creek ain't that deep here."

Anne held her breath as the driver guided the horses into the creek, and the swift water came higher and higher on the wagon wheels. Then seeing it was receding, she breathed a sigh of relief. She hadn't missed the sharp rocks jutting out of the water a little further downstream. If the wagon had been swept away in the swift current and dashed against them, she would have lost everything she owned, to say nothing of risking her life.

A few hours later, when Anne spied the tents sitting in a wooded area ahead of her, she knew it had to be the bridge camp. Thank God, she had finally reached her destination, she thought. Had she known when she left Gen. Jack's camp what a tiring, rugged trip she was getting herself into, she would have refused, and damn the consequences. But now that she was here, she was glad she had come. The camp was just about the loveliest location she had seen, sitting beneath the cool shade of the towering trees, and the cleanest, for there was no litter lying about, not even a chewing tobacco wrapper. The air had just a hint of pine in it, and from somewhere in the woods, she could hear the faint gurgling of a stream.

When the driver pulled up to a stop, the camp seemed to be deserted. In the distance, Anne could hear the sound of hammering, but it wasn't coming from the direction she had heard the gurgling. If the creek and the bridge were ahead of them, then what had she heard? She could have sworn it sounded like water. She looked about her, seeing a dozen or so tents and a long log cabin that sat off to one side. Noting the stone chimney that jutted from the roof on one side, she assumed it must be the office of the construction chief. After all, Gen. Jack had his own car. But what in the world would the chief of this camp need a fireplace for in this heat?

The driver climbed down from the wagon, and Anne did likewise. She had already learned not to wait for his help in alighting. She'd be sitting there until doomsday, for the old man had absolutely no manners. As she saw him start pulling her things from the wagon and piling them on the ground, she asked, "What's your hurry? Aren't you going to wait until someone shows up to greet us? Introduce me to the chief of construction?"

"Nope. I'm in a hurry. You got a mouth. You can introduce yourself."

"Well, at least go and tell them I've arrived."

"They'll figure it out sooner or later. Gen. Jack said to deliver you and all this stuff to the camp, and then get back as quick as I could. That's what I'm doin'."

The old man pulled her chifforobe to the end of the wagon, then said, "Come catch the other end of this dadblasted thing. It's might heavy fer one man."

Anne fought down her anger. He was undoubtedly the rudest old cougar she'd ever had the misfortune to encounter. If he'd just go tell them she was here, he'd have someone to help him. She walked to the end of the wagon, and helped him lower the chifforobe to the ground, then her mattress and wash cabinet. The planking for the floor of her tent, she let him handle himself, while she removed her suitcases and the vinegar barrel she used for a bathtub.

When everything was removed from the wagon, the old man climbed in, picked up his reins, and turned the wagon. When he came abreast of Anne standing beside the large pile, he pulled to a stop and said, "Well, good luck, gal. You talk a little too much fer my likin', but you got real grit."

Anne's mouth dropped open. The last thing she had expected from the crusty old man was a compliment, even a double-edged one. She watched in disbelief as he drove off. Then, to her surprise, he turned and called, "If you'll turn around, you'll see the boss of this outfit comin' right now."

Anne whirled around. She could barely see a figure coming through the thick woods. When the man stepped into the clearing, her breath caught and her eyes widened.

Guy was just as astonished to find Anne standing there. For a moment he thought she was just a figment of his imagination, for he had been tormented by mental visions of her both night and day. But those visions had never had the clarity this lovely one standing before him did. It was Anne! A feeling of joy shot through him, before he remembered what a fool she had made of him. An angry expression came over his deeply tanned face.

As Guy stalked across the clearing toward her, Anne took in the sight of him hungrily. He was even more handsome and masculine than she remembered, and damn, why did he have to be half-naked? Knowing he was angry at her was unnerving enough, without the sight of his magnificent bared chest and broad shoulders. Those familiar tingles were racing through her again, making her feel weak with yearning.

Guy stopped before her and asked in a hard voice, "What in the hell are you doing here?"

"I'm the new cook."

Seeing his eyes narrow, Anne quickly said, "Well, I don't like it any better than you do. If I had known you were here, I would have refused to come."

"Well, that can quickly be taken care of. You're going right back. I don't want you here."

Anne's anger rose. He was bossing her around again, still trying to send her away. For that reason, she was determined to stay. "I think not. Gen. Jack sent me here, and if I'm not mistaken, you take your orders from him, just like I do. What you personally want or don't want his no bearing on this. You requested a cook, and you got one."

"I didn't request a *female* cook. Christ, what in the hell was Gen. Jack thinking when he sent you, anyway? This camp is no place for a woman. Any woman! It's even more dangerous than his headquarters are."

"Damn you! Don't bring up my sex again. It has nothing to do with this. I'm a cook! It's as simple as that. Just forget I'm a female. I don't want or need any special consideration. And I can take care of myself as well as any male cook."

That might well be true, Guy admitted to himself. His last cook had been a total coward, scared of his own shadow. Why, he wouldn't even go out into the woods to collect water, without a guard to protect him. But it was going to be damn hard, if not impossible, to forget Anne was female, he thought, his eyes skimming over her curvaceous figure. Damn, why couldn't Gen. Jack have sent Big Bertha, if he had to send a woman? Or someone like her? Why *Anne,* whose feminine appeal had already given his male pride a low blow. He didn't know if he could trust himself not to succumb to her seductive beauty a second time. Just the sight of her had made his loins ache, and it was all he could do to keep from taking her into his arms.

When Guy remained silent for so long, Anne asked impatiently, "Well, are you going to risk Gen. Jack's ire, or do I stay? But remember, if you send me away, he might not send you another cook."

Guy needed a cook desperately. The men had been doing their own cooking since the last one quit, and morale was running low. But he didn't like Anne's holding Gen. Jack over his head. Dammit, he wouldn't let her threaten him, or push him into a corner by demanding a decision he might not be able to retract. "We'll give you a try. If my men like your cooking, and you can prove you're up to the job, you can stay. If not, you go. I think even Gen. Jack would agree that's fair."

He thought she'd fail, Anne thought. Well, she'd show him! She smiled smugly and answered, "Yes, that sounds fair." She turned and looked about the camp, then asked, "Which tent is the cookhouse?"

"It's not in a tent. The men sleep there. That log cabin holds both the dining room and the cookhouse. I decided they needed a decent, substantial place to eat, and since we were going to be here for a while, and there was plenty of wood around, we built that. It also serves as a kind of recreation hall, a place where the men can go to play checkers or cards in the evening, since their sleeping quarters are so crowded."

"And I suppose they get drunk?" Anne asked in disapproving voice.

"Drinking and Irishmen just naturally go together, Anne. I allow them liquor, just like they do at the bar at Gen. Jack's headquarters, but I limit them to two drinks. They're on their honor, and so far, it's worked out very well. They're aware I could forbid it. Many of the outlying camps do. So they're very careful to stick to the rules, for fear they'll loose their privileges. Besides, they don't want to get roaring drunk. They just want to relax a little bit."

Guy glanced at the pile on the ground and said, "Well, I see you brought your living quarters with you. That at least saves me the trouble of having to scare up another tent, since the last cook slept with the men. I'll have it set up beside mine."

Anne was alarmed. Was he planning to seduce her again? Over her dead body! "You'll do no such thing!" she said in outrage. "I want it understood right now that this is going to be strictly business."

"I wasn't suggesting anything else," Guy answered angrily. "I was thinking of your protection in the middle of the night. There are wild animals out here, you know."

"I'm not afraid of wild animals." Anne turned and looked back at the camp. One tent was set across the camp from the others, and she assumed it was Guy's. Since it was set a good distance from the cookhouse, she said, "I'd like my tent set up on the other side of the cookhouse, in that vacant area."

"For God's sake, I told you I wasn't going to try anything! I'm just as anxious as you are to keep this strictly business. But *that* area sits just off a trail the animals use to go to a watering hole at

night. At least let me put you on the other side of the camp."
"No, I want it placed there, where it will be close to the cook-house."
"All right, godddammit, have it your way! I'll get a couple of the men to set it up for you."
As Guy turned to walk away, Anne asked, "Can I go with you?"
Guy pivoted around. "Why?"
"I'd like to see the creek, and the bridge you're building."
"Well, I guess that's reasonable. And I've got to introduce you to the crew sometime. It might as well be now. Come on."
They walked through the camp and then the thick woods behind it. When they came into a clearing, Anne didn't see a thing, until she looked down. The creek sat at the bottom of a deep chasm, and far below her she could see the men hammering away at what was the beginning of a trestle. "I have to go all the way down there to get water?" she asked in dismay.
"No, we get all of our water from the stream that runs through the woods that I was telling you about. It's spring fed and perfectly clear. That water down there is muddy as hell. We don't even bathe in it. We use the stream."
Anne was vastly relieved. Not only was the chasm deep, but its banks were terribly steep. Hearing the sound of axes and saws coming from further down the gorge, she asked, "Are you cutting your own wood?"
"Yes. No damn cottonwood on this bridge, thank God. With all the timber about, we can afford to be choosy. The men fell the trees, saw off the limbs, then drag them down to the creek with a team of mules. So don't be surprised if you hear a godawful noise in the morning a few hours before sunrise. It's just those damn mules braying for their breakfast."
"What time should I plan to serve breakfast?"
"I like to have the men out here as soon after sunrise as possible."
Anne was accustomed to getting up about sunrise. But if she was going to prepare breakfast, she'd have to get up much sooner. She was glad to hear about the mules. They would be her alarm clock. "How many men will I be cooking for?"

"Thirty, including me. Think you can handle that?"

It was going to be a challenge, but Anne wasn't about to admit that to Guy. He'd probably start gloating, thinking she would fail. "Yes, I'm sure I can," she answered confidently.

Guy wondered. It was going to be a hell of a job, cooking meals for thirty men three times a day. Strange, he'd never stopped to think what a chore it might be with the male cook, even though the man constantly griped about how hard he worked. "Well, you've got a helper," he informed her. "One of the bridge monkeys washes the dishes and totes wood and water, then comes down to the bridge to help when he's finished in the cookhouse."

Anne was surprised. She had expected to have to do everything. "And how do I go about ordering supplies?"

"When we get low, give me a list of what you'll need, and I'll send one of the men in a wagon back to Gen. Jack. But don't let it get too low. It takes almost a week back and forth, you know."

Anne knew. She had already made the long trip one way. She was glad she was staying. She'd hate to make that trip again. "What about fresh meat? Do you have hunters who deliver it to you?"

"No, we have to shoot our own game. I send a small hunting party out every morning. With all the game around in these woods, it doesn't take them long to find something."

Guy stepped forward, called down to the men at the bottom of the chasm, and motioned for them to come up from the river. They dropped what they were doing, grabbed their rifles, and scampered up the steep cliffs. Anne didn't know if they were expecting to see Indians, or what, but they clearly weren't expecting to see her. Their mouths flew open in surprise.

When all of the men had gathered around them, Guy introduced Anne and explained that she would be the new cook, and that he expected every man to treat her with the utmost respect. No man doubted his word for one minute. There was a hard warning look in the construction chief's eyes that sent shivers running up their spines.

Guy turned to Anne and said, "I won't introduce each man by name now. We can do that tonight."

Anne smiled at the men, a smile that totally captivated them. "That's all right. I'm sure I wouldn't be able to remember them all anyway. I'll just have to become acquainted gradually."

"Does that be meanin' we get a real meal tonight, Cap'n?"

"Miss Phillips will have to answer that question," Guy answered. "She's the cook."

Anne glanced at the sun. She figured she had about three hours before it set. "I'll certainly try," she answered.

"Ah, lass, even spuds would be welcome, as long as they ain't burned."

Anne laughed. "Well, I'm sure I can manage that."

Guy assigned two men to set up her tent and dismissed the others. As they walked back to the camp, Anne asked, "Why did that man call you captain?"

"He was using my old army rank. Don't ask me why, but it seems to be in style now. Maybe the men just associate the man in charge with their old officers, and figure they should have a title. Look at the way everyone calls John Caseman Gen. Jack. Personally, I'd prefer to be called Guy. I've even told the men that much. But they persist in calling me captain."

Guy took Anne into the log cabin. It was much larger inside than it looked from the outside, and the floor was planked. Two long log tables stretched almost to the end of the large room, with rough hewn benches on both sides, and on one side of the room sat a big, stone fireplace. Then Guy led her into the smaller room that served as a kitchen. Anne looked about her, seeing the big stove, a wood box filled to the brim, open cabinets on two walls, a door which she assumed led to the pantry, a big sink, and a table sitting in the middle of the room with a small bench on each side. But what caught her attention was the open windows, one on each side, and from each she could see a lovely view of the woods outside. She walked to one window, looked up, and saw a planked shutter which could be closed when it rained, then turned and gazed about the kitchen. Why, it looked like a castle compared to the boxcar she had been working in! "This is . . . very nice," she said in an awed voice. "And you say you and your men built it?"

"Yes, there are a few men who worked as carpenters back in Ireland, and we're accustomed to working with timber. We figured if we could build a bridge, we could manage a log cabin and some crude furniture."

"But how in the world did you find the time?"

"With thirty men it didn't take long. In two Sundays we had it completed. Like I said, it's been good for the men's morale. Stuck way out here in the wilderness, they deserve something in the way of comfort. To tell you the truth, I didn't realize just how much it would mean to them in the beginning. What brought it all on was a couple of fights in their quarters. But they're very proud of their accomplishment, and it's the closest thing they've had to a home since they left the old country. They're a good bunch of men. Oh, every now and then, they get a little rowdy. Fighting and drinking seem to be second nature to Irishmen. But they never fight in here. It's an unspoken rule they made for themselves. If they have a disagreement they think needs to be settled with fists, they got out into the woods to settle it."

"You said you were going to be here for some time. How long do you anticipate?"

"Probably until spring."

Anne was a little taken aback. She hadn't expected to be in the camp for that long. For a moment, she was assailed with doubts. Maybe she should have gone back. Not only would she had to contend with a hard winter in the mountains, but Guy, too, and as much as it provoked her, she still found him terribly attractive.

"Are you having second thoughts?"

There was a smug look on Guy's face that totally wiped out Anne's doubts. She'd be damned if she'd let him send her back, neither would she run from him. "No, but isn't that rather long to build a bridge?"

"Anne, there are some places in this country where it has taken years to build a bridge, although I'll have to admit that the bridges we've built so far on this railroad haven't taken that long. None of the rivers we've crossed have been that large. But now that we're coming to the mountains, things are going to be slowing up a little bit. We're running into what the C.P. has been dealing with all along. That gorge out there isn't all that wide, but it's deep. During spring thaws, it's got to withstand a tremendous amount of floodwater coming down from the Rockies, so it's got to be built extra strong. To add to the problem, the banks don't set at the same level. So it's going to be tricky."

Guy turned and motioned to a door at the back of the room. "There's a small porch out there where you'll find a covered water barrel. What supplies aren't in the pantry, you'll find in the tent next door. Do you know how to operate a wood stove?"

What did he think she was, an idiot? Damn him! He didn't think she could do anything. "Of course, I can. That's what I cooked on back home."

There was a sharpness in Anne's voice that irritated Guy. Christ, he had just asked a simple question. "Well, then I guess you can manage from here," he snapped.

"I certainly can," Anne answered frostily.

Guy glared at her a moment, then spun on his heels, and took a few steps. He hesitated for a moment, then turned back around. "Look, if you can't manage a full meal tonight, don't worry about it. Like Mike said, potatoes will do. I realize you don't have much time."

His surprising consideration made Anne realize that she had been acting a little overdefensive. Why, most construction bosses would have just pointed out the cookhouse and gone back to their work, but Guy had taken the time to show it to her and tell her where things were. Feeling a little ashamed of herself, she smiled and answered, "I'll manage something."

As soon as Guy had left, Anne looked in the pantry to see what she had. Spying a few tins of corned beef and some sacks of potatoes, onions, and carrots, she quickly made her decision of what the menu would be. Then she set to work lighting the fire and peeling potatoes and onions and scraping carrots like mad. Heaping them in the roasting pans along with the corned beef, she slid them into the oven. She glanced out of one of the windows, wishing she could see the sun and guess at how much time she had left. Certainly not enough to bake pies. Then her eyes lit up. But she could bake a cobbler. She had seen a box of tinned milk in the pantry and some baking powder. It could be cooking while the men where eating their meal.

Anne had the table set when the men walked into the dining room. Hearing their heavy boots on the wooden floor, she walked to the door and said, "Have a seat, gentlemen. I'll have the food on the table in a second."

As she set the platters of corned beef and heaping bowls of steaming potatoes, onions, and carrots on the tables, the men stared at them in amazement. Then Anne stood back and said, "I'm sorry there isn't bread, but there will be tomorrow."

The men sat perfectly still, still staring at the food in amazement. Anne laughed and asked, "Well, are you going to eat it, or just look at it?"

The hungry men didn't need any further prompting. They dug in. Anne returned to the kitchen and brought out a big pot of coffee. Seeing her, one of the men dropped his fork and jumped to his feet, saying, "I'll pour that for you, lass."

"No, you won't. This is my job. Now sit back down and eat, before your food gets cold."

By the time the men had finished eating, every platter and bowl was left clean. All praised her cooking lavishly, and Anne thanked them sweetly. Then as they started to rise, she said, "Oh? Aren't you going to wait for the peach cobbler? I just took it out of the oven."

Anne might as well have thrown a bomb into the room, for the surprised looks that came over the men's faces. But the look she relished the most was the one on Guy's face. She had never in her life seen such a dumbfounded expression.

Anne turned and walked back into the kitchen, a smug smile on her face. She guessed she'd shown that domineering brute a thing or two. Just let him try to send her away now. Why, his men would tear him to pieces!

Chapter Eighteen

That night, alone in her dark tent, Anne wasn't feeling quite so smug. She wasn't accustomed to the night sounds of the woods. Back at Gen. Jack's camp, she was used to hearing the loud snores of the men in the sleeping cars, the muted clatter of the night cooks preparing breakfast, and the boisterous laughter, yells, and gunshots that came from the Hell on Wheels town beside the camp, but here in the woods, crickets cheeped, and the wind sighed through the trees. Ordinarily those might have been soothing, restful sounds, but it was the noises beneath them (that she could barely hear) that disturbed her. She heard every snap of a twig and rustle of a bush, and remembered what Guy had said about the path behind her tent that the wild animals used to go to water. Not knowing what kind of an animal had made those sounds—some small, harmless mammal or a very large dangerous one—kept her nerves on edge. It was a long time before she finally slept.

Several hours later, she was awakened by the loudest, most startling animal sound she had ever heard. She sat bolt upright in her bed, her heart racing in her chest, looking wildly about the dark tent. Then she realized it was the mules braying for their breakfast, her signal to rise. Wearily, she climbed from the bed, lit her lantern, and dressed.

She was well into preparing breakfast when Guy walked into the kitchen. While stirring a huge pot of oatmeal, she looked at him and asked irritably, "What are you doing here? Checking to make sure I'm on the job on time?"

Guy wasn't feel so hot himself. He, too, hadn't had much sleep. First, he had been worried about Anne's safety on the other side of the camp, and then, as usual when he thought about her, he had remembered the night he made love to her and became aroused. It had been a long time before he'd finally slept. "No, I like to have a cup of coffee in the mornings before the others arrive, while it's still peaceful. Do you mind?" he snapped.

"Well, you'll have to help yourself," Anne snapped back. "I'm busy!"

Guy picked up a tin cup, walked to the stove, and poured himself some coffee. Then he walked to the table and sat down.

"Can't you sit in the dining room?"

"I always sit here and drink my first cup of coffee."

"Well, maybe the other cook didn't mind, but I do. I need that table to work on."

"As far as I know, I'm still the chief in this camp—and I can sit any damn place I want to!"

Anne was tempted to tell him that he might be boss of the camp, but she was boss in this kitchen, but held her tongue. God, she'd give anything if she could go back to bed. She wasn't normally this irritable in the morning. She poured herself a cup of coffee and drank a few quick sips, then set it aside.

"This is good coffee," Guy commented grudgingly. "It's strong, just the way I like it."

"If there was one thing I learned from Bertha, it was how to make coffee. She always said if it wasn't strong enough to stand on, the men would throw it back at you."

"Bertha? Why do you call her that, and not Big Bertha?"

"Because I think it's rude to refer to her large size. She can't help it if she's built big."

"She doesn't seem to mind."

"Maybe not, but I do."

Anne walked to the storeroom, picked up a big slab of salted bacon hanging on a hook there, and carried it back to the table. She slammed it on the table so hard that Guy jumped. Next she picked up a wicked-looking butcher knife and started quickly slicing the meat. Guy had to jerk his hands off the table to keep from being cut.

"Watch what you're doing!" Guy threw out in annoyance. "You damn near cut my hand off."

"I told you I needed the table to work on."

Anne looked Guy straight in the eye, clearly issuing him a challenge to stay put at his own risk. Guy was determined he wasn't going to sit in the dining room. He retrieved his cup of coffee, rose, and walked to the sink, leaning on it while he sipped his coffee.

Anne put the sliced bacon on a platter and placed it on the top of the stove. "I hope you aren't going to expect meat and vegetables at breakfast. I know they serve that back at the main construction camp, but they have a night crew of cooks. I'm the only one here. I can't be expected to work both day and night."

It seemed to Guy that Anne had learned a lot more than how to make strong coffee from Big Bertha. She'd picked up her sassy ways, too. "I didn't say I expected you to work day and night! An ordinary breakfast will do."

"That's good. Because that's what I planned on, coffee, oatmeal, bacon, tinned fruit, and biscuits."

"Biscuits?" Guy asked in surprise.

"Yes. If you don't like them, you don't have to eat them."

"I didn't say I didn't like them. It's just that the other cook never baked anything but bread, and that was as hard as rock."

"Then what was the baking powder doing in the pantry?"

"Hell, I don't know. Maybe the clerk that fills the orders for these outlying camps just automatically sends that stuff."

Anne opened the oven door, peeked in, then picked up a big dish towel, and removed a huge pan of biscuits. As she carried them to the table and set them on it, Guy's mouth watered. He hadn't had biscuits since the last time he had been home. And his mother's were never that large. Why, they were a good two inches high.

Anne covered the pan with a dish towel to keep them

warm, then placed a frying pan on the fire and began to fry bacon. "While we're discussing what is and isn't in the pantry, there are a few things I'd like to order."

"Have you looked in the tent next door? It seems to me that we're pretty well stocked up."

"I doubt if what I need will be in the tent. What I want are some spices and some baking pans. Do you realize the only pans around here are bread pans? Why, I had to bake that cobbler last night in a roasting pan. Maybe that's why the other cook didn't bake. He didn't have anything to bake in."

Guy seriously doubted that. He was a lazy bastard. "You don't have to do all that much baking. It's time-consuming. I know that from my mother. Besides, all these men want is something to fill their bellies. There's no sense in you knocking yourself out. They wolf it down so fast, they don't even taste it."

Anne took pride in her cooking, particularly her baking. It was one accomplishment she felt she excelled at. And if she was going to get experience for her restaurant someday, she'd have to serve something more than meat and vegetables and bread. "I enjoy baking. I don't even mind baking pies, now that I don't have to bake two hundred a day."

God, she was stubborn, Guy thought in exasperation. He'd given her an out, one that he would have thought she'd jump at, and she'd turned him down flat. "All right, suit yourself. As soon as you have the list ready, give it to me, and I'll have one of the men go back for it. If it's not heavy stuff, maybe he can bring it back on a packhorse. It would be quicker that way."

"You have horses here, too?"

"Yes, we have two teams for our wagons. We have to go back every now and then for building supplies. They're terrible riding horses. Their gait is so rough it just about knocks your teeth out, but they will accept a saddle, which is more than most work horses will."

Guy set his cup down on the sink, walked to the table, and lifted the dish towel. As he reached for a biscuit, Anne said sharply, "Keep your hands off those! They're for breakfast."

Guy was stunned at her stern reprimand. "But I just wanted one."

"You'll get your share at breakfast. Just because you're the chief here, doesn't give you special privileges."

When Anne turned her attention back to the bacon, Guy was tempted to snitch one, then thought better of it, no matter how delicious they looked. He'd be damned if he'd steal like some kid. He turned and walked from the kitchen, thinking that Anne had changed. She certainly wasn't the same girl who had stepped off the train that day in Cheyenne. Besides having developed a tendency to be a little snippy, this woman was much more confident and self-assured. Oh, sure, she had been spirited then, anxious to try her wings at independence. But this Anne had flown, was still flying. Despite how she exasperated him, he was proud of her.

Over the next two weeks, Anne discovered that she loved her new job. Being able to pick her own bills of fare—as menus were called in that day—and cook a variety of foods, was more stimulating than standing at a table and making pies. And cooking for thirty men wasn't nearly the chore she had thought it would be, since she didn't have to bother with washing dishes or collecting firewood or toting water. Her helper even mopped the dining room for her everyday and carried the trash off into the woods. She usually had her meal going by mid-morning or mid-afternoon, and her baking done early in the morning. That left her a few hours to do things for herself, like washing her clothes or cleaning her tent or taking a walk through the beautiful woods around her. She realized that she was a lot more fortunate than some farm women, who had big families to cook for, plus all the house cleaning, washing, mending, canning, and performing small outdoor chores, like caring for the chickens and milking the cows. She didn't know how in the world those women ever managed it all. And she was even being paid for what she did!

What Anne liked the most about her new job was her

kitchen. It was her own little private domain. After her helper left, she had it all to herself, and there was no sour Henry at the other end of the table pounding on his bread, and no Aunt May peaking over her shoulder and telling her she was doing it all wrong. Even Guy stayed out of it and never interfered. In fact, the only time they had been alone was when she gave him the list of supplies she needed. Oh, she saw him at every meal, but she might as well have been a chair for the way he acted. The other men always greeted her and were friendly with her, but Guy never said a word and just wolfed his food down. One minute he would be there, and the next he was gone.

Anne had mixed emotions about Guy. She told herself that she was glad he was letting her be her own boss and keeping his distance. She didn't want any personal relationships with him. Yet, his ignoring her hurt. She wanted him to pay attention to her, and yet she didn't.

On the ninth night in camp, Anne lay in bed listening to the men in the dining hall singing. Twice before she had heard them, but their evening songs weren't rousing railroad tunes. They were songs about Ireland, and they all had a sad, lonesome sound to them. Strange, she thought. The big, tough men were incredibly homesick, and she hadn't suffered one pang of it. They must have come from warm, loving families.

Anne wondered what her parents had been like. It was something she had wondered over and over throughout the years. She had absolutely no recollection of them. She had been two years old, when they were killed in a coach accident. What was it like to held in your mother's arms and cuddled, or sit in your father's lap and have him read a story to you, to be tucked into bed with a kiss, to have someone soothe your little hurts, to have someone to share your laughter and your tears, to have someone make a big to-do over some little accomplishment, to have someone answer all of your questions no matter how silly they might be, to know that no matter what you did, you were loved and accepted? It must be wonderful. With this yearning thought in mind, Anne went to sleep.

She was awakened by the sound of heavy footsteps outside of her tent and a grunting sound. Then she caught the whiff of a strong, fetid smell, and knew without a doubt that some wild animal was out there. She tossed back her sheet and flew from the bed, for the noises had come from just the other side of where it sat. She fumbled for her lantern, lit it with trembling fingers, and looked wildly about for her carbine. Then she heard a ripping sound and a loud roar that shook the tent, making her jump almost out of her skin. She turned and saw the tent was being shredded to pieces by unbelievably long, razor-sharp claws. She let out a blood-curdling scream, then stood frozen in terror when the huge bear stuck its head and massive shoulders through the ripped canvas. Anne stared at its gleaming sharp teeth, glittering golden eyes, and the huge paws with their sharp claws reaching out for her.

Anne never knew how fast Guy arrived on the scene. The time passed like an eternity to her. She knew she was looking death in the face, but was powerless to move. Guy tore into the tent and pushed her aside, then emptied his Spencer into the bear. The bear was knocked backwards by the impact of seven bullets hitting its chest at close range. The beast fell with a loud thud, shaking the ground as its heavy weight hit.

Guy pulled Anne to him with one arm and held her tightly, the other hand still holding his smoking carbine. She was shaking like a leaf. Two bridge monkeys carrying guns ran into the tent in their faded long johns and looked around wildly. Spying the shredded canvas, one of them asked, "What was it, Cap'n?"

"A grizzly. You two go around back and make sure it's dead."

"Hell, Cap'n, ye put seven bullets in it. I counted 'em meself."

"Sometimes grizzlies are harder than hell to kill. Go check it out. If it isn't dead, put a couple of bullets in its head, then drag it off in the woods until we can dispose of it in the morning."

Guy could hear the other men who had come running, asking questions about what had happened. As the two bridge monkeys walked out, he said, "And tell those other men to go on back to bed. The excitement is over with for the night."

The two men informed the crowd of men standing in front of the tent about what had happened and passed Guy's message on. The crowd turned and walked back to their tents, many of the men yawning sleepily, while the first two Irishmen went behind the tent and pulled the dead bear away.

"Why didn't you shoot it?" Guy asked, still holding Anne close to him.

"I couldn't see my gun in the dark. Once I had the lamp lit, everything happened so fast!"

Guy didn't want to let Anne go. When he had heard the bear roar and her scream, he had been up and running as soon as his feet hit the ground, snatching up his gun as he passed the door of his tent. The run across the clearing to her tent had seemed to take forever. He had never been so terrified in his life, and now that he had Anne in his arms, he wanted to keep her there forever, but he knew that would be sheer folly. Already his body was responding to the feel of her soft curves pressed against him. He didn't just want to hold her. He wanted to make love to her, his desire so strong it bordered on desperation.

By sheer will, he forced himself to drop his arm, step back from her, and focus his attention on the gaping hole in the canvas behind her bed. Anne felt a pang of deep disappointment when he stepped away from her. She had felt so safe in his arms.

"Do you have a blanket anywhere around?" he asked.

"Yes, there are several on the top shelf of my chifforobe."

Guy placed his rifle on the washstand and walked to the chifforobe. For the first time, Anne noticed that he was only wearing a tight-fitting pair of knee-length underwear that left nothing to the imagination. As he walked, she found herself staring at the muscles in his taut buttocks and long legs. Her mouth turned dry and her heart raced. My God, she thought, how could she think of *that* at a time like this? She was a shameful creature.

Guy turned from removing the blanket from the chiffo-robe. "If you can find me some safety pins, I can pin this to the canvas to cover that hole for tonight."

Anne forced herself to look at his face. But it did her little good. She could still see his muscular shoulders and broad tanned chest with its mat of dark hair. But even more discon-certing was the fact that she could see the dark hair at his groin through the material, and against one leg, the bold out-line of his manhood.

Having no idea why she was just staring at him, and think-ing she was in shock from her fright, Guy said, "I asked if you have any safety pins?"

Anne jerked her head to the side and answered, "Yes, there are some in one of my suitcases. I'll get them for you."

Anne rushed to the corner of the tent where she had piled her suitcases. By the time she had found the pins and turned back around, Guy had pulled the bed away from the tent and was standing with his back to her. Holding one corner of the blanket up against the canvas, he reached back with one hand and said, "Hand me one, will you?"

Anne opened a pin and handed it to him. When Guy had pinned the blanket completely at the top, he pinned the sides, stepped around the end of the bed, and pushed it back. Looking at the blanket, he said, "I guess that will do for the night, but it will have to be repaired tomorrow."

"How can you repair it?"

"We have a tarpaulin that we use to cover our tools and building supplies on the bridge site. We can cut off some of it to patch this with."

Guy turned to face her and said, "I'd exchange tents with you tonight, except all I have is a hard cot to sleep on. You'd be much more comfortable here in your own bed. If you're afraid to stay here by yourself after what happened, I can spread a blanket outside of your tent and sleep there tonight."

Anne was afraid. She had never had such a fright in her

life. But she didn't want Guy giving her any special consideration because she was a woman, especially not after she had insisted that she didn't need any. She smiled wanly and answered, "No, I don't think that's necessary."

Guy knew it was time to leave, but he couldn't force his legs to move. He stood and stared at Anne, thinking she looked so beautiful with her hair hanging around her shoulders and her cotton nightgown clinging to her curves. He was acutely conscious of her breasts rising and falling, and could see the darkened area of her nipples through the material. Her sweet scent drifted across the few feet that separated them, and he longed to bury his face in the soft nook between her neck and shoulder, and breathe deeply of that intoxicating scent.

Anne stared back, her yearning for him almost more than she could bear. If he didn't either leave, or take her into his arms, she'd scream.

With a tortured groan that seemed to come from the depths of his soul, Guy swept her into his arms and nuzzled her throat, saying "Oh, God, Anne. I don't want to leave."

A sob of gladness escaped Anne's throat. She slipped her arms around him and answered, "I don't want you to."

The barriers they had set up between them came tumbling down. Guy covered her face with feverish kisses, then his mouth closed over hers as he kissed her hungrily, telling her eloquently of his longing. Anne kissed him back, standing on her tiptoes and straining against him, thrilling at his exciting kiss, and the proof of the intensity of his wanting her, hardening and lengthening against her thigh.

He unbuttoned her gown and pushed it off of her shoulders, leaving a trail of fiery kisses across her collarbone and over her upper chest. As he nuzzled the cleft between her breasts, Anne dropped her arms, and the gown slid from her to puddle at their feet. Guy cupped one creamy breast in his hand and bent his head. Anne arched her back to give him better access, and cried out softly as his teeth gently raked the throbbing peak, sending a bolt of fire rushing to that hidden place between her legs. She clung to his shoulders, each wonderful, powerful tug of his mouth sending tingles through her and making her legs tremble with weakness.

Suddenly, her knees buckled. Guy caught her, carried her to the bed, and placed her on it. As he stripped off his underwear, Anne watched, admiring the powerful muscles in his shoulders and arms as he bent to shove the tight garment down. Then when he stood, her breath caught as she saw his manhood standing bold and proud before her, seemingly throbbing with a life of its own. It was Anne's first good look at it. When he had made love to her before, she had been too engrossed with all the new sensations he was making her feel to notice. Her heart raced with a mixture of both fear and excitement.

Then she became aware of Guy taking in her nakedness, his dark eyes hot and hungry as they roamed over her, lingering at her breasts, then staring at the triangle of curls between her legs. His avid, almost devouring look made a flush slowly rise from the tips of her toes to her head. Then he tore his eyes away and gazed deeply into her eyes, and Anne gasped, for his eyes were blazing with the heat of his desire.

He sat down on the bed beside her and stroked her side from shoulder to thigh, running his fingers lightly back and forth over her, as he said in a husky voice, "You're beautiful, Anne. Even more beautiful than I remembered. God, I've been dreaming of this so long. Ever since that night in the hills."

His admission gave Anne the courage to do something she had been dying to do ever since he had stripped off his underwear. She reached out and ran her hand over the powerful muscles of one thigh, then felt them trembling beneath her touch. Then tentatively, she reached for him and took him in her hand, feeling just a little shocked at her own boldness. But the minute she touched that hot, rigid flesh, she knew Guy wasn't averse to her touching him there, even though she felt him jerk. His groan of pleasure told her differently. Instinctively, she stroked him, thrilling at the feel of him lengthening and growing even harder, and the sound of his breath rasping in the air.

Suddenly, he stilled her hand with his and pushed it away. Anne started to object. She was enjoying exciting him. But when he lay down beside her and took her into his arms, kissing her deeply and passionately, all thought fled. Her senses reeled.

She was floating on a warm, rosy cloud when Guy covered her body with kisses, his hands and mouth seemingly everywhere and leaving tiny fires in their wake. When he hands stopped their roving, and he ran his fingers lightly up and down one thigh while he kissed and nipped her neck, Anne sobbed in frustration, wanting him desperately to touch her where she was throbbing. Then when his fingers slid between her legs, she tilted her pelvis in anticipation, feeling a wetness slip from her.

It was even more wonderful than it had been before, those shimmering waves of pleasure washing over her as Guy's fingers worked their magic there. Then, when they peaked with an intensity that made her shudder, leaving her still aching there, she was sorry it was over, and wished he would do it again. She knew from the last time that that was the best part of it.

When Guy slid down her body, dropping torrid kisses at random over her skin as he did so, then knelt between her legs and slipped his hands under her buttocks, she felt a keen disappointment that the end was so near. Then she gasped when he lowered his head, and sensing what he was about to do, cried out in shock, "No!"

Guy paused and looked up her body, then said in a thick voice, "You don't know what you're saying. You liked what I did with my fingers, didn't you?"

"Yes . . . but—"

"Then hush. I can pleasure you even more with my mouth."

Anne thought it was shockingly indecent, but she soon found out that Guy's promise was true. What he had done with his fingers was nothing compared to what he was doing with his mouth. My God, where had he learned to use his tongue that way? It was like a fiery dart, here, there, circling, stroking, driving her wild. When her legs relaxed, and Guy released them and slid his hands up her body to caress her breasts, Anne gave herself up to sensation. Indecent or not, it was the most wonderful thing she had ever felt. She was drowning in a thick, warm syrup. She was burning from her hips to the soles of her feet. The intense pleasure rose, wave by exquisite wave, each more powerful than the last. Her breath came in ragged sobs; her heart pounded in her chest. She feared she would go out of her mind if he didn't stop, yet didn't want him to. And then the pleasure crested, and she convulsed, seeing a burst of stars behind her eyes.

Guy slipped into her while those spasms of delight where still rocking her body. He clenched his teeth against the feel of her hot muscles contracting on his own feverish length, fighting down a wave of pleasure that threatened to engulf him with sheer willpower. When she opened her eyes, he smiled down at her and asked, "Well? Was I correct? Didn't I give you more pleasure that way?"

Anne hated to admit it, but she couldn't deny it. "Yes. It was wonderful."

"Not as wonderful as this is going to be."

He gave a slow thrust, and Anne's eyes widened as she felt a bolt of fire go through her. But she still doubted his words. Nothing could be more wonderful than what she had just felt. To her utter astonishment, Guy quickly proved her wrong. Each slow thrust sent powerful electrical tingles rushing up her spine. Then, when he quickened his pace, Anne wrapped her long legs around his hips and pulled him even deeper. Her senses were swimming, her heart pounding, her blood flowing like liquid fire. A fine sheen of perspiration covered her skin as she met him stroke for stroke. Hot shock wave after shock wave traveled up her spine with each deep, masterful stroke. That same terrible, urgent pressure she had felt before was building higher and higher, intensifying until she thought her skin would burst and her heart would leap from her chest. Then it burst through, and she was thrown into a spinning vortex of blinding flashes of light and swirling colors.

Guy hovered over her, watching the expressions on her face as he carried her up those rapturous heights, holding back his own passion with an iron will, in his determination to see that she reached her fulfillment. Not until he saw her eyes fly open with the wonder of it, heard her cry of ecstasy, and felt her spasms contract on his own feverish, pulsating flesh, did he allow his steely control to break. With a cry of exhalation, he gave one deep, powerful thrust and followed her to his own shattering, mind-boggling release.

For a long time they lay, their breaths rasping in the silence of the tent, still locked in that sweet embrace, Guy's dark head buried in the crook of her neck. Finally, he kissed her ear and raised his head to look down at her face.

Anne looked up at him dreamily and stroked his damp shoulders. "You were right," she said in an awed voice. "It was more wonderful. More wonderful than I would have ever dreamed. But why didn't it happen before?"

"Because you were a virgin. Making love was new to you. And then, too, maybe I didn't give you enough time. That's new to me."

"What do you mean?"

"Anne, I'm sure you must know that there have been other women before you."

Anne was suddenly filled with a consuming jealousy. "This is hardly the time to mention them."

"No, Anne, that's what I'm trying to tell you. *They* didn't mean anything to me. I didn't particularly care if they received pleasure or not. I was only interested in my own." He rolled to his side and pulled her to him, laying her head on his shoulder. His fingers lightly stroked her back, as he said softly, "I told you I cared about you, Anne. I meant it. I won't out and out say I love you. What I feel is too new to me. But I've never felt this way about a woman before. Not only do I desire you and want to give you pleasure in return, but I want to protect you. That's why I wanted you to go back East so bad. I was afraid something would happen to you. Tonight, when I heard that bear roar and you scream, I must have died a thousand deaths before I got to you. I was never so terrified in my life."

It was hard to imagine Guy being afraid, but his admission told her the depth of his feelings. "Oh, Guy, I care for you deeply, too. But your wanting to send me back East seemed so uncaring. It seemed to me, if you really cared for me, you wouldn't be sending me away. Then I felt betrayed. I thought you had only used me to satisfy your lust."

"Lust? Christ, Anne, if that's all I had wanted, I could have gone to any whore. But I can't deny that I desire you, Anne. Wanting you and caring for you seem to go hand in hand. I can't separate one from the other."

Anne ran her hands over the damp hairs on his chest and answered, "I know. I feel the same. I guess it's shameless of me to admit that."

"No, Anne, it's called honesty, and I admire you for it. At this point, it would be ridiculous for either of us to deny our passion for one another."

Indeed it would, Anne thought. And she wouldn't sink to that hypocrisy.

Guy pulled his arm out from under her and rose. As he blew out the lamp, Anne was filled with disappointment, thinking he was going back to his tent. After tonight, her bed would feel even more lonely.

Then as he lay back down and pulled the sheet up over them, she felt a wave of relief. At least, he wasn't leaving quite yet.

Taking her back into his arms, he said, "I don't want to leave you alone, until we've patched that tent. I'll sleep here until those damn mules start braying, then go back to my tent. Isn't that about the time you get up anyway?"

"Yes. As a matter of fact, they're my alarm clock. But . . ." Anne's voice trailed off.

"But what?"

"But what if the man who goes to feed them should see you leaving my tent at that hour?"

"He won't. No one goes to feed them. We just all roll over and go back to sleep. You see, they're old army mules and used to being fed that early, but that doesn't mean we have to bow to their demands. We keep hoping that they'll break themselves of the habit, if we ignore them long enough." Guy paused, then said, "But you've got a good point. I think it would be best to practice discretion around the others. I'm not ashamed of our relationship. I'm not trying to hide it. But it's simply none of their damn business. It's personal, just between us."

Anne was in perfect accord. She didn't want the men snickering behind their backs, and trying to make something dirty out of what they doing. It felt too beautiful, too right, to have it besmirched like that.

She snuggled closer to Guy. Just as she was about to drift off to sleep, he nuzzled the top of her head with his chin and asked, "Anne? Are you asleep?"

"No," Anne muttered sleepily.

He tightened his arms about her and said softly, "I'm glad you came."

Guy felt her lips curve into smile against his bare chest where her head was laying, then heard her murmur, "So am I."

Chapter Nineteen

Anne was feeling absolutely wonderful the next morning, despite the fact that she hadn't had much sleep. She could hardly contain her happiness, and it took all of her self-control to hide it from the men at breakfast and behave as she normally did. Other than thanking her when she poured his cup of coffee, Guy, too, behaved much as he had been, showing her no particular interest. But Anne knew he was just as aware of her as she was of him. She could feel the electricity between them.

When he walked into the kitchen, after the men had finished eating and left, Anne was surprised. She glanced out the door at her helper, who was picking up the dirty dishes in the dining room. "What are you doing here?" she whispered. "I thought we agreed to be discreet."

"I don't see why that means we can't have a civil conversation within their hearing," Guy whispered back. "After all, you're the cook and I'm the boss. It only stands to reason that there are things we need to discuss. I've been thinking about your tent. Instead of repairing it, I've decided to replace it with a log cabin. I'd feel a lot safer. Besides, with winter coming, you're going to need something more substantial."

Anne glanced back into the dining room and saw her helper was at the other end of the room. "Are you crazy? Don't you think the men will think that suspicious?"

"In view of what almost happened last night, they're as concerned about your safety as I am."

"Why? Because I'm a woman? I thought I told

you I didn't want any special consideration."

"Dammit, Anne, you're not going to start that again, are you? You *are* a woman. It's a fact none of us can ignore, and men feel protective about women. It's a part of our nature. I'm doing this as much for their peace of mind, as mine."

"I don't want to be a liability," Anne answered.

"You *aren't* a liability!" Guy answered in exasperation. "You're an asset. Why, you're probably the best damn cook working for this railroad. We don't want to lose you. Think of it of that way, as nothing but a purely selfish interest on our part. Hell, Anne, if our last cook had been as good as you, we would have done the same thing for him."

"That wouldn't have been necessary. He was a man. He could take care of himself."

"Like hell he could! He almost shot his own foot off trying to kill a harmless grass snake. Then when he discovered a spider in the pantry, he wouldn't go into the kitchen until one of the men went in and killed it. My God, all he had to do was step on it! He was scared of his own shadow. You've got more courage in your little finger than he had in his whole body."

Anne chewed on her lip, then said, "It's just that I hate to see you take your men away from their work. You're here to build that bridge, not build a cabin for me."

"With all of us working on it, it wouldn't take more than a couple of hours, not if we build it the same size and use the flooring you already have."

"Oh, all right then!" Anne snapped. It seemed that if she didn't agree, he's stand here arguing with her all day, and neither one would get any work done. Then she added, "On one condition."

"What's that?"

"That you let me help. If I'm going to be the one to benefit from it, then I should do something."

Damn her and her fierce independence, Guy thought in exasperation. "All right, you can fill in the gaps between the logs with mud in your spare time. That's the most time-consuming part of it."

* * *

Within the the hour, the men were dragging logs into the camp. When Anne glanced out of her window and saw that they were building her cabin right next to the big one, she rushed outside and said to Guy, "I thought we agreed to move my quarters to the other side of the camp?"

It was an agreement that Anne and Guy had made that morning, before Guy had gone back to his own tent. "I got to thinking about that. I didn't like the idea of you crossing the camp in the dark in the mornings, to say nothing of bad weather. That's a pretty good distance. If we leave it here, you'll be just a matter of a few feet from the front door of the dining room.

Seeing Anne frown, one of the Irishmen said, "Ah, lass, 'twould be unlikely fer ye to get attacked in that short a distance, but if that's what yer afraid of, we could run a stockade between the two buildings."

"That's not what I was thinking. I'm not afraid to walk that little stretch. It's just that I was hoping you'd put windows in it, like you did the kitchen. But if you're going to set it right next to the big cabin, that would cut off the—"

"Ah, 'tis a view, ye be wantin'," the Irishman interjected. "Well, that can be arranged. We can put a window at the back and the other side. Will that do?"

"I wasn't thinking so much about a view," Anne informed the man. "It was ventilation that I was thinking about. But that would be wonderful!" Then seeing Guy scowl, she asked, "What's wrong?"

"I hadn't planned on putting windows in it."

"Oh," Anne answered, disappointment written all over her face. "I suppose it is more work."

"No, it's not that much work. We'll do it, but I am going to put a stipulation on it. I want the shutters on those windows closed at night. A bear might be too big to get through, but a mountain lion or a lynx wouldn't be."

A shudder ran through Anne at the thought. "I'll keep them closed at night. I promise. It's not hot then. It's only in the daytime that it's so stifling."

* * *

Shortly after Anne returned to the kitchen, the hunting party returned with her fresh meat for the day. Anne was surprised to see that there were eight fat sage hens. It was the first time they had brought her poultry, and she hadn't even been aware that there were big birds around. But she was glad to see them. That meant she could cook the men two special meals, in appreciation of their labor in her behalf. For dinner, she'd have stewed hens and dumplings, and for supper that night, roasted hens and dressing, since it would take a while to dry out some bread for the dressing. She remembered the gallon tin of pie cherries she had found in the pantry. She had been saving them for a special occasion, and decided this was it.

Anne was so busy preparing her meal that she didn't even notice how rapidly the cabin next door to her was going up. Even when the sawing and hammering stopped, she didn't notice. She was just slipping the pies into the oven, when Guy stuck his head through the doorway and said, "You'd better come see if we have the furniture arranged like you want it."

"You're through already?" Anne asked in surprise.

Guy grinned. "I told you it wouldn't take long."

Anne hurried outside and into the small cabin. Then she stood looking about her in amazement. Everything was arranged just as she'd had it, right down to her suitcases. Guy must have done that, she realized, a little surprised that he had been so observant the night before.

"Everything okay?" Guy asked.

"Yes, but are you sure it isn't bigger? It looks it."

"That's just because the walls aren't sagging like that tent's was, and it's a little taller."

Anne glanced out the window at the back, then at the one to the side. They both had lovely views of the woods, and she could feel a slight breeze. Why, it was much, much cooler than her tent had been. And she wouldn't have to contend with that musty odor of the canvas either. The scent of fresh-cut pine was delightful. She was glad Guy had thought of it. This was a palace compared to what she had been living in.

"Well," Guy said from the door, "if everything is all right, we're heading for the bridge."

"No, wait!"

Anne hurried to the door and stepped out of the cabin, then said to the men standing around her, "It's beautiful. Thank you so very much."

" 'No, lass, don't be a-thankin' us. 'Twas our pleasure," one big Irishman answered, and the others quickly agreed.

As the men walked away, Guy said, "See? They wanted to do it. I told you it wasn't just me."

"But just because I'm a woman."

Guy shook his head in exasperation. He wished she would stop being so damn defensive about her sex. "No, Anne. They appreciate you for the person you are. Your being a woman has nothing to do with it. They respect you. They value you. *You!* Not the body you walk around in."

Before Anne could respond, he hurried off to catch up with his men.

Tears shimmered in Anne's eyes. The Irishmen had given her the esteem that she had never received from any of her family, not even her brother. It was a warm, shimmering feeling that she had never known. And knowing, deep down, that it had been given because she earned it, made it all the more beautiful.

Anne spent every free moment she had during the next few days, shoving mud into the cracks between the logs of her new cabin. It was a tedious, time-consuming chore, but she was very careful that she didn't leave any holes. She didn't want any creepy little creatures in her cabin.

The third night, she heard a soft knock on her door. She opened it and saw Guy standing there.

"The men think I've gone to bed early. Am I welcome?"

Anne melted at the warm look in his eyes. "You know you are," she answered and stepped back.

As soon as he had closed the door behind him, Guy took her into his arms. After giving her a fierce, hard kiss, he ran his mouth up and down her neck, saying, "Oh, God, Anne,

I've needed you so much. Knowing you were so close, and yet, so faraway, has been an agony for me."

"Then why didn't you come sooner?"

"I was afraid it would be too obvious."

Anne pushed herself slightly away, so that she could look at his face. "Guy, we can't hide our feelings for each other indefinitely. Besides, I think the men suspect something. They're not fools, you know. Oh, I admit, I didn't want them to know at first. I always thought of them as being crude and rough. I was afraid they'd snicker behind our backs, try to cheapen our relationship. But after what happened with this cabin, their being so generous, I know better. Their roughness is all on the outside. Deep down, they're sensitive, caring people. I should have realized that before by their songs. I don't think they're going to criticize us in any manner. Of course, that doesn't mean we have to throw it in their faces, but we don't have to avoid each other like the plague either."

"You're probably right," Guy admitted. "No one looked particularly surprised when I said I was going to bed early. If anything, they looked relieved. I guess my restlessness was wearing on their nerves, too. No, I don't they'll be critical either. They have too much respect for both of us. I think they'll realize this isn't just a physical arrangement, that we really care about each other. If anything, they'll probably envy us. They're lonely men, hungry for female companionship, female gentleness. It's a hunger that can never be satisfied by those rough whores they visit, and yet, I think that's what they're really searching for."

Now that Guy mentioned it, Anne was in agreement. The Irishmen talked surprisingly a lot about their mothers, sisters, and the sweethearts they had left back in the old country, and there was always a yearning quality to it.

Guy led her to the bed and sat on it, then pulled her to his lap. For a few moments they talked quietly, then he began to make love to her. It was a slow, leisurely loving, for their having decided not to got to extremes in keeping their relationship a secret from the men had taken the urgency from it. They savored each kiss, each touch, rediscovering the secrets of each other's bodies as if it were the first time for them.

Slowly, ever so slowly, they stoked the fires of their mutual passion, stroking, caressing, exchanging kisses; gasping, moaning, muttering endearments.

Even when he entered her, there was no urgency, no blind rush to fulfillment. For long moments, they held each other in their arms, and relished the feeling of their joining. To both, it seemed nothing short of a miracle that they fit together so perfectly, mouth to mouth, chest to chest, abdomen to abdomen, thigh to thigh, her velvety softness sheathing his rigid hardness as tight as a glove. But it was inevitable that they couldn't hold their passion at bay indefinitely. Guy led her up those spiraling, lofty heights with a sweet savageness that climaxed among exploding stars.

He stayed with her that night, making love to her once more before they slept in each other's arms, and Anne thought that was the best part of it, laying with her head on his chest and listening to the beat of his powerful heart, with his strong arms around her. His not wanting to leave her even after his passion had been sated spoke volumes. She knew in her heart that he loved her.

The next morning while they were dressing, Anne said, "There's something I've been wondering about since the day the hunting party brought me those sage hens. Hens lay eggs, and I'd dearly love to have some to cook with. If I had eggs, I could cook custard pies, cakes, puddings, flapjacks, all kinds of things. Do you have any idea where I might find their nests?"

Guy frowned. "I don't want you going into the woods and snooping around under bushes, Anne. Snakes like eggs, too. But I will tell the hunting party to keep a look out for them. How many would you need?"

"Well, cakes take three or four apiece, and if I baked three, that would be a dozen."

"I don't know if they'll be able to find a dozen at one time, but they do keep for awhile. I'll also tell them to keep an eye out for turkey eggs, but they'll be harder to find."

Anne had never even thought about turkey eggs, but they

would be even better, since they were bound to be larger. "Why do you say that?"

"Turkey hens are very ingenious about hiding their nests, since the cock destroys the eggs if he can find them, and a hen only lays one brood a year."

"How do you know that?"

"I'm a farm boy, remember? We raised a few turkeys."

Anne smiled. She had forgotten. "Any kind of egg will do."

A mischievous glimmer came into Guy's eyes. "Any kind? What about snake eggs?"

A horrified expression came over Anne's face. "No! Absolutely not! I'm not that desperate."

As Guy walked to the door with a big grin on his face, Anne shrieked, "Don't you dare tell them to bring me snake eggs!"

Guy turned at the door and chuckled. "Don't worry. I think they'd balk at that. They aren't that desperate either."

From then on, the hunting party brought her eggs. Usually it was it was only three or four a day, in which case Anne hoarded them until she had a sufficient number. One time they found a bonanza, a turkey nest with twelve eggs in it, and it was just as Anne had suspected. The eggs were twice as big as chicken eggs. The next morning, the men found something on the table that they hadn't seen since they had left Omaha—scrambled eggs. Each man got only a large spoonful, but the eggs were a big hit.

Guy asked the men who had found them where the nest was, and they told him. "You might look around in that area again in about two weeks. In all likelihood that hen will lay another dozen or so."

"But I thought you said turkeys only laid once a year?" Anne objected.

"They do, unless their eggs are destroyed or stolen. Then they lay again. They seem to be driven by a compulsion to hatch a brood."

"Is that a fact, now?" one the Irishman on the hunting party asked. "Well, we'll look again, Cap'n, and keep a-lookin' in the future. He laughed. "We'll have that poor, flustered hen a-workin' up a storm fer us."

When the hunting party delivered two big gobblers later that morning, Anne said, "I wish you could find turkey hens. They're much more tender."

"No, lass, no more hens from now on," the same big Irishman who had spoken up that morning answered. "We can't risk a-killin' our layin' hen. 'Tis a shame we can't find a few more nests," he said wistfully. "I'd give me right arm fer a half-dozen eggs fried sunny-side up."

Anne's mouth watered at the thought. She loved fried eggs. When the Irishman handed her the three eggs they had found that day, she was sorely tempted to cook them for herself. Then she felt ashamed of herself. Like everything else in her pantry, the eggs belonged to the crew as a whole, and no one was going to get special treatment, including herself.

The two weeks that passed since Guy had come to her cabin was a time of perfect happiness for Anne. During the daytime she threw all of her energies into her job, but at night, she was Guy's, body and soul. He came every evening. Sometimes they talked or played checkers before going to bed, a quiet, companionable times that both enjoyed as much as their exciting, fiery moments in bed. Sometimes they were so hungry for each other that they tore their clothes off in a frenzy, almost as soon as Guy stepped into the cabin. Sometimes they didn't even make love, being content to just sleep beside the other, for there was an intimacy, a special closeness in sharing a bed and the long night that was more meaningful than even the act of passion. It was a time when man was by his very nature the most vulnerable, when all of his defenses were down, and to willingly share that vulnerability took explicit trust.

Chapter Twenty

One day in early September, Anne looked out of the window in the kitchen and saw something purple blooming in the woods behind the camp. Curious to see what it was, she walked from the kitchen and out into the woods. When she reached the flower, she bent to examine it closer. Anne had never seen a Fringed Gentian before. They didn't grow where she had come from. The purple petals of the flower were covered with tiny silky hairs that gave them a velvety feel. Thinking they would look very pretty in her cabin, she picked the flower and then went hunting for more.

Since the flowers were just starting to bloom, her search led her far into the woods. As she was bending to pick another for her bouquet, she sensed something was watching her. She jerked upright and glanced warily about the thick woods all around her, but could see nothing but trees and bushes. Still, the feeling persisted, stronger than ever. She knew something was out there, and she had a uncanny certainty that it was big. The memory of the night the bear had attacked her flashed through her brain. She turned and tore off for the cabin.

As she ran, she could hear the sounds of bushes rustling and twigs breaking, and knew that whatever it was, it was following her. She ran even faster, not even bothering to look back over her shoulder as she darted past trees and around bushes. She didn't have to look back to know it was running after her. She could hear the muted sounds of its feet on the thick mat of pine needles and rotted leaves on the forest floor.

Her breath rasped in the air, and her lungs burned; there was a painful stitch in her side, but she forced herself to keep going. She flew through the clearing behind the big cabin, pushed open the back door, then slammed it shut, throwing the bolt in for good measure. Then she leaned against it, drinking in deep draughts of air, her heart pounding in her chest.

Anne heard heavy steps on the back porch, then the rattle of the lock. Then it pounded on the door. It had to be a bear, she thought. Wolves and big cats didn't pound. Or did they? She glanced at the open window to one side of her, then darted to it and yanked the shutter down. She whirled around to go the window on the opposite side and froze in terror. Standing there and looking in at her was an Indian.

Anne stared at him, and the Indian stared back. Then he grinned, a grin that looked more like a leer and very threatening to her. Spying her carbine from the corner of her eye, Anne reached out and yanked it from where it was leaning against the wall. She pointed it at the startled Indian and fired just as he ducked, the loud sound of the shot bouncing from wall to wall and the carbine smoking.

Anne didn't know if she had hit the Indian or not. All she knew was that she could no longer see him. Suddenly, the front door of the cabin was flung open, and she heard someone running into the dining hall. She pumped the lever of the gun, whirled around, and shot blindly into the larger room, then heard the sound of a body hitting the floor.

"For God's sake, Anne, put down that goddamned gun before you kill somebody! It's me!"

Guy? Oh, thank God, he was here, Anne thought in relief. Another horrible thought came fast on its heels. Oh, my God, she must have shot him! She threw the carbine down and ran into the dining room. She reached Guy just as he was rising from the floor and asked anxiously, "How bad are you wounded?"

"You didn't hit me. I dove for the floor as soon as I saw the muzzle of the gun pointed at me."

"I'm sorry. I thought it was that Indian, or another one."

"Yes, I figured that out. Christ, I hope you didn't kill him!"

"What do you mean you hope I didn't kill him?" Anne asked in a mixture of confusion and anger. "I hope to hell I did!"

"That's Blue Feather. He's a friendly Ute that brings us game every now and then."

"Well, if he's friendly, why was he spying on me in the woods, and why did he run after me like that?"

"He was probably trying to give you the game he brought us."

"How do you know it was him? It could have been any Indian. Why, I could have been dead by now!"

"Anne, calm down."

"Calm down?" Anne shrieked. "I've just had the daylights scared out of me, and you're telling me to calm down?"

"I know it was Blue Feather, because I saw him passing through the woods. That's why I came back to the camp, to warn you. But he must have come across you in the woods and followed you here. Where was he when you shot at him?"

"Outside the kitchen window. He was standing there leering at me."

"I'd better go check up on him."

Guy walked outside. Anne returned to the kitchen. Seeing him through the window, she asked, "Well?"

"He's not here, "Guy answered, looking about the ground around him. "I don't see any blood, either, so you must not have hit him. I'll go and see if I can find him."

While Guy was gone, Anne seethed silently. She didn't care if the Indian was friendly or not, he didn't have any business scaring the wits out of her like that.

About ten minutes later, Guy walked in and placed six rabbits on the kitchen table, then said, "Well, I found him hiding in the woods. He said if we didn't treat him any better than that, he wasn't going to bring us game any more."

"Well, that's fine with me!" Anne threw back angrily. "Those rabbits are so scrawny they won't make one pot of stew, much less three."

"That's not the point. The point is he's friendly and trying to help us, and the railroad wants us to make as many Indian friends as we can. You'd be surprised, insulting just one of them can have repercussions with their entire tribe. He's out back. Can he come in? We usually give him a plate of food in appreciation, but he says he won't come in unless you agree. He's afraid you'll shoot at him again."

"All right, let him come in!" Anne snapped, then added sarcastically, "I certainly wouldn't want to be accused of starting an Indian war." She picked up a tin plate and lifted the lid of the venison stew she was cooking, then said, "But don't blame me if he doesn't like what I serve him. The meat is still half-raw."

"That won't bother him. That's the way the Indians eat it anyway."

By the time Guy returned with the Indian in tow, Anne was setting a plate of stew, a couple of slices of bread, and the jug of syrup on the end of the dining room table. The two men stopped beside her, and Guy said, "I explained that he frightened you, and that you didn't know he was a friend. He's forgiven you."

Well, I guess that explains the stupid grin on his face, Anne thought. She forced herself to smile back, despite the fact that the Indian smelled to high heaven.

Guy said something to Blue Feather and motioned to the food. The Indian shook his head, pointed to Anne, and said something in the same guttural language.

"What did he say?" Anne asked suspiciously.

"He said he would rather have *you* as payment," Guy answered with a perfectly deadpan expression on his face.

Anne was furious. "Oh, he did, did he? Well, you tell that grinning bastard that I not only said no, but hell no!"

Guy chuckled and said, "Now, don't get your dander up again. He didn't mean it as an insult. Besides, it's your own fault. You shouldn't have smiled at him."

"You said to be friendly!"

"I didn't mean that friendly. You see, Indians read a lot more into a woman's smile than white men do. He thinks you're attracted to him."

Anne looked at Blue Feather. He was a good four inches shorter than her and stocky. His braids were greasy; his teeth half-rotten. His nose was so flat it looked like someone had stepped on it and permanently mashed it, and he reeked. "Him? Why, that's the most preposterous thing I've ever heard!"

Anne turned and walked back into the kitchen in a huff. Guy diplomatically told Blue Feather that white men did not barter their women, and again made his offer of food.

With a sigh of disappointed resignation, the Indian sat down at the end of the table. Guy turned and walked back into the kitchen, where Anne was slamming pots and pans around. "Have you got a spoon for Blue Feather?"

It irritated Anne to no end that Guy was being so solicitous. He had terrified her, then insulted her, and Guy was treating him like some honored guest. "I put a knife and fork out. What does he need a spoon for?"

"If you'll look in the dining room, I think you'll know."

Anne peeked into the dining room and saw that Blue Feather had broken his bread over his food and was pouring syrup over the entire plate. He kept pouring until everything on the plate was swimming in syrup, and the sticky liquid was dripping off the sides. "My God!" Anne exclaimed in horror. "He isn't going to eat that revolting mess, is he?"

"He is. He does it every time. Indians are notorious for their sweet tooth."

Just the thought of it made Anne nauseous. She handed Guy a spoon and said, "You take it to him. I can't bear to watch."

Blue Feather not only ate his food, but to Anne's absolute disgust, he licked every bit of the syrup from the plate. Then he stood, rubbed his stomach, and said in English, "Heap good."

His English took Anne by surprise. How much of it did he understand? she wondered. Oh, God, did he know she had called him a bastard? As Blue Feather walked to the door, Anne said nervously to Guy, "I thought he didn't speak English."

"As far as I know, those are the only two words he knows. I think someone must have taught him that he was supposed to say them after eating."

"Like who?"

"I don't know. Maybe he did some hunting for mountain men or prospectors, before we came on the scene. 'Heap good' isn't exactly good English. But he always says it."

"Where did you learn to speak his language?"

"There was a Ute in the surveying party I was with, who took care of our packhorses. I learned enough Ute to get by from him."

"Well, I'm glad Blue Feather is gone." Her nose wrinkled at the rank odor that still lingered. "But it will take me all day to air out the dining room. My God! Doesn't he ever bathe?"

"That wasn't body odor. It was the bear grease he smears on his hair to keep the flies and mosquitoes away."

"Well, it must be effective," Anne answered in a biting voice. "Given a choice, I wouldn't go within a mile of him!"

Guy chuckled as he walked from the cabin. Anne would never forgive the Indian for giving her such a fright. But he couldn't really regret that she had shot at the Indian, as long as she hadn't harmed him. It proved she wasn't afraid to defend herself, and better able to take do so than he had thought. Yes, she was turning into a very self-assured, self-reliant woman.

Sunday was a day of rest in the camp. The men slept late, then spent the morning washing and mending their clothes or tending to more personal needs, such as bathing, cutting their hair, or trimming their beards and mustaches. In the afternoons, they whiled their time away playing horseshoes or just lounging in the sun. For Anne, however, it wasn't a day of rest and relaxation. She still cooked three full meals a day.

One Sunday, when the men had left the dinner table, she looked at it and said to Guy in exasperation, "Look at all that food they left. You'd think since I went to all the time and trouble to cook it, they could at least eat it."

"My God, Anne, they just ate breakfast four hours ago. They're not that hungry."

"Are you suggesting that I serve all of the meals later, just because they eat breakfast late on Sundays? "Why, I wouldn't get out of the kitchen until way after dark!"

"No, but you could back up dinner an hour or two. Then don't bother to cook an evening meal. If they get hungry, they could eat leftovers."

"Leftovers? Why, they'd have a fit if I served them leftovers! Besides, those have to be warmed. I might as well cook a meal."

"Anne, the men simply aren't that hungry on Sundays. They're not doing the hard work they do during the rest of the week. And I'm not suggesting that you warm up the leftovers. Just leave everything on the table, and cover it all with dish cloths. If they get hungry, they can help themselves. A cold meal once a week won't hurt them, and the food won't spoil. You deserve a little time off, too. God knows you work as hard as the rest of us."

"That's fine for you to say. You may not mind eating cold leftovers, but they might."

God, she could be stubborn, Guy thought. "All right. Suppose we ask them?"

Guy led Anne from the log cabin and summoned the men. When they were standing around him and Anne, Guy said, "I put a proposal before Anne, but she doesn't think you're going to like it. I'd like to know what you think about it. I suggested she serve dinner an hour later than usual on Sundays, then leave all the leftovers on the table, so that anyone who gets hungry can help themselves. That way, she wouldn't have to bother with an evening meal, and she could have some time off, too."

A big giant named Pat stepped forward. " 'Tis a grand idea, Cap'n." He turned to Anne and said, "To tell ye the truth, lass, I always feel a wee bit guilty, a-loafin' with ye in there a-workin'so hard. Ye deserve the time off as much as us."

"You'd be willing to eat *cold* leftovers?" Anne asked in disbelief.

"Aye."

Another man stepped forward and said, "We've eaten worse than that, and aye, there was many a day when we didn't eat at all back in the old country. I can remember me stomach a-rubbin' me backbone. I ain't too proud to eat cold leftovers."

"Particularly, if they be yers," another man added.

"We'll put it to a vote," Guy said. "Every man who agrees, raise you hand."

The men didn't only raise their hands, they cheered. Guy grinned and said, "We'll, I guess it's settled then. From now on Anne gets Sunday afternoons off."

After the crowd of men had dispersed, Guy asked Anne, "Well, what are you going to do with your afternoon off?"

"I don't know. I haven't had time to think about it."

"Would you like to take a long walk in the woods with me?"

It sounded delightful to Anne. "Yes, that would be nice. Let me take off my apron and cover the food, and I'll be right with you."

They strolled leisurely through the sun-dabbled woods, following the murmuring, shallow stream that meandered through it for awhile, then cutting back toward the creek. "How is the bridge going?" Anne asked.

"Great. Would you like to see how far we've progressed?"

When they reached the gorge and Anne looked down, she said in surprise, "Why, it's almost halfway to the top!"

"Yes, I'd like to get the skeleton structure up before winter sets in. Then we can concentrate on reinforcing it."

"It doesn't look like just a skeleton to me," Anne commented.

"You really can't tell much about a bridge's structure looking down on it. But from the bottom of this gorge, you can see a lot of gaps that have to be filled in. Come on. Let's walk down to the bottom. I'll show you what I mean."

Guy helped Anne down the rocky path to the narrow muddy stream. When Anne looked up, she could see the gaps in the trestle that she hadn't been able to see from above. "What's it going to look like when it's finished?"

"Sit down here on the bank beside me, and I'll draw you a picture."

They sat on the sand, and Guy picked up a small stick and drew as he explained the various beams that needed to be added or those already standing that needed to be reinforced.

Anne looked from the drawing and up at the trestle, back and forth as he drew and talked. When he had finished, Anne could clearly envision how the bridge would look when it was finished. Now she knew where the term "designing" a bridge came from. The timbers weren't just thrown up at random. Each beam had to support a certain amount of weight and bear a certain amount of stress. But what amazed her even more, was that Guy's bridge wasn't just a work of engineering, but with its flowing, graceful lines that towered into the air, a work of art, too. Still gazing up and seeing the bridge in her mind's eye, she said in an soft voice, "Oh, Guy, your bridge is going to be beautiful!"

Guy shot her a sharp, surprised glance, then admitted, "I hope so, because that's what I had in mind when I designed it. I don't see any reason why a bridge can't be sleek and graceful, as well as utilitarian. There are a lot of engineers who would disagree with me, who think a sound, strong bridge should look sturdy, that the more bulky timbers used, the better. That's not true. It's where you place the timbers that determines its strength. There are a lot more engineers who would out-and-out laugh at me for even suggesting that a bridge should have artistry and grace. They're the men who can't be bothered with aesthetics, who leave eyesores all over the country to mar the natural beauty of the land in the name of progress." Guy laughed self-consciously, then said, "I don't know. Maybe they're right. Maybe I am just being silly. Maybe nobody will even notice or care."

If they didn't, it would be a shame, Anne thought. "You really prefer building bridges, don't you?"

"Yes, they're much more challenging than building a road over a flat area, or even one that requires going around curves and up inclines. Each and every trestle presents a different set of problems to be overcome, whether it be over a gully or a deep gorge like this one. You have to take into consideration not only the depth and width of the span, but the degree of the incline of its banks, the type of soil you're building on, the amount and force of the water that will flow under it, and on and on. Then, too, I think it's exciting to build something that defies gravity, even when a great stress such as the weight of a train is placed on it. I hope to someday become one of the best bridge engineers in this country, or maybe even this hemisphere. This is the first bridge where I've been allowed to not only design it, but actually have full responsibility for its construction. I probably won't get another opportunity on this project to do both again. For that reason, it's going to be as perfect as I can possibly get it."

And Guy's bridge would be perfect, as well as beautiful, Anne thought, as they walked away and climbed back up the gorge. Years and years from now, people who knew anything about bridges would point to it and say, "Guy Masters built that bridge," for Anne knew that Guy was going to be a tremendous success in his chosen field. She felt immensely proud of him, and deeply touched that he had shared his confidences and dreams with her. She sensed that these were things that he had never revealed to anyone else. His sharing of them with her had told her the measure of his feelings for her. He didn't have to tell her he loved her. She knew.

Chapter Twenty-one

When Anne and Guy reached the rim of the gorge, Anne saw the deep scowl that came over his face. "What's wrong?" she asked. "Why are you frowning so?"

Guy nodded towards the western horizon and said, "I don't like the looks of that."

Anne turned and saw the line of dark, angry-looking thunderheads rolling over the mountains in the distance, they were laced with jagged flashes of lighting. "It looks like we're in for a storm."

"Yes, and from the heavy look of those dark clouds, I'd say there was a lot of water in them. Damn! Of all the rotten luck! Why does it have to rain *now?* Why couldn't it have waited for another week or two? That bridge isn't strong enough to sustain flood waters yet."

"But maybe it won't rain that hard," Anne objected.

"I hope not, but from what I've heard from some of the old mountain men, this country is known for its cloudbursts. Come on. Let's get back to the camp before it hits."

Despite the fact that they rushed, they didn't outrun the storm. The wind that preceded it blew their clothing and hair around wildly and buffeted the limbs of the trees they were passing under, twisting them this way and that, as if a giant hand had reached down from the heavens and was shaking them. Thunder rolled and lighting crashed all around them. Then the rain came, torrents of it, drenching them to the skin within seconds.

They took refuge in Anne's cabin. While Anne changed

clothes, Guy stood at one of the open windows and stared out at the storm, a grim expression on his face. "Don't you want to take off your wet clothing?" Anne asked, seeing the puddle of water at his feet. "The air is a little chilly. You might catch cold."

"I've never had a cold in my life," Guy answered in a distracted voice.

Throughout the storm, Guy stood at the window and watched. The rain was so heavy that it looked like a sheet of water falling from the heavens, and he couldn't even see the woods around them. It pounded on the roof, adding its deafening noises to that of the loud cracks of the lightning and crashes of the thunder. Then, as suddenly as it came, the storm passed, and the sun came out, leaving the trees glittering as if thousands of diamonds had been scattered over them.

"I'm going down to the bridge," Guy announced, turning from the window.

As he walked rapidly to the door, Anne said, "Wait a minute! I'll go with you."

Anne had to practically run to keep up with Guy's quick strides, splashing water from the deep puddles on both of them. When they reached the rim of the gorge and looked down, Anne saw the bridge was still standing, and that the water in the creek had risen a few feet. "See, it wasn't as bad as you thought it would be," she said with relief. "You did all that worrying for nothing."

"It's not the water draining from the surrounding area that's worrying me, Anne. It's the water that fell in those mountains in the distance. They're made of solid granite, so the water doesn't soak in like it does here. And this creek is the main tributary that drains those mountains. I won't know for hours just how much water will come down."

Anne stayed with Guy while he anxiously paced and waited to see what would happen. Several of the men from the camp who were also concerned joined them. The sun sank lower and lower, until it was obscured by the mountains in the distance, making their jagged purplish crests look as if they had been gilded in gold, and casting a rosy color over the sky. Then Anne heard it, a rumbling noise in the distance that grew louder and louder, until it became a distinct roar. She stared upstream, in a curious anticipation that was a mixture of both excitement and dread. But even though she was expecting it, Anne wasn't really prepared for what she saw. A tremendous, thirty-foot wall of water came thundering down the deep ravine, carrying limbs and uprooted trees that bobbed up and down wildly in the rolling water. It hit the trestle with a loud crash, and swept away the entire structure as if it had been made of sticks, instead of heavy timbers. Anne stared down at where the trestle had stood just seconds before. All she could see was muddy, thrashing water. But even though she had seen it with her own eyes, it still seemed impossible to believe. She would never have dreamed that water could be so forceful, so destructive.

"Jesus, Mary, and Joseph!" one of the Irishmen muttered, a shocked expression on his face. " 'Tis gone, just like that, in the snap of me fingers." He paused, then asked, "What are we goin' to do now, Cap'n?"

Anne glanced at Guy. The expression on his face tore at her heart, for all of the distressing emotions he was feeling were briefly revealed there: anger, disappointment, sadness at his loss.

He stared at the swirling waters for a moment, then answered grimly, "There's only one thing we can do. Rebuild it."

"Aye, but we'll never get it done on time, not with with winter comin' down on us!"

A fiercely determined expression came over Guy's face. He turned to face the men and said, "Like hell we won't! This bridge is going to be standing and ready for those trackmen when they arrive, if I have to kill all of us to see it done. Now get to bed and get some rest. Starting tomorrow, we've got a lot of catching up to do."

Guy meant his words. He not only drove his crew from sunrise to sunset, but kept them on the construction site for hours after darkness had fallen, working by the light of huge bonfires. No longer was Sunday a day of rest. The men worked at a frenzied pace seven days a week, eighteen hours a day, and fell into bed at night exhausted.

To Guy's credit, he worked right beside his men and drove himself even harder, which was the reason his crew didn't rebel. He came to Anne's cabin every night, but was so tired that he could hardly mutter a word, much less summon the energy to make love to her.

One night, when he arrived, he staggered to the bed and sat on the edge of it. His appearance tore at Anne's heart. He hadn't taken the time to shave in days, and there were dark circles under his eyes. His face had a lean look about it from the meals he had skipped, and he looked so weary, that she marveled he didn't fall asleep on his feet.

"I guess you wonder why I even bother to come here," Guy said, his words a little slurred from exhaustion. "Besides being no good to you as a lover, I'm lousy company."

Anne's eyes twinkled mischievously. "Oh, I'll admit I wondered. I decided it was my soft bed you came for."

Guy was only able to manage a weak smile to her teasing.

"Lie down, and I'll take off your boots," Anne said, giving his shoulder a gentle shove that sent him tumbling backward on the bed.

"You're too good to me, Anne," Guy muttered, while Anne was tugging on his boots. "Too damn good. I'm not worth it."

Anne set the boots aside and turned, seeing Guy was dead to the world. She smiled and pushed a lock of dark hair from his forehead, whispering, "You're wrong. You're worth every bit of it."

The next day Anne visited the bridge site for the first time since the flood. She was surprised to see that the destroyed trestle had not only been replaced, but the timbers almost reached the top of the deep ravine. She watched as the men worked, thinking that bridge monkeys was an apt description of them. They scampered up and down the trestle, and swung arm to arm from one beam to another, as agile and as unconcerned at the terrifying heights as the animals they took their names from, making their dangerous job look like child's play. From where he was helping two men hammering a beam high up in the framework on the opposite side, Guy spied her and waved. Anne waved back. Then, to her surprise, he made his way across the structure toward her, making her gasp in fright at the death-defying leaps he took from one timber to the other.

As he climbed over the edge of the ravine and came to a stand beside her, Guy asked, "What are you doing here?"

"I was just curious to see how far you had progressed. I had no idea you'd accomplished so much."

Guy beamed with satisfaction. "Yes, in another day or two, we'll be back on schedule. Then we can take a few day's rest."

Anne looked at Guy. He didn't look at all weary today. But she knew it was a false impression. Before he had been running on sheer willpower, and now on the adrenalin being pumped into his bloodstream from his elation.

Anne's estimation was correct. When Guy called a halt two days later, the crew had a brief, but roaring celebration that night in the dining room. When the adrenalin wore off, not even the liquor they were downing could keep them going. They collapsed in utter exhaustion, a few not even making it to their tents, but sleeping with their heads on their folded arms at the table. It was left to Anne to rouse them enough to stagger to their cots a few hours later, and then, for well over thirty hours, she was the only being stirring in the camp.

The next Sunday afternoon, Guy and Anne took a walk through the woods, carrying a blanket and a small picnic lunch. The woodlands had taken on their fall dress, and Anne admired the quaking aspens with their golden leaves and the scattered oaks with their brilliant scarlet. Even the pine and fir leaves seemed a richer, deeper green. The squirrels were everywhere, scampering up and down tree trunks, leaping from limb to limb, bounding across open spaces from one tree to the other, in their search for acorns and pine cones to last them through the coming winter.

"I can't believe winter is just around the corner," Anne commented. "We had that week of brisk days, but now the weather is so warm and mild again."

"It won't last, Anne. This is probably the last warm spell we'll see. That's why I particularly wanted us to go for a walk today. The place I want to show you won't look nearly as pretty in the winter, to say nothing of it being too far to walk in the cold."

"What place is that?"

Guy smiled, then answered mysteriously, "You'll see."

They followed the shallow stream through the deep woods,

its crystal clear water sparkling where the sunlight hit it and making soft, gurgling noises as it rushed over rocks. Then the terrain became more rugged, the hills steeper and steeper. When they veered away from the stream, Anne objected. "Why are we going this way? Why don't we stay closer to the stream, where we can get water when we're thirsty?"

"We'll see it again in a little bit."

They climbed another hill, this one even steeper and rockier. In several places Guy had to climb to the top of ledges made of sheer stone, and then help Anne up. Then Guy turned sharply and led her through a woods that was so thick that only shafts of golden light could penetrate here and there, and the air was pungent with the smell of pine and rotted leaves.

When they suddenly stepped into a clearing, Anne's breath caught. A small waterfall cascaded down a solid wall of rock to a deep pool of water. She glanced quickly around at the meadow where the pool sat, and saw where the stream again narrowed in the distance, meandering off into the woods.

"Is this the same stream?" she asked.

"Yes."

Anne looked about her. "Oh, Guy, it's lovely. It was worth the walk."

"I discovered it when we were surveying this area for a possible route through here. As you know, we set the line a ways over, where it wasn't quite so rugged, but I never forgot this place. It has a certain charm about it."

Enchantment, you mean, Anne thought. "Then the others don't know about it?"

"No, I never mentioned it to them."

Anne's eyes settled on the pool. The water was crystal clear, not muddy like all the rivers and creeks she had seen out here. That was why she had foregone bathing in any of the streams the railroad had come across. She would rather take a cramped bath in a little clean water, than a river or creek so full of dirt it would defeat her purpose. And she had stayed away from the stream behind the camp, because she knew the men bathed there. "I wish I had known about it before now," Anne said. "Do you have any idea of how tired I am of bathing in that stupid little vinegar barrel? Why, I haven't had a decent, honest-to-God bath since I left Cheyenne."

Guy frowned. Maybe it had been a mistake bringing her here. He didn't dare say it would be too dangerous for her to come out here alone. Saying anything was too dangerous to Anne, was like waving a red flag in front of a bull. He chose his words very carefully, "Anne, I wouldn't want you to come out here alone. It's much too far from the camp and too isolated."

Anne's fierce independence flared briefly. Then she was forced to admit that it would be foolish to venture this far by herself. If an Indian should come across her and she had to make a run for it—like she did because that stupid Blue Feather—it would be a long run. Besides, she probably wouldn't be able to climb that last hill without Guy's help. She wasn't half-monkey, like he was. "I suppose you're right, but I wish you had thought to bring some soap and towels with us, since you knew we were coming here. I'd dearly love to take a bath in that pool."

"If I had brought soap and towels along, it would have ruined my surprise. That was the fun of it, seeing the expression on your face when you first saw it. Besides, you're not dirty. You took a bath this morning."

He still didn't get the point, Anne thought. She might be clean, but she longed to immerse herself in water, to be able to stretch out her arms and legs in it, to be able to luxuriate in the feel of water all around her.

Anne walked to the edge of the pool and gazed longingly at it, while Guy spread their blanket out on the ground, removed his gun from his hip, and placed it at one corner. As he walked to Anne, she heard his footsteps behind her and said, "Well, if I can't bathe in it, the first thing I'm going to do is take a dip."

Guy's warm hand brushed her throat, as he pushed the hair in her hair net aside and softly kissed the nape of neck. "Can't it wait? I had other things in mind."

When Guy slipped one arm around Anne's slim waist and pulled her back against him, and his mouth slid to her throat, Anne knew with a certainty what things he had in mind. A part of her wanted it, too, but another part of her desperately longed to plunge into the pool. The two desires struggled within her. She steeled herself to the feel of Guy nibbling on her earlobe and reached for the arm that held her, intending to pull it away, but Guy slipped his other arm around her, his hand cupping, then stroking one breast. She could feel his heat surrounding her like a warm cocoon, and his scent engulfing her, an exciting masculine scent that always sent her senses reeling. His thumb brushing back and forth across her nipple made her legs tremble with need. When his tongue darted into her ear, her bones melted.

Completely forgetting the enticing pool, Anne turned in the circle of Guy's arms and looked up to see his black eyes smoldering, a look that made her heart race. Sliding her hands over his broad shoulders, she lifted her head, her lips aching for the feel of his. Guy's warm mouth covered hers, his tongue playing teasingly at the corners, before it slipped inside to ravish the heady sweetness there. Sensation erupted in Anne. A moan of desire rose from deep inside her as she pressed her body closer to his, a thrill at the feel of his hard readiness against her added to the excitement of his plundering kiss.

Anne was trembling all over when Guy stepped back and undressed her, caressing and kissing each inch of skin he explored. He dallied at her breasts, his swirling tongue laving the soft mounds, his lips nibbling, then again at her navel and thighs. By the time the last garment fell to the ground, Anne was a quivering mass of jelly.

Guy's gaze hungrily swept over Anne's rosy, naked flesh. God, she's beautiful, he thought, every curve and hollow a perfection.

Anne knew by Guy's warm, ardent gaze what he was thinking, and flushed with pride that he thought her beautiful. She wanted to be so, more for his sake than her own. Then she realized that *he* was still clothed, and felt suddenly cheated. She wanted to see him, too. She stepped up to him and began unbuttoning his shirt, a little shocked at her own boldness, for other than removing his boots, she had never undressed him. With trembling fingers, she pushed the shirt off his shoulders and down his arms, thrilling at the feel of those powerful muscles under her fingertips. Guy stood perfectly still, excited by her stripping him, yet hesitant to move for fear she would turn shy on him.

She struggled with the heavy belt buckle, awkward in her frustration, acutely aware of the huge bulge straining at Guy's pants just below her fingers. Finally, the stubborn buckle gave way, and she unbuttoned his pants. The feel of her fingers against his bare, feverish skin came as a surprise to her, for she hadn't known until then that he wasn't wearing his underwear. Her discovery fueled her growing excitement, for that was one less awkward garment for her to have to contend with, and she was anxious to see him in all his naked glory.

At the feel of Anne's fingers lightly brushing across his aroused sex, Guy's mouth turned dry. When her hands slid down his thighs as she pushed his pants down, he sucked in his breath sharply, both at the feel of the long, excruciating caress and that of his erection springing to attention, as it was suddenly released from the confining material. His breath came in ragged gasps as he lifted one foot, then the other, for her to remove his boots and socks, then slip the pants off and toss them aside, too.

Anne sat back on her heels and looked up. Her breath caught in her throat. With Guy's powerful, muscle-ridged body bathed in the bright sunlight, and his eyes blazing with the heat of his own desire, he looked like a proud, fierce, magnificent god.

He's beautiful, she thought in awe, absolutely beautiful. Her eyes locked on the blatant proof of his masculinity, and seeing it lengthen another inch under her bold appraisal, felt an incredible thrill run through her. She reached for him, taking the hot, throbbing organ in her hand and stroking it sensuously.

Guy's legs turned so weak he feared they wouldn't support his weight. He brushed her hand aside and lifted her to her feet, then quickly led her to the blanket. Capturing her mouth in a hot, torrid kiss that gave full rein to his passion, he drew her to the blanket with him, his hands roving impatiently over her back, her hips, her rounded thighs. Anne, too, was seized with an urgency as her hands feverishly ran over him and she kissed him back. When he entered her with a swift, deep thrust, she welcomed him with a cry of gladness and threw her long legs around his slim hips, pulling him even deeper.

Guy felt Anne's legs around his hips like a tight vise, and the muscles of her warm, damp depths squeezing on his rigid flesh like tiny greedy hands. Fearing he would loose control right then and there, his big body trembled, and he muttered, "Easy, sweetheart, easy. There's no hurry."

But to Anne there was. She was filled with a pressing urgency, her need for release so intense she thought she would burst. She writhed beneath him, clasping him with her arms and legs as if she were intent upon taking *every* inch of him into herself, just as she had his manhood. She reined hot, torrid kisses over his face, his neck, his shoulders. When she tried to make the first movement, Guy hissed sharply, then held her hips still. Feeling frustrated beyond her endurance, she nipped his shoulder and raked his back with her nails, sobbing "Damn you! Finish it! I can't stand this."

Then suddenly, the pressure within her exploded, and a convulsion wracked her body. Stars exploded behind her eyes. She opened her eyes to see Guy still hovering over her, his forehead beaded with perspiration and an agonized expression on his face. Dazed, she wondered what had happened, then, becoming aware of his rigid organ still inside her, realized that he was still holding back. "I'm sorry," she muttered weakly. "I couldn't wait for you."

Feeling Anne's legs relax around his hips, Guy finally regained control of his own raging passion. He smiled down at her and said in a teasing voice, "Jesus, sweetheart, now I know what they mean when they say a woman is a man-eater. I thought you were going to squeeze the life from me, if you didn't suck all of me up into you."

Anne felt her passion on the rise again, and she had thought it sated! And she *had* wanted to take all of him into herself, absorb him right through her skin. My God, she did have a voracious appetite for him. But she couldn't seem to help herself. "I am shameless, aren't I?"

The teasing twinkle in Guy's eyes quickly disappeared, to be replaced with a deadly earnest one. "No, don't ever say that about yourself! I love your honesty in our lovemaking. I don't want any restraints on it. I want it to always remain free, spontaneous, uninhibited. That's what makes it so beautiful."

As Guy started his movements—slow, exquisitely sensuous thrusts—Anne thought it was beautiful the way their bodies could communicate with one another without a word being spoken. As he quickened his movements in bold, powerful thrusts that sent her blood racing through her veins like liquid fire, she matched him stroke for stroke, whimpering little animal sounds that told him of her pleasure. They climbed those lofty, spiraling heights until they reached the trembling peak. Guy held them there at that white hot crest, their hearts pounding against the other in intense anticipation, before they went spinning out into space and exploding in a shattering release that seemed to shake the earth around them.

They lay a long while drifting in the warm afterglow, before Anne became aware of the sheen of perspiration on her skin. She laughed softly and said, "I guess it's a good thing I did wait for my dip in the pool. I might not have needed it then, but I certainly do now."

Guy glanced over his shoulder from where he was still laying over Anne and saw his body glistening in the sunlight. "I'd say we both could use a dip." Then he grinned, adding, "Besides, if I stay like this, my rump is going to get sunburned."

As he pushed himself away from her and rose to his feet, Anne thought Guy's words probably not too far from the truth. He was deeply tanned to the waist from going without his shirt so much, but from there down his skin was almost as white as hers.

When Anne stepped into the pool, a shiver ran over her and she said, "I didn't realize it was so cold."

"It's spring-fed, remember? You'll get used to it."

By the time Anne had reached hip-depth, she had serious doubts about adjusting to the cold. There was gooseflesh all over her body, and her teeth were chattering. "I think I'll skip the dip, after all."

As she turned to wade back out, Guy put his hands on her shoulders and pushed her down until the water covered them, saying, "You can't adjust until your entire body is submerged."

Anne's breath caught as the icy water surrounded her. In a flash, she jumped to her feet and, hugging herself tightly, said, "No, I've had enough! I'm getting out."

She hurried from the pool, hearing a splash behind her. At the bank, she turned and saw Guy swimming across the pool. He's insane, she thought, swimming in that ice-cold water. "You're going to catch cold," she called.

Guy turned and treaded water. "I've already told you. I've never had a cold in my life."

Damn him, why did he have to be so healthy and strong? He was making her look like a weakling. "Then you'll get cramps in your legs. Don't expect me to come rescue you, if that happens."

"It won't. The water doesn't even feel cold anymore."

He's lying, Anne thought. He couldn't have possibly adjusted that quickly. She peered closer, expecting to see he was turning blue or shivering beneath the water. She saw neither, irritating her even more.

She turned, hurried to the blanket, and sat on it, wrapping it tightly around her and watching rather resentfully as Guy swam the length of the pool several times, looking like he was enjoying himself immensely. When she had warmed up, she pushed the blanket back and began removing her hair net. Hearing a splash, she looked up and saw Guy wading from the pool, the water sliding off of his glistening, muscular body and the water drops in his dark hair glittering in the sunlight. A familiar heat suffused her. Damn him! she thought. Why did he have to be so utterly male and so blasted virile? Couldn't he have just one weakness? Why did he have to be so irresistible? Why, just one look at him sent her heart racing, and reduced her to a quivering mass of jelly. He had no right to hold such a power over her. She jerked her eyes away and forced herself to concentrate on the knot in her hair net.

Guy fell to his knees beside her and asked, "What are you doing?"

"I'm trying to undo this hair net," Anne answered irritably. "My hair got wet when you pushed me down, and it's dripping down my back."

"Here, let me get it for you," Guy said, reaching for the knot."

Anne slapped his hand away and said, "I'm perfectly capable of undoing it myself!"

Guy had no idea why Anne was angry with him. "Well, you

don't have to be so snappish about it," he retorted. "You were the one who wanted to take the dip, remember? I didn't force you go in."

"No, but you forced me down in the water, and that's what got my hair wet," Anne answered in an accusing voice, glaring at him.

"And that's what you're so damn mad about, because you got your hair wet?" Guy asked in exasperation.

Anne pulled the net loose, tossed it aside, and shook her hair. She heard Guy's sharp intake of breath and glanced at him, seeing a warm look coming to his eyes.

He raised a hand and smoothed down her hair on one side, his fingers trailing down her arm. "Your hair is beautiful, Anne, even with the ends wet. Did you know that it's not just one color, that in the light, its strands are gold and red."

"Just in the sunlight," Anne answered, fighting the weak feeling coming over her at Guy's admiring gaze.

"No, not just in the sunlight. In any bright light. I first noticed it in the lamplight, that night we dined in Cheyenne."

And she had thought he hadn't even noticed her that night, Anne thought in surprise.

"Look up," Guy commanded her softly.

"But why?" Anne asked in confusion.

"Just do as I ask."

Anne looked up.

"Now down," Guy requested.

Anne looked down.

"Now to the side."

As Anne glanced to the side, Guy smiled and said softly, "Fascinating, absolutely fascinating."

"What?"

"Your eyes. They change colors when you move them; the light catches them from different angles. I noticed them that night, too. I was so fascinated I could hardly tear mine away."

Guy's complimenting Anne on the two things that she felt were her greatest flaws totally disarmed her. When he pushed her back on the blanket and began to kiss and caress her, she offered him no resistance. She realized that while he held a power over her, she held one over him also, and it was a heady knowledge, almost as heady as his deep, drugging kisses and tantalizing caresses.

And when he carried her once again up those thundering heights, she gloried in her powerful, virile lover, who could bring her such exquisite delights, whose strength and endurance could take her to heaven and beyond. Never had she felt so vitally alive, so powerful herself, as if each deep, masterful stroke Guy made infused her with his own omnipotence. Her blood sang, her spirits soared, and every nerve ending in her body was taut with breathtaking sensation, as she neared the soul-shattering crescendo.

Guy felt Anne stiffen in his arms and knew she was on the verge of attaining her release. "Open your eyes!" he commanded sharply.

Anne's eyes flew open, not at Guy's command, but at the wonder of the earth-shaking sensations she was experiencing. Guy looked down at her eyes and felt himself drowning in the kaleidoscope of swirling blues, greens, and grays. A powerful force seized him, rushing from the tips of his toes like a monstrous wave that threatened to blow the top of his head off before he exploded inside her with a scalding release that made him momentarily loose consciousness.

It was a long time before Guy could summon the strength to even move. He had never felt so incredibly weak or totally drained in his entire life. He nuzzled Anne's neck where his head lay on her hair and muttered, "I love you, Anne. I love you so damn much, it hurts."

When Anne failed to respond, Guy lifted his head and saw that she had drifted off to sleep. He smiled, thinking that the words had really been unnecessary. By now, Anne should know that he had fallen in love with her.

He lifted himself from her and rolled to his side, careful not to disturb her slumber. Then he held her tenderly in his arms, feeling a deep contentment and marveling at the happiness she brought him.

Eventually, Guy dozed off, too, and the warm autumn sun beamed down on them.

Chapter Twenty-two

The day by the pool was the last warm day Anne and Guy saw. The next day, the weather turned cold and blustery, and they were forced to use the fireplace in the dining hall for the first time. For several weeks they never saw the sun. The sky stayed gray with low-hanging, leaden clouds, and if it wasn't sleeting, there were snow flurries. But the construction on the bridge continued, despite the fact that the slippery ice on the timbers made the work even more dangerous. Huge bonfires were lit at the creek bottom, where the men could go to briefly warm up before scampering back up into the trestle.

Anne was busy, too, first making a long list of staples and smoked meats to tide them through the winter, then after delivery, rearranging the pantry and storage area to hold everything. Several times, she found the water barrel sitting on the lean-to frozen over with ice in the mornings, and had to pound on it with her rolling pin to break it. Deciding she had had enough of that, she pushed the barrel until she got it into her kitchen, where it was warm. Then it got so cold that even the stream froze over, and the men had to bring her chunks of ice, instead of buckets of water.

Anne was glad that she was in the nice, big warm cabin during the daytime, and not outdoors like the men. Even her small cabin was warmer at night than their tents, for she not only had the insulation of the logs to protect her from the biting cold, but her small stove, too. But still there was always a little chill in the air, and she dove for the bed as soon as she undressed, burrowing beneath the covers.

Climbing in beside her one night, Guy chuckled and said, "You're just about the most cold-natured person I've ever seen. You must have thin blood."

"I have nothing of the sort," Anne replied tartly, snuggling up to his warmth. "I'm just not half-Eskimo like you are."

Guy put his arms around her and said, "Sometimes I think that's the only reason you want me in your bed, to warm you up."

"Oh, I'll admit that is a distinct advantage. But there are other reasons." She bent her leg and sensuously rubbed her soft thigh up and down his hair-roughened one.

Guy's breath quickened, and he tightened his arms around her. "Is that an invitation?" he asked in a husky voice, running his mouth up and down her neck.

"What do you think?"

"I think it is, but I'm afraid I'm going to have to disappoint you. I'm a little tired tonight."

Anne was disappointed, and a little miffed. If he was too tired, then why had he encouraged her that way? She pushed away from him and flounced over on her side with her back to him.

Guy chucked, rolled to his side, slipped his arm around her waist, and said, "You give up too easy. I was only teasing."

"And what did you expect me to do when you said you were too tired?" Anne asked irritably. "Seduce you?"

"I wouldn't be adverse to it."

"Well, you can forget it. I'm too tired now," Anne answered stubbornly.

She felt rather than heard Guy's chuckle, for he had moved so close that his chest was pressed against her back. "You have got to be the most obstinate woman I've ever had the misfortune to meet. All right. Have it your way. I'll just have to seduce you."

"Don't bother. It won't work."

When Guy's hand slipped up to cup her breast, Anne pushed it away and quickly rolled to her stomach. Undaunted, he pushed aside her long hair and dropped featherlike kisses at the nape of her neck, then over her shoulder blades, then down her spine, his hand smoothing over her hips and thighs. Anne had completely discounted her body's reaction to his touch. It came unbidden and unwanted, and she cursed her treacherous body beneath her breath. She tried to steel herself against the feel of his licking her buttocks, then the backs of her thighs, but his tongue felt like a flaming dart, and her heart raced. She sighed in relief when he lifted his head, then felt his scalding breath beside her ear, just before he kissed it.

She jerked her head away and said, "Stop it!"

"Oh, you don't like that? Then maybe you'll like this better."

He nibbled on her shoulder, the tiny bites sending little thrills through her. Then she gasped as his hand slipped between her thighs. "No, don't!" she cried out, trying to roll away from him.

Guy hooked his muscular thigh over hers to hold her down, licking her shoulders and back, as his fingers delved into her warm moistness. Anne tried to twist away, but it only made what his teasing, taunting fingers were doing there worse. Then she sucked in her breath as he slipped them inside her, moving in and out in a sensuous rhythm that made warm shivers of delight run over her. "Please, stop," she begged.

"No."

"Then I give up. Let me turn over."

"No, you were the one that picked this position."

"But I want to kiss you, touch you."

"I don't need to be kissed or touched. I'm already excited."

He shifted his weight, enough so that Anne could feel the hot, throbbing length of his erection against her thigh. With that part of him scorching her and his fingers moving inside her, Anne squirmed in frustration. It was heaven, it was hell. She didn't want him to stop, and yet she wanted to kiss and touch him, too!

"Please let me turn, please," Anne begged.

As he withdrew his hand, Anne sighed in relief. As soon as

he had rolled her over, her fingers tangled in his dark hair and pulled his head down. She placed hot greedy kisses over his face, neck, and shoulders, her hands sweeping over her broad back, reveling in the feel of those powerful muscles contracting under her fingertips and his chest hair tickling her breasts.

Guy caught her roving mouth with his; their tongues meet and danced. The kiss grew wilder as he kissed her hungrily, his tongue an instrument of soft, sweet savagery that sent both of their senses reeling, and their blood coursing hotly through their veins.

He kissed her throat, slowly descending. As his warm tongue drew lazy circles around her breast, she moaned in anguished anticipation, then cried out softly as his mouth closed over the hardened peak, his tongue rolling it, then flicking, sending a bolt of fire racing up her spine.

Anne couldn't stand it any longer. She reached for him and guided him to her. He drove into her, his thrust deep and true. Anne's legs trembled; her breath caught at the feel of him, immense and throbbing inside her. Then suddenly, he withdrew, and Anne sobbed in frustration.

"Please, Guy, no more," Anne pleaded as the hot tip of his swollen shaft teased and tormented at the portal of her womanhood, then circled the ultrasensitive bud, so close to where she wanted him, and yet so faraway. "I can't stand any more of this tormenting."

Guy plunged into her the second time, then groaned as he felt her hot, greedy muscles contracting around him. Anne locked her long legs around him, pulling him deeper, determined that he wouldn't get away from her this time.

Guy was her willing prisoner. The time for teasing was over. His own passion rose white hot. He captured her mouth in a deep, consuming kiss, and he moved inside her, taking her by storm, harder, deeper, swifter, sweeping her up to the heights of heaven, then climaxing in a sweet intense rush of sublime ecstasy as his arms tightened convulsively, and he shuddered in his own exquisite throes of release.

It was some time before reality returned for either of them.

The first thing Guy became aware of was that the wind had picked up considerably. He raised his head and cocked it, listening closer.

"What's wrong?" Anne asked, still feeling dazed.

"The wind. It wasn't blowing that hard earlier."

"We don't care," Anne purred in contentment. "We're warm and cozy here."

Guy smiled at her remark. He relieved her of his weight and rolled to his side. Anne snuggled back up to him. He absently stroked her back with one hand for a minute, then said, "Now, don't take offense, Anne, but you've got to learn to stop taking everything so seriously. You're too intense, too sensitive. There's a light side to life, too."

"What are you talking about?"

"I'm talking about my teasing you. You either get angry or hurt, and I don't mean it either way. I come from a family where teasing was part of our everyday relationships, a way of showing affection. Oh, we worked hard, but we never took life so seriously that we couldn't laugh a little, too."

Anne could have pointed out that she hadn't come from a warm, affectionate family, and certainly not one where laughter or lightheartedness was nurtured. She had tried to do a little teasing with Guy, but she still didn't feel comfortable with it, especially when she was the one being teased. She misinterpreted it as criticism, for that was all she had ever received at home, and got defensive.

"And another thing," Guy continued. "Independence is fine, but sometimes you carry it to extremes. You seem to think every time I offer to do something for you, I'm insinuating that you aren't capable. It's not that. I'm proud of how self-sufficient you've become. But no one is an island, Anne. No one stands totally alone. No matter how strong we are, we need someone's help every now and then, and even if we don't need it, we don't have to refuse it. Doing small things for others is another way of showing caring."

And that, too, went back to her upbringing, Anne thought. She was determined to be a success in everything she did, and to do it on her own. "I guess

I'm just trying to prove my worth."

Guy's arms tightened around her. "You don't have to prove your worth to me, Anne. Believe me, there is no one who values you as much as I do. I think you're absolutely wonderful. And I've never been so happy in my life, as I've been these past few months."

A warmth spread through Anne, not a superficial one like the heat she felt when Guy made love to her, but a deep one that warmed her soul. "I've never been so happy either," she admitted with tears in her eyes, "and I'll try not to take everything so seriously. But it won't be easy for me. It's against my nature."

Guy wondered why it was against Anne's nature, but decided not to probe, for fear she would throw up her defenses again. He was a little amazed that she hadn't gotten angry at what he had said, or at least resentful. Apparently, she was opening up to him, and that pleased him.

Much later that night, Anne was awakened by a sudden cold draft. She looked up to see Guy crawling from the bed. Groggily she raised herself on her elbow, and asked, "What's wrong? Why are you getting up? I didn't hear the mules."

"How could you, over that noise?"

It was then that Anne heard the wind howling. And the air in the cabin was icy. She yanked the covers back and huddled into them. "Did the fire go out?"

"No, it's still lit."

"Then why is it so cold in here?"

"I imagine the temperature outside must have dropped drastically, and that little stove can't contend with it," Guy answered as he lit the lantern. "It sounds like we've got a blizzard on our hands."

He dressed quickly, then walked to the door and opened it. A blast of icy air and a cloud of swirling snow came into the cabin. One look was all it took. In the gray, predawn light, all he could see was whirling snow. He pushed the door to, having to fight the force of the wind to do so.

He turned to Anne and said, "You'd better get up and get dressed. I'll take you to the big cabin, then go and round up the men. They can't stay in those flimsy tents without any heat in weather like this."

Anne pushed the covers aside, then yanked them back up again. "Will you hand me my clothes?" she asked, a shiver running over her. "I'm going to dress in here where it's warm."

Guy passed Anne's clothing to her and watched with amusement while she struggled to dress in bed. Not until she had everything on but her shoes did she venture from beneath the covers. Then she slipped them on quickly and made a beeline for her shawl and cloak, wrapping the shawl around her head like a scarf. As she slipped on her gloves, Guy said, "You'd better tuck the ends of that shawl into your cloak, otherwise the wind will rip it right off you."

Guy slipped on his sheepskin jacket, then his hat, pulling it low on his forehead. He walked to the bed and yanked the blankets from it, then handed one of the pillows to Anne. "What's this for?" she asked.

"There's a good likelihood that we'll have to sleep in the main cabin tonight. You'll need a pallet and a pillow."

"What about you? Won't you need a pillow?"

"No, I slept for years without a pillow when I was in the army."

He turned and walked to the door. "What about the fire in the stove?" Anne asked. "Aren't you going to put it out?"

"No, it will burn down," Guy answered over his shoulder, "but you can blow out the light."

Anne never got the chance to blow out the light. As soon as she had lifted the chimney on the lantern to do so, Guy opened the door and a blast of frigid wind did it for her.

Anne was shocked when she stepped outside of the cabin. All she could see was snow swirling around her, and the icy wind was so strong it almost blew her over. She turned her head toward the main cabin, but she couldn't even see a faint outline of it.

It took all of Guy's strength to close the door of the small cabin securely. Then he took Anne's hand and yelled over the wind, "Grab my belt, and don't let go. I'll lead the way."

Anne was glad she was following Guy. Since he was walking straight into the wind, his body shielded her to some degree. But still the snowflakes blew in her face, and they didn't feel like the soft, powdery stuff she was accustomed to, but more like sharp ice crystals that stung her skin. Within minutes, they had crusted so heavily on her eyelashes that she couldn't see a thing, and every breath she took burned her lungs. She buried her face in her pillow and stumbled after Guy, the wind tearing at the shawl wrapped around her head and wildly flapping the blankets he was carrying.

When they reached the big cabin, Guy grabbed the door handle. As soon as the lock cleared the latch, the door was torn from his grasp by the wind and banged open. He stepped in, pulling Anne in behind him, then forced the door closed. As soon as he had lit a lantern, he turned to Anne and asked, "Do you think you can get a fire going in the fireplace, while I rouse the men?"

Anne was shivering so hard she could hardly answer. "Of course! Who the devil do you think lights it every morning?"

Guy grinned as he walked back to the door. He was glad to see Anne was still feisty. When he had told her he thought she was too sensitive, he hadn't meant to squelch her high spirit, just tone down her exasperating independence a little. If she became too amicable, things would get downright dull.

Anne had a terrible time trying to get the fire going in the big stone fireplace. Just as she would get the match lit, the wind coming down the chimney blew it out. She was groaning with frustration, her bare hands feeling like two blocks of ice. Throwing them up in disgust, she rose, picked up the lantern, and walked into the kitchen, deciding to light the fire in her cook stove first. It didn't have an open chimney on it. Then when she had that fire going, she caught the end of a stick on fire and carried it into the dining hall and used it to light the kindling in the fireplace.

She was feeling very proud of her ingenuity and was lighting the lanterns in the dining hall when the door banged open and half a dozen men rushed into the room, carrying their bedrolls with them. No sooner had they closed the door than they stomped their feet and shook off like a pack of dogs, making a small snowstorm of their own.

The huge bridge monkey named Pat walked over to the fireplace, stripped off his gloves, and spread his hands out over the flames, saying to Anne, "Ah, lass, 'tis glad I am we built this cabin. Otherwise we would have froze our . . ." He paused and a flush rose on his face. He had been about to say balls. ". . . our noses off in this storm."

Anne looked at his nose. It did look awfully red. As did his earlobes, sticking out from underneath his sweater cap. She wondered how long it took for frostbite to occur. Guy wasn't even wearing anything over his ears. Like the rest of him, he swore they never got cold. Damn him! It would serve him right if they froze and fell off. Then maybe he wouldn't be so cocky.

She turned and saw that the men had piled their blankets and wraps on the tables. She wondered where she was supposed to serve breakfast. Seeing the dismayed expression on her face, Pat guessed what she was thinking and said to the men, "Here, now, lads. Let's not be a-clutterin' up the tables with our stuff. Pile 'em in the corners, where they won't be in the way."

Anne smiled gratefully at the big Irishman and walked to the kitchen, saying, "I'll have a pot of coffee ready in just a few minutes."

By the time Anne returned with a big pot of coffee, at least two dozen more men had arrived. Pat asked if there was anything he could do to help, and remembering what Guy had told her earlier, Anne answered, "Yes, there's a tray of cups in the kitchen you can bring in."

As the men were drinking their coffee, Anne asked Pat, "Where are Guy and the others?"

One of the late arrivals answered her question. "They're securin' the tents, a-pounding the stakes deeper. They were a-flapping an' a-snappin' something awful in that wind. 'Tis lucky we'll be if they don't blow clean away."

Anne returned to her kitchen to prepare breakfast. She kept peeking through the door into the dining room to see if Guy and others had arrived. The more time that passed, the more worried she became. Then, just as she was serving breakfast, they finally arrived, looking half-frozen.

She walked up to Guy, in the group huddled around the fireplace, and asked him, "What took you so long?"

"The snow was falling so thick we got lost there for awhile. We couldn't even see our hands before our faces. We yelled, but I guess no one in here heard us over that wind."

Anne glanced at one of the Irishmen. His face was still ashen with fright. "Then how did you finally find your way?"

Guy laughed. "I closed my eyes and pretended it was dark, then let my instincts guide me, like I did on those dark, moonless nights during the war. It turned out we were only twelve feet from the door."

They could have frozen to death out there, Anne thought, her heart dropping to her feet. Seeing Guy rub his ears, she asked in alarm, "What's wrong with your ears? Did you get frostbite?"

"They'll be okay. I rubbed snow on them."

"They're freezing and you rubbed snow on them?" Anne asked sharply.

"That's the treatment for frostbite, Anne. Believe it or not, snow is just a little bit warmer than that wind, and you're not supposed to warm them up too fast. The idea is to let the circulation return slowly."

He hadn't learned a thing, Anne thought crossly as she walked back to the kitchen. He would still be running around with nothing over his ears. And he had the audacity to call *her* obstinate!

That day the construction crew thought the blizzard was a big lark. No sooner had the table been cleared of the breakfast dishes than they brought out their cards and checkers. The games went on all day long, the gambling hot and heavy. A few of the men even took to pitting their strength against the others in arm wrestling, and bets were even placed on that.

That evening, after the supper dishes had been cleared, Pat sat at the end of one table with a forlorn look on his face. As Anne passed, he asked her, "Ah, lass, could I interest ye in a game of checkers?"

"Won't any of the others play with you?"

"Nay."

"Why not?"

" 'Tis sore losers, they be. Now I ask ye, can I help it if I'm on a winnin' streak?"

"If you're on a winning streak, why would I want to play with you?"

"Ah, but that's just it. Maybe me winnin' streak is broken. We won't be a-knowin' until we try."

Anne laughed. Undoubtedly that was how Pat had suckered the others into playing with him. Winning streak, my eye, she thought. He won because he was an expert at the game. "All right, I'll play a game with you."

Anne won the game, and she knew it was only because Pat allowed her to win. He leaned across the table and asked, "What do you say to a-placin' a wee bet on the next one, lass? 'Twould liven things up a bit."

Anne laughed. "Oh, no, you're not going to have me owning you my next three months' salary, like these men here. I'm saving my money for important things."

"Like what, lass? If ye don't mind me askin'?"

Anne didn't truly know if she still wanted her own restaurant or not. Since Guy had come into the picture, she didn't know what her future held, and he had given her no inkling into what he had planned for them. She had only told Pat she was saving her money to discourage him. "Well, I was sort of toying around with the idea of buying my own restaurant someday."

Pat's blue eyes lit up. "Why, 'tis a grand plan, lass, providin' ye'd be doin' the cookin'. Why, then it would be bound to be a big success. I'm a-tellin' true, now, lass. I'd walk twenty miles fer one of yer meals."

"Thank you."

"An' if ye'll take me advice, put it in a railroad town. Ye

can't beat railroad men fer hardy appetites."

Anne laughed. "How well I know that."

Pat grinned across at her and said, "Now, what do ye say to a penny a game? Sure and alive, that won't break ye."

"All right. A penny a game."

Anne didn't notice Guy sitting a few feet away, nor did she realize that he had overheard the entire conversation.

The next day the blizzard was still going strong. If anything the wind was stronger, sounding more like a shriek than a howl, and the shrill noise played on everyone's nerves. Besides that, the men were growing restless. They paced the hall like caged tigers. By late that afternoon, tempers were flaring. Then, right after supper, fists flew between two men. The next thing Anne knew it had turned into a free-for-all.

Guy tried to stop it, stepping between two men. All he got for his efforts was a good cuff on the chin meant for someone else. Seeing him staggering backwards, Anne was infuriated. "Stop it!" she screamed at the top of her lungs. "Stop this brawling this minute!"

The men didn't even hear her with their yelling and turning over benches as they scuffled. Snatching up her broom, she stepped on a bench, then the table, and began to beat on them, screaming, "Stop it! Do you hear me? Dammit, I said stop it!"

She gave the nearest man a good whack on the head. The man happened to be Pat. The big Irishman's fist stopped in midair, and he looked up with a bewildered expression on his face, then seeing the broom, he said, "Watch it, there, lass. Ye could hurt a man with that thing."

"You're damned right I can! And if you don't stop this fighting this minute, I'm going to beat the tar out of every single one of you!"

By now, Anne had gotten the attention of half of the men. The other half were still fighting. Pat bellowed out, "Settle down, lads! The lass is upset with us. 'Tis time we mind our manners."

Those who were still fighting turned, surprised looks coming over their faces when they saw Anne standing on the table with a furious expression on her face and her broom ready to swing. All except two, that is. They kept pounding at one another. With a snort of disgust, Pat walked over to them, caught each by the collar, literally raised them off the floor, and shook them.

"Behave yerselves, or I'll lay ye both out!" the big Irishman threatened.

Apparently both men believed him. When Pat set them back down—their faces a little blue from being half-strangled—both men were subdued, settling on just glaring at each other.

Pat turned to Anne and said, " 'Tis sorry we are."

"I should hope so! Look at you! I've never seen such a mess of black eyes and bleeding noses in my entire life. And your friends did it to you. Not your enemies. Your *friends!*"

The men looked sheepishly at one another. "Aye, 'tis true, we're a bloody mess," Pat agreed. "But what's a wee disagreement between friends? No one is a-holdin' a grudge." He turned back to Anne and said, "Ye, see, lass, we're bored. An' when Irishmen get bored, they fight. 'Tis a grand way to relieve boredom."

"That's the most ridiculous thing I've ever heard! There are other ways of relieving boredom than half-killing one another."

"Like what?"

Anne racked her brain, then said, "Well, like singing."

"Do ye be a-meanin' our songs about the Emerald Isle?" one Irishman asked.

"No, something more boisterous, something that you can release your energy through. Like this song." Anne launched into the railroad song about the Tarriers. The Irishmen joined in wholeheartedly, and apparently they knew all the verses. Once she had them started, she climbed down from the table and walked into the kitchen, where she found Guy holding a handful of snow on his bruised jaw.

"How bad is it?" Anne asked.

He removed his hand and gingerly moved his jaw from side to side, then answered, "Well, I don't think it's broken, and there aren't any teeth missing." His expression warmed. "You were wonderful in there, the way you tore into them. They'll be talking about you and your broom for months."

Anne felt a twinge of shame for getting so violent herself. "You mean about what a shrew I am?"

Guy chuckled. "No, about how fierce and furious you looked, about how one woman armed with just a broom stopped thirty brawling Irishmen. That's quite an accomplishment, you know."

"Well, someone had to stop them."

"Yes, and obviously I couldn't," Guy said, rubbing his bruised jaw.

He listened to the men singing at the tops of their lungs and said, "That was a good idea. It's a good release for them."

Anne wasn't so sure. The noise was worse than their fighting. For some strange reason, they seemed to prefer the verses about blasting to all the others, particularly the line; And drill! And blast! And fire!" They shouted those words and pounded their fist against their other hand to emphasize them, the deafening noise almost raising the roof.

An hour later the men were still going strong, and Anne marveled that they hadn't shouted themselves hoarse. Lying on her pallet in the kitchen, she fervently wished she hadn't made her suggestion. Her head was pounding, and each "And drill! And blast! And fire!" felt like someone was hitting it with a sledgehammer.

The next day the blizzard ended, and the men had to shovel their way from the main cabin. Guy kept them busy that day, shaking the snow off the tents that had been all but buried in snowdrifts, and clearing walkways covered with three feet of snow. Soon the camp looked like a maze, with all the tunnels running here and there.

When Guy came into the big cabin to get a cup of hot coffee that afternoon, Anne asked, "What about the horses and mules? All they all right?"

"Yes, I just got back from checking on them, and they're fine. We keep them in a small cave, so they were pretty well sheltered."

She noticed the thin scar at his hairline was red from the cold. She stepped up to him and lightly ran her fingers over it. "Where did you get that?"

"During the war. A bullet grazed me."

He had come that close to being shot in the head? Why, he could have been killed, or left like poor Johnny. A fear for him seized her. He lived too dangerously, both then and now.

"What are you looking so serious about?" Guy asked.

She wanted to ask him to be more careful, more cautious, but she knew without his daring, his boldness, his fearlessness, he wouldn't be Guy, the man she had fallen in love with. Besides, he'd just laugh at her again. "Oh, I was just thinking about those poor animals. It would have been a shame if they had frozen to death," Anne lied smoothly.

Long after Guy had left, Anne thought about the risks he faced in his job: crawling over high, slippery trestles; working with dangerous explosives; braving avalanches, rock slides, and flash floods. She wondered if she could live a lifetime of worrying about him. But if it meant giving up the man, she knew she had no choice. It was the price she would have to pay, and no price was too high for Guy.

That night, when Anne heard that Guy had decided to let the men sleep a few more nights in the main cabin until the weather warmed a little, Anne insisted upon returning to her lodgings, for fear of a repeat of the previous night. But it turned out she needn't have worried. The Irishmen were so exhausted from moving tons and tons of snow all day that they couldn't even muster the energy to talk, much less sing.

Chapter Twenty-three

The second week in February, the warm, dry Chinook winds blew down from the Rockies and melted the snow. Water dripped from the eaves of the roof in the big cabin, as snow melted in the daytime, then froze again at night, leaving long icicles hanging from the roof. The steady drip, drip, drip filled the cabin, and to this was added the soft plopping and dull thudding sounds of the snow falling from the trees. By the end of the third week, all that was left of the blizzards that had plagued them off and on throughout the winter, was scattered patches of snow in the hills around them.

As soon as the warming trend occurred, Guy had his men in the trestle working to shore up the bridge before the spring floods came. By the time the water came tumbling down, the bridge was almost completed, except for a week or so of reinforcements on the main beams.

One evening when Guy and the men came in for supper, they found the meal on the table, but Anne wasn't in the building. Thinking it odd, Guy went looking for her. He found her lying in her bed in her cabin, doubled over in pain.

He sat on the edge of the bed and asked in concern, "What's wrong?"

"Nothing. I've just got terrible cramps."

"Do you think it was something you ate?"

An embarrassed flush rose on Anne's face. What ailed her seemed so intimate, so personal. She averted her eyes and answered, "Not those kind of cramps. Women's cramps."

"Are they usually this bad?"

"Oh, Guy, just go away and leave me alone."

"No, I won't leave you alone," Guy answered in a firm voice, "not when you're hurting. And there's no need for you to be embarrassed in front of me. For God's sake, Anne, I have four sisters and a mother. I've known women have monthlies and that sometimes they're rough since I was a kid. It's a fact of life. Now, answer me," Guy said softly. "Are the cramps usually this bad?"

"To be perfectly honest, I've never had them before in my life. But I know that's what it is. It must be so bad this time because I missed my last few monthlies."

Guy's heart slammed against his chest. For a moment, time seemed to be suspended. Then he asked, "Have you ever missed before?"

"No."

"How many months have you missed?"

"Two, I think."

Guy lay down beside Anne and took in her his arms. "Have you had any other symptoms?"

"What do you mean—symptoms?"

"Are your breasts more tender than usual? Have you felt nauseated in the mornings?"

"Well, I did feel a little poorly in the mornings the past few weeks, but it always passed by midday. And I thought my breasts being a little sore was from your . . . your lovemaking."

It *was* caused by his lovemaking, Guy thought, inadvertently. He cursed himself for being a complete fool. Not once had he stopped to think that they might be risking pregnancy. No, he was too wrapped up in his happiness and his passion for Anne. He should have been more careful, withdrawn at the crucial moment, or better yet, kept his blasted hands off of her. And now she was suffering because of him, and the poor girl didn't even know what was wrong with her. Dammit, why hadn't someone told her? He'd never realized she was that innocent, that naive.

Anne saw the anguished look on Guy's face. "Guy, what's wrong?"

"I'm afraid you're pregnant, Anne."

"Are you saying I'm carrying a baby?" Anne asked in a shocked voice.

"Yes, but this doesn't look good, this cramping you're doing. I'm afraid you're about to miscarry."

Anne clasped her hands even more firmly over her lower abdomen, saying in a terrified voice, "But I don't want to loose it! I want it!"

Guy was deeply touched by Anne immediately feeling fiercely protective over their baby. She had barely gained knowledge of it and she wanted it, which told him volumes of how she felt about him. And now that he knew about it, he wanted it, too, even if it was something he hadn't planned on. "Sssh," he crooned, stroking her arm, "getting upset will just make it worse. I want it, too."

Anne clenched her teeth as a terrible cramp seized her. Perspiration broke out on her forehead. The cramp was shortly followed by another hard contraction. From then on, they came in such rapid succession that they seemed to blend into one long, wrenching pain.

Other than wiping the perspiration from her brow, there was nothing Guy could do but hold Anne and try to comfort her. He wished she wasn't trying so hard to be so brave, that she would scream, moan, do something other than chewing her lip and gasping. It was agony watching her writhe in pain. If only he could take the pain from her, transfer it to himself. Then he remembered the small bottle of laudanum in the medical kit the railroad had issued him. He slid his arms from Anne and started to rise.

Her hands flew out and clutched his arms. "No, don't leave me!"

"I just remembered the laudanum in the medical kit in my tent. I'll be right back."

There was a frantic, terrified look on Anne's face. "No, don't leave. Please, don't leave me alone!"

"Anne, it will ease the pain, and I'll only be gone a second."

Her fingernails dug into the flesh of Guy's arms. "No, if you leave me, I know I'll loose it. I know it!"

No matter how much Guy tried to reason with her, Anne wouldn't let him leave. She clung to him with a wild desperation. Realizing it was just distressing her more, Guy lay back down again and took her into his arms, soothing her with caresses and muttering promises that he wouldn't leave.

When the bleeding finally came it was almost a relief for Guy, for he couldn't stand watching her hurt any longer. The sooner it was over the better, for he had known for some time that it was inevitable. Then the new horror began. There wasn't just a rush of blood and then it was over. It keep coming, seemingly torrents of it! No sooner had he placed a fresh rolled-up-sheet between her legs than it was soaked. He had never seen so much blood in his life, and he had never felt so utterly helpless. He was afraid she was going to bleed to death right before his eyes, as the color drained from her body, her lips turned blue, and her skin became cold and clammy. When she first realized she had lost the baby, she sobbed, but now she lay very still, and there was a glazed look in her eyes that terrified him.

He held her in his arms, desperately trying to infuse some of his heat, his strength into her, pleading for her not to die and saying silent, fervent prayers. Finally, the bleeding subsided until it was practically nothing. Then Guy stripped off her bloody clothing, washed her, changed the soiled linens and put a warm gown on her, tending to her needs as if she were a baby.

"I'm cold," Anne muttered.

It was the first sound Anne had made since she had stopped sobbing, and that seemed eons ago to Guy. Encouraged, Guy felt tears of relief at the back of his eyes. He sat on the bed and tucked the blankets closer, saying in a teasing voice, "You're always cold."

"I told you, I'm not half-Eskimo like you are."

The words had been said weakly, but there was pertness about them that encouraged Guy even more. Even near death, Anne was feisty, and Guy loved her for it. She's a fighter, he thought. She's going to make it.

He kissed her forehead and asked, "Would you like a cup

of hot tea? It would help warm you."

"Not now. I'm too tired. All I want to do is sleep."

Guy sat on the side of the bed while Anne slept and watched her like a hawk, still half-afraid she might slip away from him. Shortly after he heard the mules braying, he walked from the cabin in the gray, predawn light to one of the tents and shook the shoulder of one of the men sleeping there.

Pat raised himself up on one elbow, shook his head to clear the sleep from it, then asked, "What's wrong, Cap'n?"

"Sssh," Guy whispered, "I don't want to wake up the other men. Step outside."

The two men walked a distance from the cluster of tents, Pat running his fingers through his tossed hair, his baggy long johns hanging loosely on his huge frame. Guy turned to him and said, "I'm going to have to leave camp today. I'm putting you in charge. I'm taking Anne back to Gen. Jack's headquarters."

"A-taking her back?" the Irishman asked in surprise. "But why?"

Guy wondered briefly if he should tell Pat the truth, then decided that it would be pointless to try and make up some illness. The men knew that he and Anne were lovers, and lying to them would cheapen their relationship. "Anne had a miscarriage last night. She lost a lot of blood. Hell, she almost died!"

"Ah, Cap'n, 'tis sorry I am to hear it," Pat said with genuine sincerity. "Poor, little lass. An' I guess that explains why ye look like hell yerself."

Guy felt like he had been to hell and back. Nothing he had ever done had left him feeling so drained, so exhausted, neither working on the railroad nor any of his long rides back to the lines during the war when he went for days on end without sleep. But the ordeal wasn't over yet, not until he had Anne someplace where someone could take proper care of her. "It's going to take her quite a while to recover her strength, and she's so weak she'll need someone with her all the time at first. I can't do it. I've got this bridge to finish. So

I'm taking her back to Big Bertha. Do you know her?"

Pat laughed. "Aye. Everyone on the U.P. railroad knows that tough redhead. I'd rather tangle with a fierce she-bear than her any day. But ye're right, Cap'n. The lass needs the healin' hand of another woman. When are ye leavin'?"

"As soon as I cook us some breakfast and hitch the mules to the wagon. You men are going to have to fend for your own food again."

"We'll survive. But we're gonna miss the lass somethin' awful. There's nothin' like a woman to make a place seem more homelike. It's not just the cookin'. It's just the bein' there. The gentleness. The warmth. The smiles." A twinkle came into the Irishman's eyes. "Aye, an' the beatin' the tar out of ye when ye be a-needing it. Now, who else would be a-carin' when a wild bunch of no-good Irishman are a-killin' each other, unless it's a woman with a tender heart in her."

Pat turned and walked away, a dark, hulking shape fading into the gray.

Anne refused the oatmeal and toast that Guy tried to get her to eat, but to his relief, drank the cup of hot tea that he had laced with laudanum, complaining that the sugar he had put into it to mask the drug's bitter taste was too sweet. Guy didn't have any qualms about drugging her. He knew if Anne realized that he was going to take her back to Gen. Jack's headquarters she would argue with him, insisting that she would be fine in a few days and able to resume her duties as cook, and that would have been wasting energy she didn't have to expend. He knew only too well how stubborn she could be and how determined to be a success at her job.

As soon as she had fallen into a deep slumber, Guy hitched the mules to the wagon and wrapped her snugly in the blankets. Lifting her in his arms, he held her tightly against her chest and whispered, "I'm sorry, Anne. I know you're going to be furious when you find out what I've done, but it's for your own good."

Guy placed her on the pallet he had made at the back of

the wagon and crawled over the seat. The morning star was just beginning to fade, and the sun was just tinting the eastern horizon in soft mauves and pinks as they drove from the camp.

The drive to the construction headquarters seemed like an eternity to Guy. On one hand, he was worried at how still Anne was, on the other, afraid she would wake up and he'd have a fight on his hands. Since Gen. Jack had moved his headquarters up to the end of the line several times since Anne had come to Guy's camp, they rolled into the busy terminus about one-thirty that afternoon.

Big Bertha was enjoying a moment of quiet and relaxation alone in the cookhouse after the hectic preparations for the noonday meal, when she looked up and saw Guy carrying Anne up the stairs to the cookhouse. Seeing how deathly pale Anne's face was against the blanket wrapped around her and that her eyes were closed, Big Bertha dropped the cup of coffee she was drinking and slammed to her feet. "My God! She ain't dead, is she?"

Guy stepped inside the cookhouse and answered, "No, but almost."

Big Bertha supported herself by leaning on the table. Her legs were trembling badly from the fright she'd had. "What happened?"

"Is there someplace I can lay her down? Then I'll tell you everything."

Big Bertha led Guy to her sleeping quarters in one corner of the car and pushed aside the curtains. Guy walked past her and gently placed Anne on the bed. Big Bertha watched with a worried look on her face, then asked, "Is she sleeping or unconscious?"

"She's drugged," Guy answered, unwrapping the blanket around Anne and placing it over her. "I slipped some laudanum into her tea this morning so she wouldn't fight me about coming here. You know how seriously she takes her job."

Big Bertha nodded in agreement, then as Guy rose, said, "Come on. We'll go sit down at the table to talk, so we won't disturb her."

"Won't your cooks be coming back pretty soon? There's more privacy here."

"No, I told them to go on a break for an hour or so until we have to start the evening meal. They're probably down at the bar having a drink. It's about the only time they have it all to themselves. Speaking of drinks, you look like you could stand one yourself. I've got a bottle stashed away in my trunk that I've been saving for celebrating when this damn railroad is finished. It's good Kentucky whiskey, not that rotgut they sell over at the bar. I can break it open for you."

"No thanks."

"Then how about me dishing you up a plate of food? You look beat."

"No thanks, but a cup of coffee would taste good."

Big Bertha poured two cups of coffee, and they sat down on the stools at the end of the table. Guy took a couple of swallows of the hot liquid, then said, "Anne had a miscarriage. She almost bled to death. That's why I brought her back here. She's going to need someone to look after her until she regains her strength, someone that can be close by all the time for awhile."

Big Bertha shot him a sharp, questioning look. Guy looked her straight in the eye and said quietly, "Yes, it was mine. I take full blame for what happened."

If Guy expected to see any condemnation in Big Bertha's eyes, he didn't find it. If anything, the big woman was feeling a little guilty herself. She knew Anne and Guy were attracted, had deliberately sent her to him, but she hadn't expected this to happen.

"Christ, Big Bertha," Guy said, running one hand through his thick hair, "I didn't realize she was so innocent, so uninformed. She seemed so self-sufficient, so capable. I thought she knew the facts of life. But she didn't even know she was pregnant. I had to tell her when I found her doubled over with cramps and found out she had missed a few monthlies."

Big Bertha felt another twinge of guilt. "I reckon that was my fault. I knew her aunt didn't tell her nothing, but we just never got around to that part of it. I reckon she was pretty upset, losing the baby and all."

"Yes, very upset." Guy was silent for a long moment. Then he shook his head and said, "I don't know what in the hell I was thinking. I guess I thought Anne and I could just drift along indefinitely. I never even thought about children. This shocked me to my senses."

Big Bertha frowned. "What are you saying?"

"I'm saying I should have never fallen in love with Anne, that we should have never become lovers. I knew marriage was out of the question for me. I'm a railroad construction engineer. I make my living working in isolated, dangerous areas where it's unfit for a woman to live. But Anne seemed so strong, so capable, that I got to thinking it might work out after all."

"Well, maybe it would work out," Big Bertha objected.

"No, I was only fooling myself for my own selfish reasons. I wanted my career, my dream to become a great bridge engineer, and Anne, too. But it wouldn't be fair to her, constantly on the move, never having a home, having to live under the harshest conditions. Even if I set her up in a nice home back East, that wouldn't be a marriage. She deserves a real husband, someone that will be there when she needs them, not just some man popping in and out every year or so."

"Well, maybe you ought to leave that decision up to her. Maybe a home ain't all that important to her."

"A home is important to every woman. You all have strong nesting instincts. It comes second nature to you."

"Not to me, it don't. I couldn't care less."

"All right, so you're the exception to the rule, but I happen to know for a fact that Anne wants a place to put down roots, a stable place where she'll feel she belongs. Hasn't she ever told you about the restaurant she's saving her money to buy?"

A surprised expression came over Big Bertha's face. "No, she ain't never mentioned anything about a restaurant to me."

"Well, I overheard her telling one of my men. She's getting tired of wandering from pillar to post, and no wonder. That's no kind of life for a woman. It's even worse for children, being dragged all over the country. They need the security of a real home and the love and support of a full-time father." Guy paused, then said, "I had a lot of time to think while I was driving here. I considered giving up my dream and getting a job with one of the engineering firms back East. But I know I wouldn't be happy, sitting behind a desk and drawing plans. I want to be in on the actual building, right there at the construction site, and I want to build railroad bridges in challenging, impossible places. Eventually my unhappiness and discontent would spill over into our marriage, and in the end, I'd only make Anne unhappy, too."

He was probably right, Big Bertha thought. Dreams died hard, and sometimes they didn't die at all. If Guy's dream really meant that much to him, he'd always wonder if he should have given it up for Anne. If he was miserable with his lot in life, Anne would be miserable, too. "Are you gonna tell her all this?"

Guy set his coffee cup down before he answered. "No, for the same reason I didn't tell her I was bringing her here. She'd argue with me, and she simply doesn't have the strength to expend on something so futile. What has to be done, has to be done. She might think she doesn't care, that she loves me enough to make any sacrifice, but I know deep down in my heart that what I'm doing is what's best for her."

Guy rose from the stool he was sitting on, walked to the open car door, and gazed out.

"So you're just gonna walk out on her with no explanations, no nothing?" Big Bertha asked angrily.

Big Bertha's angry question cut deep. Guy knew she was reacting in Anne's behalf. What he was doing was going to hurt Anne. But she was strong. She'd get over it and him. Better a quick, clean hurt than a lifetime of misery and regretting. He turned from the door and answered, "No, I'm not that big a bastard. I thought I'd leave her a note. You can give it to her when you feel she's strong enough to take the shock. But I'm not going to tell her everything I told you. I'll tell her that I just don't think things will work out between us.

The less particulars she knows, the better."

"But she's gonna think she's just been used! That's gonna make her furious."

"I know. And then she can hate me. She'll get over it quicker that way."

"Then come back and tell it to her face."

"I can't do that." When Big Bertha just stared at him, Guy said in an anguished voice, "Christ, don't you know how this is tearing me up? I feel like a part of me is being ripped out. I've never known the happiness I've known with Anne. I don't want to give her up! And I couldn't pull it off if I had to face her. I'd back down. When it comes to her, I'm incredibly weak. Then I'd be right back to being a selfish bastard putting myself before her good. She deserves better than that."

He's already hurting, Big Bertha thought. And he'd go on hurting, probably a lot longer than Anne. She'd have her hate to sustain her, but all he'd have would be memories to haunt him. He was doing what he thought was best, but Big Bertha wasn't so sure it was the right thing. Seemed to her when two people loved each other they should be together, no matter what. Nothing was worse than losing the person you loved with your whole heart and soul. It left an emptiness that could never be filled. She knew. She'd walked that road. But it wasn't her place to interfere again. And she no longer trusted her judgment. Her interference had almost cost Anne her life. Dammit, why did life have to be so complicated?

When Guy asked if she had a pencil and a piece of paper, Big Bertha didn't argue. She watched while he labored over the brief note, then accepted it when he handed it to her and slipped it into her apron pocket. Guy rose from the table, his eyes drifting to the blanket-enclosed area where Anne was sleeping. He seemed to be fighting a silent struggle with himself, then admitted in an emotion-choked voice, "I can't go back in there to tell her good-bye. You will take good care of her?"

It was a question that both knew was unnecessary, but Big Bertha answered anyway. "Yes." She paused, then asked hopefully, "Are you sure there ain't nothing you want me to tell her?"

"No, just give her my note. I'll send her tent and things back in a day or two."

"What are you and your crew gonna do for a cook?"

"We won't be there much longer. In another week or so, we'll be finished and moving on up the line to join another bridge crew. We'll make do until then."

"Then we won't be seeing you again?"

"No. I'm going to make myself scarce."

Big Bertha stuck out her hand and said, "Well, so long then. Good luck to you." A deeply concerned look came over her face. "And you take care of yourself. You hear?"

Guy lightly shook the cook's huge hand and smiled weakly. "Don't worry about me." He dropped Big Bertha's hand, and his eyes again drifted to the back of the car. "Just take care of Anne for me."

The tears Big Bertha saw shimmering in Guy's dark eyes brought tears to her own. Then he whirled, bounded down the steps, and climbed into the wagon. He drove away in a flurry of dust, whipping the horses to a furious speed. Big Bertha knew he wasn't rushing away because he was anxious to get back to his camp, but that he was desperate to put distance between himself and Anne before he changed his mind.

Tears streamed down the big woman's face as she muttered, "You big lug. I hope to hell you know what you're doing."

Chapter Twenty-four

Anne awakened about an hour after Guy had left the camp. She looked around in a daze, then seeing Big Bertha sitting beside her, asked, "What are you doing here?"

Big Bertha smiled. "You should be asking it the other way around, honey. You should be asking, 'What am I doing here?' " Big Bertha paused, feeling a twinge of dread at having to tell Anne that Guy had tricked her, then said, "Guy brought you back to Gen. Jack's camp."

"But when?" Anne asked in confusion. "I don't remember anything."

"He drugged you. Slipped some laudanum into your tea." Seeing the furious expression come over Anne's face, Big Bertha quickly came to Guy's defense and said in a firm voice, "Now, don't you go getting mad at him. He did what was best for you. He knew you'd raise a ruckus, and he couldn't take care of you up at his camp. He's got a job to do."

"He had no right! I'll be fine in a day or two. Why, I'm fine now!"

Anne tried to sit up. Everything went spinning around her before a dark curtain fell over her eyes. When she regained consciousness, she muttered, "What happened?"

"You passed out cold there for a minute. See, honey? You're so weak you can't even sit up, much less stand up. You've lost a hell of a lot of blood. It's gonna take you awhile to recover."

"Then he told you what happened?" Anne asked, feeling suddenly shamed.

A sad look came over Big Bertha's face. "Yeah, honey," she said in a gentle voice. "I sure was sorry to hear about you losing the baby."

Anne's shame disappeared like a whiff of smoke in a strong breeze. She should have know that Big Bertha would never condemn her, that she would understand. Tears welled in her eyes and spilled down her cheeks. "I didn't even know about the baby until I was losing it. I wanted it, Big Bertha. I wanted our baby so bad. I don't know what I did wrong. I didn't lift anything heavy that day."

"Now, let's get one thing straight right now," Big Bertha said in a stern voice. "Don't you be getting any ideas in your head that it was something you did and feel guilty. These things just happen."

"Maybe there's something wrong with me," Anne said in a distraught voice, as the horrifying thought came to her. "Maybe I can't carry children."

"And don't you start thinking along those lines either! I know lots of women who have had miscarriages and did have children later. Hell, my own ma lost her first one, then had fourteen." Big Bertha took Anne's hand in her big, roughened one. "I know you're hurting, honey, and it's hard to accept. But don't go blaming yourself. It's hard enough to take without that, and there ain't no call for it. It was something you had no control over."

Big Bertha rose and said, "Now, we're gonna get you back on your feet. It's gonna take a little while though, so don't you be giving me a bad time. You can stay here until you get strong enough to fend for yourself. That way, I'll be close by in case you need me."

"But where are you going to sleep?"

"Hell, I'll throw down a pallet."

"But—"

Big Bertha silenced her by raising her hand and saying, "There you go! Arguing with me. And I just finished telling you not to give me a bad time."

"I'm not trying to give you a bad time. It's just that—"

"I know," Big Bertha interjected. "You're independent, just like me. You want to stand on your own two feet. But like it not, honey, there are times when you have to accept a little help, and this is one of them. And that's what friends are for. You'd do the same thing for me, wouldn't you?"

"Yes, of course!"

"See?"

Anne chewed her bottom lip, then said, "I suppose you're right. It's obvious I'm too weak to care for myself, and the sooner I get better, the sooner I can get back to my job at the bridge camp."

"No, honey, you ain't gonna get well that fast. It takes time to build your blood back up, and Guy said they'd be finishing up in a week or so and moving on to another bridge site with another crew."

Anne had realized that the bridge was nearing completion, but she'd never stopped to wonder if she'd still be needed as cook. Probably not, if Guy's crew was going to merge with another who already had a cook, particularly since this had happened. "Does that mean I don't have a job?" she asked in an alarm.

"No, honey, you're still working for the railroad. And we never did fill your old job. Henry and I have been doubling up and doing it. You can have it back."

Anne couldn't muster up any excitement about having her old job back, but a job was a job. She suddenly became aware of pots and pans being rattled on the other side of the blanket. "What about them?" she asked in a lowered voice, nodding her head toward where the cooks were preparing the evening meal. "What are you going to tell them about me?"

"You mean what's wrong with you? I don't reckon it's anyone's business. But you're right. They're gonna ask questions, and so is Gen. Jack." Big Bertha paused, pondering over a solution, then said, "I'll them you had a bad bout of influenza that left you so weak you can't get out of bed. That can happen, you know. I got it one winter and didn't recover until that summer. Thought I never was gonna get over it." Big Bertha grinned and said with a conspiratorial twinkle in her eyes, "And maybe you can cough every now and then, to make it look good."

It was several days before Anne could stand on her feet without passing out, and another week before she could stay up for more than a few hours without getting incredibly weak. During this time, Big Bertha fed her so much beef broth and meat that Anne feared she would pop. Bertha also poured a vile-tasting concoction down her that she claimed was her grandmother's secret tonic. Even the other cooks tried to help Anne regain her strength by preparing tempting little side dishes for her, and Henry bought her a bouquet of wildflowers, touching her deeply and making Big Bertha gape in disbelief.

Everyone showed concern for her, from the water boys to Gen. Jack, who visited several times, but Anne neither saw nor heard anything from Guy. She couldn't understand why he hadn't paid her a visit. Of all people, he should be the most concerned about her, and there wasn't that much distance between the two camps that he couldn't have made the trip. By horseback, it was only a few hours' ride, or less, considering how skilled a horseman Guy was. When two weeks had passed and he hadn't shown up, she remarked on it to Big Bertha when the two women were alone in the cookhouse.

Big Bertha wondered if Anne was strong enough to accept the shock of Guy's note. The head cook had been dreading the day she had to give it to the young woman. Deciding that *she* wasn't up to it herself quite yet, Big Bertha said, "Why, honey I imagine he and his crew have moved up the line by now. Why, he's probably in Utah. You may not realize it, but the big race is on. This railroad is almost finished, and both the C.P. and U.P. are working like mad to see who can lay the most track at the end. Why, he's probably so busy he ain't got time to turn around."

Anne did know that the railroad was almost finished and that both companies were working at a feverish pace to lay as much track as they could. Gen. Jack had told her on one of his visits. For the directors of the companies it was a matter of money. Every mile of rail bought sixteen thousand dollars in government subsidiaries to the company on flat ground and forty-eight thousand dollars in the mountains. For the men working for the railroads, it was a much more personal matter. A fierce competitiveness had risen between Crocker's Chinese Pets and Gen. Jack's Irish Tarriers, each side determined that they would prove themselves the better men. "I know all of that," Anne answered irritably. "But Guy was bound to have had a few hours before he left. He could have come to see me then, particularly if he knew it was going to be some time before we saw one another again, or he could have sent some kind of word to me. There are supply trains going back and forth from this camp and the outlying ones all the time."

Big Bertha could see where her delaying action wasn't going to work. The time to give Anne Guy's note had come, whether she herself was ready for it or not. She took a deep breath, pasted an innocent expression on her face, and said, "Well, by golly, now that you mention it, he did leave you a note before he left here that day, but I plumb forgot about it."

Anne's heart raced in excitement. "Where is it?"

"I put it in one of my apron pockets." Big Bertha rose from the stool she was sitting on beside the big table. "Give me a minute, and I'll see if I can find it."

Big Bertha walked into her sleeping quarters in the corner of the car and returned a moment later with the note in her hand. Hoping Anne couldn't see the dread she was desperately trying to hide, she handed it to the young woman.

Anne read the note. Big Bertha watched as her expression turned from excited happiness to puzzlement. Big Bertha felt like a heel, but she didn't want Anne to realize that she had known all along the terrible news. In the first place, Guy had told her he didn't want Anne to know his real reasons for walking out on her, and Big Bertha felt that to tell Anne the truth would be breaking his confidence. In the second place, Big Bertha didn't want Anne getting angry at her for keeping the news from her. Then Anne would feel betrayed by her as well as Guy, and the young woman was going to need a friend to lean on. "What's the matter, honey?" Big Bertha asked, hoping she looked innocent, but feeling guilty as hell. "You look baffled."

"I am," Anne answered in a dazed voice. "He said the miscarriage had made him do some serious thinking, that he doesn't think things would work out for us, that he thinks we should go our separate ways from now on and not see each other again. I don't understand. I know he loves me. I *know* it!" Anne ended in an anguished voice.

Big Bertha struggled for something to say that wouldn't give Anne false hope. "Well, honey, I hate to say it, but men are strange creatures. You never know what they're gonna do. Maybe it's for the best."

"But I love him!"

Big Bertha's heart went out to the young woman. She took Anne in her arms and muttered, "I know, honey. I know." To the head cook, her words sounded terribly lame, but for the life of her, Big Bertha couldn't think of another thing to say that would comfort Anne. She had never felt so helpless or so utterly useless in her entire life.

Anne was still in a state of shock when Gen. Jack moved his factory up the line the next day. She had read Guy's note over and over, and was no closer to understanding why he had said what he had than first time she had read it. Could someone stop loving another, just in the snap of a finger? she wondered. And what had her miscarriage to do with it? Did he only want her when she was strong and healthy, did her suddenly being dependent upon him make him see her as an unwanted burden? Then why had he been so kind to her that night, so caring? Was it guilt that had motivated him? Over and over the questions flew through her mind as the train sped over the newly laid rails.

As the train raced down the line, she got a glimpse through the thick woods of two cabins sitting in a clearing beside the track, a large and a smaller one. She recognized that abandoned camp even before the train raced across the beautiful bridge that spanned the deep gorge. The memories of her time with Guy came rushing back, and a terrible pain welled up inside her, then spilled over as the tears finally came. It was over between them, she realized. Guy had walked out on her, putting his back to her just when she needed him the most. A fierce anger came to her defense. Damn him! she thought. She had let him make a fool out of her, not once, but twice. She had stupidly fallen for all of his smooth talk, his vows of caring. He didn't give a damn about her. He had just been using her again, and then tossed her away as callously as if she were an old rag. He didn't take her back to Big Bertha because he was concerned for her. It had only been a handy opportunity to get rid of her, so he could cowardly slink away while she was still drugged. The treacherous bastard! She hated him! But she hated herself even more. She should have stuck to her vow to keep their relationship strictly business. She didn't need him then, and she didn't need him now. She was perfectly capable of taking care of herself. She didn't need Guy—or any man—cluttering up her life.

Over the next week, Anne threw herself into her work, as she had before when Guy had hurt her. But this wound was much deeper, and there was too much time to think. Her job of baking pies was incredibly boring and took no mental concentration. She had done the task so often that it came automatically, and she could have performed it in her sleep. The evenings were even worse, for no matter how exhausted she was, she couldn't stop herself from remembering, as she lay in her lonely, empty bed, the same bed that she and Guy had shared.

In the end it was her writing that was Anne's salvation. She resumed her journal on the railroad, telling of her experiences in the bridge camp (again making no mention of Guy), then keeping a day-to-day account of her activities. But even that couldn't keep her mind busy. She began hounding the other cooks for stories they knew of the building of the railroad, then questioned Gen. Jack, who provided her with a wealth of information. She planned her writing during the daytime while she was baking, then wrote everything down the same night.

Soon her growing journal became more than just a means to keep her mind occupied. It took on a life of its own. She hounded everyone for stories, from the water boys to the trackmen, and it was from the rough construction men that she gained the stories of exciting, sometimes humorous happenings that had occurred in the Hell on Wheels towns that were forbidden territory for her. When the Tarriers learned that she was writing a history of the building of the railroad, they held back nothing, and she discovered that they had a knack for story telling that rivaled their remarkable singing ability. Through their lips, the gamblers, the pimps, the outlaws, the pitiful drunkards, the aimless drifters, even the whores, took on a lifelike quality, and those chapters were filled with rough and tumble fistfights, terrifying gun duels, tense card games that lasted far into the night, as well as unbelievably funny and terribly sad tales.

Still Anne wasn't satisfied. She branched out, seeking stories from the engineers, the firemen, even a conductor who had come to the end of the line to see the exciting work being done. From them, she not only gained new information on the building of the transcontinental railroad, but exciting stories from their experiences on other railroads: terrifying tales of derailments, runaway trains, attacks by bandits, exploding boilers, blizzards and avalanches that buried entire trains. She came to realize that those who worked on railroads were an incredibly hardy and brave lot of men, who had their own superstitions and their own growing folklore. They were one and all a group of hard-drinking, hard-fighting, tough men who shared a brotherhood of sorts, an esprit de corps that bound them as close as any family, and that brotherhood extended to the few females among them. For Anne, who had never had any strong sense of family, that was every one a heartwarming revelation. For the first time in her life, she felt she belonged. The railroad was firmly entrenched in her blood, and its people were her people.

The U.P. reached Sherman Summit, Wyoming, 8,200 feet above sea level. General Dodge telegraphed the directors of the C.P., boasting that while the C.P. had transversed the Sierras, the U.P. had crossed the highest point of either railroad. The competition between the two companies was even fiercer than before, each pushing their men to their limits in order to get to Utah first and get the edge on the Mormon's lucrative business. One day the Tarriers laid eight miles of track, an unheard-of record. Farther west, a U.P. bridge crew was driving fifteen-hundred feet of piles into the Bear River. The bridge was completed in a week, yet another seemingly impossible feat.

Stories began to drift back to Gen. Jack's camp at Grouse Creek. The graders of the two rivaling companies had met. The work had come to a standstill as the Irishmen and Chinese had looked at one another. Each race decided they didn't like the looks of the other. The Chinese pushed a big boulder down over their embankments onto the Tarriers working below. The next day a blast of U.P. powder shot into the air, taking a few Chinese with it. The Chinese returned evil for evil. The two groups had declared open warfare. Not only did they blast the other without warning, but there were several times when the two broke ranks and met in open combat, slinging fists, picks, and shovels.

On April 7th, Gen. Jack's rolling factory made its last move through the Rockies. It was the most beautiful ride that Anne had taken yet. Here the mountains lifted snow-covered, jagged peaks above deep gorges and leaping waterfalls, and enclosed flowered meadows that were carpeted with a rainbow of wildflowers. They sped through dark tunnels and crept around roadbeds that hugged the mountainsides over terrifying drops to the purpled valleys far below, then raced onto the Utah flatlands and flew across the new bridge over Bear River. There, on the west bank of the river, they came to a stop, and Corinne, a new Hell on Wheels town, sprung up beside them.

Shortly after they settled down in their new camp, General Jack came lumbering up the stairs of the bakery one day, and seeing Anne and Big Bertha, said in a booming voice, "Well, there you are. I've been looking all over for you ladies."

Big Bertha cocked her head suspiciously. Since when did the big ape call her a lady? she wondered. "What do you want?" she asked curtly.

"I have a gentleman here I want to introduce to you two." He turned and said to someone standing at the foot of the stairs, "Come on up, Phil. They're in here."

A tall, pleasant-looking, sandy-haired young man walked up the stairs. "Ladies, this is Phil Johnson. He's a reporter for the *New York Times*. He didn't know that the railroad hired any woman cooks, and he'd like to interview you."

There were reporters from the East swarming all over the place, but none had paid any attention to Anne or Big Bertha. Big Bertha thought it high time someone took notice of them. After all, they had done their part in building this railroad, too, and she highly resented seeing all of the glory go to the construction crews. "Well, it's about time one of you reporters asked us something," she said bluntly. "It may come as a surprise to you, but we cooks work twice as hard as those big apes out there. What do you want to know, young feller?"

Phil's blue eyes twinkled with amusement. He pulled out his notebook and pencil. "First of all, your names."

"Well, I'm Big Bertha and this is Anne Phillips."

"Bertha what?" Phil asked, his pencil poised in the air.

"My last name don't matter. Everyone just calls me Big Bertha, and I reckon that's what you ought to call me, too.

Otherwise, nobody is gonna know who you're talking about."

As Phil asked questions, Big Bertha answered them with enthusiasm. Anne, however, was reluctant to give much information, particularly personal information. Phil was vastly disappointed. He had been shocked to step into the car and find a beautiful young woman standing there. And it soon became obvious that she wasn't a rough, backwoods woman like Big Bertha. Her voice was soft-spoken, and there was a sadness about her striking hazel eyes that gave her beauty a haunting quality. He was immediately attracted to her, and wanted to get to know her better.

Over the next several days, Phil came to the bakery often, using the excuse that he just dropped in for a visit with the two ladies. Big Bertha knew better. It wasn't her that he was coming to see, but Anne. The good-looking, personable reporter couldn't keep his eyes off of the younger woman. However, Big Bertha wasn't adverse to his calls, even if they did interrupt their work. He always had something interesting to relate.

One day, as soon as Phil had sat down, Big Bertha asked, "Well, where have you been snooping around today?"

Phil chuckled and answered, "I told you, Big Bertha, I don't snoop. I look around, ask questions, then report what I've seen and heard."

"Yeah, well that's what I call snooping, but I didn't mean it as an insult. Where did you go today?"

"Over to Junction City."

"I've heard of that place. It's supposed to be one of the worst Hell on Wheels towns that's popped up yet. You better be careful nosing around there."

"Yes, it's a rough one, but I didn't go to visit the town. I went to see the grading camps. Believe me, that valley where they sit is a lot more dangerous than any Hell on Wheels town. Both the U.P. and C.P. are lifting whole ledges of limestone from the Promontory Mountains there, and hurling them hundreds of feet in the air, scattering rock and debris for half a mile in every direction. And they still aren't warning each other when they're going to blast. To make matters even worse, the U.P. is using homemade nitroglycerin, and that stuff is dangerous as hell even under the best of conditions. There have been many unnecessary accidents. I've heard the federal government is getting alarmed about the situation and is considering stepping in and setting a point for the two railroads to meet."

"Well, maybe it would be for the best," Big Bertha commented. "Before those Irish apes and Chinese monkeys all kill each other." She paused, then asked, "Did you hear about Crocker boasting that his Pets could beat the Tarriers record for laying more track in one day?"

"It's gone past just boasting. He says he's going to prove his Chinese can lay ten miles of track in one day. Thomas Durant bet him ten thousand dollars he can't do it. Crocker accepted the bet and has picked the spot and the day. He's invited U.P. officials to come and watch the expedition. Of course, all of us reporters are invited to watch, too."

"Well, you're gonna be in for a big disappointment," Big Bertha responded. "Those little Chinamen can't begin to lay track the way our men can. When it comes to building railroads, the U.P. has got it all over the C.P. Crocker is gonna make a jackass out of himself."

The big day arrived, and every one in the U.P. camp anxiously awaited news of how Crocker's Pets had fared. No one thought the Chinese could possibly break their record of eight miles in one day. When the news was finally telegraphed backed after darkness had set, there was a stunned silence in the camp. The Chinese had laid an unbelievable ten miles and fifty-six feet of track in eighteen grueling hours! The news had a terribly demoralizing effect on the Tarriers, for word had already arrived a few days previously that the Federal Commission had set the meeting place at Promontory Point, less than ten miles away from the U.P. end of the line. The Tarriers knew they would never get the chance to try and break the new record.

The next day when Phil came to visit, Big Bertha said, "Well, I guess you came to rub our noses in those Chinamen breaking our record."

"No, it was a remarkable feat, but not quite as remarkable as it sounds," Phil answered. "Crocker had been getting ready for the expedition for a week. All the ties were there beforehand. All he had to do was lay rails. But the U.P. still lost their bet."

"Well, I wish Crocker had issued his challenge sooner. That way we may have had a chance to break his Pets' record. Hell, if we had sleepers already laid, we could lay twelve miles of track in a day."

Fortunately Phil knew that "sleepers" were what the railroad people called ties, or he might had been confused by Big Bertha's boast. "I'm afraid U.P. is going to have all they can do to reach Promontory Point by May 10th. They still have a tremendous amount of grading to do. They should have accepted C.P.'s offer of their grading behind the U.P. lines, particularly that fill the C.P. made over that deep gorge halfway up the east slope of the Promontory Mountains. Building that big trestle there cost the U.P. a lot of valuable time."

"We don't want their grading!" Anne said hotly, surprising Phil, for she rarely said anything around him. "We've built this railroad this far without their help. We don't need it or want it. We don't want anything from them!"

"That's right!" Big Bertha chimed in. "It'd be just like them to say we could have never finished it without their help, the sneaky bastards. Why, it would surprise me if Crocker didn't deliberately wait until the meeting point was set to issue his challenge. Seems to me a little suspicious that those ten miles cut us just short of coming back and beating his record. But we'll show him, and everyone else on the C.P. We'll get to Promontory Summit before they do, come hell or high water. You mark my words."

"I sincerely hope so, Big Bertha," Phil answered. "As a reporter, I'm supposed to remain unbiased, but as a man

I've been secretly rooting for the U.P. ever since I met you ladies."

Big Bertha thought she knew why. The reporter was smitten with Anne and wanted to see her happy. She wasn't in the least surprised when he turned to the young woman and said, "I'm going to take a drive over to Salt Lake City. It seems ridiculous to come all this way and not even see the Mormons' biggest city. It will be an all-day excursion, and I'd love to have your company."

Anne knew that Phil was attracted to her. Despite the fact that it helped soothe her battered ego, she had deliberately kept her distance. She wanted nothing further to do with any man. "Thank you, but I don't think so. I have work to do."

"Nonsense!" Big Bertha said to Anne, butting in. "You've said time and time again that you'd love to see the city. This is a perfect opportunity for you. Now you two go ahead. I'll take care of any work on this end."

Anne could have kicked Big Bertha. It was true that she had said she would love to see Salt Lake City. Her journal seemed incomplete without something in it about the flourishing city the Mormons had built in the middle of a desert. And she didn't dare take off on her own, not without a man to protect her. Besides, she'd probably get lost. But she had gone to all of this trouble to discourage Phil, and now Big Bertha was throwing her at him.

Seeing her hesitate, Phil said, "I'd consider it a privilege if you'd accompany me. We can make a visit to the Great Salt Lake, too. I've seen it, but it's something everyone should see. It's the biggest inland lake in the West, you know."

Anne suddenly remembered why she had come West, to see new and exciting things, and here she was foolishly turning down an opportunity to do just that. Phil posed no threat to her. Oh, if she had met him before Guy, he might have appealed to her greatly. He was a nice-looking, pleasant, well-traveled young man who was a very interesting conversationalist. And he was a gentleman to the bone. She knew he wouldn't make any improper advances.

"Well, are two gonna go, or do I have to boot you outta here?" Big Bertha asked impatiently.

Anne laughed and said, "Well, it looks like I'm going. I'd be a fool to turn down a day off when my boss absolutely insists on it."

As the two drove away shortly thereafter, Big Bertha watched them and smiled. Anne deserved a holiday, and maybe Phil was just what she needed to get over Guy. Oh, Anne had bounced back remarkably well, but Big Bertha knew that deep down there was an emptiness inside her. Big Bertha had never found a man to fill the void that the loss of her husband had caused her, had never looked for another very hard, but Anne was a different kind of a woman. Big Bertha was content with just her independence, but for Anne that would never be enough. There were some women who just weren't whole without a man to love and to love them in return. They needed that giving and taking, that sharing, like the flowers needed the sun and the rain, and Anne was one of those women.

Chapter Twenty-five

Almost from the moment they drove away, Anne didn't regret her decision to go with Phil. He kept a lively conversation going, telling her fascinating little facts that he had unearthed about the country they were passing through.

As they followed Bear River, he said, "This is one of the most amazing rivers I've ever seen. It starts in the Unita Mountains in the far northeast corner of Utah, and twists and turns for five hundred miles to cover a distance that would be only ninety as the crow flies. At one place it makes a lake, and there have been recent sightings of a huge sea serpent in it, reputed to be ninety-feet long."

"Do you actually believe that?" Anne asked.

"I didn't when I went to investigate. But after talking to some of the people who had seen it, I'm not so sure it doesn't exist. They were clearly terrified. I kept hoping it would make an appearance that day, but it didn't."

When they reached the point where the Bear River emptied into the Great Salt Lake, Anne gazed out in wonder. She had never seen such a large lake. She couldn't even see the other side of it. There was a fair wind that day that kicked up good-sized waves on it, and then hearing a cawing coming from above her, she looked up and asked in amazement, "Are those sea gulls?"

"Yes."

"But how did they get out here, way in the middle of nowhere? There's not an ocean for hundreds of miles from here."

"I assume they've always been here. The Great Salt Lake is supposed to be what is left of an ancient inland sea. The

Mormons revere the gulls, and have a strict rule against anyone killing them. It seems that shortly after they had settled here, their crops were threatening by hordes of crickets. Then, out of the blue, the sea gulls came from the lake and ate the crickets, thereby saving the crops. Since their entire venture to settle this land would have been destroyed without those crops, the Mormons considered it nothing short of a miracle."

"Is the lake really salty?" Anne asked.

"Yes, it is, so salty that nothing can sink in it. Of course, fish can't live in it either. The Bear River and Blue Creek are the only two streams that empty into it, and they can't sustain it. Every year a little more of it evaporates, so that it's slowly shrinking. On the other side of the lake you can see the evidence of this happening. That's where the great salt desert is. It's fifty miles of nothing but hard-packed salt, the glare from the sun reflecting on the white flats so strong it hurts your eyes, with not a drop of water to be found, and littered with broken-down wagons and the bleached bones of those who didn't make it."

They drove away from the lake across the dry, alkaline flats. Then they started passing through cultivated areas, but the green plants that were just sprouting were too small for Anne to recognize. "What grows here?"

"Mostly grain, and on the irrigated land, sugar beets and cotton. I seriously doubt that anyone but the Mormons could have made this desert the productive land it is now. But they were desperate. They had to succeed. They had been chased from civilization because of their religious beliefs and had nowhere else to go. That's why Brigham Young, their leader, chose this land for their home. It was an arid, alkaline land that no one else wanted."

They passed Mormon farm cabins, cotton mills, sugar factories, and irrigation canals, then drove through an area that was uncultivated where the cactus, sagebrush, and creosote was covered with a thin coating of alkaline dust. Seeing a pile of bleached bones, a shiver ran over Anne as she asked, "Do you think they're human?"

"No, there're too big. They're probably oxen. One of the

oldest wagon train trails to California passes through here. In the days of the gold rush, the towns in this valley were the last stop the forty-niners could make to stock up on provisions before crossing the Sierras, a trade that turned out to be quite profitable for the Mormons."

Anne smiled. "With the railroad coming, there won't be anymore wagon trains."

"No, probably not," Phil agreed. "The railroad is going to change the West forever."

"You don't sound very happy about it," Anne remarked.

"Don't get me wrong. It's not that I'm against progress. But I kind of hate to see it come to this land. It means the last of the great buffalo herds, the last of wagon trains, the last of old mountain men, the last of the Indians, the last of those rugged pioneers that blazed the trails through the wilderness. It's sad in a way."

Anne laughed. "Well, the West is hardly going to get tamed overnight."

Phil chuckled. "That's true. The West has a lot of wild and woolly years left. Why, it will probably take a good fifty years or more to civilize it, and then I'll bet there will still be areas out here that will remain unchanged, remote areas that are too rugged to be reached by roads of any kind."

Salt Lake City sat between the Great Salt Lake and a smaller lake known as Utah Lake, along a stream the Mormons had named the Jordan River. The city was laid out in great blocks that were ten acres square, and had wide streets lined with shops and homes that were mostly made of stone. They stopped where the Mormon Tabernacle was being built and watched for a while.

"I understand Young designed it, but it's being built by Henry Grow, a bridge builder," Phil informed Anne.

"A bridge builder?" she asked in surprise. "Why would he have a man who builds bridges construct a tabernacle?"

"Young wants it to have perfect acoustics for the choir he's founded. Maybe Grow was the only man who appreciated how the Mormon leader felt and thought he could give it to him."

Anne remembered Guy had said he wanted his bridge to

be perfect. If Grow was as talented, as committed to grace and beauty as well as utility, she thought she could understand Young picking him. The thought caught her by surprise, but she couldn't take it back. No matter how she felt about Guy personally, she couldn't deny that he was an extremely talented engineer.

They left the Tabernacle and the Great Temple, which was also in the process of being built, and a while later passed by a large building that Phil identified as the Salt Lake Theater. "But I thought the Mormons were a very strict people, like the Puritans," Anne objected.

"No, they practice temperance in that they don't use tea, coffee, tobacco, strong drink, or profanity, but they love music and dancing and drama. And they don't run from a fight either, as the government found out when they tried to expel them from Missouri. They fought back to defend their homes and their right to practice religious freedom, until a state of civil war actually existed. The climax came when a company of militia murdered twenty Mormons. The Mormon leaders, including Young, were arrested on charges of treason, murder, arson, burglary, robbery, larceny, and perjury, an utterly ridiculous list of charges. They were kept in prison without trial for months under terrible sufferings. The government knew it couldn't possibly convict them on the charges that were made against them. In a fit of anger, the governor of the state had literally thrown the book at them. To save face, he permitted them to escape."

Phil drove down one street, then another, then another. Seeing him crane his neck to look around, Anne asked, "Are you looking for something in particular?"

"Yes, the Lion House, Brigham Young's home. I understand it has so many gables on it you can't miss it."

"Then that long stone house up there must be it. I've never seen so many little gables on a house. Each room seems to have one!"

"Yes, I've been told that each of his wives' rooms is marked with a gable."

"How many wives does he have?"

"It's rumored to be twenty-seven."

"Why, that's outrageous!"

"Yes, it's the Mormons' practice of polygamy that has aroused so much public outrage against them and been one of the major reasons for them being so persecuted. Actually very few ever practiced polygamy, and back in '62 when Congress passed a law against it, many Mormons who did have more than one wife were disfranchised and imprisoned. When Young still refused to proclaim against it, the Corporation of the Church of Jesus Christ of the Latter Day Saints was dissolved and its property confiscated. That seems to be a favorite way for the government to punish them, taking away their wealth, but as you can see, they're still here and they're still working on their temple and tabernacle, and Young is still governor of the territory and still has his wives."

"Then why doesn't the government remove him as governor?"

"They tried that once, back in the fifties. Young issued a proclamation forbidding U.S. troops in Utah. When they came, 30,000 Mormons evacuated their homes and cities and prepared to move on. It panicked the federal government. Pres. Buchanan knew that Utah would revert back to a useless desert if they left, and one of the major trails to California would wither and die. They backed down, and Young was reinstated as governor. Then when the Civil War came, he surprised everyone and sided with the Union, proving his loyalty to the federal government despite all of the bitter, bloody disputes he'd had with them over the years." Phil paused briefly, his expression thoughtful, then said, "It's a shame the Mormons persist in holding the practice of polygamy. They're a hard-working, thrifty people whose amazing industry should rightfully bring them public respect, and Young is a genius when it comes to colonizing. But he insists that its matter of religious beliefs, and not legality. It leaves the federal government with only one remaining method of punishing them, refusing them statehood."

"How did you come to know so much about the Mormons and their history?" Anne asked him curiously.

"I've been talking to them as well as the railroad people. The more I learned, the more I came to realize that they have been a very misunderstood people."

Phil's information put an entirely different light on the Mormons for Anne, too. She had always thought of their refusal to give up what she considered an immoral practice as pure stubbornness. But if they really and truly believed that they were defending their right to religious freedom, had borne and were still bearing persecution, she had to admit to a grudging admiration for them.

They ate at a small restaurant in Salt Lake City before making the return trip to Corinne, this time passing through Ogden, Utah's second-largest city and named for the fur trapper who founded it long before the Mormons arrived on the scene. From there they followed the U.P. tracks to Corinne. The sun was setting, making the Great Salt Lake in the distance look like a band of burnished silver and throwing long azure shadows over the valley they were passing through.

As they rode, Phil asked, "How did you come to work for the railroad, Anne?"

Anne laughed. "You asked me that once before."

"Yes, and you never answered me. I'm not asking as a reporter this time. I'm just curious."

"I came with my brother, who had been hired as an engineer. We were under the mistaken notion that the railroad provided living quarters for their employees' families. When we found out differently, my brother wanted me to go back East, but by then I was so enthralled with the exciting things going on out here that I refused and hired on, too."

"Then you have a brother out here?"

"No, he was killed in a blasting accident."

Phil heard the hint of sadness in Anne's voice. "I'm sorry to hear that."

"It was a long time ago, or at least it seems like it was."

"But you stayed on?" Phil asked in amazement.

"Yes. By then seeing this railroad completed had become a very personal thing."

Phil smiled. "A month ago I wouldn't have been able to understand that answer, but I do now. With every railroad person I've talked to, it's the same. For them, it's not just a job, a livelihood. Seeing this railroad completed has become a personal challenge, and each and everyone of them seems to feel an ownership for it. The railroad bigwigs may thing it belongs to them, but in essence it belongs to the railroad people, those who built it and run it. I've never known any business enterprise where the employees take such a possessive interest, where they show such pride in their accomplishments, where they have so much loyalty to one another. There's a certain spirit amongst railroad people that I can feel, but eludes me when I try to put it down on paper."

Anne smiled. She knew only too well what Phil was trying to say. It was that railroad brotherhood, a sense of belonging that extended not only to the members that made up their unique family, but to every tie, every rail, every station house, every locomotive, everything associated with the railroad. And why not? The railroad itself was that family's home, their pride and their joy.

It was well after dark when Phil drove the wagon up to Anne's tent and came to a stop. After helping her down, he followed her to the tent door. There Anne turned and said, "Thank you for taking me. I really enjoyed the entire day."

"I did, too," Phil answered softly.

When he took Anne in his arms and kissed her, she wasn't particularly surprised. His lips were warm and questing, a pleasant kiss, but nothing more. There was no fire, none of the wild excitement that she had always felt when Guy kissed her. There wasn't even a tingle of warmth.

When Anne didn't respond, Phil broke the kiss and stepped back. "You didn't feel anything, did you?" he asked softly, in obvious disappointment.

"No. I'm sorry, but I didn't."

"I'm sorry, too. I had hoped you might be a little attracted to me. But I hope it won't keep us from being friends."

When Anne made no comment, Phil said, "I'm a lonely man faraway from home. You don't know how much I enjoyed your company today, having someone to talk to, to share my explorations. I'd like very much to do it again."

Anne had enjoyed the day, too, and it would be silly to refuse Phil's offer of friendship. He was an intelligent young man whose company was stimulating, if not exciting. And she knew—even more so now—that she was in no danger of falling in love with him. She felt a little pang of regret. It seemed a shame that he had come into her life too late.

Anne smiled a little sadly and answered, "I see no reason why we can't be friends."

Chapter Twenty-six

The next day, Gen. Jack moved his rolling factory to the end of the line. The following morning, Anne looked up from her pies and saw Phil standing there.

"What are you doing here so early?" she asked. "I told you I only get Saturday afternoons off."

"I had nothing to do today, so I came early. I thought maybe we could decide where we're going to go today, while you're finishing up."

"Wherever you choose will be fine with me."

Phil heard the slight hint of annoyance in Anne's voice. "I'm interrupting your work, aren't I?"

"Well, to be perfectly honest with you, I can get done a lot faster if I don't have anyone distracting me. Why don't you wait . . ." Anne hesitated. She hated to say outside. Friends should be treated with more hospitality ". . . in my tent?"

"If you don't mind, I don't." He turned, saying over his shoulder, "See you in a few hours."

When Anne walked into her tent, she found Phil sitting on the side of her bed and reading her journal. She walked across the tent, jerked it from his hands, and said angrily, "How dare you! How dare you snoop into my personal things!"

Phil rose and said, "I wasn't snooping, Anne. It was sitting here on the bed, and I just picked it up and started leafing through it out of boredom. It's not like it's a diary, or something. It didn't seem all that personal. Then I got so fascinated with it, I couldn't put it down."

"Well, it's personal to me. Something very private."

Phil frowned. "It shouldn't be, Anne. Everyone should have the opportunity to read it. Like I said, it's a fascinating collection of amazing stories. I'd like to see it published."

"Now you're making fun of me."

"No, I'm dead serious."

Seeing she was still doubtful, Phil said, "Anne, I'm a trained journalist, and I do know something about writing. You've got a natural knack for it. Your descriptions are so vivid and your characters so real, that I felt I was right there with them. I'd like to send it to my editor."

"But it's not a novel. They're just railroad stories."

"Precisely, and right now the public back East is going crazy over anything about railroads. The building of this transcontinental line has fired their imaginations and honed their craving for excitement. Why do you think there are so many reporters out here? We can't give them enough. The entire country has railroad fever. It's almost become a mania with them. But this journal is full of exciting stories that none of us have ever heard, not just stories about this railroad, but railroads in general. Do you remember me telling you that railroad people had a certain spirit that eluded me when I tried to put it down on paper? Well, you've captured it, Anne, and you did it because you're one of them. Please, let me send it to my editor."

"I didn't write it to have it published."

"Maybe not, but it would be a crime not to publish it. You've been out here, you've experienced all the exciting things happening, but there are others who aren't that fortunate, people who long for excitement and adventure and can only find it in reading. Do you really feel justified in denying them? Is it so terribly personal that you can't share it with others?"

Put in that light, it did make Anne feel a little selfish. But she was still hesitant. "It's not finished. It won't be until the last rail is lain."

"You can send that story in later if my editor decides to buy. And, Anne, I really think there's a good chance of it. I have a strong feeling that he's going to be as fascinated as I was."

Phil waited patiently while Anne worried her bottom lip in indecision. Aware of his steady eyes on her, she finally consented with little enthusiasm, "Well, all right then. I suppose it won't hurt."

Phil laughed and said, "You're unbelievable, Anne. Most people would be tickled to death to get something published."

"I suppose it is thrilling, but I just don't happen to think that it's good enough to publish."

"Well, I don't agree." He took the journal from her hands and said, "I'd like to get to it my editor as soon as possible. I have a colleague going back to New York this afternoon. I'm sure he'll deliver it for me. That way it can be on my editor's desk in just a few days." Phil laughed. "But you can be sure I'm not going to tell my friend what it is, for fear he'll try to steal it. He's from a rival newspaper. I'll wrap it up in plain brown paper good and tight. Hell, for all he'll know, it could be books I'm sending back, or dirty laundry."

"Then you're going to take it right now?"

"Yes, if you don't mind us skipping our excursion this afternoon, I'd like to get it back before his train pulls out. Then I can telegraph my editor and tell him to be on the watch for it."

"But shouldn't it be rewritten? It's kind of messy in places."

"I didn't have any trouble reading it, and I'm sure my editor won't either." He turned and started walking toward the tent opening, saying, "I've got an interview set up for tomorrow, but I'll see you Monday."

Anne watched in dismay as Phil pushed back the canvas flap and he and her journal disappeared. She felt as if she had just said good-bye to an old, dear friend that she might never see again.

True to his word, Phil returned the next Monday afternoon. He found Anne and Big Bertha in the cookhouse, and as soon as he stepped into the car, he asked, "What's all the excitement about? I've never seen this camp in such a frenzy of activity."

"Of all the dad-blasted times for you to come snooping

around, why did it have to be today?" Big Bertha asked him curtly.

Seeing the stunned expression on Phil's face, Anne quickly came to his defense. "You should be ashamed of yourself, Big Bertha. Phil isn't going to go back and tell anyone on the C.P. what's going on here. Just because he's a reporter doesn't mean he breaks confidences."

Phil's reporter's curiosity overrode any hurt feelings he might have had at Big Bertha's almost rude brusqueness. He smelled a story. A big one. An almost avid expression came over his face. "What's going on?"

"Gen. Jack got wind that the C.P. is going to extend its temporary spur into a complete siding at Promontory Summit tomorrow, so they can claim the historic site as a C.P. terminal," Anne informed him.

"Yes, I heard rumors to that effect. Some of my fellow reporters said they were going to go over to the C.P. lines tomorrow, to see if there was in any truth in it."

"Well, Gen. Jack said he ain't gonna let them steal it from us," Big Bertha said hotly. "We're going to get our own siding there first."

"But you don't even have a temporary spur to extend," Phil objected, "and there's just a few hours of daylight left."

A big grin came over Big Bertha's face. "We ain't gonna stop at sunset. We're gonna keep building all night."

"In the dark?" Phil asked in disbelief.

"We've got plenty of lanterns and lots of coal oil to make torches from," Big Bertha answered.

As Phil turned and rushed down the stairs, Big Bertha yelled, "Where are you going? Back to tell those nosy friends of yours?"

Phil turned and laughed. "I'm not going anywhere. A team of wild horses couldn't pull me away from the U.P. lines today. I've got an exclusive story here. Who knows? Maybe it will turn out so good that I won't look so bad to my editor up against Anne."

As Phil hurried off, Big Bertha asked, "What in the hell is he talking about, up against *you?*"

"Phil talked me into letting him send my journal to his editor. He's got some crazy idea that his newspaper might publish it."

"Why, honey, that's the most wonderful news I've ever heard! Ain't you just thrilled to death?"

Anne had tried not to get excited about it, but it was hard to do. The more she thought about it after Phil had left, the more thrilled she had become. She had finally had to take herself firmly in hand. "I don't want to get my hopes up and then be disappointed. Phil is my friend. He's probably prejudiced. Besides, there are all kinds of stories going in now about railroads from professional writers, and I'm not even what you could call an amateur writer. I'm just someone who scribbles things down on paper to have something to do with my spare time."

"Well, even if they don't publish it, it was a big compliment. Phil ain't no amateur."

"Yes, it was one of the nicest compliments I've ever had," Anne admitted.

All during the night, the U.P. crews worked laying ties and rail at a feverish pitch. Anne, Big Bertha, and the other cooks kept a steady stream of hot coffee and sandwiches going out to the end of the rail to sustain their energy. By dawn, they still had half a mile to complete, but since the C.P. was nowhere in sight, they kept building. As soon as the siding was finished, Gen. Jack had his rolling factory pulled up and placed on it, and then ordered a one-room station house quickly thrown up. When the C.P. engine came puffing up the line, its flat cars loaded down with rails and pig-tailed trackmen, the U.P. crews were waiting for them. As the astonished C.P. engineer brought his locomotive to a screeching halt, a resounding cheer came from the Tarriers that could be heard for miles around, and despite their exhaustion, they launched into a celebration. The C.P. had stolen their thunder by beating their track-laying record, but the U.P. had claimed the historic site as their terminal. Even more important, the U.P. had won the long race across the country and reached the Summit first.

* * *

Promontory sat in a circular valley surrounded by mountains and dotted with sagebrush and cactus. No sooner had the two railroads laid their sidings there than a new Hell on Wheels town appeared beside them. Fourteen tent houses on each side of the tracks sprung up, offering the sale of "Red Cloud," "Red Jacket," and "Blue Thunder." A rough board main street was laid where hastily constructed shacks were thrown up housing shops, dance halls, and even more saloons. Only two buildings were of any substance, The Pacific Hotel and a one-room restaurant.

Spectators poured in long before the great day. Indians, Mexicans, mountain men, prospectors, a few ranchers came to see the show, as well as workmen who drifted in from down the line. During this time the main track was lain by both railroads, the two lines stopping a rail length apart. Between them, all ties were laid except for the one in the exact center. When that was finished, Gen. Jack built a second siding behind the first, and moved his factory to it, making Big Bertha complain bitterly that if he moved them any farther away, she and Anne were going to have to walk a mile just to see the show.

On May 7th, the day before the big event was scheduled to take place, Phil walked into the cookhouse and said to the two women, "Well, I've just heard some disappointing news. The festivities for tomorrow have been canceled. They've rescheduled them for Monday, the 10th."

"But why?" Anne asked.

"It was at the U.P.'s request. It seems there was a washout of U.P. track at Devil's Gate Bridge in Wyoming, and they're going to have to replace the track before Thomas Durant and the special train of dignitaries he's bringing can continue the trip."

"Well, I guess it must be raining over there as much as it has been here," Big Bertha commented.

Phil grinned. "That's the official story. Would you like to hear the real one, just between friends?"

"What do you mean the real story?" Anne asked.

"That story about the washout is just something the U.P. made up as an excuse for the delay. What really happened was Dr. Durant was kidnapped at Piedmont, Wyoming, when his train stopped there."

"Kidnapped?" Big Bertha asked in a shocked voice. "By who? Bandits?"

"No, by a gang of Irish tie-cutters who carried him off in a wagon. It seems they were angry because they haven't been paid since January and decided to handle their dispute with the U.P. in their own way. Needless to say, Durant has promised to pay them the $253,000 the railroad owes them and has been released, but he won't be able to make it here by tomorrow, and naturally we can't have the ceremony without the Vice President of the U.P."

"How embarrassing for the U.P.," Anne commented. "I can understand why they don't want everyone knowing it. But how did *you* get wind of it?"

Phil smiled a sly smile. "I have connections."

"Are you going to send the story back to your paper?" Big Bertha asked, her voice tinged with resentment.

"No. Sooner or later the story will leak out and be printed, but I see no reason for me, or any reporter, to do it now, despite the fact that we're committed to keeping the public informed. It would ruin the big day for them, and that would be a serious injustice. What they've done is a remarkable feat, an engineering marvel that deserves worldwide acclaim, and I don't think anything should put a flaw on their day of glory."

Anne smiled warmly at Phil and said, "Thank you."

"You don't have to thank me. I'm not doing it as a favor to anyone." He directed his words directly at Big Bertha, "It may come as a surprise to you, but despite our snooping, reporters have ethics, too."

A flush rose on Big Bertha's face. "Aw, I'm only teasing you when I say you snoop. Why, if it weren't for you, we wouldn't know anything that's going on around this place."

On the 8th, the day the ceremony was supposed to have

taken place, the directors of the C.P. and other dignitaries arrived from California, looking a little shaken, for the train had almost been swept off the track by an avalanche. Big Bertha and Anne, along with everyone else in Promontory, went out to greet them, then ogled at the elaborate, gilded private cars and the gentlemen and ladies who were dressed to the hilt in their finest.

Phil shouldered his way through the crushing crowd to where Anne and Big Bertha were standing. As he came to a stop beside them, Big Bertha said, "Would you look at that train, Phil? I ain't never seen such fancy scrolling and so much gilding. Why, even the engine's cab is covered with it!"

"Personally, I think it's a little overdone," Phil answered, "but then, it doesn't surprise me. The C.P. directors are still adjusting to being wealthy men and haven't learned the difference between being tasteful and gaudy. You see, they're all ex-storekeepers who made their wealth during the gold rush days."

Anne looked at the large group of California men standing beside the C.P. engine and asked, "Just which men are the directors? They all look wealthy to me."

"Leland Stanford, that heavyset, slow-moving man with the straight black beard is one of them. He's also the Governor of California. Charlie Crocker, that fleshy, corpulent man with the flowing goatee is the C.P. Chief of Construction and made his fortune on dry goods. The dour-looking man between them is Huntington. He made a mint selling hardware and is the driving force of the group. His partner in business, standing to the left of Governor Stanford, is Mark Hopkins, the last of the Big Four." Phil paused, then said, "They all look pretty unconcerned. I wonder if they don't know about the riot going on over at Victory yet."

Victory was the name the C.P. had pinned on the place where their historic track-laying had taken place. "What riot?" Anne asked.

"Well, technically it's more of a tong war going on between two rivaling Chinese gangs. Several hundred men of the See Yup and Teng Wo companies got into a row over fifteen dollars one company owed the other. That's where I've been, and I've never seen anything like it. They attacked each other with every conceivable weapon. Spades, crowbars, spikes, picks." Phil shuddered and said in a grim voice, "Don't let anyone ever tell you those Chinese can't fight. That seems to be a common misconception because they're so small and stay to themselves. Everyone thinks they're cowards. But I've never seen anyone so fierce, or so vicious. Several shots were fired, and one man was seriously hit. Strombridge, Crocker's chief of staff, and several of his men, and some of the leading Chinese finally managed to stop it. But I hope like hell the man who took that bullet doesn't die, or the battle will start all over again."

The next day the U.P. finished a track to a switch opposite the C.P.'s. That afternoon, the U.P.'s engine number 66 arrived from the East with the two Casement brothers, numerous contractors, and others. As they had the day before, everyone in Promontory went out to meet the new arrivals, the ladies from California daintily picking their way through the mud, while the rugged railroad people just sloshed through it. The U.P. engine came to a halt less than a hundred feet from the C.P.'s number 62 Whirlwind and let off steam. The Whirlwind replied with its whistle. Anne and Big Bertha watched as the construction chiefs, their subordinates, and contractors of both roads shook hands, then curiously examined each others' engines. These were radically different, one being a coal burner and the other a wood-burner.

Big Bertha shook her head in disgust and said, "Ain't that just like a bunch of men? No one but them can get excited about a stupid machine."

Anne was wondering where Phil was. She hadn't seen him all day. Then suddenly she was turned, and Phil picked her up and whirled her around, saying in a jubilant voice, "Congratulations! I knew you could do it!"

As Phil whirled her around, Anne was acutely conscious of people staring at them curiously. As soon as he set her on her feet, she pushed herself from him and said irritably. "What in the world is wrong with you? Have you gone insane?"

Grinning from ear to ear, Phil waved a telegraph wire in her face. "Do you know who this came from?" he asked in an excited voice. "My editor! He wants to publish your journal, Anne. It's just like I thought. He's crazy about it! And he said to tell you if you wrote any more material on railroads, he wanted to see it."

Anne was shocked speechless, but not Big Bertha. She let out a big whoop, making everyone in the crowd around them jump in surprise, and then hugged Anne so tight she almost cracked her ribs. Holding Anne back, she said, "Oh, honey, I'm so happy for you, I could just pop!"

Suddenly tears of happiness welled in Anne's eyes. "I can't believe it."

"Well, it's true," Phil said, his eyes shining with pride and happiness for her. "He didn't name a price, but I'm sure the paper will pay you a nice sum. They're going to run it as a serial. Why, you can probably quit working for a few years."

Quit working? Anne thought. She didn't want to quit working for the railroad and leave her family.

"He wants you to get back to him as soon as possible," Phil continued, "so you can iron out all the particulars. I'll give you his address before I leave today."

"Leave?" Anne asked in a shocked voice. "But I thought you were going to cover the big event tomorrow."

"I was, but my editor said to let Harriman handle it."

"Who's Harriman?"

"He's another reporter my paper sent out to cover the event. He arrived a few days ago."

"I sure am sorry to hear about your leaving," Big Bertha said. "I was kinda counting on breaking out that bottle of bourbon I have tomorrow and having a few snorts with you to celebrate, since Anne won't touch the stuff."

"I'm sorry I'm going to miss it, too," Phil answered.

"Why is your editor calling you back at this point?" Anne asked angrily. "You've been covering this for weeks, and now, when the big event we've all been waiting for is almost here, he's telling you to go back and let another reporter do it. I don't think that's fair!"

"Whoa, Anne, don't get mad at him. I've been hounding him for years for an overseas assignment. It seems one of our correspondents in Europe suddenly resigned and there's an opening available. My editor says if I want it, I'd better get back on the double."

"But it's just one more day," Anne objected.

"One day can make a big difference when you're traveling by boat, and he's already booked passage for me in five days. You don't want me to miss my boat, do you, either literally and or with my career? This is something I've been wanting for a long time."

"No, not in that case," Anne admitted.

"Would you mind going to station to see me off? I'd really like that."

"Of course, I don't mind. Why, next to Big Bertha, you're my best friend, but are you sure there's a train going back East today?"

"Yes, I checked on it when I went over to pick up this telegram. The U.P. is sendin' another trainload of workers back, and I can hitch a ride on it."

"*More* workers?" Big Bertha asked in surprise. "Hell, we ain't hardly got anyone left to cook for as it is. Why, I'll bet there ain't a fourth of our crew left." A scowl came over her face. "And I don't think it's fair of the U.P. to be sending them all back at the last minute and making them miss the big celebration. It was the Tarriers who built this railroad with their sweat and toil. It should be their big day, too."

"That's the trouble," Phil explained. "The Irishmen have been doing too much celebrating in advance. It's only the drunks the railroad is picking up and sending back, and it's for their own protection. There have been twenty-four killings in the boomtowns in this valley over the past twenty-five days. That's to say nothing of the workers who have been beaten up and robbed. It's better to be disappointed at missing the big day, than dead."

"Yeah, I reckon you're right," Big Bertha conceded. "Besides if they're that soused, they probably wouldn't even know what all the celebrating was about."

Phil turned to Anne and said, "I'm going to go back to the

hotel to pick up my things before I go to the station. Shall I meet you here?"

"No, there doesn't seem to be much going on here now," Anne answered. "Meet me back at the bakery."

"Yeah," Big Bertha agreed, "you can only do so much looking at fancy cars and fancy-dressed people. Besides, it looks like it might rain again."

Phil arrived at the bakery an hour later, carrying his suitcase. He reached into his coat pocket and handed Anne a piece of paper, saying, "Maybe you'd better put this someplace where you won't lose it. It's the name and address of my editor."

Anne took it, walked to where her apron was hanging on a hook on the wall, and slipped it into her pocket. Phil helped her don her cloak, saying over her shoulder to Big Bertha, "Would you like to come along?"

Big Bertha knew Phil wanted some time alone with Anne before he left. "No, I'll stay here where it's nice and warm." She stepped up to Phil and offered her hand, saying, "Well, good luck, Phil. I sure hope everything turns out for you just like you want it. You should be a real success. You're just about the best dad-blasted snooper I've ever known."

Phil chuckled and shook the big woman's hand. "Good luck to you, too."

Phil and Anne walked to the station. In the distance, where the two rails met except for the missing tie, the crowd had dispersed, the Californians going back into their lush cars, while the train was being switched to a side track, and the others drifting back to their work or the wild boomtowns.

Anne and Phil walked in silence, both dreading their parting. When they reached the station, the east-bound train was already waiting there, being loaded with U.P. workers being taken back. Those who could be brought to their feet (in the wagon that had collected them from Promontory and the neighboring boom towns of Deadfall and Last Chance) staggered as they were led to the train. Those who could not stand were carried by their foremen and the firemen into the train and roughly dumped into their seats.

"With all those fumes floating about, I'll probably be drunk, too, before we reach the Utah border," Phil quipped in a effort to lighten their mood, as they stood on the wooden platform beside the train.

Anne forced a laugh. "Well, maybe it will make the trip to Omaha pass faster."

The engine blew its whistle. "All aboard!" the conductor called.

Phil turned to Anne and said, "Well, I guess this is it."

"I'm going to miss you," Anne said.

"I'm going to miss you, too." A wistful expression came over his face, and Anne knew then that he loved her. "I still wish it could have turned out differently for us. We would have had a great time exploring Europe together."

"I'm sorry it couldn't have turned out differently, too," Anne answered in all sincerity.

He stared at her for a long moment, as if he were trying to memorize her features, then took her in his arms and kissed her lips softly. Anne slipped her arms around his shoulders and kissed him more warmly. When she stepped back and saw the surprised expression on his face, she said, "That was thank you."

"For what?"

"For being such a good friend, for believing in me, for sending my journal to that editor."

An earnest expression came over his face. "You keep writing, Anne, no matter what. Like I said, you've got a natural knack for it."

The train started chugging away from the station. Seeing it, Phil picked up his suitcase and said, "Hell, I'm not going to miss my boat. I'm going to miss my train!"

"Good-bye, Anne," he called, already on the run.

"Good-bye!" Anne called back as he tore down the boardwalk to catch the train.

Phil made a running leap for the door of the last car, caught hold, and pulled himself in, banging his suitcase on the entrance. Then he turned and waved, and Anne waved back.

The train blew its whistle again as it sped away. For that reason, Anne didn't hear the rapid footsteps behind her. Suddenly she was whirled around to see Guy standing there. A tremendous wave of longing swept over her, making her knees weak, before she noticed the furious look on his face.

"Who in the hell is that man?" he demanded.

Anne's own anger rose. He hadn't changed one iota, she thought. He was still an arrogant brute. "That's none of your business!"

"Like hell it isn't! He kissed you, and I saw the look on his face before he did. He's in love with you."

"So what! It's still none of your business."

Guy caught her shoulders, his fingers biting into the soft flesh. "Are you in love with him?"

Anne couldn't force herself to lie, nor would she give Guy the satisfaction of knowing Phil was only a dear friend. She held her silence.

Guy shook her lightly and thundered, "Dammit, answer me!"

Furious, Anne pulled away from him. "I don't owe you any explanations! Just because you don't want me, doesn't mean other men don't. And what I feel for them is none of your concern. It's over between us. You were the one that made that decision. Remember?"

Guy had spied Phil and Anne walking to the train station and followed, hungrily devouring the sight of Anne. She was even more beautiful than he remembered. He had stood just behind the corner of the station and watched her, where he could see, yet not be seen by the two. He hadn't intended to make his presence known to Anne. All he wanted to do was feast on the sight of her for a brief moment. But when Phil had kissed her, and Anne had kissed him back, he had been filled with a consuming jealousy that made him forget all caution. Anne's reminder that it was he who had made the decision for them to part brought him to his senses. He dropped his hands and stepped back. Even then it took all of his willpower to keep from crushing her in his arms and kissing her so fiercely, so possessively that she would know he had put his seal on her for life.

Anne watched as a hard, closed expression came over Guy's face. "You're right, Anne. It was my decision, and this isn't any of my business."

As Guy stiffly pivoted and walked rapidly away, Anne felt his turning his back on her like the lash of a whip. Pain and fury welled up in her. "You bastard!" she muttered. "I hate you!"

She turned and rushed back to the bakery, the tears in her eyes almost blinding her.

Chapter Twenty-seven

When Anne rushed into the bakery, her teary eyes glittering with fury, Big Bertha took one look at her and said, "God-almighty! What got you so riled up? You look mad enough to chew nails."

"I am mad. No, I'm furious! Guy saw Phil kissing me good-bye at the station and had the audacity to be angry with me about it!"

Big Bertha's eyebrows rose at this surprising bit of information. She hadn't noticed Guy in the crowds, and he was a man who stood out. "Well, honey, I think I can understand that. I reckon Guy was jealous."

"But that's just it! He doesn't have any right to be jealous. He didn't want me. No, he used me and then tossed me aside like I was dirty rag. Then he turns around and gets angry because another man shows interest in me. What I do is none of his damn business. He's nothing but an arrogant brute, sticking his nose where it doesn't belong." Anne paused, her breasts heaving with anger, then asked "What's he doing here in Promontory anyway?"

"Why, I reckon he came for the big celebration tomorrow, just like everyone else. After all, he's worked hard to see this railroad competed."

"Well, I've worked hard, too, and now he's ruined it for me," Anne answered bitterly. "If he's going to be there tomorrow, I'm not going. I don't want to ever lay eyes on that bastard again!"

Big Bertha scowled, then said in a stern voice, "Now you

just back up there. One of the things I always admired about you was the way you didn't go around spewing out your bitterness about what happened between you and Guy, and I ain't gonna stand here now and listen to you calling him ugly names. It's just natural for a man to get jealous when he sees another man kissing the woman he loves."

"But he doesn't love me! He never did!"

"No, honey, you're wrong there. You got the idea in your head he just used you, but I happen to know the real reason Guy walked out on you. We did a lot of talking the day he brought you from the bridge camp, or rather he talked and I listened. He didn't do it because he'd stopped loving you. He did it because he thought it was what was best for you, and it was tearing him up something awful. You see, he didn't feel it was fair to ask you to drift from pillar to post with him while he went around the country building bridges. He thought you deserved a real home. And he's under the impression that you want to settle down someplace real bad. He said he overheard you telling one of his men that you were saving your money to buy a restaurant. Is that true?"

Anne was a little stunned by the things Big Bertha was telling her. "Well . . . well, yes, I did," she admitted. "But buying a restaurant was just an idea I toyed around with for a while. And it wasn't because I wanted to settle down. I was thinking more in terms of being my own boss, being more independent. But I've changed my mind. I don't want to leave the railroad. It's in my blood. I like the excitement of it, and I like the people. I would have told Guy all of that, if he had bothered to ask me," Anne said, her anger on the rise again. "He should have talked it over with me, instead of just walking out the way he did."

"I told him that, but he was afraid you'd argue with him, then somewhere down the line you'd realize you had made a serious mistake and regret it. Like I said, he really thought he was doing what was best for you."

"Dammit, he's always trying to make me do what *he* thought was best for me, treating me like a child who hasn't got enough sense to come in out of the rain. It was that way from the very beginning. He never gave me credit for being mature enough to know what I want." Anne paused, then asked, "If you knew all of this, why didn't you tell me sooner?"

"Guy didn't want me to tell you. He *wanted* you to think he had just used you and then tossed you aside. He figured that way you'd hate him, and it would make it easier for you to accept. I didn't know if he was doing what was right or wrong, but I felt like I'd be breaking his confidence to tell you, and I didn't want to do that, until today, when you started attacking him. I flat couldn't take that. I know he loves you, and I know he's been hurting, too."

Big Bertha watched Anne while the young woman pondered over everything she had told her, then asked bluntly, "What are you gonna do about it?"

"I don't know if there is anything I *can* do about it. He may have been jealous, but when I reminded him that it was he who had made the decision for us to part ways, he made it quite clear that he hadn't changed his mind. He turned his back on me and walked away again."

"You love him, don't you? You still want him?"

"Yes, of course."

"Then I reckon you're gonna *have* to do something about it."

"Like what? I can't force him to change his mind, and I'll be damned if I'll go begging. I do have some pride, you know."

Big Bertha threw her hands up in exasperation and asked, "Is your pride gonna keep you warm at night? Is it gonna make you happy? Is it gonna give you children? Is it gonna comfort you when you're hurting? Is it gonna be a companion to you in your old age?" When Anne just stared at her, Big Bertha said in a hard voice, "I told you a long time ago, if you want something real bad, you have to go after it with all you've got, you have to fight for it. If you ain't willing to do that, then you don't deserve it. You want Guy? Then go get him, and to hell with your silly pride! But if you ain't got the guts to do it, then don't come bellyaching to me about it."

With that, Big Bertha turned and left the bakery.

For a long while, Anne stewed over what the big woman had said. It was true, she didn't deserve Guy if she wasn't willing to fight for him, and no one else could fight her battles for her. If they were going to get back together, it was going to be left up to her. But Guy wasn't going to be easy to convince. The arrogant bastard always thought he knew so much more than she did, particularly about what was best for her. Well, by God, she wasn't going to take this sitting down. He might walk out of her life again—but she was going to make it damn hard for him to do!

Filled with determination, Anne left the bakery, making a beeline for her tent.

An hour later, Anne walked down one of the narrow boardwalks that lined the main street of Promontory. Even though it was still daylight, the wild boomtown was already revved up for the night. Anne could hear the clink of glasses, the rattle of casino games, the tinny piano music, the drunken laughter, and belligerent curses of the men as she passed the long line of hastily constructed saloons, then the deafening noises coming from a dance hall across the way. The street was crowded with curious sightseers, wandering from saloon to saloon and souvenir shop to souvenir shop, as well as those who had come to drink, gamble, and taste the forbidden delights that the town offered. Glassy-eyed drunks staggered from bar to bar; shifty-eyed gamblers slinked from one saloon where they had just fleeced a table of men and ducked into another in hopes of finding more prey: pickpockets jostled the men walking down the streets, smiling innocently while they deftly practiced their trade; painted floozies openly solicited, inviting men into the their little tents with curtain-enclosed cubicles.

Everyone stared at Anne as she passed, men and women alike, for it was clear that she didn't belong here. Most of the stares were in disbelief, for none had thought a respectable woman would dare to venture into this dangerous, sinful place. But Anne dared. She was a woman with a mission, who would let nothing or no one deter her. She walked with a determined set to her face, her eyes straight ahead.

Only twice was she accosted. The first man to step in her path backed down when Anne stared him straight in the eye. The second man to block her way was of another breed, a mean-eyed brute with a well-worn six-shooter on his hip, who

Anne pegged as an outlaw. Her legs trembled, but Anne refused to show her fear. She raised the gun she was carrying beneath her cloak and said, "Step aside. I have a loaded six-shooter pointed at your chest, and I won't hesitate to use it."

The man glanced quickly down and saw the muzzle of the gun tenting Anne's cloak. He started, then glanced up at Anne's face as if to judge if she would actually follow through with her threat. "I mean it," Anne said in a deadly calm voice, looking him straight in the eye.

As the filthy, heavily bearded outlaw seemed to be pondering what to do, Anne asked, "Why risk it? At this close range, I can't miss. There are plenty of willing women around here, and if it's money you' re after, I'm not carrying anything on me but this gun."

Deciding she meant what she said and that it wasn't worth the risk, the outlaw stepped aside. Anne walked on, giving the appearance that the confrontation hadn't unnerved her in the least, despite the fact that her heart was racing.

When she reached the Pacific Hotel, Anne walked into the two-story building and right up to the desk clerk. The man gaped at her as if he didn't believe his eyes. Anne smiled pleasantly, bewildering the man even more, then asked, "Can you please tell me what room Mr. Guy Masters is staying in?"

Anne waited patiently while the man pulled out the register from beneath his desk and read it. There was no doubt in her mind that Guy was staying here. It was the only halfway respectable hotel in the valley. The clerk looked up from the book and said, "He's in 203, ma'am."

"Thank you."

Anne walked to the stairs and up them, totally ignoring the desk clerk who was still gawking at her. When she reached the second story, she turned down the hall and stopped at the door that was numbered 203. She shifted the heavy gun to her other hand and started to knock. For a brief moment she paused, with her knuckles hovering over the door. Then firming her resolve, she tapped on the door.

"Who's there?" Guy called.

Anne refused to answer, for fear Guy wouldn't open the door to her. She knocked again, even louder.

A moment later, Guy answered the door. Anne wasn't surprised to see a .45 pointed at her, but it wasn't the gun that caught her attention. It was the expression on Guy's face. He looked so shocked that it was all she could do to keep from laughing.

Not wanting to give him time to recover and perhaps deny her entrance, Anne walked past him, saying, "Well, if you won't invite me in, I'll invite myself."

As Anne passed him, her scent drifted across to Guy, that sweet, womanly smell that always intoxicated him. Combined with her unexpected appearance, he felt stunned and closed the door in a daze, then turned and saw Anne taking off her cloak and placing it over the back of a straight chair. When she stepped away from the chair, his eyes focused on the gun she had placed on the seat, its long, black muzzle poking out from underneath the folds of her wrap.

Seeing him stare at the gun in surprise, Anne said, "You didn't think I'd be foolish enough to come into this town without some means of protection, did you? I bought it from the factory's general store before I came. The clerk was even kind enough to show me how to load it and give me a few pointers about shooting it."

Guy frowned. He had come to realize that Anne was becoming more and more self-reliant, but there was a hint of brittleness in her voice that disturbed him. Yet it didn't sound like anger. It was almost as if she were issuing him a challenge of some sort and had already thrown up her defenses. "Why did you come here, Anne? What do you want?"

You, Anne thought, but she wasn't quite bold enough to come right out and say it. "I came to prove something to you."

The strange glitter in Anne's hazel eyes made Guy feel even more uneasy. "What?" he asked suspiciously.

"That you love me. That you still want me."

Guy sucked in his breath sharply. His eyes hungrily swept over her enticing curves before he realized what he was doing, and he jerked them away to focus on her face. "No, Anne, you're wrong. It's over between us."

"You were jealous this afternoon when you saw another man kissing me," Anne pointed out.

"That was just a spontaneous reaction. It didn't mean a thing."

"I think you're lying. I think you want me as much, if not more, than ever."

It took all of Guy's will to keep his eyes focused on Anne's face. "No, I don't! Now please leave."

Guy's denial was too adamant, and there was a frantic look in his eyes that told Anne he was fighting his feelings tooth and toenail. She almost felt sorry for him, until she remembered what she had come to accomplish. She reached for the buttons on her bodice.

Seeing her unbuttoning her dress, Guy asked, "What in the hell do you think you're doing?"

"I told you. I'm going to prove something to you."

Guy watched in disbelief as Anne slipped the dress from her shoulders, and it dropped to puddle on the floor at her feet. Again, he sucked in his breath sharply. She hadn't been wearing a stitch of underclothing and stood before him stark naked.

Anne smiled smugly at the shocked look on Guy's face, then said, "You see, I came prepared for your arguments. I know how stubborn you are. Now tell me you don't want me."

Guy tried to keep his eyes from her beautiful bare body, but it was impossible to do. Even staring at her face, he could see her lovely shape from his peripheral vision. His breath turned ragged. For the life of him, he could not say a word. If was as if the sight of her nakedness had paralyzed his vocal cords.

"Has the cat got your tongue?" Anne taunted softly, pulling the net from the back of her head and shaking her long hair loose, so that it tumbled down around her shoulders in a golden reddish, shimmering waterfall. She slipped off her slippers from one foot, then the other, and stepped up to him, standing so close that Guy could feel the tips of her breasts through his shirt. "It's probably just as well. I wouldn't believe you. I can see how fast your heart is racing here."

When Anne placed the fingertips of one hand against the racing pulse on Guy's throat, he flinched at the burning sensation they caused. And her breasts seemed to be boring a hole into his chest right through his shirt. As Anne's fingers slid up his neck to toy with his earlobe, he trembled. He stood rooted to the spot as Anne began to unbutton his shirt with her other hand, then slipped it off his shoulders and down his arms, leaving his skin tingling everywhere her fingers touched. When she started placing scorching kisses over his chest, he clenched his fists (to keep from taking her into his arms) and finally managed to find his tongue. "Stop it, Anne!" he said harshly. "You're acting like a whore!"

Anne's eyes flashed. Then as quickly as it came, her anger was gone. She smiled, saying, "No, Guy, it won't work. I won't let you make me angry. You told me once you wouldn't be adverse to my seducing you. Well, I'm just taking you up on your invitation."

She slid her hands up the length of his arms and around his neck, then pressed her naked breasts against his chest. Guy stiffened and asked through clenched teeth, "And what if I won't let you seduce me?"

Anne laughed softly, her warm breath fanning his neck. "Oh, Guy, you can't fight me and your passion." As Guy opened his mouth, Anne silenced him by cutting across his words with, "No, don't bother to deny it. I know you're aroused." She pressed herself against the hot, rigid proof of that arousal, and Guy felt his treacherous manhood lengthen yet another inch.

Guy's senses spun as Anne forced his head down. Her soft lips captured his in a fiery, devastating kiss that left him so weak he couldn't even summon the strength to push her hands aside as she unbuttoned his pants and slipped them and his drawers down. Anne was relieved that he had been barefooted, for removing his boots would have been time-consuming, and she didn't want to give him the chance for recover from her sensual assault. She had him where she wanted him now, exactly where he'd had her so many times, trembling with need and drugged with passion.

She pushed Guy back on the bed, where he lay sprawled and staring at the ceiling with glazed eyes while Anne dropped torrid kisses over his face and shoulders, then nipped his chest. Her small tongue whipped out and lashed his flat male nipple, making Guy hiss in pleasure and bringing a smile of satisfaction to Anne's lips. She traced his ribs with her tongue, her hands running up and down his arms, the sides of his chest and lean hips, his hair-roughened thighs, glorying in his utterly male magnificence and her power over him.

From some small corner in the back of his mind, Guy told himself to stop her. A man who allowed a woman to inflict her will upon him was no man at all. But he seemed to be helpless against her onslaught of fiery kisses and tantalizing caresses. The feel of her licking his thighs while she stroked his rigid hardness left him trembling, and his breath came in short, rasping gasps. Then Guy felt her warm breath fanning his straining manhood. He looked down and saw her mouth poised over him and her hair falling around his hips like a silken waterfall. As she lowered her head, he stiffened in shock. She wouldn't! he thought. She had never made love to him with her mouth. Surely, she wouldn't go to such lengths to bring him to his knees.

He thought to pull her head away, but again his body betrayed him. His arms refused to obey his mind's command, and instead his muscles quivered in intense anticipation. As her agile tongue danced over his throbbing length, each touch jarring his burning nerve endings, Guy fought against the wild excitement that was filling him. Then, when her devilish tongue circled the tip of him and she took him into her mouth, he gave himself up to sheer sensation, her willing, eager captive.

Seducing Guy and making love to him so totally uninhibited had excited Anne unbearably. She'd had to work up her nerve to taste him as he had tasted her so many times, but had found it terribly titillating. Knowing she was giving him immense pleasure only intensified her excitement. She, too, was trembling with need and burning for fulfillment. She abandoned her ravishment, straddled his hips, and lowered herself over him, slowly taking him in inch by inch. Delicious shudders wracked her as his pulsating, rigid heat entered her. She felt as if she were riding on the edge of a lightning bolt.

As Anne began her movements—each slow thrust making her gasp in pleasure as nerve endings inside her seemed to explode—Guy gave up his passive role. His hands swept over her thighs, her hips, to fondle her breasts. In a sudden, quick movement that took her completely by surprise, he flipped her to her back, and captured her mouth in a hot, plundering kiss that not only robbed her of her role as aggressor, but of her senses as well. Guy plunged into her over and over with a wildness that bordered on fury, making her quiver from head to toe, taking her breath away, stilling her heart, filling her with wonderful electrifying sensations, and lifting her to paradise, reaching for her very soul, then pouring himself into her.

When it was over, they both felt shattered, yet reborn. For a long while they were content to drift in that warm languidness, their arms still curled around one another. Neither spoke, feeling there were no words to express what they had just shared. This is where I belong, Anne thought, here in Guy's arms. This is my home. The only home I want.

Anne's thought reminded her of her purpose in coming here. She stroked Guy's sweat-slick back and kissed his shoulder softly, tasting his saltiness before she said in a low, throaty voice, "See? You still want me. You still love me."

Guy lay where he had collapsed over her, with his head buried in the crook of her neck so still and so silent that Anne thought he must have fallen asleep. Abruptly he pulled away from her and rolled from the bed. Anne watched in dismay as he picked up his pants and jerked them on, keeping his back to her as he quickly buttoned them.

He turned to her, a solemn expression on his face, and said, "All right, Anne. I still want you, and I still love you, but nothing has changed. I felt that way when I left you with Big Bertha, but I wouldn't let it influence my decision. Neither will I let what just happened change it. I still think it's time for us to go our separate ways. You could have saved yourself the time and the trouble and both of us the pain of having to part a second time."

Anne's anger came to the fore. "And I have no say in this decision?"

"I'm doing what's best for you, what's best for both of us in the long run."

Anne sprung from the bed and stood before him, so furious she was trembling. "Dammit, I'm sick and tired of you deciding what's best for me. I'm not a child. I'm a grown, responsible woman. I know what I want. I want you, not some stupid home!" Seeing the surprised look come over his face, she continued. "Yes, I know what you're thinking. Big Bertha finally told me. You overheard me telling Pat that I wanted to buy a restaurant and assumed that meant I wanted a place to settle down. Well, that had nothing to do with it. I was thinking of how to support myself, and that I wanted to be my own boss. A home had nothing to do with it. But I don't even want a restaurant anymore. I don't want to be stuck in some dull little town where the biggest thing that ever happens is a change in the weather. I just got out of a town like that. No, there are too many new, exciting things to see out here, and you can't see them unless you move around. Don't you understand? I don't mind moving from place to place, and I don't give a fig about a home."

"All right, Anne, maybe you wouldn't mind, but what about children? Did you ever think of that? What would happen to our family? That's no kind of a life for kids, constantly moving about, never having a place where they felt they belonged. They deserve the stability of a real home. A wanderlust life may be fine for us, but it's no kind of a life for children. To inflict that on them would be just pure selfishness on our part."

That's why her miscarriage had brought this all on, Anne realized. He had been thinking of children as well as her. It was a sobering thought.

Guy picked up Anne's dress and handed it to her. She accepted it and dressed, still mulling over what Guy had said. When they were both dressed, Guy placed her cloak around her shoulders and said, "I'll take you back to the camp."

His apparent anxiousness to get rid of her brought Anne's anger on the rise again. "That's not necessary!" she snapped, picking up her gun from the chair. "I found my way here with no help from you, and I can find my way back."

"Dammit, Anne, this is no time to be stubborn!" Guy answered in exasperation. "It's growing dark out there, and this town is too dangerous for you."

Anne's eyes flashed. "I've told you over and over that I don't need your protection! I don't need anything from you, but what you refuse to give me. You're the one who's being stubborn."

A look of total disbelief came over Guy's face. "Stubborn? For Christ's sake, didn't you hear anything I said?"

Anne walked to the door and opened it. She turned and said in a biting voice, "Oh, I heard what you said. It all sounded very logical, until I got to thinking about it. You're wrong, Guy. You have a mistaken impression of what a home is. It isn't a place. It isn't a house. It isn't a town. I know, because I lived in the same house, on the same piece of land, in the same town, all of my life, and I never felt I belonged, that it gave me any sense of security. And do you know why? Because there was no warmth, no love, no caring in that house. There was no one to cuddle me, no one to encourage me, no one to soothe my hurts and fears, no one to laugh with me, no one to guide me, no one who gave a damn. That's what makes a home, Guy. Not the place, but the people in it. It doesn't matter if it's a tent or a palace. If there isn't love there, it's not a home. It's nothing but a place of emptiness, as barren and useless as some of the deserts we've passed through. It may sustain life, but it doesn't make life worth living."

Anne stepped into the doorway and turned. "Think about that, Guy. If you change your mind, you know where to find me."

Anne closed the door, leaving Guy standing and staring at the wooden panel with a deep scowl on his face.

Chapter Twenty-eight

The next morning the weather was cold and bleak, and there was ice on the water puddles scattered about the valley. A stiff breeze snapped the flag hanging over Promontory Summit and whipped the Great Salt Lake into foam- tipped waves. But the cold and a threat of rain didn't stop the spectators from gathering at the site long before the noontime celebrations. They huddled together, shivering in the cold wind and waiting in excited anticipation.

Anne and Big Bertha left the railroad camp around ten, fearing if they didn't they wouldn't find a place close enough to see the uniting of the two railroads. Red, white, and blue bunting hung from every tent and building, and Gov. Stanford's private car was decorated with banners of the same colors, all flapping in the brisk, cold wind. When the two women reached the spot where the celebration was to take place, they were shocked to see almost a thousand people had already crowded around the two rail heads.

"I guess we should have come earlier," Anne said in disappointment. "We won't be able to see anything from back here."

"The hell we won't," Big Bertha answered in a determined voice. "Those spectators didn't have nothing to do with building this railroad. We did! This is our day, and there ain't no one gonna cheat us out of it."

Big Bertha took Anne's hand and roughly shouldered their way through the crowd of men and women, glaring at anyone who looked like they might object. When they stood at the front of the crowd, Anne glanced about, hoping to see Guy. All night she had waited for him to come to her tent, to tell her that he had changed his mind. When he didn't appear, she had pinned all her hopes on his joining them at the celebration, but Guy was nowhere in sight, and with his height he would have been easy to spy. Had he decided to skip the festivities and left town? Anne wondered in despair. Had he walked out of her life, once and for all?

Damn, Anne thought. She'd tried. She'd buried her pride and boldly—no, brazenly—gone to Guy to fight for what she wanted. She had proved he still wanted her, tried reasoning with him, did everything but get down on her knees and beg, and it had all been for nothing. She had made the biggest gamble of her life and lost. Now she was right back where she'd started, facing a future that looked bleak and empty.

Then Anne took herself firmly in hand. Stop it, she scolded herself furiously. You're not going to let it ruin what you've strived so hard for all these months. This is the great day you've been waiting for. Tomorrow you can mourn, but today you're going to enjoy every minute, even if it kills you.

She forced herself to direct her attention to what was going on around her. The excitement that hung in the air around her helped, for it was contagious. When the first of the two excursion trains from the East arrived between ten and eleven, and the engines already sitting on the side tracks blew their whistles, she cheered just as loudly as everyone else, then watched as the spectators poured out, the men dressed in high silk hats and Prince Albert coats and the ladies in their finest. There were even a few children among them. Vice-President Durant's special train arrived a short time later, bringing more whistling and cheers, and came to a stop on the side track, spilling out army officers, government and railroad officials, and four companies of the 21st Infantry Tenth Ward Headquarters Band.

The soldiers formed ranks and marched to the site, sloshing through the mud puddles and playing a rousing tune. Suddenly, the sun came out, making the golden tubas and trombones sparkle, and the crowd went wild. Photographers jostled for places to set up their tripods, then squeezed the rubber balls on their clumsy boxlike contraptions, trying to catch the excitement of the moment for prosperity.

For a while, the crowd settled down, while the band continued to entertain them. Railroad officials, with the help of soldiers, cleared the main track for the big event. Then the Union Pacific No. 119, a dark green and gold coal-burner with a tall, narrow coffee-grinder smokestack, steamed to the end of the line, while the Central Pacific's Juniper, a red and gold engine with a broad Dolly Varden smokestack, chugged up to the meet it, bringing another loud cheer from the crowd of onlookers.

Those who were to take part in the ceremony stepped up to the ties between the two engines. Gen. Jack and Charlie Crocker, the two superintendents of construction, picked up the last tie (made from California laurel) and put it in place, to the accompaniment of more excited yells. The Union Pacific's last rail, carried by a crew of burly, grinning Irishmen, was brought forward and laid on the ties, bringing not only cheers but ribald calls from their fellow workmen who hung from the engines and cars. Six Chinese, dressed in their dark pajama-like outfits and large straw hats, with their long pigtails hanging down their backs, picked up the Central Pacific's last rail. "Shoot!" called a nearby cameraman to his crew. The Chinese looked up with terrified expressions on their faces, dropped the rail, and ran away as fast as their short legs could carry them, bringing gales of laughter to the crowd.

It took awhile for the Chinese to return. They had to be argued back by Crocker, who finally convinced them that no one here meant them harm. But even as they carried the heavy rail and placed it, they kept looking about nervously.

Dr. Durant, Gov. Stanford, and several other notables stepped forward with silver hammers in their hands. Everyone waited impatiently while Gen. Dodge and Gov. Stanford gave brief speeches, then a prayer was said. Three spikes—two silver and one silver and gold—from Montana, Utah, and Nevada were placed and made fast by various notables. Then the big moment everyone had been waiting for finally came. The last spike, a pure gold one from California, was placed. Gov. Stanford stepped forward with his silver hammer, to which telegraph wires were attached, so that the blow that drove in the last spike that united the country could be heard over the land. The Governor missed his mark, bringing a howl of laughter from the workmen. Nonetheless, the telegraph operator tapped out DONE in morse code, a signal that set off a celebration all over the United States. Cannons were fired at San Francisco and Sacramento. A hundred-gun salute was given in Omaha, and yet another in New York City. In Philadelphia, the Liberty Bell was joyously rung; in Buffalo, the "Star Spangled Banner" was sung, and in Salt Lake City, the Tabernacle was filled to overflowing.

The cerebration at Promontory Summit followed a moment later when the golden spike was finally pounded into the earth by the embarrassed Governor. The crowd went wild. A deafening cheer rang out and echoed in the surrounding mountains. People clapped each other on the back, danced in the streets, and hugged one another. The two engines moved across the last rail until their cowcatchers met. The engineers shook hands, then poured champagne over the rails and each other's engines.

When the last spike had been pounded into the ground, Big Bertha let out a loud whoop and grabbed Anne, hugging her so tight in her elation that she almost smothered the younger woman. Then she stepped back and said, "Oh, honey, we did it! And we did in one year less than everyone thought it would take. Ain't that something? Ain't you just tickled to death?"

Anne *was* thrilled. She wouldn't have missed it for the world. "Yes, I feel wonderful. Absolutely wonderful!"

The band started playing "Auld Lang Syne." A sudden hush fell over the crowd, and everyone joined hands and sang. Standing between Big Bertha and a strange man, the melancholy tune had a disastrous effect on Anne. No longer could she keep her thoughts from Guy. The memories of their time together came rushing back in a tremendous wave that overpowered her. A terrible pain rose in her and spilled over as tears streamed down her cheeks. She was so lost in her misery that she didn't notice when someone broke the handclasp between her and the stranger and took her hand. Even when the music died away and Big Bertha dropped her hand and moved away with a big grin on her face, Anne stared into space, thinking death would be better than the terrible emptiness she felt.

"What about it, Anne?" Guy asked softly and gently squeezed her hand. "Do you think we can forget the past and start over fresh, like the lyrics say?"

It was Guy's voice, but Anne couldn't believe it. She feared her mind might be playing some cruel joke on her. She was afraid to turn and face him, for fear he wouldn't really be there.

Guy stepped in front of her, still holding her hand in his. "I thought over what you said. In fact, I almost missed the celebration because I was so busy thinking. You're right, Anne. It's the people that make the home. I never thought of it that way. I guess because I came from a warm, loving family, I always thought they were one and the same." He smiled, a little, apologetic smile that tore at Anne's heart. "I got to thinking that there are a lot of people who move around a lot. Army people for one. The wives follow their husbands from post to post, and yet one of the closest knit families I've ever seen was that of my superior officer in the army. He'd hit about every isolated post in the West, and yet the hardships and the dangers he and his family had faced seemed to bind them closer, and their children hadn't seemed to suffer. They were the most rugged, self-sufficient individuals I'd ever seen, and yet, there was a deep love there. You could feel it every time you stepped into their quarters."

Anne didn't say anything. She couldn't. She was too full of happiness.

"I'm willing to try it, if you still are," Guy said. "And if the trash that follows the railroad can pick up its saloons and gambling halls and move them, I see no reason why we can't move our house. After all, I'm an engineer. I should be able to figure out some kind of a collapsible structure that we could carry along with us."

"I don't care where I live," Anne answered, finally finding her tongue, "whether it's a tent, a cabin, or a cave. Just as long as I'm with you."

Guy now had both her hands. He looked her deeply in the eyes and said, "I love you, Anne. I'd be miserable going through life without you. But there is one thing I want to ask. I want you to give up your job with the railroad. I'm selfish. I don't want to share you with anyone, not even as my crew's cook. I want a full-time wife."

Anne didn't really mind. As his wife, she'd still be a part of the railroad family, and that would give her more time to devote to her writing. It would be the perfect life, seeing all the new and exciting places in the West at Guy's side, and writing down everything she'd seen and heard. "I don't mind. I imagine I can find enough to keep me busy."

Guy was vastly relieved. He'd been afraid Anne would give him some argument on that score. "The Union Pacific is planning on putting in a spur to Denver," he informed her. "I've already signed up with them and been promised some challenging bridge assignments of my own. But I don't have to report to work for six weeks. I understand the U.P. plans on opening regular transcontinental service within a few days, with luxurious Pullman coaches and dining cars. We could get married here—that minister who said the prayer could perform the ceremony—then go to Sacramento on the first train going through, and spend our honeymoon there. We might even make a side trip to San Francisco. I understand it's an exciting city. It seems ridiculous to get this far and not see the Pacific."

Anne was so thrilled at his exciting plans that she couldn't even speak. She nodded her head eagerly.

Guy slipped his arms around her. "Is it settled then? You'll marry me? But remember, Anne," he cautioned, "it isn't going to be easy. We'll have some tough times ahead of us, living in some rugged, isolated wilderness most of the time. This is your last chance to say no. So think it over carefully."

"I'll marry you, Guy," Anne answered without the slightest hesitation. "There's nothing to think over. I'm not afraid of hardships. I'd go to the moon with you, if you asked me to."

Guy beamed at her answer, feeling a tremendous happiness filling him. He tightened his arms around her and bent his head. Anne met his lips midway, her arms sliding around his broad shoulders.

The ladies and gentleman from the east- and west-bound trains turned and walked back to their luxurious cars, to read the congratulatory telegrams pouring in from all over the country and to dine on a sumptuous feast that had been prepared for them. Railroad workers passed bottles around and clapped each other on the back, bragging boisterously of their accomplishment as they walked back to their camps. The other spectators in the crowd turned and strolled back to the Hell on Wheels towns scattered about the valley to seek their own means of celebrating. Two children ran through the dispersing crowd, playing tag. The dogs in the cabs of both the C.P. and the U.P. engines barked furiously at each other. The warm spring sun shone down brightly. The flags overhead snapped in the breeze, and the band played on.

But the couple who were embracing and kissing were oblivious to it all. They were locked in a wild, sweet world of their own making.